Mom's Night Out

A Novel

Lara Shea

Mom's Night Out

Edited by Jenny Jensen
Cover design by Hadleigh O. Charles

To my husband, John Shea,
for believing in me more than I believe in myself.

One

Sucker punched. That's how I felt, like someone had knocked the wind out of me. In my case that someone just happened to be an extraordinarily good-looking cop sitting in my kitchen. I shook my head, mentally kicking myself for not being ready. Most of the time I could depend on my imagination—exhausting, childish imagination, my husband would say—to keep me on my toes, but I guess I was getting soft. Things had been going smoothly for too long now, four or five years at least. Instantly I began to worry; don't these things usually happen in threes?

It was Tuesday, the last week of February, and although the typical seventy-degree winter days in Hermosa Beach were nothing to complain about, this particular day was different. The sun seemed higher, stronger. The temperature was supposed to reach eighty-five. The air was crystal clear without so much as a hint of haze or smog or Southern California's impending June Gloom. The day screamed *summer*.

This type of occasional perfect day amidst a winter of other near-perfect days had a strange effect on my fellow denizens who, like me, ran on solar. It made them smile more easily, relax and slow down, as though we had all just been through one doozy of a winter and we knew that finally—*finally!*—the big thaw was right around the corner. We'd soon be able to shed our bulky long-sleeved T-shirts in exchange for something capped.

I felt it so much that I decided our four-year-old, Casey, would play hooky from his parent-participation preschool (naturally after first checking to make sure he wasn't missing anything mega important like his share day or my day to bring snack) and loaded him and our two-year-old, Griffin, into the double Bob along with a bag of sand toys, two large plastic shovels, Casey's Razor and Griffin's Mini-Kick, their helmets, towels, boogie boards, snacks, drinks, books and an assortment of action figures.

I pushed the button on the garage door, letting the sunlight slide in. "The sunshine's gonna kiss your toes!" I teased. The boys squealed and kicked their bare, zinc-oxide Fred Flintstone piggies at the rays as my heart surged. I wanted to gobble them up, they were my pure, unadulterated joy. I kissed them both on their silky heads, slid on my visor, tightened my ponytail, wound the stroller leash around my wrist until it hurt, flipped up the break and pushed us off.

I blinked in the bright sunlight, quickly adjusting the stroller to shade the boys, and began the half-mile jaunt down the hill to the beach. The jasmine I had planted a few years back made the air honey-sweet and the squawking of a flock of wild parrots punctuated the calmness of our neighborhood. I took it in with a deep, relaxing breath, making it a whole block this time before my reoccurring nightmare kicked in—the one where I trip and the stroller goes careening uncontrollably into the heavy traffic on the Pacific Coast Highway and is hit by a truck while I am dragged by the leash across the asphalt screaming helplessly.

"Those worries are totally normal," my OBGYN told me when I confessed them a few months after Casey was born. It was embarrassing, like I was a delusional, mentally unfit mom. "They'll taper off once he's a little older."

But they didn't. They got worse, in fact, once Griffy was born—now I had to choose which boy to save. The theory is that nightmares like mine typically affect new moms who are anxious about their child's safety. They generally occur in a dream and it's the subconscious' way of creating a situation that would startle the dreamer awake so she could then process the problem and solve it consciously, effectively preparing her for anything that could possibly happen in real life. Simple enough.

Except my subconscious and conscious seemed to be in cahoots, and my nightmares occurred both day and night and long after the six-month mark. At the beach I'm prone to visions of tsunamis, attack seagulls and sharks the size of *Jaws*. At home there are earthquakes that could bring down ceiling beams and knife-wielding serial killers who creep in through the windows. Elsewhere there are child abductors, African killer bees, mass shootings, tainted food, faulty toys, and of course, that good old fashioned abandoned well into which one of my boys was sure to fall. You could say I am a worrier.

While I hate these nightmares, I also credit them for keeping me consistently on my guard. I am not the mom relaxing on the park bench updating my Facebook page as my kids play. I am not the mom so obsessed with throw pillows at Pottery Barn that for seven minutes she didn't notice her child had wandered out of the store and over to me and my boys to pitch pennies into the fountain. I am innately, instinctively and unapologetically the mom who is on guard and actively engaged (hyperactively, some have said) one-hundred percent of the time.

It's exhausting, but I honestly can't help it. I tried, I really did, but anytime either Mark, my husband, or myself were not in complete control of the boys, I had panic attacks and broke out in hives. There are just too many accounts, almost weekly, of children made victim by gruesome chance: the baby ripped from his grandma's arms by the family pit bull, the unsupervised child drowned in the pool at the birthday party, the kid who fell off the three-story balcony. The headlines alone bring tears to my eyes and make me nauseated. If I could put my boys in bullet-proof, fall-proof life-sized floating hamster balls until adulthood, believe me, I would.

Four hours later, exhausted but happy, I hauled us all back up the hill from the beach looking like Max, the Grinch's dog, as he lugged the overstuffed sled to the top of Mt. Crumpit. I wheeled us through the automatic doors of Ralph's market and closed my eyes for a moment to soak in the blast of air conditioning as it hit my face. We had recently entered a new stage where Griff was able to stay out longer, without needing a nap or having a meltdown, and I was reveling in it. Today there had been no fights, no major tantrums, and I was thinking I was doing a pretty good job of both figuratively balancing the needs and wants of two very active little boys while literally balancing our mammoth of a stroller. I even found myself humming the theme song from Rocky as I grabbed a gallon of organic milk from the cooler and headed to the check stand.

And that's when it happened.

In the split second of signing my name on the credit card machine and not having both hands white-knuckled on the stroller, both Griffin and Casey spontaneously jumped out to get a closer look at a toy that was situated in a display a few feet from them. Their sudden dismount upset the delicate balance of our Beverly Hillbillies-esque contraption, dumping everything—groceries, scooters, helmets, and sand toys—all over the checkout space. Milk splattered, the rotisserie chicken skidded like a hockey puck toward the automatic doors, plastic action figures flew like confetti and juice boxes projectiled into the next checkout lane. In my mad dash to get it all back together and leave the store with a shred of dignity, I forgot my wallet on the counter. By the time we got home, noticed it was missing and retraced our steps, it was gone.

"You canceled your credit cards, right Mrs. Birkby?" Officer Tewksbury asked me an hour later as we filled out the police report. He sat on the edge of a bar stool next to my kitchen island, the lemonade I poured for him untouched as I hovered next to him like an anxious Chihuahua.

I nodded diligently and drummed my nails on the granite. "Probably within forty minutes of losing it. And please, call me Kelly." He was disarmingly handsome. Mid-30's, fit, a head of soft brown hair that feathered slightly on its own. His muscular forearms were tan and the hair bleached from the sun, clearly a surfer. When he came to our door I could see the superhero version of him reflected in my boys' eyes.

"That'll help," he said with both a shrug and a lifting of both his eyebrows, "but it wouldn't surprise me if whoever took it has already used it. And you should start monitoring for identity theft since they got your I.D." He caught the widening of my eyes as my fingers stopped mid-drum, and he began to ramble.

"Oh yeah, stuff like that happens daily around here. Just last week we busted a clerk at the Vans store who was lifting credit card numbers from customers. We catch shoplifters all the time at Jack's Surfboards, Becker's, True Religion, Big Lots. Happens everywhere."

"You're kidding," I replied, my voice going up in pitch. "Here?"

Hermosa Beach and the two other beach towns that enveloped it, Redondo to the south and east and Manhattan to the north, were known to be some of L.A.'s safest, most family-oriented communities. It was the main reason we had chosen to buy a home here instead of one of the larger coastal cities like Venice or Santa Monica, which would have been easier for Mark's commute to Century City.

These three towns made up the South Bay and were like a bubble. There were no gangs. They had great police forces. There were neighborhood watches and everyone looked out for each other. There wasn't even a homeless problem, although I had heard the cops popped them in an Uber and sent them up to Santa Monica. The politicians ran on the safety platform. It was supposed to be a priority. *The* priority. It dawned on me that my relentless, obsessive worrying may have missed the mark completely. I made a mental note to open a safety deposit box to hold the boys' social security cards.

"Oh yeah," he continued almost boasting, seeing he had an attentive audience in me. He flipped back through the pages of his notebook as if refreshing his memory for more material. "We've caught people driving up and down the streets with pick-up trucks, dashing into open garages and swiping bikes, lawnmowers, tools. Whatever isn't tied down that they can quickly grab. There are several people making a living off the bikes and strollers they steal at the beach. They know there are only a handful of cops patrolling the streets, and we're usually dealing with the drunk and disorderlies on the promenade. We can't be everywhere, so they take their chances."

"But that's so bold, so risky," I said, my brow now tightly furrowed. "Right in the open, in the middle of the day?"

He nodded and made a face, then lowered his voice a little so my boys, who were playing nearby, couldn't hear him. "You want to talk about bold, just last week a woman who was high on meth poured gasoline around her bed with her boyfriend sleeping in it then lit the entire thing on fire." He straightened up, his badge catching the sun, then went back to his normal voice. "They both made it out okay, but the whole condo went up. It was in her name, too. Insurance does not reimburse you when you burn your own house down on purpose, especially when you're high on meth." He winked as though this was his personal little nugget of insider wisdom that I should take to heart.

My jaw dropped and I covered it to stifle the gigantic gasp I accidentally let slip.

"What's wrong, Mama?" Casey said, looking up. Following his brother's lead, Griffin looked up from playing trains on the floor, a concerned look on his sweet, baby face.

"Oh, sorry, sweetie," I said, trying to compose myself. "Officer Tewksbury was just telling me, uh, how far he has to run every morning to stay in shape for his job."

"That's right, boys," he said, playing along. "If you want to be a police officer you need to run all the way from the Hermosa pier to the Manhattan pier and back."

"Wow," Casey said. Griffin quickly following with his own mini version of "wow." They spent five minutes injecting all sorts of stats on how far they could run and who they knew who could run and then demonstrating what fast running looked like by running in the house to the front door and back several times, Griffin pushing Casey when he got passed, then crying because he didn't win.

I settled them back down, gave them each a few fig bars and some milk and returned to Officer Tewksbury. For the next fifteen minutes, he regaled me with story upon story of arrests the police had recently made for things I never would have dreamed could happen in our small, quaint town: car jackings, kidnappings, all sorts of theft and drug deals, multiple incidences of indecent exposure to minors in park bathrooms, assaults with a deadly weapons, extortion, grand larceny and homicides. It was as if he were describing Tijuana and not the town that was voted "Best Beach Town for Families" by Time Magazine five years in a row; not where Santa was spotted surfing each December and the hometown fair thrived on both Labor Day and Memorial Day. It couldn't be the town where free concerts from bands covering the Beach Boys and Neil Diamond took place every Sunday during the summer by the pier, where the AVP hosts its largest volleyball tournament of the year broadcast by NBC and where, if you wanted to live within a block of the beach it would cost you a cool $2 million for a 1500 square foot fixer with no yard.

"It's the economy," he said as I walked him to the door. "Hits us two-fold. People in other communities lose their jobs or can't make ends meet so they come to the more affluent communities to steal or sell drugs. We, in turn, don't have the budget for enough officers to counter. It's a downward spiral. Hell, I'm only part-time. I only do this because it's a good way to meet clients. My bread and butter comes from selling real estate. I love referrals," he smiled and handed me his card. Looking leading-man-Hollywood-handsome, he put on his aviator sunglasses and wished me a good afternoon, leaving me feeling blindsided.

I closed the door and quickly latched the deadbolt. Slowly I made my way back to the kitchen as all the crime scenes he had laid out for me, scenes that included everything you see on four season's worth of *Law and Order*, replayed in my head. It just didn't compute. Yes, I knew there was crime in L.A., but I had never, ever imagined it happening here, in safe and secure Hermosa Beach, let alone my own *neighborhood* and on a regular basis. I could imagine if someone was being chased by the police and got lost on the freeway then tried to hide out in our tiny little beach streets. A one-time event like that I could certainly imagine. But not someone from our town who was so messed up on drugs that they stumbled into traffic, pointed a gun at a motorist and carjacked them in broad daylight. This having taken place two blocks from our house, right in front of the Ocean Diner where we got pancakes on the weekends and cupcakes after ArtZone classes.

I watched the boys playing, laughing and being silly with each other. They were so very perfect, so innocent all round, and sweet-smelling, every inch sweet and delicious. Conception had not been easy for us. It had taken years to have a viable pregnancy. There had been so many heartaches, that one awful heartbreak. I apparently had fragile eggs. I had no idea they were so fragile back in my single days when I was on the pill and trying *not* to get pregnant. I'd miss a pill and freak out. Little did I know I had almost zero chance of actually getting pregnant the old fashioned way.

So naturally in my mind my two little boys, the strongest of the fragile eggs, sole survivors if you will, would be fragile little people in need of total and constant protection. And that was my job, which I took very seriously. I was driven by it, this fear that enveloped me like a fine mist, that something awful would happen to them, to us, our little family we'd worked so hard to have. Even just *witnessing* a crime like a carjacking, could potentially have a horrible effect on their fragile little psyches, and I couldn't let that happen. I wouldn't let it happen.

"You're overreacting. It couldn't possibly be that bad," Mark said taking off his tie as he trudged up the steps from the garage. It was almost nine and he had just walked in the door after a late dinner meeting, his shiny light brown hair was ruffled as though he'd run his fingers through it more than once and his green eyes were bloodshot from the long day. I'd met him at the garage door and before he even had a chance to kiss me hello I started to feverishly repeat every detail the officer had given me and kept at it as he continued up the stairs with me on his heels.

"What are you talking about?" I said, my voice on the edge of a shriek, my eyes bulging as I watched him get out of his Brooks Brothers button-down and into an old Duke's Fish Shack t-shirt. "How can a *shooting* that resulted in *murder* in the middle of the day half a mile away from our house be considered *overreacting*?"

He moved to the bathroom, I followed. "That was an isolated event," he said reasonably, grabbing his toothbrush while looking past me and squinting as though he was trying to retrieve some information from the back of his brain. "I remember reading about it, took place last November, right? The guy who was shot was working construction on those condos on PCH? It was a dispute over money, something to do with gambling," he said, the lawyer in him trying to get all the facts straight as he applied toothpaste to his SonicCare.

"So?" I said, looking astonished at him in the mirror. "That's right down the street." I grabbed my toothbrush as well, turned it on and began brushing as though plaque was an enemy of the town.

"So," he replied evenly, "the guy wasn't even from around here. That doesn't happen every day. Manhattan has at least one shooting a year, Redondo probably a few more."

"So you're willing to put up with that?" I asked, accidentally spraying the mirror with little dots of toothpaste. I rinsed and spit, wiping my mouth with a tissue. "One a year is acceptable says the man who isn't constantly strapped to the Double Bob dodging bullets as he makes his way to Farmer's Market? What about all the other stuff? The meth lab that was busted on Bonita Ave? The woman who lit her boyfriend on fire? The fraud at the Vans store? The abducted and missing waitress?"

"You said she lit the bed on fire, not the boyfriend," Mark said.

"And that makes a difference?" I snapped, grabbing some Windex from beneath the sink and quickly wiping down the mirror. "There was a woman. In our neighborhood. Who was bat-shit crazy enough to soak her bed with gasoline while her boyfriend was sleeping on it and then she lit a match!"

"Just pointing out a little technicality, and you said he was fine," Mark said, looking at me out of the corner of his eye.

Mark always said that people got into the worst trouble by letting their emotions get the best of their judgment. I'm not sure if it was because he saw this behavior every day, or if it was just his personality. He tended to be Mr. Mild-Mannered, Mr. Even Keel, Mr. Reasonable in just about every circumstance. I took a deep breath and stifled the urge to roll my eyes.

"Ok, but what about all the other stuff? The attempted kidnapping? The robberies?"

"Eh," he shrugged, leaning forward towards the mirror and rubbing a patch of his cheek he had missed shaving. "I guess I can see it."

"What?" I turned and stared him down, mid-floss. "None of this surprises you? Upsets you?"

"I'm just not sure how much of it really affects us. There's crime everywhere, sweetie. Hermosa's not going to be any different."

"Our community, *our family*, is in serious danger, and you respond as though I'm complaining about graffiti or gum on the street."

"No, I'm not. I just don't know what getting upset about it is going to accomplish. We live on a safe street. We have a neighborhood watch. Our town is as safe as it gets here in L.A., without living in a gated community. We don't interact with drug addicts or dealers or kidnappers or thieves. We don't employ nutcases. Sure, we need to pay attention to our surroundings, maybe a little more now that we know about this. We need to be smart about things, make educated, informed decisions up front, but that's the best you can do. We don't live in the hood. There isn't a bad side of the tracks that you need to avoid anywhere in the South Bay as far as I know. Random, bad things are going to happen. There's not much you can do about it. It's a waste of time and energy to stress out about it."

He looked so relaxed, borderline aloof, in his T-shirt and boxers, his attitude only made me more agitated. I spit out my fluoride rinse. "It is not a waste of time to be concerned about this. Hermosa should be completely safe. I'm talking one-hundred-percent-leave-your-doors-unlocked-at-night-knowing-nothing-will-happen-here for one very good reason. We live here! I'm telling you that there are felons living amongst us! Murderers! Drug dealers!"

"I highly doubt that Chuck is a murderer," he quipped as I

followed him to bed and he flipped on the TV.

Chuck was our eighty-year-old neighbor who liked to both work on and drive around in a candy-apple red Corvette while wearing tube socks pulled up to his knees, plaid shorts and nothing else. A month or so ago he had shuffled across the street to brag to me that his 1970's era house had recently been appraised at $2.2 million and from the looks of things, he was using his newly available reverse mortgage to pick up a certain young, scantily-clad clientele in his hot rod. *He may not be a murderer, but he's definitely a john,* I thought to myself, not wanting to get the discussion off track. *Add prostitution to our town's litany of problems.*

"Make all the jokes you want, but I'm in complete and utter disbelief. How could we not have noticed this?"

"I'll give you two answers," he said, adjusting the covers. "One of them is four and the other just turned two."

He was right, of course. Ever since having kids I had lost my awareness of the world at large, my focus was them. By choice, of course. Being a mom was what I wanted more than anything. But still, they had replaced any personal interests I may have had at one point. I no longer read the paper, or got news online or read anything for that matter unless it was child or parent-oriented. Instead of answering emails, I updated my blog with recent photos and stories of what the boys had been doing for Mark's and my out-of-state parents. I hadn't been to a yoga class or on a run without a baby or a stroller in years. The only friends I now had were the ones who also had kids and our get-togethers usually included our kids and the topic of conversation was almost always about our kids. The boys had taken over my life with a vengeance.

We could afford a babysitter, but I had waited so long to have my babies and had watched jealously as my friends had theirs that I was hell bent on being the one who was there for them—*always*—especially with our conception difficulties. I had tried, at the beginning, to maintain some semblance of balance, but Casey had had other ideas. I remember having him on a playmat when he was six-months old, I was answering emails and paying bills while he wailed, his fat feet kicking the little stuffed giraffes and elephants that dangled above and were supposed to keep him entertained. I got up from my desk and laid down next to him, putting my feet up as well and demonstrating how much fun it could be to kick the hell out of a giraffe. "See? Isn't this awesome?" He stopped crying instantly and looked at me with the sweetest blue eyes I had ever seen.

"So this is how it's going to be, huh?" He smiled, his eyes lighting up as he gurgled his response with adorable spit bubbles that melted my heart like chocolate in a hot car. In that moment I gave in to him completely and I felt my shoulders relax as though I was giving up the fight. "Okay then, munchkin," I vowed as the two of us stared at each other. Another smile, more bubbles. And my world got very, very small.

Now that Casey was older and I got the rare twenty minutes where he could play independently while Griffin napped, it was always used to catch up on logistics like emptying the dishwasher. Never did I think to use my time to check the police report. But still, an increase in crime like the one the officer had described should have been headline news in my opinion, especially in our local paper, the South Bay News. And people should have been talking about it on the playground at preschool. The only thing I'd heard people get riled up about lately was that one of the Kardashians had been spotted looking at real estate.

I looked at Mark, a giant version of our two boys. They would grow up to look just like him. That is, if they survived. "Exactly. And if we want our four-year-old and two-year-old to make it to kindergarten, don't you think we should do something? Aren't you worried about them? Worried for their safety?" I tried not to glare but the instinct was too strong.

He looked at me with his head cocked and a don't-be-ridiculous expression on his face. "Alright," he conceded, taking a deep breath, "what should we do about it? I don't think they make bullet-proof strollers, and I know you won't drive places that are walkable. Do you want to move?"

The question took me by surprise. Ever since meeting Mark and landing here at the beach ten years ago I've felt like I finally found my place in the world, that this would be our home forever.

"No, of course I don't want to move," I said reflectively. "I just want this to be a safe place to raise our family."

"As do I," he said, pulling me into him, clearly tiring of the conversation. "So why don't you fish around and find out why we don't have a better police force. Talk to someone on City Council or someone from one of those mom groups you're in. Better yet, call Mayor Arvid. We pay enough in property taxes, we shouldn't have to rely on realtors for protection for Christ's sake."

This fact, I think, bothered Mark more than the issue of the rising crime. It didn't bother me as much because, after spending almost a year house hunting in the South Bay, I had met a whole lot of realtors and they were not only tenacious, but they could also be cunning and sometimes even downright vicious. So maybe we needed to convert *more* realtors into part-time cops in order to fight fire with fire. Plus, there were so many of them, they were literally everywhere.

That got me thinking, as I stared at the ceiling unable to sleep, both worried about the dangers that lurked outside my window and annoyed by Mark's seeming indifference as he snored away beside me. I realized I knew some people who could be equally tenacious, equally cunning, and probably even more vicious, particularly when it came to the security of their children and homes. And they carried stylish diaper bags.

Two

The next morning I woke up with a plan. I had to sound the alarm and alert the people of Hermosa Beach to my new-found information, but I couldn't run around like Chicken Little. I needed to alert the ones who would be concerned the most and would help the most. The ones who had temerity, were innovative, and could work well together. The folks who were problem solvers, assiduous and more than anything else, the ones who were the eyes and ears of our town. I needed to alert the moms.

I figured once I got all the moms I knew together, I'd lay out the news the same way the cop/realtor had laid it out for me. The moms I knew were all glued to their phones. Once they knew, I reasoned, they could then call or text their friends and word would spread faster than conjunctivitis in a daycare. We could then meet with the city council, the mayor, and the police force and figure out a solution to this disaster. Maybe form a committee or a task force or something. I was hell bent on not letting a bunch of criminals take over my beloved Hermosa. Our town could, and *would*, be saved. Even if it killed me.

I needed to get everyone together and the best way I knew was to host the mother of all Moms' Night Out. Over the past five years I had orchestrated plenty of these MNO's. I'd become the "go-to" mom for organizing them and I loved it, it was like a small throw back to days as a producer (plus it enabled me to control everything so I could work around Mark's schedule so he could watch the boys). My guest list at this point was pretty vast. It included all the moms I'd met from several years' worth of Mommy and Me classes, Mom's Club, Casey's preschool, My Gym and others from the park or playground. I wasn't all that picky for these big group events; basically you just had to be a mom and live in the general area.

My goal had been one a month, but I usually missed a few during the summer and skipped December all together. So far we'd been to every new restaurant in the South Bay, seen plenty of chick flicks (anything with Johnny Depp got a huge response), gone rock climbing, dressed up and watched the Oscars at my house, learned to surf on one occasion and paddle board on another, chartered a sail boat for a booze cruise, sang karaoke at a dive bar near LAX, scouted for celebrities at the Beverly Hills Hotel, and bar hopped up and down the Strand dressed as pirates while riding our kids' scooters, one of my all-time favorites.

But *this* particular MNO, this one would have to be different. This one mattered. I wasn't getting us all together for a little camaraderie or some grown-up entertainment. I wasn't getting us out of our houses, ponytails, and mommy clothes just for a much needed drink. We had serious business to discuss. I *had* to make people think this one was not to be missed. The first thing on my agenda, therefore, after getting the boys breakfast, refereeing three arguments, unloading the dishes, and changing Griffin's post-breakfast diaper, was to send out an email inviting everyone to my house.

I allowed the boys twenty minutes of Mickey Mouse as I sat down at the computer with my cold coffee and high hopes for the subject line of my eVite. It needed to be compelling, invoke action and convey urgency. I was aspiring to use words that would have teeth and be alarming, something like "Lice Outbreak!" or "Measles Epidemic!" but without the medical slant.

I considered something gossipy like "Johnny Depp Casting Middle-Aged Moms for New Pirates Movie!" I'm not above lying to get some attention. My words needed to make the moms read my email *now*, even though they may have a child pulling at them or dinner boiling over on the stove. The subject line couldn't be benign. Let's face it; e-Vites like those don't get opened for days. Sometimes not at all.

Unfortunately the best I could come up with was a disappointing "Emergency MNO!!!!" which was generic and lame, I had to admit, but Casey was having a major meltdown because Griffin was messing with his Legos and in the hysteria that was taking place in my living room, I just couldn't think. 'Emergency', I figured, was one of those words that made moms' ears perk up no matter what and I crossed my fingers that it would be enough to do the trick. I tossed a few extra no-brainers into the body like 'community crisis' and 'extremely dangerous living situation' for added firepower along with more than my fair share of exclamation marks, shot it out to my database of 73 moms and crossed my fingers.

That was the first part of my plan but I needed a pre-emptive strike. I needed to get my closest friends together beforehand and pronto, to see if they knew anything. I wanted it to be immediate if not sooner, which in our case took three days.

We decided to try this new Mexican place called "Samba!" on the promenade by the pier. It was hip and swanky and had replaced a tired, old fish shack run almost single-handedly by a Vietnamese woman, one of several older businesses that had recently fallen to glossy, fresh ones with their correlating crowds. The promenade was alive with people spilling out from open air bars and restaurants, cyclists whizzing by, tourists window shopping as they made their way to the pier.

I led our group of five to the restaurant like a mother duck. We followed the hostess past the bar and tables filled with mostly 30-somethings, men in jeans with bling on the back pockets and surfer T-shirts, sometimes with a short-sleeved button down over the top, and ladies in spaghetti-strapped tiny dresses and big heels. Everyone sun-kissed and beautiful, laughing and having fun, soaking up the chic décor along with the Cadillac margaritas as if they didn't have a care in the world. As if they were *safe*.

Mark and I had been that way, once upon a time. Back before we were parents, before we were homeowners, living in his tiny Strand apartment. We'd cruise north in his old, cherry-red convertible Saab up the coast highway for seafood in Malibu and end up continuing to Santa Barbara to stay in a B & B for a weekend of wine tasting. We'd throw parties on his deck and invite random passersby to join us. We did dinners out with friends, just like these people, all over L.A. and never once thought to bring up local crime stats as a topic of conversation.

The petite blonde hostess with a dolphin tattooed on her shoulder seated us at a table with a beautiful tile mosaic pattern near the back, per my request, where I hoped it would be quieter. The wall next to our table was stylishly sleek and made entirely of river rock with water trickling down. It would have been a really cool place for an MNO, I thought, had the circumstances been better.

We sat around the table, my three closest friends plus Ramona, catching up on small life events and commenting about the menu, the clientele and the beautiful twenty-something wait staff as we ordered. Finally Lexie, my best friend, had had enough.

"Okay. We're set," she said impatiently, gesturing dramatically to the table. "We've all got water, silverware, napkins, margaritas, chips, salsa and we've ordered. Can you spill the beans now? What's got your panties all up in a wad?"

Lexi looked gorgeous as usual, her honey blonde hair falling in loose curls to her shoulders as if she'd actually spent time styling it when I knew she'd probably had it up in a scrunchie all day and barely thought to run her fingers through before heading out. She wore a light cottony top with a blue flower print that made her crystal blue eyes almost glow, like a husky. Her only accessories were a few rubber band bracelets her kids must have made and her wedding ring, a four-karat princess-cut that gave her eyes a run for their money in the sparkle-category.

I stared at her and raised one eyebrow. "My panties are not in a wad or any other shape that's—"

"Ignore her," Lisa cut in from my other side. "She's just upset you're not telling us what your problem is." Lisa was the only one of us who had a full-time job and from the looks of her silk paisley Ann Taylor shirt tucked tightly into a dark pencil skirt with a matching jacket she had draped over her chair, she hadn't had time to change since she got home hours ago. I felt a tinge of guilt for pulling her away from her family on a weeknight when she had already had such a full day. "Go ahead, we're all ears."

I took a deep breath and tried to relax into the conversation. "Well," I began, looking at the four ladies who were, for the most part, waiting patiently, encouragingly. "Remember how on Tuesday it was super warm, like summer? Well it was so beautiful I let Casey play hooky from preschool and took him and Griffin to the beach."

"Skipping class already? In preschool?" Jackie interrupted. "Tsk, tsk. What kind of message is that sending?" Jackie was the youngest of us all by more than a decade and her choice of 'going out clothes'—a designer T-shirt, tight jeans and flip-flops—accentuated that difference. Her dark skin was radiant and she had her hair pulled back into a colorful headband. A string of beads and chandelier earrings complimented her outfit perfectly. Jackie had recently quit her job as a Disneyland Imagineer, one of the truly talented people who make the experience of the Magic Kingdom so magical, in order to stay home with her one-year-old daughter. Her creativity was unrivaled, like Martha Stewart with ADD, and without an obvious outlet it was emerging in oddball ways, like now as she turned a free South Bay Magazine she had grabbed from the bin at the front of the restaurant into a funky, cool collage.

I smiled and was about to continue when Lisa cut in again. "Hold on. Is this story, this issue you want to discuss, is it about your kids?" She took a sip of her margarita and looked eagerly over the salted rim.

I looked at her sideways, cocking my head. "Kind of, but not directly."

"Does it, by chance, have anything, anything at all what-so-ever to do with the City Council?" she continued.

I thought for a second, picking up a chip and nibbling the corner. "No, why?"

She smiled and turned to Lexie and held out her palm. "Fork it over."

Lexie smirked and dug into her purse. "Gladly," she said, whipping out a five-dollar bill and handing it to Lisa.

"Wait a minute," I said, taking in the scene, "did you guys *bet* on my problem?"

"Maybe," Lexie said with a smile that said that's what you get for keeping secrets from your best friend.

"And what exactly did you bet I wanted to discuss?" I asked.

Lexie was smug. "I was pretty sure it was going to be your usual. How lame our City Council is and how they can't get anything done."

I slumped in my chair and glared at her. Lisa patted me on the knee. "Don't take it personally, Kel. Lexie here was driving us crazy. She was texting every hour with ideas of what your problem could be. It was the only way I could make her stop, she's like a little kid. I had to do something. Besides," she added, "not that I don't think your problem is an emergency, but if it were a true life-threatening event, you would have told us immediately. So go ahead."

I didn't know where to even start now. Part of me wanted to say forget about it but another part knew she was right, I did rant an awful lot about the City Council and even this was somewhat related since they were in control of the budget for the police. I decided I couldn't even hint at that right now but instead took a sip of my marg and blurted out the whole wallet story, including how within an hour of losing it someone had already charged $3500 worth of sporting goods to my American Express.

"So there ya go," I said, dipping a chip in the fabulous house-made guacamole, "murder and mayhem have arrived in Hermosa Beach. I was just wondering if you guys have heard about any of this, because it basically blindsided me." I plopped the chip in my mouth.

The concern around the table was genuine, nobody shrugged me off like Mark had and I loved these ladies for that. Instead, they began their own accounts of incidents.

"My neighbor's car was broken into just last night," Ramona was the first to offer. "Right in front of her house. Car alarm never even went off. They just seemed to rummage around the glove box. I found her manual and service records littered on her lawn this morning when I was walking Smedley." Ramona was the newest member of our little group and by far the oldest. I guessed she was somewhere north of 80 and had pretty much been a hermit up until Jackie befriended her and started bringing her along to all our MNO's. She reminded me of that smartass old lady on the Hallmark cards.

"They were probably looking for a gun or prescription drugs," Lisa said. "I saw that on *60 Minutes*. Most car alarms are simple software so crooks can now download the codes to unlock them off the internet for twenty-five bucks. They just have to walk around the neighborhood finding a match."

"That's horrible," I said, my brow furrowed. "So you can have your car locked and alarm set and still get broken into? How do you even protect yourself from that?"

Lisa shrugged. "They don't know."

"That's awful, but check this," Lexie said. "Did you read in the Beach Reporter about the lady whose car was stolen at the gas station in South Redondo while she was at the kiosk paying? She wasn't even *inside* paying. She was right there and her toddler was inside! Luckily they found the car and the baby half a mile away."

We all together gasped, I shook my head. Just the thought was unimaginable.

Jackie knew of a friend of a friend who had been stopped at a traffic light when a man pulled up next to her and had pointed a gun at her. "She's totally freaked out now, doesn't want to leave the house," she said.

"I would be, too," I said, shaking my head. "Who does that?"

"But you're not even safe in your own house," Lisa said leaning in, her voice dropped conspiratorially. "Did you guys hear about that woman whose house was broken into just the other day with her in it? She's on Monterey Place and the guy claimed to be the police."

"What did she do?" Jackie asked, wide-eyed. "Did she have a gun?"

"No, she apparently was very cool headed or just really confused and the guy eventually left. I think he just took some random stuff on his way out, like a vase or something. I think she was really old."

"Wow, she's lucky she wasn't hurt," Jackie said.

"Old people are generally confused," Ramona said.

"Not all old people, just you," Jackie said with a wink.

"That would have been smart, to fake like you're confused or just go along with him," Lexie said, her face flushing red with animation. "I'd fake it right up to the point where I'd show him our safe in the closet and while he was rifling through it, I'd hit him over the head with Stosh's baseball bat."

I shook my head, staring at Lexie. "Oh my God, could you really do that? Hit a guy over the head with a baseball bat?"

"Hell yeah," she said, her eyes narrowed, determined. "In a heartbeat. I wouldn't think twice."

"Wouldn't you be scared he'd have a gun?" Jackie asked.

"Uh, yeah," she said in a *duh* tone. "That's why I'd have to hit him over the head with my bat. Beat him to the punch," she said as if this sort of logic should be obvious to everyone. I made a mental note to buy some bats.

"You know who I'd like to hit over the head," Lisa said, "the guy who tried to sell Scarlet and her friends drugs."

My head swung swiftly to Lisa. "What?"

"Yeah, right down here at the promenade. Cute guy apparently, but a total snake. She was down here with two of her girlfriends, just hanging out after Junior Guards. I guess this twenty-year-old sidled up next to them, started to flirt a little, then asked them if they wanted to have a little fun. When they asked him what he meant, he showed them a bag of pot."

Jackie's jaw dropped. "What did they do?"

Lisa scrunched up her face a little. "Well, that's the weird part. They didn't buy it, but they didn't exactly tell him to go the hell away either. It sounds like they were flattered by the attention."

"Nice tactic," Ramona said, sneering.

The rest of the dinner was spent telling story after story of people we knew or had heard of that had been burglarized, vandalized, or attacked in some way. I was glad to see the others shocked by these stories, their frequency, the violent nature of many of them. Taken individually it wouldn't have been so disconcerting, but collectively, we agreed it was a major problem, one that needed fixing, and soon.

I decided there was no better time than the present.

We paid the bill and walked to my car, my friends settling back into their casual chit-chat while I quietly schemed. One of the stories told over dinner involved the middle school recently being vandalized, like within the last twenty-four hours. I had it in my head that if the story were true, then we would indeed need to declare war on this new criminal element, go on full-scale alert. But if it weren't, then maybe the sky wasn't falling, and maybe we could get by with implementing some hard-core neighborhood watches. Either way, I needed to know and I wanted my friends with me. I once read this article in one of my parenting magazines that said if a task took less than five minutes, you should do it right then and there instead of adding it to your to-do list because the time you spent worrying and thinking about it would be more than the five minutes to just get the thing done. The detour I had in mind would take more than five minutes, but the gist was the same.

We got into my black Toyota Highlander and headed up the hill. I gripped the wheel as we got to Ocean Drive where, if I were driving us all home, I should continue straight up the hill. I exhaled, knowing I needed a diversion when I spotted the Christie's sign in the yard of the house across the street.

"Hey," I said over my shoulder, "did any of you hear Britney Spears was looking at that Strand property? The one by the 90210 beach house?"

I was totally making this up, but knew everyone had strong opinions about Britney and sure enough, the car erupted. I made the odd left turn, stealing a glance in the rear view mirror to see if anyone had noticed. Nothing. They were all still gabbing. *Maybe* a flicker of recognition washed across Ramona's face as she gazed outside, she probably didn't even know who Britney was, but when she looked back to me I put my eyes on the road before we could make eye contact.

I saw the mission-style church up ahead, the stucco painted the color of Pepto Bismol, even in the dark it was impossible to miss. I withheld the urge to cut my lights until I pulled into the parking lot and drove around back. I knew it was right above the school and was happily surprised when I found that none of the lights from the street made it back into this part of the parking lot. Assuming no one saw us drive in, we were in the excellent position for sneaking out of the car and down the pathway unnoticed.

I braced myself for any pushback I might get considering I owed them for bending over backwards to get out tonight in the first place. They had rearranged their schedules, hired babysitters or called husbands home early from work to cover the evening routine, not to mention *showered,* something that I knew first hand could take some serious finagling. I shook off the guilt, promising myself I'd make it up to them at some point then cut the engine, which in turn cut the conversation causing everyone to glance around and then at me.

"What are we doing here?" Lexie asked.

I turned to face them and raised one eyebrow. "Going on a mission."

Three

The church parking lot was just above the school's ball field. The boys and I had discovered a worn path of short switchbacks cut into the hill connecting the two when we were playing on the campus one weekend. I led the way.

The night air smelled of eucalyptus and the sea. A fine mist had already moved in from the ocean making the path slippery. We held on to each other as we moved along in the dark, those in sandals (me and Jackie), keeping those in heels (Lexie and Lisa) upright while everyone looked out for Ramona (really old clogs).

It took just a minute for us to reach the edge of the blacktop at the back of the school where we stopped to brush off the bits of dirt and wood chips that were stuck to our shoes. Before anyone could move toward the building, I told them to hold on as I set my bag down and began to dig through it.

"Viola!" I said, holding up a bottle of 2007 Justin Isosceles I'd tucked in before I left home, not knowing where the night might lead us. To my surprise, not a single person had complained about the detour, but I still felt compelled to make our investigation as fun and social as possible. I handed some plastic cups to Jackie to pass around, found my corkscrew and popped it open.

"Now that's what I'm talkin' about," Lexie said. "Way to be prepared."

"You must have been a girl scout when you were little," Lisa said, taking a small sip.

"Nope, just a Brownie." I stashed the bottle back in my bag and nodded toward the buildings to get us moving.

Jackie scoffed. "How did you, Miss Overachiever, avoid the lure of earning all those badges?"

I laughed as the others fell in step with me. "If I recall, the girls were scary and mean."

"Girl scouts are like the *Heathers* of first grade," Lexie said. "If they could haze, they'd be all over it. That's why Savannah won't be joining them."

"Really? They're that bad?" Jackie asked apprehensively, probably thinking forward to the days when Sierra would be old enough to join. I envied that troop because Jackie would blow the ass off their Arts and Crafts program.

"That's not why," I interjected, shooting Lexie a scolding look for trying to scare Jackie. "She's just teasing, Jackie. The truth is Josh won't *let* Savannah join because he knows Lexie here will try to take over the cookie selling operation for the entire South Bay and the Williams family would never see their wife or mother again."

"Like they need any help selling those things," Lisa said with disgust. "Let me tell you one thing: There is nothing "thin" about Thin Mints. You cannot lose baby weight with boxes of cookies around. I still blame Thin Mints for me being fat five years later."

"You're not even close to fat," Lexie scoffed. "And you're right, Kelly. I would sell those cookies and I'd sell the shit out of them. We're not talking a card table in front of a grocery store. We'd go big, baby. Hit the places with money. We're talking Rodeo Drive, the law offices in Century City, all the golf clubs. I'd launch a Smart Phone app, Facebook page, Twitter account, corporate matching program—"

"And this is why we're all lucky Savannah doesn't even want to join the scouts," I said, barely getting the last word out of my mouth because we had just reached the courtyard of the campus and the damage nearly took my breath away.

The school was basically two buildings. In the front was your typical mid-century U-shaped design, one story, boxy and all brick except for the windows, which were designed to be high enough to let in light while not allowing the kids any distracting views. Two classrooms were able to fit side by side going down the sides of the "U" with two more at the base, although those were used as offices. The empty space in between the "U" was used as a covered courtyard where the kids ate their lunches on picnic tables near the bottom and grew a garden toward the top. Beyond the garden was a wall that separated the school from a fairly busy street. Juxtaposed in the rear was the new addition, a two-story all-glass modern building that was more or less your basic rectangle starting from the middle of the U but then jutting out to one side. It housed the library, art and music rooms, computer and science labs, as well as the classrooms and lockers for the older grades. The blacktop, playground and soccer fields sat to one side of both structures. The whole campus probably took up five acres right smack dab in the center of town.

When Lisa told us over dinner earlier that the school had been vandalized, I had hoped that it was just some kids having a little fun as a class prank or something, lots of kids did that. But this, this was way beyond something silly and fun. This knocked the wind out of me—another stinking sucker punch.

We walked slowly around the perimeter of the different buildings, taking in the mess in complete silence, a rarity for us. Spray paint was everywhere and cubbyholes had been pried off the wall. Every trashcan in sight had been overturned.

We eventually made it back to the central courtyard where all the picnic benches had been over-turned and posters and papers lay scattered all over the ground. Turning over a few picnic benches, we sat, all of us suddenly sober, trying to make sense of it all.

"Who would do this?" Jackie whispered.

"Punks," Ramona said. "Bored, teenage punks."

"Assholes," Lexie added. "Shitty, fuckhead assholes."

"There is no way we're going to be able to hide this from the kids until it gets cleaned up and fixed," Lisa said, putting her hand on Lexie's knee. It was considered the middle school of Hermosa Beach because it contained sixth, seventh and eighth grades, but it also was home to the third, fourth and fifth graders and so was partially an elementary school. Both Lexie and Lisa had children who attended school here. Lexie's oldest was in fourth grade and Lisa's older two were in eighth and fifth. The kids had today, Friday, off as a developmental day for the teachers so no one had yet to see the damage.

"This is going to require one hell of a fundraiser," I said, trying to size up the cost of the repairs. I was struck, again, by how easy it was to destroy something, just like with my wallet. It took the thief a second or two to swipe it and would take me weeks to replace my driver's license and every credit card, reward card and membership card. Not to mention finding time to hit the mall to get a new one and deal with the unauthorized charges.

We sat there, astonished and sickened, assessing the damage and mulling repairs when we heard a small noise near the entrance of the school.

"What was that?" Lexie asked, as all our heads went up like prairie dogs. We watched each other, frozen, listening. Seconds later we heard loud footsteps from several pairs of feet—heavy, men's feet—heading our way and fast.

Now I knew this school like the back of my hand. Almost every Saturday I took my boys here to play before we hit the beach. We'd run around the playground, play hide and seek in the courtyard, investigate all the nooks and crannies and look in the classrooms. Casey loved the place so much he wanted to skip straight to third grade instead of going to Pre-K this fall.

So I knew we could have quickly ducked down the corridor that led to the south side. I knew there was a safe place back there where we could have called the cops and reported the suspicious sounds without being detected while we waited safely for the police to arrive. But something had changed in me. Ever since the officer stood in my living room and told me offhandedly that my town was going to hell and there really wasn't *anything to be done about it* I had started to feel a little nag, both in the pit of my stomach and the back of my brain. That sensation had been growing, metastasizing, with each new horrific crime story I heard and it was that feeling that was now in control.

"C'mon," I whispered, grabbing everyone before they had time to argue, herding them to the side of the courtyard where we could hide behind some thick azaleas next to the wall of the front office. Ramona tripped on one of the branches and ended up falling on top of Lisa who landed on her face in the dirt with an audible thud. The rest of us were quick to get them up and settled so we were still as statues when four men hastily crept into the quad.

They wore black gloves and dark clothing. Two wore baseball hats, one had his sweatshirt hood up and the other had a crew cut. The one with the hood had a crowbar in his hands. They were quick and moved like a unit, entering the courtyard single file. They seemed to be scanning the graffiti for information, reading it as if it was a clue. "In here," one of them called, motioning to the others to join him by a window near the front office. We watched in horror from twenty feet away as the man with the crowbar smashed the window. I had to put my hand over Jackie's mouth because she let out a little scream that, lucky for us, was covered by the sound of breaking glass. I held my breath worried the men could hear my heart pound.

The guy with the crew cut hopped through the opening and unlocked the door for the others. Seconds later they were out, holding two laptops and a desktop computer that they set on the ground outside the office. They moved on. "Over here!" one of the baseball capped men said, looking at the graffiti and moving toward another office. Again, the man with the crowbar smashed the window as we all winced, watching helplessly as another man hopped through and opened the door. They were quick, only inside for seconds then out carrying more computer equipment, a file drawer and some iPads, which they placed next to the first pile. "This way!" the man with the crowbar ordered as we all strained from our perch behind the bushes to watch them disappear down the hall toward the library.

"I can't believe this!" Lexie whispered to us all a look of complete shock and disgust on her face.

"What do we do?" Jackie whispered back.

"I'm calling the police," Lisa whispered. She had already pulled out her phone and was dialing. We heard another window being smashed and from the sound of it, I figured it was either the library or the computer lab, both of which were on the other side of the hall from the courtyard.

"Follow me," I whispered, crawling along the wall toward the street. I stayed low and went slowly so as to not make any noise, staying behind the bushes the whole way until we reached the end of the brick building by the garden. I quickly checked to see if the coast was clear, then stood up and began to slide with my back across the east side of the building, staying in the shadows as the others followed suit. When we were close to the corner at the front of the school I stopped and we all huddled together, peeking around the corner to where we had first heard the men. Sure enough, an empty white Toyota truck with oversized wheels was now parked under a eucalyptus tree by the bike racks and the courtyard entrance, out of the lights of the parking lot. And, to add insult to injury, it had run over several azalea bushes, left tire marks in the grass, and was parked on top of the geraniums the 3rd graders had recently planted in the flower beds.

"Looks like we found the getaway vehicle," Lexie said.

"There's a sedan on the street that wasn't here before, too," Ramona added. "Maybe a Chevy Nova." We all strained to see the street over the four foot wall. Sure enough, at the edge of the school grounds there was another car.

"Good eye," Lisa noted.

"Did you get through to the cops?" I asked Lisa, glaring at the pick-up truck as if it was to blame.

"Yeah, the dispatcher said she was sending officers over immediately and that we should stay safely out of the way and wait for the authorities," Lisa replied.

I looked away from her and back at the truck. That would have sounded reasonable to me a week ago. But as I stared at those once bright geraniums all gnarled under the big fat wheels of the truck, pinned down as if they were gasping for air. I envisioned the little kids coming here on Monday, seeing the school they were so proud of completely wrecked, and I imagined the expressions on their faces as their entire sense of well-being dissolved. And that little visual put me over the edge.

"Fuck that," I said, my voice surprisingly steady. "We're taking these losers out."

Four

When I looked from the truck to my friends I must have had a determined look on my face, like the stay-at-home version of Jason Bourne, because nobody argued with me.

"What do you have in mind?" Lisa asked.

"Here," I said, handing Lisa my keys. "Take Jackie and Ramona and get my car. Stay hidden. Follow whoever gets away. Lexie and I will stay here and try to get as much information on these guys as we can. Maybe even try to slow them down."

"Be careful," Lisa warned. "They look like they know what they're doing. I bet they're armed."

We all nodded. Lisa took my keys and the three of them took off running over the soccer field and into the night.

"Ok, Wonder Woman," Lexie said, turning to me, "what's the big plan?"

To be honest, I didn't really have a plan. All I knew was that somehow we had to stop these guys. I figured as moms we were good at winging it, plus we had the element of surprise on our side, which as far as elements go, was a really good one.

"Come on," I said, grabbing Lexie's hand and creeping out from the safety of the wall toward the back of the truck. I knew we had to get as much information on the men as possible, which meant trying to be close to them when they came back out in order to get descriptions. It also meant getting the make, model and license plate of each car. But even that didn't seem to be a sure thing, a guarantee that they would be caught. And at this point, I was hell bent on a guarantee. We reached the back bumper and I bent down and began digging through my bag. "Cover me," I whispered.

"What does that mean, 'cover you'?" Lexie whispered back. "I don't have a gun."

"It just means," I said looking up at her, "to look out for the bad guys and let me know if they're coming. Now get down a little and shhhhh!" I pulled her down so she was at least hiding behind the truck and not standing there like she was waiting in line for a latte. I finished rifling through my bag until I found what I was looking for. "Aha!"

Lexie looked down. "Duct tape? Who keeps duct tape in their bag?"

"Casey's obsessed with it," I said tearing off several strips. "Give him a little duct tape and it buys me some time as we grocery shop."

"I bet Griffin loves that," she said, her head scanning the grounds back and forth like a sprinkler.

"Rule number one of the duct tape is he can't use it on his brother." I took the strips and began taping my phone to the inside of the truck's back bumper. "There, now we can track them if we have to." We heard another window smash in the distance and we both flinched.

"Are you crazy? What if they find your phone? They don't strike me as the type of people who would just return it nicely to your doorstep."

I knew she was talking about all the personal information my phone contained: where I lived, what my kids and husband looked like, who my friends were. Nasty people could do serious damage with that. It was a risk and a big one. I took a deep breath, knowing that with this act, I was fully committing to this cause. "I know, I know," I said, praying that the cops would be here any minute, knowing, though, it could be a while.

We ran crouched down back toward the wall, waiting for the men to appear, but halfway Lexie stopped and ran back to the truck. I watched her grab something from its bed and then catch up to me by the wall holding a tire iron. We were both slightly out of breath, more I think because we were scared than because we were out of shape.

"What are you going to do with *that*?" I asked, my eyes wide with surprise. I tried to take in slow breaths to control how shaky and scared I felt, but they weren't working. I could still hear my heart pounding in my ears.

"I don't know, but I feel safer holding it. Here, you should have a weapon, too." She looked around, then, finding nothing, grabbed my bag and took out the wine bottle. She popped off the cork and began pouring wine out into one of the flower beds.

"Hey! What are you doing?" I cried. "That's a 2007 Isosceles!"

"Well," Lexie said, putting the cork back into the bottle and handing it back to me, "I doubt the thieves will know the difference between that or Two-Buck Chuck if you have to crack them over the head with it. Now do you want to defend yourself or have a tasting?"

I took the bottle. "I just don't see how it's any better of a weapon empty, that's all," I said. I looked the bottle over, remembering the Paso Robles tasting room where Mark and I had first discovered this winery before Casey was born. Never in a million years did I think I'd be doing anything with the bottle other than pouring wine out of it, certainly not brandishing it as if it were a light saber the way I was now. I tried lightly pounding myself on the forehead to see how much it would hurt, and was surprised by how much it did. "Ow," I said, rubbing my head as Lexie folded her arms across her chest and gave me a look. Clearly I needed a little training and I looked at her a little sheepishly. "Do you really think they're armed? Like with guns? Real ones?" I said, rubbing an emerging goose egg.

"No, I'm sure they're just armed with sticks and stones, grumpy faces and potty mouths," Lexie deadpanned. "Of course I think they're armed with guns. *Real ones*. I sure wish I had a real one right now," she said, looking around.

"Could you really shoot somebody?" I asked, taking the bottle into both hands and practicing swinging it baseball-style into a tree branch in slow motion.

"Hell yes! Not to kill anyone, of course. I'd aim for their legs or crotch or something. I'm just as sick of this bullshit as you are, especially when it comes to messing with our kids." A car passed and we jumped back into the shadows and clung to the side of the building.

"Hmmm," I murmured.

"What's, '*hmmm*' supposed to mean?" Lexie replied. "Couldn't you shoot someone?"

"No! I mean, I don't think so. Maybe. I don't know, it would depend on the circumstances." Lexie's comment about weapons had triggered a thought and I dug into my bag. "Hey, look at this!" held up my Swiss Army Knife. "I totally forgot about this. Come on."

I took Lexie's tire iron from her hands and dropped it with my wine bottle in the grass by the building. I could hear the men at the very back of the school, so I knew we had at least a minute or two. I grabbed Lexie and practically pulled her arm out of its socket as I rushed her toward the wall by the street. "Up you go," I said, grabbing her foot and giving her a haphazard boost over the short wall, making a mental note that should we ever attempt this again, to give people a dress code that did not include heels. Lexie stifled her protest, glared at me, then took hold of the wall and pulled herself up and over. I grabbed the top and with my biggest effort, hoisted myself up and over, landing right beside Lex.

"There's a gate right there," she pointed down the fence twenty yards.

"Yeah but you can see it from the courtyard. Too risky," I said, pulling Lexie low to the ground on the sidewalk and running over to the car Ramona had pointed out that we thought belonged to the men. I took out my knife and began to slash the tires. "I've always wanted to do this," I whispered, struggling with the tool as I tried to saw the tire back and forth. "Christ, this is harder than it looks."

Lexie scoffed. "Some criminal you'd make. You put it in the side, silly, not the tread. Like this," Lexie took the knife from me and quickly and easily sliced through the smooth side of the front tire. The wounded rubber let out a loud smelly hiss. "This better be one of their getaway vehicles, or we just bought someone a brand new set of tires."

"How do you know how to slash tires?" I asked, both surprised and impressed by my best friend.

Lexie just shrugged. "TV? Movies? Maybe you should borrow my Eminem cd and listen to a little more rap and a little less ABBA."

I let the ABBA comment slide because whether they would help my street cred or not, they were still a really good band. Taking the knife, I went to work on the back tire and listened with intense pleasure as it gave off a loud hiss. As it subsided we could hear the men coming so we had no time to slash the pick-up's tires. Instead we bolted over the fence again and ducked back into the shadows where we grabbed our make-shift weapons, making ourselves as flat as possible against the wall. "Where the hell are those cops?" Lexie whispered. "I swear, they're right on you the second you jaywalk or your parking meter expires, but have a *real* emergency and they take their own sweet time."

"They're understaffed, it's the City Council's fault, shhh!" I whispered, having learned more than I ever expected about the inner workings of the Hermosa Beach police department earlier this week. "Here they come now, get ready!"

We plastered our bodies to the wall, heavily camouflaged by the nearby bushes and trees as all four men walked by, moving quickly and with armfuls of computer equipment. When they'd passed us, we knelt down and peered through the bushes, watching as one by one they piled the stuff in the back of the truck and the one with the crew cut got in and started the engine. The other three turned and ran double-time back into the school. They were back in seconds to finish loading the stolen equipment. One of the men with a baseball hat got in the passenger seat while the one with the hood tossed the crowbar into the bed and banged twice on the side with his hand. Good to go. The truck slowly rolled through the flowers crawled off the curb and into the parking lot. When it pulled out onto the road, the driver turned on the headlights and I felt nauseous as I watched my phone roll away. I prayed that Lisa would be there to follow them and cursed myself for not doing something more to have slowed them down.

The other two men didn't wait to watch the pick-up leave. They had already turned and were quickly walking to their car on the street, the one with the hood pulling out his keys. They noticed the slashed tires immediately. The one with the baseball hat pounded the top of the car. Both looked around as if to spot the guilty culprit. They began arguing but stopped when they heard sirens in the distance. We watched them from around the corner and the safety of the building as they exchanged a few more words before jumping in, starting it up and driving as quickly as they could down the street on only two good tires. We ran from the shadows and peered over the fence, my heart sinking as the car slowly drove down the road.

When they were a few blocks away however, a cop car suddenly came out from a side street blocking them, its rollers switched on, brightly lighting up the street and surrounding homes. Two officers got out and stood behind their doors, guns drawn and pointed. One officer yelled at them to get out of the car slowly and to put their hands on their head.

The sedan stopped and nothing happened for what felt like forever as Lexie and I looked on, stunned, from behind the wall. Then the two men got out of the car and began to put their hands up, but the next second they took off running back toward the school—straight toward us—with the police giving chase.

"Holy shit!" Lexie whispered. "What do we do? What do we do?"

I sucked in a huge breath and pulled Lexie back. This, I felt, was my second chance. I had watched a million crime shows, was addicted to action flicks, played cops and robbers and spies and super heroes countless times with my kids, which, I figured, was good enough preparation for this situation. It was time to take the training wheels off.

"I bet they cut through the school and disappear up the hill by where we parked. You and I," my hands on her shoulders, I looked her straight in the eye, "are going to take these assholes down."

"What? Are you serious? Did you see them?" Lexie balked,

glancing quickly back toward the men. "They weigh three times as much as us. They're probably armed, remember?"

"They've got my phone, Lexie!" I practically shouted back at her. I was already on my feet and pulling her with me, holding on to her hand as we ran the thirty feet or so back to the front of the building. "If they cut through the school, they'll probably round this corner," I shouted, marking their possible path with my hand. "We'll totally take them by surprise, they won't have time to pull a gun and the cops are right behind them anyway. Here, take your crowbar thingy and hide behind that tree. When they run by, clobber 'em!"

She begrudgingly took the weapon as I pushed her toward a nearby Pepper tree, her eyes wide. *"Clobber 'em?"* she hissed back at me, running the best she could in the wet grass to the tree. *"That's your big, swell plan? Just clobber 'em?"*

I could feel her glaring at me but didn't have time to argue. I ran to another tree about twenty feet away. I could hear Lexie whispering to herself, "This is crazy, this is crazy, this is crazy," as I took a deep breath and tried to calm my nerves.

We had about ten seconds so I quickly wiped my sweaty hands on my jeans and tightened my grip on the wine bottle. I positioned myself so that my back was to the tree and turned my head so I could better hear. I closed my eyes to focus, just like Jason Bourne does when he's in that field and tracking the other hit man, and to both my surprise and delight, it worked. I could tell they were on the sidewalk and rapidly approaching the school. I knew we had to get at least one guy. At least one. He would be able, I reassured myself, to tell us where the others were going so I could get my phone back. My family wouldn't be endangered, and we could save the school's computers.

As I heard the men rounding the corner by the wall, I steadied myself. They were cutting through the schoolyard as I suspected. I was filled with adrenaline, every single one of my senses heightened.

And then they were on us. I glanced around the tree to see the hoodie man taking the corner at full speed, like a man being hunted. He was so close I could see his eyes scanning the field, searching for the best way out. He was in mid-stride, maybe two feet from where Lexie lurked behind her tree when she jumped out at him, timing her assault perfectly, swinging the tire iron through with all her might, letting it go at just the right time and catching him in the ankle. In a blur of motion he screamed, tumbled and rolled, unable to get his arms down, taking in a face full of mud and grass as he skidded to a stop. He let out a guttural cry and flipped over, grabbing for his ankle while he rolled on the grass in agony.

The other man was right on his tail, almost tripping on him. He was able to regain his footing, fingering the grass to keep himself upright and was just starting to look away from his friend and forward again, when I made my move. I jumped and positioned myself directly in his path, aimed at his head and swung the bottle with all my might, screaming, "Hiyah!!" just like I do with my boys when we surprise each other in a game of *Kung Fu Panda*. I underestimated his height and missed, hitting his shoulders instead, knocking him off balance but his momentum still carried him into me as though I were a tackling dummy and we tumbled together a few yards. He was quick to get up and I heaved myself at him and grabbed his foot, holding on with all my might. He dragged me a foot or two across the grass until he kicked me in the face to get me off. I screamed and let go, taking his shoe with me. He quickly gained his speed again and was ten yards out, about to reach the blacktop and disappear, when I made my last ditch effort. Crawling on my knees to reach the wine bottle I hurled it as hard as I could, tomahawk-style, over my head. "Ahh!" I cried, using the extra force of my voice to give it everything I had. Exhausted, in pain, and on all fours, I watched the bottle travel seemingly in slow motion, end over end, before finally making contact, and this time I didn't miss. It landed squarely on the back of his head, knocking him off his feet and causing him to skid, face first, across the hopscotch court. By now the two cops giving chase had caught up while another two patrol cars came flying into the school parking lot, lights blazing and sirens blaring. The place looked like a war zone. The first two jumped on the suspects, yelling orders at them and cuffing their hands behind their backs.

Lexie ran over to me and helped me up, brushing the mud and grass off my shirt and pulling it out of my hair. She got me to my feet and over to a bench just inside the school, out of sight of the men. We sat down and when I looked at her she had utter shock and amazement mixed with a huge grin on her face. I was dazed from the tackle and kick to the face and she left me for a moment, returning with my bag and began pulling out diaper wipes.

"Holy shit, Kelly," she was laughing while wiping my face, "when you said 'clobber 'em,' you really meant it. Is this what you had in mind?"

I grabbed one of the wipes from the package and spit some mud, grass and blood into it and grinned back at Lexie, showing off a mouth that was still filled with the soccer field. Lexie held her hand up and I gave her a weak high-five, letting my hand rest in hers and giving it a squeeze.

"Minus the minor injuries, grass-stained jeans and my brand-new-and-now-ruined Free People shirt, yeah, I guess that's pretty much what I had in mind."

She hugged me and I fell into her as we both took a couple of deep breaths. I could feel the raw anxiety swelling up in me, the stress of the night about to overflow as tears began spilling out of my eyes. "You were awesome," Lexie said, giving me a tight squeeze and then pulling back. She looked me in the eye and gave me one of the highest compliments I could have received: "Jason Bourne would have been proud."

I smiled wide through my tears and began to laugh and cry at the same time. I had to stop because it hurt like hell from my ribs to my head. Groaning, I grabbed a few more wipes for my nose and when I brought them down they were filled with blood. I looked at Lexie in horror, and with shaking fingers gently touched my lip, nose and jaw, which felt plastic and foreign, completely numb.

"Here, don't touch," she said, switching into full-on mom mode. "I'm sure it feels worse than it is, facial injuries always do. Put your head back."

I did as I was told and sat still on the bench with a pounding headache as Lexie went through my brand new package of wipes, giving me a little sponge bath right there on the bench.

"Jesus Christ, Kel," she laughed out loud as she worked, "for someone who barely weighs a buck ten, you're quite the badass."

"I'll second that, said a deep voice. We both looked up to see an officer holding out two bottles of water. He was mid-thirties, fairly tall, ruggedly handsome and vaguely familiar. I watched out of the corner of my eye as Lexie subtlety tried to pull lipstick from her pocket and apply it. The officer introduced himself as Sam Hogan and once he said his name, I remembered where I'd seen him before: the Ocean Diner, just down the street from my house.

"You're a Buckeye," I said, taking the bottle of water. He looked at me closer, trying to place me, then it hit him.

"And you're married to one," he said with a smile, remembering the day I had worn Mark's oversized Ohio sweatshirt down to the diner to pick up breakfast. He and his partner were getting off their shift and we had started up a friendly conversation about being from the Midwest.

He commended both Lexie and me on our brave work, saying he had seen it all from his car right as he pulled up. "That's quite a swing you've got there," he told Lexie, who laughed and remarked that she was better with a golf club. "And I don't ever want to do battle against you," he said, looking at me. I smiled weakly, keeping my mouth covered with a wipe.

He got out a pad and pen and started to jot notes. "So, do you two lurk in the shadows all the time, popping out to assail suspects just at the right moment? Or were you just out taking a nice stroll at, er, one a.m.?" he said, looking at his watch then looking back at us with a raised eyebrow.

"Oh my God it's late," I whimpered. "The boys are going to be up in a few hours. I am going to be toast today."

Lexie nudged me with her shoulder. "I'll bring you a Red Bull and double espresso for lunch. That always helps me when I pull all-nighters." I smiled with my eyes only and wondered vaguely how many all-nighters she pulled in order to have a regular morning-after routine.

We began to give the officer the details of how we had come to the school to look at the vandalism, hoping to organize a fundraiser when the men arrived and began smashing the windows and stealing the computers. Upon hearing the words out loud, we both looked at each other and shouted, "The computers," in unison.

"Shit. How could we forget?" Lexie asked.

"We?" I scoffed. "Hello? Mild concussion," I said pointing to my head.

"Alright," she conceded, rolling her eyes. "Alright, alright, you got me this time."

We both quickly stood up and started talking over each other, telling the officer about the truck, how Lisa and the gang were hopefully following it, the stolen computers, and my phone that was duct taped to the bottom of its back bumper.

"Can I borrow your cell phone?" Lexie asked Officer Hogan.

"You've got a computer in your squad car with internet, right?" I asked.

Officer Hogan nodded yes to both queries and the three of us were immediately up and jogging towards his car. Lexie ducked into the back trying to dial Lisa while I sat in the passenger seat and instructed Officer Hogan how to track the phone online.

"Crap," Lexie cried, "I can't remember her number. Do you know it? I've got her programmed and always just hit her name."

I thought I knew it and after a few wrong numbers, Lexie was able to connect, just as I brought up the phone tracking website and located my phone. "Lisa, it's me, Lexie," I heard her say from the back seat. "Where are you guys? Were you able to follow the truck?"

"Lexie, where the hell have you guys been?" Lisa screamed from the receiver so loud both Officer Hogan and I could hear from the front seat. "We've been calling you and Kelly for the last half hour."

"It's a long story, I'll fill you in later. Were you able to follow the truck?"

"Yeah, we're still behind it but we can't follow this thing all night, it's like the O.J. ride from hell. We've got to get home and we're getting low on gas. What if they go to Vegas or something? This could go on forever." I could picture the three of them, wild-eyed and intense, trying to stay close to the truck but not too close.

"Okay, we're with a cop now. Where are you?"

"I see them," I cried, pointing on the screen to a little dot that was moving along a map while patting the officer's shoulder about five times in one second. "There they are. Damn, I can't believe this worked. Ask Lisa if she's just passing the five freeway now."

Lexie asked and indeed they were. My heart was now pounding again, but in a completely different, joyous way. We gave the make, model and color of the truck, along with the license plate number to the officer who relayed it to his dispatcher on his radio. We told Lisa to hold tight for a few more minutes, that help was on the way. Then the three of us sat in the squad car watching a real-life drama unfold before our eyes both on the soccer field, as well as on the car's computer screen: An ambulance came and paramedics checked out the handcuffed, swearing, spitting pissed-off suspects before loading them up and taking them away. Lexie and I ducked down so they couldn't see us, which was both terrifying and simultaneously funny. Before they left the paramedics tried to look at me and while I was waving them off, a reporter from the Beach Reporter who had been listening to the police radio interviewed Lexie. Then Officer Hogan got another call—domestic disturbance—and had to take us home.

Later, we learned from Lisa, the Harbor City police pulled along side of them on the freeway. The three of them, Lisa, Jackie and Ramona, began frantically pointing and waving at the truck that was a few cars ahead of them, unrolling their windows and trying to shout loud enough so the cops could hear, "Arrest them!" and "Computer thieves!" The officer nodded and apparently gave Lisa a thumbs up and Lisa backed off as three squad cars surrounded the truck, two on the side and one in front and hit their lights. As soon as Lisa saw that, she took the next exit and turned back for home.

By three a.m. all the chaos was over. Officer Hogan had our information and said he would follow up with us in the morning as he dropped us at Lexie's house. Lexie drove me home and told me she'd call me in a few hours, holding out her fist for a bump. "Here's to Mama Power."

"Mama Power," I said in return, thinking that the catchphrase she used all the time now had a whole new meaning. It was just shy of four a.m. by the time I dragged my exhausted body to bed and snuggled up close to Mark. He grunted a little, mumbling something about the time, then wrapped his arm around my waist and pulled me close. I wanted so badly to wake him, to tell him everything that happened, but I was dead tired and I knew this would be at least an hour-long conversation and I was going to need every minute of sleep I could get. My story could wait until the morning.

I closed my eyes and thought about what a crazy, scary, horrible, and yet exciting night it had been. My emotions were all over the place. We had done something—actually done something!—to stop some of the madness. It felt nothing short of exhilarating and I fell asleep smiling and thinking. *Moms 1, Bad Guys 0.*

Five

Two and a half hours later, I woke up to someone pushing gently on my fat lip. I opened my eyes slightly and was nose to nose with my two-year-old.

"I have to go potty. You have a worm on your face."

My lip and nose were throbbing and the rest of my body felt like it had been hit by a truck. I looked at the clock, six-twenty three a.m. It was uncanny how this little boy could wake up precisely at the same time every day without an alarm clock.

"Honey," I groaned, feeling with my foot for Mark who was still snoozing next to me.

"Hmmmmm?" he said.

"I need a mommy-sleep-in-day."

"It's not Sunday," he murmured back.

"You've stored up over four years more sleep than me. I'm calling one in."

I prayed for some action on his part, unsure if he heard me or not, then could feel him stretching and mumbling, "Okay, but this makes us even." I felt him sit up, rub his eyes and get out of bed. Then I heard him pick Griffin up and whisper, "Hey, champ," as they padded down the hall.

When I woke three hours later, the house was eerily quiet. I stayed in bed for a moment, listening, trying to gauge where everyone was. There was no screaming from downstairs, no thumping of feet running from the kitchen to the living room, no singing or banging or crying. The TV wasn't even on. *This could not be good,* I thought and made myself get up even though lying in bed all day sounded like heaven.

In the bathroom I checked out my face. My lip looked better than I expected given Griffin's assessment and the fact that it felt like a rubber hose, and my nose looked only slightly swollen. The worst thing was my eyes. They had either gotten much blacker, or I was really, really tired.

I put on my robe went downstairs to the kitchen where the smell of Peet's was in the air. I wondered for half a second how fresh it was before I grabbed a mug, poured in a little milk and topped it off with coffee. As I was gently taking my first sip, Mark came through the front door wearing jeans, a T-shirt and flip flops. He smelled of cool, fresh, salty air.

"Finally, you're up. What the hell happened last night? Are you okay?" He made straight for me, tossing the paper on the table.

"I'm fine," I said embarrassed about how I looked, feeling like I wanted to have this conversation wearing a ski mask.

"What were you thinking, Kel? Let me look at you." I closed my eyes so I didn't have to see the anxiety in his, but when I felt him kissing my cheeks and brushing the hair out of my eyes, I had to look at him.

He already knew the logistics because Buckeye Sam had dropped by after his shift to check up on me and to deliver my phone that the Harbor City officers had retrieved, which Mark now produced from his pocket.

"My phone," I squealed, practically dropping my coffee and grabbing it out of his hands. I gave it a hug and a kiss before turning my gaze to my husband. "Mark, you would not have believed how awesome we were," I felt the excitement rise up in me as I retold the story. He listened intently, taking in all the details, nodding every so often which I knew was going to be the extent of his ability to get excited.

"You guys made the paper," he said when I was done, and he handed me a copy of the weekly Beach Reporter. The reporter must have just made deadline in order to get in his one, tiny paragraph about the bust hidden in the Crime Reporter. "The story is light on details but Lexie got in an interesting quote. Was she lit or what?"

I took the paper and sat down at the kitchen table with my coffee that I'd decided to drink with a straw and started to scan the short article with Mark hovering over me. When, where, what, who, the basics were covered just like he'd said. Both Lexie and I were identified only as "two local women" who had assisted in the arrest, something Buckeye Sam had suggested in order to protect our identities. But either the wine or the adrenaline had compelled Lexie to say, "Moms have incredible power. We are faster than a two-year-old darting into traffic, more powerful than a strong-willed child, and able to stay one step ahead of a sneaky teenager."

I put my hand over my mouth to keep from spewing coffee and giggled. I had no recollection of her saying any of that to the reporter. Mark sat down next to me as I finished the article, smiling when he saw that I'd read the quote.

"I can't believe she said that, she sounds insane. I don't think she was drunk, I think she was just high on, well, 'Mama Power' or something."

Lexie was all about the "Mama Power." Years ago, after having her first child, she started an online boutique selling designer T-shirts, canvas totes, pajamas, yoga pants and various other things. Each item had her "Super Mom" logo, a cartoon brunette who looked like she could take care of business as well as her kids. Her hair was in a high ponytail and one of her perfectly tweezed eyebrows was raised. She had a grin that was half warm, half menacing. She wore yoga pants and held a baby on her hip with one hand and brandished a frying pan like a weapon in the other. A blankie draped around her neck served as a cape and her utility belt held a cereal bar, a bottle of hand sanitizer, a water bottle, a cell phone and wipes. Lexie took half the money she earned and invested it back into her store. The other half she gave to various charities, particularly ones that helped women and children.

Mark shrugged. "Mama Power must be potent stuff."

I nodded as he went on to tell me that according to Sam, the men we nabbed were involved in an identity theft ring. The officers following the truck ran the license plate which matched one the FBI had associated with a huge interstate case. FBI agents ended up questioning the guys with the stolen computers which led them to a big warehouse in Barstow where they found tons of stolen equipment from all over, even as far as Florida.

"That's crazy," I said, my jaw dropping as wide open as it could given my fat lip.

Mark nodded in agreement. "The police think their M.O. was to scout out places as vandals first, marking targets with graffiti. Then they'd come back if there was something worth stealing. These guys hit offices, schools, churches, you name it. They'd strip the computers of personal info—social security numbers, addresses, birthdays—then clean them up to sell. But the real money is in the personal information; they take out credit cards, buy stuff online then resell it."

I was dumbstruck. I didn't know what to say as Mark sat across from me, took my hands and began massaging them. I looked up to see him looking intently at me. "The boys and I need you in one piece, okay? They love their mommy and I love my wife. I know you have this alter-ego-superhero right-all-the-wrongs thing going on, but let's be a little more careful. Those guys were serious felons. You were really lucky you or your friends didn't get hurt..." he said as his eyes wandered over my face causing me to blush, "...worse."

"Okay, I know," I said sheepishly, squeezing his hands. "Believe me, it wasn't premeditated. It all just kind of happened. My adrenaline and temper took over. Plus there was the wine..."

"That's what I'm afraid of," Mark said, the seriousness of his tone showing up on his face. He forced a smile. "In the future, let's just use your phone to call the cops. Not strap it onto some thug's bumper and go all James Bond on them. Deal?"

I smiled back. "Deal. Where are the boys anyway?" I asked, suddenly aware that they weren't around.

"Your friend Ramona, stopped by to check on you, see if you

needed any help this morning. She has them down at the diner. We went for second-breakfast pancakes, they're probably still talking her ear off."

I blinked at him. "You just let a virtual stranger take our kids?" I knew Ramona, but Mark certainly didn't. His willingness to just hand over Casey and Griffin sorta freaked me out. I stood up and started for the door.

"Please, she's like 80, I hardly think she's going to abduct them. She knew all about last night and I've heard you talk about her so relax, they're fine. Plus she brought sock puppets. The boys were hysterical, you should have seen them."

"Still," I said, holding onto the door handle while putting on my flip-flops, "what if there's an armed robbery? Or a kidnapping? She can't protect them. She's like 80, remember?"

"I don't know, she looks pretty capable. Did you know she was a Merchant Marine? That's pretty badass. Anyway, I've got some work to do," he said looking at his watch and getting up, "but maybe we could walk to beach the later and have dinner?" He kissed me again on the head and hustled upstairs to shower.

I stood there, speechless, processing. No, I didn't know she was in the Merchant Marines, the woman hardly talks. If I were a Merchant Marine—whatever the hell that was—I'd have that tattooed across my forehead so no one would mess with me or my family. It seemed odd, her not mentioning it. Was she hiding something or just shy? I wanted to know more because maybe her training and experience could help us right now. But maybe she had PTSD or something from her time spent…doing whatever you spend your time doing in the Merchant Marines and she didn't like to talk about it. I'd have to ask Jackie.

I grabbed my phone and began to get the boys when it rang in my hands.

"Hello?"

"Hello yourself, crazy. Are you okay?" It was Lisa.

"I'm fine," I said, checking my watch and sitting on the arm of the couch. I touched my tender nose, "nothing a little Advil won't cure."

We chatted about the night, how incredible the whole thing had been, how insane it was that we not only caught the SOBs but also made the paper. Then she sprung a little morsel on me. "So did I ever tell you I have a friend at the FBI?"

"No," I said, completely intrigued. "No you did not tell me you had a friend at the F.B.I."

"Well, I do. We taught English together in Japan aaannd…"

Everyone knew I was fascinated by the undercover agent world. I loved any book, movie or show where seemingly average people were kicking serious bad-guy ass in exotic locations. I suppose I imagined myself in that role, it was just so different from my domestic existence. I'd said it time and time again, completely joking of course, how as a mom I have the perfect cover for an undercover agent. No one would ever suspect, for example, that I was doing surveillance while pushing my boys in the stroller. No one would ever check Griffin's soiled diaper for a jump drive filled with secret files that I'd sewn into the lining. Of course I knew that in reality no good mom would ever risk taking her child into the field with her. And no good agent could focus on work while having to tend to a child. But still, a part of me thought a little alter ego and stealth lifestyle might be fun, and maybe just a tiny bit possible.

"And?" I said, taking the bait. Lisa was not one to tease unless it was something really good.

"And her beat is Gang Violence. Apparently Lexie's little quote sounded a little, uh, "gangy," for lack of a better word, so it triggered their radar. She called me to see if I knew this woman and well, now she needs to meet us all to clear the file. Strictly routine stuff. What do you have going on this afternoon?"

"Are you kidding?" I said, practically jumping off the couch. "I'm hanging with the FBI!"

A few hours later, the boys and I arrived at Lisa's. We were late because Griff needed a nap, which I had to wake him from so he was still sleepy and not wanting out of my arms. But I had a new stomp rocket and tons of snacks in hopes of entertaining them and the other kids for at least thirty minutes while I got to meet my very first

FBI agent. I settled them outside with the other kids without too much drama and slowly edged my way to the door and the sound of familiar voices.

Everyone was sitting around Lisa's kitchen table, talking about last night's adventure. "Is she here?" I interrupted, not even trying to hide my excitement. "Your friend from the F.B.I.?"

"Kelly, have you considered switching to decaf," Jackie asked, a question I'd heard more than once in my life.

"What? I had two cups," I looked at my watch, "like ten hours ago."

"Here, spaz," Lexie said pouring me a glass of wine. "It's not Justin Isosceles."

"Gee, thanks," I said, accepting it. "Seriously, though, is she here?"

"Yes, she is," a voice said and we all spun around.

Rachel Wilson was tiny, like barely five feet tall, and couldn't have weighed more than ninety-five pounds soaking wet. She was of Thai descent and had flawless brown skin and shiny, jet-black hair that was bobbed. She was dressed in a casual business suit with Jimmy Choo heels, a white button-down top and had designer sunglasses pushed up on her head. She went to Lisa first, gave her a quick hug and apologized for letting herself in, then looked at the rest of us. "So this is the Mama Power gang," she said, pulling up a chair. "I've heard a lot about you."

I stared at her in disbelief looking her up and down as my words poured out without me even having a chance to filter. "You're an agent? *For the FBI?*" I couldn't believe that someone so cute, so sweet, so *perky,* could work for the country's top bad-guy busting agency. She looked like someone I could take, maybe with one hand tied behind my back. All I'd have to do is sit on her.

"I know, can you believe it?" she laughed, showing a set of perfect pearly whites. This woman belonged on a soap opera, not the SWAT team. "I'm sure you all feel much safer knowing the Thai-version of Dora the Explorer is hard at work protecting the denizens of Los Angeles."

We all laughed, but Lisa was on her. "Don't underestimate Rachael, it's her secret weapon," Lisa smirked, watching Rachel from the corner of her eye. "She may look friendly, but she's a third degree black belt, was an Elite gymnast, ex-military and has a masters in Computer Programming. And she speaks four languages."

"Five," Rachel corrected with a smile. "They sent me to school to learn Farsi. So I hear you all have been up to a little mayhem lately?" she said, switching the subject seamlessly and looking at us. We all mumbled and nodded, stumbling over our words as she reached for a clean, yellow pad from her sleek, black Furla tote, then set the pad on the table in front of her and took out an expensive-looking pen. "So," she said, cutting us all off, "which one of you is the ring leader?"

Everyone looked at me and Lexie even pointed and said my name. "What?" I gasped, slightly horrified. "I am not. We did this together. All of us, I thought," my voice dwindling as they all glared, "mostly." I had, up until that moment, thought that it was pretty much a group effort. That none of us deserved more or less credit—or blame—than anyone else because we had all taken part, all played a role. But sitting there in the hot seat, with everyone's eyes and Lexie's finger pointing at me, my mouth began to get cottony. I felt like I'd been sent to the Principal's office.

"Ok," I said defensively, feeling as though I was confessing to some great sin. "It was my idea to get us all together for drinks and to talk about all the crime problems in town. And it might have been my idea to stop and look at the school on our way home."

"Sweetie," Lisa noted, "you drove us there and told us we could either check it out or walk home."

"That was just a joke," I said. "I would nev—"

"And you shoved us in the bushes," Jackie said.

"Shoved? Give me a break, I might have nodded that we go hide behind the bushes…"

"Might? Ha!" Lexie said, "You practically pulled my arm out of its socket getting me in there."

"Oh, that is not true," I huffed. "I did not—"

"Alright," Rachel said, looking me over. I wondered if she were psychoanalyzing me. I was sure that was part of an agent's training. I wondered if she could tell, just by looking at me, from the little details of the way I dressed or wore my hair where I was born, what my socio-economic and religious background was, what my parents did for a living, and what, if any, sort of deviant behaviors I partook in. I tried to be stone-faced, a blank slate, just to see how good she truly was, but she took me off guard when she gave me an empathetic smile and said without a hint of condescension, "So you're the one with the wine bottle. I read about it in the report. That's some shiner you got. You took quite a hit."

I nodded, feeling my cheeks starting to get hot and red. Again, she smiled. "I've been on the receiving end of a wine bottle once, it's not fun. See these?" she said pointing to her perfect, white teeth, "All fake."

I couldn't believe it. She was commiserating with me, comparing battle wounds, like we were equals! I thought she was going to give us—me really—a huge lecture on how we should stay out of "police business." How we should call the authorities and let the experts do the hard lifting, just like Mark had this morning. And she did, later, as she was wrapping everything up. But right now, she was doling out the accolades and, whether this was her intention or not, I took them to heart. I took her words to mean she felt I (and therefore the rest of our little team) had the guts, the instinct, the raw materials it took to be on her level of the game. It was as though she were telling me indirectly she would have no problem going into the field with me as her partner, or at the very least, her sidekick who stays in the car and calls for backup, which is still an important role. My blushing subsided and I began to beam as she continued.

"Now, why don't you all tell me how this started," she inquired.

Relaxed and at ease, we all began telling her our story starting with how we parked above the field. Each of us told a part, then the others would add in details, some of us laughing at the things that were scary then but now, in hindsight, were a little funny. Naturally, Rachael had plenty of stories of her own and even though she prefaced her stories with disclaimers about how long she had trained, I found myself completely intrigued.

Or more accurately, inspired.

Six

Normally on Mom's Night Out I could count on eight to twelve ladies to show up, and that was when I gave three week's notice. The numbers would spike to fifteen or even twenty if the venue was especially cool or we were seeing something with Johnny Depp. But when I checked my eVite responses this morning, Friday, a week after the school incident, I had forty-one *"Will be there with bells on!"*, twenty-five *"Has anyone seen my bells?"*, and only seven *"Bummer, my bells are broken."*

I'm sure I got the boost in numbers from the publicity and general buzz around the school incident. That was great because right now, after taking Mark's advice and looking for the mayor all week while simultaneously hunting down city council members who were as scarce as Tickle Me Elmo in Christmas of '96, I had finally caught one at my Partners of the Park meeting.

Councilman Sharpe was all business as he answered my questions about our police force. As I listened, I felt my gut churn, his words leaving me speechless as he delivered the third sucker punch in less than two weeks. I knew these things happened in threes. And now, as I watched him walk away through the parking lot of city hall with my jaw wide open three words kept repeating in my head: *we are doomed.*

I had hoped that maybe there was just a budget problem, a little kink in the system that with a tremendous amount of public support could be ironed out and we could hire more cops. But something had happened. Something bad and major and I realized with a sinking feeling that it really was going to be up to me and the other moms if anything was going to change. And I wasn't even sure that would be enough.

I snapped out my trance and ran for home, hoping to catch Mark before he went to pick up the boys so I could tell him the news, cursing myself for wearing flip-flops instead of running shoes as I sprinted up the hill. I could hear the TV on in our bedroom upstairs and used the last of my reserves to get me up there, two steps at a time. I burst in wild-eyed and out of breath to find Mark getting out of his tie and slacks while watching Sports Center.

"Oh…my…God…honey!" I gasped, bending over to try and stop a raging side cramp, gulping as much air as I could get. "So…glad…you're…home!"

"Now that's the kind of greeting I deserve every night," he said smiling but without so much as taking his eyes off the screen. "Where are the boys? I'm in charge tonight, right? You've got your Mom's Night Out thing here?"

"Mayor…Arvid," was all I could get out between my huge gasps for air. I bent over, putting my hands on my knees to steady myself.

"Mayor Arvid has the boys?" he asked. I could hear the suspicion in his voice but was focusing on my Lamaze-style breathing in hopes that would prevent me from passing out.

"AdventurePlex," I uttered, making a mental note to have our carpet cleaned.

"Mayor Arvid has the boys at AdventurePlex?" Mark asked incredulously, finally tearing himself from the TV bending over to look at me with one hand on the small of my back. "Are you okay?"

"No," I said, shaking my head, then adding, "I mean yes, I'm okay, but no." I stood up and waited a second for the head rush to go away. I sat down on our window seat, took a few more breaths and blurted it all out while I still could. "Alexa has the boys at AdventurePlex and they need to be picked up in thirty minutes and you'll need to feed and bathe them and get them in bed by eight-thirty with brushed and flossed teeth and don't forget the fluoride rinse because it's really important so don't skip it even if they whine and you think it's unnecessary because it really, really isn't and Mayor Arvid just ran off with his secretary to somewhere in Central America and embezzled a million dollars of the city's money so we aren't going to get any new cops and may have to cut the ones we have and so there goes the town." I stared at him hard while panting like a dog, feeling the beaded sweat collect and drip down my face.

His response time was longer than normal, like he was taking it all in, but he finally came back with a simple, "What?"

"Yeah, you heard me. Can you believe that?" I practically shouted, finally feeling like I wasn't going to keel over.

He looked at me for a moment, but his eyes weren't focused. It was as though he was looking through me. "No, I can't. How do you know?" His tone was slightly accusatory, like I was making this up or I heard it through some dubious source.

He did this unconsciously when he was trying to get information. I assumed it was just an occupational hazard of being a lawyer, to question people as though they were on the stand and it was his turn to cross-examine. The fact that I was married to a lawyer still sometimes took me by surprise. Mark is the smartest man I've ever known, and he is kind-hearted and fair, two of the reasons I fell in love with him. He didn't like to argue just for the sake of arguing like so many of his colleagues. But when he did get into it, he was lethal. I don't think I had ever won an argument with him; he was strategic, always three moves ahead of me. I pretty much ended up backing down, either realizing I wouldn't win or begrudgingly seeing his point.

I told him everything that went down at my Partners of the Parks meeting, how I cornered Councilman Sharpe as he tried to slip out early, how he told me the treasurer had discovered the missing funds, how Mayor Arvid's wife had received a letter from him stating he was starting over in Central America with his secretary, whom he had fallen in love with, and how the police had about zero leads on his current whereabouts. When I was finished I blinked up at Mark who had not so much as glanced over at Sports Center the whole time I was talking, so I knew he heard me, but he was just staring.

"So?" I demanded, unable to stand his silence. "What are we going to do?" I wanted him to be as livid as I was. I wanted us to demand some sort of action and consequences from the city, forge a search team to track down the mayor and teach him a lesson about trust and fairness, good and evil.

I should have known better. He saw people from all walks of life do far worse things every day. He saw the Bernie Madoffs and Bill Cosbys of the world, the people who put themselves first without any regard for other people's property, feelings, or lives. Somehow, long ago, out of necessity to do his job I suppose as well as maintain his sanity, he had become reconciled to the fact that all kinds of people did horrible, unfathomable things to strangers as well as those they loved the most, and he was able to compartmentalize it.

"James Arvid," he mumbled, looking vacantly out our widow. I watched him slide into his cargo shorts and pull a T-shirt on over his tall, lean frame. He bent down, kissed me on the head and told me he was going to get the boys.

"Wait? That's it?" I said in disbelief as he headed out of our bedroom. We knew James Arvid, he was sort of a friend. We'd had him and his wife, Cindy, over for dinner once. We exchanged Christmas cards. He and Mark usually found each other at events and talked college sports and politics. Mark turned and looked at me from the top of the stairs with a shrug and sad expression, as though his emotional armor had actually been dented this time. "I don't know what to say, I'm kind of at a loss. Some people just suck."

I stared at the stairway where he had just been and let my shoulders sag. As usual, his even-keel reaction was less than satisfying. I shook my head slightly and was so glad MNO was about to take place. In sixty minutes I'd have friends here, I told myself as I stripped off my sweaty clothes and tossed them in the basket. Friends who'd be equally shocked, equally mad, equally outraged. Friends who'd feel robbed and ripped off and duped, just like I did. Friends whom earlier I had merely hoped I could convince to attend a meeting and apply some pressure to the city council to hire more police. But now, *now* that our town was left with zero options, I knew I'd have to rally them into some sort of immediate action. The worrier in me kicked in, giving me a nagging, awful feeling in the pit of my stomach that even that might not be enough because, really, when was the last time you read about of a bunch of criminals caving to a well-intentioned, volunteer, community task force?

I pushed the thought out of my head and quickly threw on a cami with a colorful, gauzy top that would hopefully draw people's attention away from my less-than-fresh face, then put on a pair of capri jeans, hopping to the bathroom as I zipped them up. I went to add a little more mascara to the sparse make-up I'd already applied for the Parks meeting and then sweated off and as I was madly whipping the wand across my lashes, my mind racing, fretting about what we were going to do, something on the tub caught my eye in the reflection of the mirror.

I stopped mid-whip and squinted into the mirror then turned around and looked directly at the edge of the tub. There, staring at me in all their cute cuddliness, were Casey's *Penguins of Madagascar* action figures: Skipper, Rico, Kowalski and Private.

I picked up Skipper and looked into his deceivingly sweet beady eyes. He was disarmingly adorable, yet I knew from the movies and the show that he was the leader of a crack team of commando penguins that took out foes with skilled precision and masterfully well-laid plans. The key to their success was the same as ours had been at the school—no one ever suspected cuddly penguins of being deadly. They simply flew under the radar. Even though I knew they were toys and their shows were outlandish, seeing them gave me an idea. I turned back to the mirror and stared at myself, letting the idea percolate.

Suddenly my spirits were higher, I felt a little hope. "Yes," I whispered to my reflection, as the idea began to take form.

I tossed my mascara into the drawer and picked up my phone, quickly texting Lexie, Lisa, and Jackie that they needed to stay late, which they always did, but this time I had something important to discuss with them. I'd have texted Ramona as well, but she didn't even own a cell phone so I had to rely on Jackie to relay the message. Then, with a slightly lighter heart, I put myself in high gear.

Nearly an hour later I'd pulled several flatbread pizzas out and set them on my kitchen island next to a few other appetizers and a dozen bottles of wine. *Good enough*, I thought as I raced to unload the dishwasher before my guests arrived. That was when the phone rang.

"Hello?"

"Are you wet?" I recognized Lexie's voice immediately.

"Huh?"

"Are. You. Wet?" she asked again.

I pressed the phone to my ear, straining to hear her. "Come again?" I asked, immediately regretting my word choice.

"Why yes!" she exclaimed, predictably. "Don't mind if I do. But, I was wondering more if you were getting off on the latest *Bon Appetit*...the one with the chocolate hazelnut torte with mocha Grenache on the cover? I figured *you'd* be having multiples by just looking at it," Lexie said.

"God, you are so gross!"

"It's a gift. Hey, what's this big thing you have to discuss with us?"

Her nonchalant tone didn't fool me, she was dying to know.

"Nope," I replied, shaking my head. "You, my friend, are just going to have to wait like the others. It's way too big to discuss over the phone, I need you in person."

"Seriously? Didn't you learn anything from last time?" she said, a little miffed. I stayed silent. "Okay, okay. I'm giving kisses then heading your way. Do you need me to pick up anything?"

"Nope, I'm good, thanks. See ya soon."

The doorbell rang, and I raced to answer, anxious to start the night. Over the next 45 minutes, the moms arrived. Some looked a little stressed and haggard, but after a few minutes of a kid-free environment and a glass of wine, they began to relax.

Even though technically we weren't going "out" out, many of the women stilled dressed up for the night, relishing the opportunity to get out of their "mommy clothes" and into something a little more fashionable which for most of them meant jeans and cute top. They carried small, stylish purses to hold their keys and cell phones, or didn't carry a bag at all, reveling in the lightness of being free from little ones and not weighed down by the diaper bag stuffed with everything but the kitchen sink.

Naturally the first thing they wanted to know was what the big emergency was. I resisted, telling everyone I'd hold the discussion once all the moms had arrived, which was as hard for them as me but we dealt. Soon everyone was off in groups of three and four, diving into the hors d'oeuvres, sipping drinks and chatting happily. I swept through the room refilling glasses, trying not to let my anxiety show, a plastic smile on my face as I nodded and made small talk while my stomach was in knots. I could hear one group discussing strategies to get their kids to stop texting at the dinner table, another was on the potty training issues and another was discussing an article that claimed having two hundred orgasms a year would add six years to your life. Lexie, of course, was in this group and, I guessed, the one to start the conversation in the first place.

Lisa had not yet arrived and I'd promised her I wouldn't start until she did, so I joined Lexie's sex conversation. I always had some annoying jingle in my head and lately, it was "Old McDonald." I couldn't even shush it while Mark and I had sex, it actually kind of got louder, and for some stupid reason, I chose to divulge this personal tidbit to the group. Lexie, of course, loved this and responded by closing her eyes, gyrating like Prince while moaning "Old McDonald had a hard-on, E-I-E-I-O-O O O My-God! O-My-God! O-My-God! Yes-Yes-Yes!"

I dropped my head and grimaced at her. "What?" she responded casually. "I'm just visualizing Old McDonald as a hot, young Magic Mike-looking kind of farmer, doing his chores in just overalls, his chest glistening with sweat, his muscles all ablaze as he lifts a bale of hay—"

"It's in the title of the song, Lex," I interrupted, knowing she'd soon be on to vulgar versions of other nursery rhymes and Wee Willy Winkie and Little Miss Muffet needed to remain pristine for my sanity. "His name is *old* McDonald, because he's old. Besides, the emphasis is on the animals and the sounds they make."

"Oh," she said, a glint in her eye. "So you think Old McDonald is old and alone and really, *really* into his animals. Hey, I was just trying to improve the song a bit but if you want to get creepy and go the disgusting route—"

"Ahhh!" I half shouted, putting my hands over my ears. "That's not what I said!" I spied Lisa slide through my front door so I walked to the front of the room. We had every eye on us now anyway, best to start the meeting.

"Old McDonald *loved* his pig, when no one was around!" she sang out happily to the familiar tune.

"Stop! Lexie, please! Seriously, some of us still sing that song!" I pleaded.

"Have fun singing it now," she said, folding her arms, a defiant grin spread across her face.

I glared at her as the others wrinkled their noses and let out a few "ew's." "And with that," I said turning to the rest of the group, "let's begin."

Ordinarily I'm a nervous wreck in front of groups. My hands shake, my mouth gets dry and I trip over my words. Even at the Partners of the Park meetings where members are either sweet little old ladies or amateur botanist goobs, I get performance anxiety. This time it was worse because I *needed* these women to agree that the sky was indeed falling so we could figure out a plan of action and *act* on it.

I positioned myself in front of the group, my heart racing like a scared hamster. I took a quick sip of water and looked out over all the oddly attentive faces.

"Ladies," I managed, without so much as a quiver in my voice, "thank you all for coming over tonight. I know how hard it can be to get out of the house so I really appreciate it. I'll get right to the point: our town is in serious trouble."

I looked at my audience and saw I had their complete, undivided attention. Some of them stood in my kitchen behind the island, some were on the sofa and others—mostly the ones with toddlers—had settled comfortably on the floor.

I took a deep breath and dove in.

"Almost two weeks ago," I said putting my hands in my pockets to steady them and leaning slightly on the corner of the island, "my wallet was stolen. Not a big deal, when taken alone. It happens, right?" I shrugged. "But when I filed the police report, the information the officer gave me blew me away."

I wanted my friends to be blown away as well. I ran through the descriptions of all the crimes the officer had mentioned.

"All this is bad, horrible, scary stuff. And that's initially why I called you all here. But since then, our situation has gotten worse. Way worse."

I proceeded to tell them how Mark had suggested I find out more about our cop situation, or lack thereof. How no one in City Council or the Mayor's office was returning my calls, emails, or texts all week, and no public officials seemed to be in their office. How I'd finally been able to track Councilman Sharpe down at my Partners of the Park meeting earlier today.

"Is this one of your city council rants?" Lexie heckled.

"Hardly," I said, wishing it was just one of my regular complaints about the city council never getting anything done. "No, I called you all here to discuss the increase in crime, especially violent crime, in our town. But, also to let you know that we won't be getting any extra help from the police, they may even have to cut the force, I don't know. And the reason I know this is because Councilman Sharpe told me just this very afternoon that Mayor Arvid has embezzled a million dollars of the city's money and has skipped town with his secretary."

The room exploded as everyone began talking at the same time. They wanted details and I gave them as much as I knew, as much as the councilman had told me. I explained that the City Treasurer had found the money missing, how it had been tracked to a bank in Panama City, then withdrawn a few days later. How Mayor Arvid had left a note for his wife explaining that he was leaving her for his secretary and not to look for him because they were starting a new life together somewhere far away from here.

After that, what was left of the evening raced by. I got out the boys' easel and wrote down all the ideas for protecting our town that we came up with. I got everyone to promise to spread the word and to attend next week's city council meeting. Someone volunteered to set up a Facebook page and a Twitter account we could all follow and text if we saw anything remotely sketchy. We all agreed to be on high alert as we went about our days, putting the police dispatcher's direct line into our phones instead of 9-1-1 so we could report problems immediately. The meeting felt productive and I was glad I had chosen to clue them all in with the sordid details of the Mayor. By the time I walked the last of my guests to the door, I was feeling a little hopeful.

I went back inside and closed the heavy Spanish door that I loved so much and clicked the wrought iron lock into place. I looked over at the four women who remained clustered around the island in my kitchen still noshing on appetizers and chatting over their wine. I relaxed a little knowing the first part of my plan had been accomplished. It was time for the second.

"So," I said, relieved that the meeting had gone so well, "can you believe all that stuff?"

"No," Lisa said frankly, dipping a carrot in hummus and taking a bite. "Mayor Arvid? Really?"

"I know, it's absurd," I said, still in denial. "Why don't you guys head into the family room where we can turn on the fire. I'll get more wine." I shuffled in my bare feet to the wine cooler in the dining room and called out over my shoulder, "White or red?"

"Yes!" Jackie called back as I heard her plunk down in the corner of the overstuffed L-shaped sofa with the impossible-to-stain micro suede fabric and click on the fire with the remote.

As Lisa sat down, an enthusiastic animated voice chirped at her. *"It's so good to meet you! Let's be friends!"*

"Ack!" she cried, pulling a Learning Puppy out from under a cushion. "I just sat on someone who wants to be friends."

"Bet you wish that happened more often," I heard Lexie say.

"So do the police have any leads on Arvid?" Lisa asked when I returned from the kitchen with two bottles of wine and a tray of cheese and grapes. Both she and Lexie scooted over, making room for me in between them as Jackie put her feet up on the leather chair where Ramona sat.

"No," I sat slowly so as not to spill any wine, tucking my feet underneath me. "They don't have the manpower to really follow-up on it, either. I think they've tried to call in the FBI."

"Holy shi...nanigans," Jackie said, catching herself in mid-swear and self-correcting. She'd been trying to give up swearing ever since her daughter's first word was a very audible *shit.* "It's so surreal that this is happening here."

"That Arvid's a louse," Ramona said, shaking her head. "Always has been, ever since he got on the council ten years ago."

"I wonder how he did it," Lisa questioned. "Can they recover *any* of the money, like through insurance? Have you talked to Cindy?"

"No," I admitted. "It sounds like no one knows much yet. I thought of calling her but what do you say to something like that? 'I'm so sorry your husband is a dirt bag who screwed you and the entire city over. Can I bring you a lasagna?'"

"I can't imagine what she's going through," Jackie said. "How could this happen here, in our little town?"

"Are you kidding?" Lexie scoffed, "This stuff happens everywhere."

"You aren't shocked?" I asked, taken aback. "Even a little?"

"C'mon," Lexie said, furrowing her brow. "Politician steals money. Politician has affair. It's not exactly an esoteric concept."

"But for our town it is," Lisa said, sitting up straighter. "And Cindy. How would you feel if Josh cheated on you? And so publicly?"

"Please," Lexie scoffed. "Josh couldn't cheat on a diet without me knowing."

Lexie's glib answer was my opening, a way for me to get the conversation started about the idea I'd hatched as I was putting on my make-up. I jumped at it. "Exactly why is that?" I asked, my eyes narrowed and head tilted to the side.

She let out a "Ha!" with a big burst of air behind it. "Seriously?" I nodded. "Because he leaves his receipts all over the house. Because he always forgets stuff in his pockets that I find before they go in the wash. Because he constantly has his email up when he rambles off to get something to eat and then returns three hours later after getting distracted by the TV and falling asleep. There are just too many ways for him to slip up."

"So you're saying your husband couldn't get away with cheating because he's a slob?" I asked.

"Ouch," Lisa said laughing out loud.

I smiled and winked at her. "Or, would it be more accurate to say that you are acutely aware of what's going on in your household? That you have eyes in the back of your head, maybe have a sixth sense?"

"Yeah, that's it," Lexie said pointing a manicured fingernail my way. "That right there. Plus," she muttered, "he is a slob. He'll drop his dirty underwear on the floor when the hamper is three inches away."

"Brian does that, too," Jackie said. "I hate that."

"But the thing about me being stealth is better," she said nodding at me.

"I'd say we all have some pretty amazing abilities we aren't even aware of," I said, sitting up straighter. "We can be sneaky when we want to. Like when we need hide Christmas presents or plan birthday surprises. And we can lie through our teeth if we need to. Like when you, Lisa, backed into that pole after swim class but told Peter it was a hit and run, or when you, Jackie, spent $1,000 at Michael's and said the stuff was for Christmas presents when it really wasn't. Both of you completely covered up your actions."

"That pole should not have been there," Lisa said.

"It's scary how easy you can spend money at Michael's," Jackie said.

"What are you getting at?" asked Ramona, who sat with her hands in her lap, her foot tapping ever so slightly.

"I'm getting at this: do you guys really think a ragtag team made up of a bunch of flip-flop wearing, beach volleyball playing, untrained Joe Citizens like our group are really going to do any sort of significant damage against the flurry of ruthless hoodlums that are taking over our town?"

They were silent, which was exactly the response I was hoping for. "I didn't think so," I said. "I mean the Facebook page, the Twitter account, all the new eyes on the streets and reporting back to police dispatch will help. It's great ground cover. But getting to the root of this problem is going to require a really unique solution. It's going to take something drastic, something out of left field, something creative. Something the criminals will not be expecting."

"What do you have in mind?" Lexie asked.

I took a deep breath and let it out slowly. "Us. The five of us, right here," I said, pointing at each in turn. "Our own little super-tight, commando, take-no-prisoners stealth team. Just like the Penguins of Madagascar."

Lisa snorted and covered her mouth just in time to catch the wine that she almost spit out. Lexie sat back, crossed her arms and eyed me suspiciously. "I'm not kidding, guys. We were awesome at the school. We were stealth and strong and smart, and it just came naturally. We were like Ninja Mamas. We were Ninjamas! Only we'd obviously need a better name. With a little training in say, martial arts or espionage, I think we could honestly be like a crack team of commando moms, defending our beloved town from the evil criminals. Just picture this: You see a mom pushing a stroller down the street. She sees someone stealing a bicycles or, or," I put my wine down on the coffee table and pretended to push a stroller, "doing a drug deal and she stops. Very stealth-like she reaches in to check on the baby but ho ho! Look at this, she pulls out a Taser from the stroller and zaps the guys. Word would get around pretty fast that Hermosa is not a place to mess with. Crooks wouldn't know real moms from the lethal moms."

"Yeah, and the real moms would get shot in the face," Lexie scowled. "You can't honestly be suggesting the five of us push strollers around all day looking for bad guys to taze. Do you know what kind of perfect timing you'd have to have to catch someone in the act? Not to mention we do have lives. Wait a minute, I know what this is about." She shook her finger at me, eyeing me suspiciously. "You've been watching those Bourne movies again, haven't you?"

"Oh, I love Jason Bourne," Jackie said, beaming over at Lexie.

"I love anything Matt Damon is in," Lisa said, nodding and swirling her wine. "He is all that."

"I'll take Ben Affleck over Matt any day of the week," Ramona said, garnering looks of surprise from everyone, which led to an impromptu game of Name That Hot Celebrity.

I watched, exasperated. "Hello?" I said, snapping my fingers, "we were talking about serious issues here. Things that affect our community and the safety of our kids. The neighborhoods we want to live in for the rest of our lives. Can we please bring the conversation back around?"

"Oh yes, please," Lexie said with a smirk and a roll of her eyes, "go right ahead with your encrypted, stealth, insane ramblings."

"It's not insane," I insisted. "Listen, we took down those guys at the school and why? Because they weren't expecting us. We have a lot of qualities that make us perfect for this job. Face it, to criminals we're just middle-aged, benign, nobodies. They don't even notice us. They look *past* us to keep an eye out for the cops."

"Like being old," Ramona said. "Nobody notices you when you're old."

"Did somebody just say something? It's like I heard a voice from the chair, but I don't see anyone over there," Jackie said. Ramona chuckled and swatted her feet.

"You're nuts," Lexie said, surprising me a little. Of all of them I figured she would be the first onboard, always ready to shake things up a bit. "Ninjamas? Really? That sounds like a new toddler show from Netflix. What are we supposed to do, carry around diaper wipes laced with chloroform? Offer a bad guy a hotdog that isn't cut up in bite sized pieces hoping he'll choke?"

I smiled to myself. *Chloroform diaper wipes!* I knew Lexie would be perfect for this type of work.

"Well who else is going to take care of the problem?" I said. "Who? Tell me? We have no budget for more cops, we may even lose the ones we have. Someone has to put a stop to all this and I can't think of anyone who would be better suited for it. And besides, aren't you sick of all this crap? Not just the crime, but all this cheating the system bullshit? I am. Crime and cops aside, what am I supposed to tell Casey and Griffin? That our mayor, the one in charge of our town, the one who took them by the shoulder and gave them a tour of his office, someone in a position of power whom we all are supposed to look up to and trust, just lied and cheated us all for his own personal benefit?"

"Not a bad lesson to learn early?" Lexie suggested with a wry smile.

"It's not funny," I said, glaring at her.

"This beach town is quirky," Ramona said, watching the fire as she spoke, her voice soft but strong. "Always has been, especially compared to Manhattan, and that used to be part of its charm." Ramona had spent the majority of her seventy-three years in Hermosa. She and her late husband, Ben, had bought one of the first homes on the hill east of PCH, back when land was sold by the acre and a good deal of the city was used for raising goats.

She told us how for years the mayor's office and city council were filled with guys who moved here to surf. They liked the "live and let live lifestyle," so they weren't very strict with the rules. They wanted to make it a place everyone could enjoy. They even did away with a good chunk of taxes for a while, which helped to attract a lot of artists and free spirits in the sixties and seventies.

"Many of those folks still live here, own businesses and are now worth a pretty penny because of the properties they bought for $20K back then are now literally worth millions. They remember Hermosa in its heyday and don't want it to change or evolve. It's virtually impossible to move the city forward without a bunch of old surfers and hippies showing up to protest. In the past decade or so Hermosa's gotten a lot more grit and a lot less quirk." She turned to me. "They could use someone with your passion and energy down in the city council, Kelly. Why don't you run for office?"

"Seriously, Kel," Lisa said, sitting forward, "what a great idea. They need people with gumption and perseverance, especially now. You'd be perfect."

"And you're kind of famous now, for the school thing," Jackie said. "That's a campaign manager's dream."

I rolled my eyes. "Please, the only real change those people can produce is to get a speed bump added, and even that's a year-long fight. I don't want baby steps. We can't afford baby steps, we don't have the time," I pleaded. "If we don't do something major and meaningful soon, the criminals are going to have the upper hand. It will be impossible to get them out if they know Hermosa's an easy target, no police force and all. We'll lose our town and never get it back."

With kids, everything was a baby step. Talking, walking, potty training, getting them to use good manners, to not freak out when using the hand dryer in the public bathroom. I didn't want to take baby steps to have a safe town, too. Now that I knew there was a problem, I wanted to fix it and fix it now come hell or high water. I hadn't really thought about it until right this moment, but suddenly I realized that if I continued to just putz around with my little organizations like Partners of the Parks and Moms for Oceans, adding shrubs, cleaning up litter, bitching about the lack of a police force, nothing *significant* would ever get accomplished. And I wanted something major. Make that *needed* something major. Something to turn us around; a paradigm shift that would make our community the cleanest and safest anywhere. And when I thought about this, about seeing this work accomplished and how it could be perfect for my family in maybe a matter of months or possibly even a year or two, I got a rush of adrenaline similar to what I felt the night at the school.

"You guys," I said, sitting up, "your lives, my life, they're tame. I practically preach tame. I make sure we eat our vegetables and follow the food pyramid. We brush and floss twice a day. We don't hit. We share. We use our words. We make safe choices. Everything I do every day with the boys is tame, it has to be. But we can't tackle this crime problem with a tame solution. Wouldn't it be great for *us* to have a project that makes an impact and is exciting and interesting at the same time? Like the night at the school, wasn't that incredible? How many times have you thought of that since? Every day? We could be doing that sort of thing *regularly*. Really take a bite out of the problem instead of just chipping away at it. Wouldn't that be more interesting to think about when you're carpooling to soccer or playing Zingo for the millionth time?"

"Hmmmmm," Jackie sat back, giving it some serious thought, "you want something exciting and passionate that gets your heart racing…"

"You guys floss twice a day?" Lexie said, her brow furrowed.

"I know," Jackie exclaimed with a big grin. "You could be a call girl."

"Ha ha, very funny," I pouted, wondering why these gals weren't taking me seriously, weren't as compelled by my idea as I was.

"You know I heard about a group of moms that did that in Redondo a few years back. They totally ran a prostitution ring out of their homes while their kids were at school," Lisa said.

"I think we can rule that out," I said. "Maybe the first stipulation is that whatever it is, it should be at least in the gray area of legal."

"How about a pole dancer?" Lexie offered with a grin. "That's legal." I tilted my head to the side and gave her a look. "Well it is," Lexie responded defiantly. "It's a great workout, too, I hear. They have classes now you can take. You'd earn a little extra money to put towards the police force, maybe Mark could come visit you at lunch time…that would put a little zing back into your love life."

"My love life has plenty of zing and you're missing the point."

"I'm not the one singing Old McDonald while—" she said. I glared at her. She held up her hands. "I'm just sayin'."

"The point," I said, cutting her off, "is about how I—and you guys—should be doing out of the ordinary stuff to fix our town before it becomes a ghetto. Or do you want your children growing up with bars on their windows and doors, being offered drugs at every intersection in town."

"I just think you're biting off a little more than you can chew," Lexie said. "Seriously, busting drug deals? Don't you watch *Breaking Bad?* I grew up around people like that and trust me, those dudes are vicious. And if you're dead or in jail, you can't go to soccer games or My Gym classes or play Zingo a million more times."

"Duly noted," I said, feeling defeated. Again.

"I'm sure you'll find some way to put all that energy to good use," Lisa said, patting me on the leg, always the one to choose the perfect, supporting words. "And when you do, let me know. I'll join your little crusade."

"Me, too!" Jackie exclaimed as Ramona emphatically nodded. "Just make sure it's fun and involves wine."

I looked at her, then at the rest of the group with their wine glasses in front of them and my eyes lit up. "That's it. Listen you guys, we should start now, on Mom's Night Out. It's perfect. Our kids are already covered, we're out together, having fun. We just need to have a mission of some kind each time we get together. We could do all the prep work like surveillance and stuff during the day, even with the kids, then the real mission at night during MNO. We could start small, with missions that aren't dangerous but still make an impact, like tracking down park vandals, who usually strike at night anyway. Then when our confidence and expertise are better, we can tackle the bigger jobs."

"Missions that included drinking wine," Jackie said, holding up her glass like she was toasting.

Lexie sighed with a "here we go again" look on her face. She'd seen me like this before. When I had heard that the battered women's shelter needed clothes, I organized a clothes drive. When I read in some magazine about "Alex's Lemonade Stand," a foundation that fought childhood cancer through front yard lemonade stands, I orchestrated the selling of lemonade by local families all summer long at the beach, raising over $5,000 for the cause. Lexie knew that when I got an idea in my head, it was in there for good and I tended to take it to an extreme.

"I don't know, Kel," Lisa, began in her calm, motherly tone, "I don't want to burst your bubble, but I don't think that's why most of the moms make the effort to get together. They're not out to save the world. They just want to relax and chat."

"I'm not talking about most of the moms. They can do the other stuff, the Facebook page, the neighborhood watch, the beach clean-up. The five of us will do the cool stuff."

"We like to relax and chat, too," Lexie added.

"Got it," I said, a spark of ideas beginning to take shape in the back of my head—accompanied by the *Penguins of Madagascar* theme song.

That night, after everyone left and the kitchen was clean, after I kissed my precious boys goodnight, letting my lips linger on their soft, downy hair, after I snuggled with Mark and heard how his evening with the boys went, I began thinking: what small, executable missions could the five of us do that would be fun, safe, exciting, relaxing, included wine, left us room to chat and would make a big difference? Nothing came to mind immediately, of course, but just letting the ideas swim around in my head stirred something in me that had been dormant for years. It was as though a perfect storm was brewing.

Seven

When I first met Lexie, I was sure we wouldn't click. It was at a dinner party shortly after I had moved in with Mark in his little apartment on the Strand. She was married to one of Mark's closest friends, Josh, who was an investment banker. We weren't seated next to each other so I didn't make a big effort to get to know her, particularly since I figured I already did. Like so many gorgeous women in L.A., I decided she was going to be interested her looks and her husband's money and nothing else.

And Lexie is beautiful, the drop dead kind. She has flawless skin, almond-shaped crystal-blue eyes that are so light they almost glow, silky golden hair that tumbles in loose curls to her shoulders, and a body that makes men cross the street for a closer look, and women think, *those can't be real.* All this even after having two babies. When I overheard her chatting with another wife about what Tom Ford did for Gucci, my opinion was sealed. I knew she would be someone with whom I could have a conversation about fashion, interior design, or celebrities, none of which I cared much about.

Months later, at Mark's suggestion, I invited her to a wine tasting I put together while he was in Europe on business for two weeks. Of the eight guests I had invited and the four who had said they'd come, Lexie was the first to arrive. I let her in with a smile and a mechanical hug and I offered her a seat on the couch where I could sit across from her and see the window so I could spring up when my other guests arrived.

Only they never did.

"So you're in sales, huh? Is that tough with two kids?" I asked, reaching for my water in order to sneak a glance at my watch. We were nearing the forty-five minute mark of small talk and it was beginning to sink in that nobody else was coming. I could feel the anxiety on my face and was desperately trying to cover it with animated banter.

She blinked slowly, her eyes purposely moving from my face to my watch and back, like a cat who had caught a mouse and wasn't sure if she wanted to play with it or eat it. She smiled, her worn surf T-shirt and jeans making her look even more relaxed compared to how awkward I felt in my maxi dress.

"It's a juggling act," she said with a shrug, "but I like it. Gets me away from the little beasts for eight hours. I think you need time away in order to be a better parent, actually."

"Really? How so?" I said it too quickly. I was actually interested in the answer, but my eyes darted to the window where I thought I saw someone, only it turned out to be a palm frond blowing in the breeze.

She eyed me again, glanced at the door and stood up. Panic and humiliation shot through me as I thought she was going to take her Estee Lauder model-looking-self home to let Josh know how Mark's new girlfriend was such a loser that no one came to her party.

But she didn't. Instead she reached down, grabbed me by the hand and peeled me off my own couch, pulling me into the kitchen saying, "Let's get this show on the road. If the others show, great," then turned to me with a wink and added, "but I hope they don't, more wine for us." She stopped short when she saw my table overflowing with carefully chosen wines, their corresponding tasting notes I'd researched and typed up on little index cards, and enough food pairings to feed a small army. "Wow," was all she said.

I felt my face go hot and mustered a weak "thanks," taking her response as a compliment even though it stung rather than soothed.

She wasted no time and dug right in, poured two glasses, picked up the matching card and read the description. "This one says it's got 'A palate that is elegant and bold with jammy, strawberry and cola aromas and a smoky, smoldering finish.'"

She mock smoldered as she swirled it, exaggerated breathing it in then popped open her eyes and wrinkled her nose. "Who writes this crap?" I smiled shyly as she took a drink and made sure to slosh it around for a good minute like it was mouthwash, she even gargled with it. Then she swallowed and smacked her lips. "I disagree," she said in her best Thurston Howell III impression, making me laugh out loud. "Rather, I believe it has delicate aromas of granite and peat moss, with a strong dandelion and manure finish."

After plowing through more than two bottles that night, and finding out to my surprise that she could talk politics, books, travel and world events, the two of us began spending more and more time together. I loved her bold irreverence and how she openly made fun of herself. We always seemed to be on the same wavelength but whereas I would keep my thoughts to my myself, Lexie tended to open her mouth and say whatever was on her mind, no matter how inappropriate.

By the time I had Casey, she had three kids of her own, including a baby that was only a few months older than mine. Every first-time mom needs a friend like her to walk them through Babies-R-Us, to tell them what they will and will not need. A friend to call to see if a temperature of 99 is normal or worth a midnight trip to the emergency room. A friend who will notice before you do that your own child is about to cut his first tooth and that is why he is so fussy.

And even though she was a middle-aged mom of three, Lexie could somehow still party like a twenty-year old, which she routinely did. She liked to go out with her old friends from her pre-mommy life whom she referred to as the "Few Crew" because they would start by meeting for a "few" drinks after work but inevitably would let the wind take them where it may and since none of them had any natural tendencies to hold back, they would wind up at a posh house in the Hollywood Hills chumming it up with celebrities or a characterless bar in some strip mall in the Valley doing shots with porn stars until closing.

And so, when my cell phone rang at one-thirty a.m., my first thought was that it was probably Lexie. The phone was half a house away, downstairs in the office off the living room, but I heard it immediately since I hadn't enjoyed the completely knocked out kind of sleep that Mark did ever since my first pregnancy. I quickly glanced at my husband, who was snoring away, then ran downstairs, tripping over an abandoned garbage truck just before I grabbed the phone.

"Hello?" I managed to get out without yelling as I held onto my middle toe that felt like it was going to explode.

"Kelly? It's me, Lexie," she whisper-shouted. I could hear music and talking in the background.

"I had a feeling," I winced. "Are you okay?" I limped into the kitchen to get a boo boo buster from the freezer then lowered myself onto the kitchen's cold, hard Spanish tile. I leaned back against a cabinet and gently wrapped the ice pack around my toe.

"I'm fine. Sorry for calling so late but you won't believe this. I'm in Culver City at that so-crappy-it's-cool bar I once took you to, remember?"

"Ew, really?" I said, remembering the night she insisted we stop for one last drink on our way home from an MNO. It was a dump. Of course she argued it had character and was so gross and terrible that it was actually fun and hip and because of that, it was a great place to spot celebrities, a pastime everyone in L.A. enjoyed. I had disagreed, had painfully attempted to drink my Budweiser, hoping I wouldn't get hepatitis, and had been thrilled when we picked up to go.

"I'm with Lauren and you'll never guess who is hitting on her," she said.

I had never met Lauren personally, but had heard plenty of stories about her. She was who Lexie would have become had she not settled down and had a family. She was an alpha female PR exec for a major film company and, like Lexie, was gorgeous. I know Lexie would never have traded lives with her, but there were clearly times when Lexie was jealous of Lauren's lifestyle, or more accurately, her freedom. She lived vicariously through her and when they did get together, the two of them took L.A. by storm, one drink at a time.

"Uh, let's see," I speculated, racking my brain for some big names who would be worth calling me for, who also seemed like they wouldn't mind a place where the Formica was peeling off the tables and the smell of smoke and Lysol permeated your pores. "Uh, Leonardo DiCaprio? Colin Farrell? Johnny Depp?" I shot in the dark, thinking she'd have every one of our friends salivating if the later was true.

"No, no, no, no one like that," Lexie said a little agitated. "Robert!"

I was silent for a moment, trying to picture who Robert could be. "Robert DeNiro? Robert Redford? Robert Pattinson?" I guessed.

"No," she hissed. "Stacy's Robert!"

"Who?"

"Stacy Williams. From Mom's Club? She has three girls. Her husband, *Robert*, is hitting on Lauren as we speak."

"No way," I said, feeling my stomach sink.

"Way."

"Oh my God," I whisper-shrieked into the phone, not wanting to wake everyone up. The shock took the focus off the pain in my toe. "Did he see you?"

"I don't think so. When we came in I went straight to the bathroom. When I came out, he was sitting next to Lauren at the bar." Apparently Lexie had stopped short when she saw him, crouched behind a wall that led to the bathroom and was now using her lipstick mirror to spy on the two of them. "He's totally leaning in to talk to her and he's got his hand on the back of her barstool. And," Lexie let out a gasp, "he's not wearing his wedding ring."

I thought about Stacy. I'd last seen her at my emergency MNO meeting. That was two weeks ago. She wasn't one of my closest friends so I didn't know what was up with her marriage. But she hadn't seemed the slightest bit off at the meeting. On the contrary, she seemed pretty upbeat about a trip to Hawaii she and Robert were taking the kids on over spring break. My guess was that she didn't have the slightest suspicion that he was on the prowl. "Tell Lauren to slap him," I said, then changed my mind. "Wait, *you* should go and slap him. Yell at him to go home."

"Like that's going to do any good," Lexie said. I could hear her shuffling and imagined her retreating back to the tiny bathroom that reeked of smoke and bleach. "He'll probably just move on to someone else. I'm thinking we should teach him a lesson, scare him straight."

"What?" I said incredulously. "That's crazy."

"Just hear me out," Lexie insisted. "I can tell he's already pretty lit, so I'm thinking we'll just sneak a Percocet in his drink, then when he's out, we'll pose him with Lauren and take some risqué photos and—"

"Whoa. Stop right there," I interrupted. "I can think of a million things that are wrong with that idea. First and foremost, where are you going to get Percocet at this hour? You need a prescription for that."

"I'm pretty sure I've got some in my purse." I could hear her rummaging around and pictured her standing in the dingy bathroom, her huge leather purse balanced on the edge of the dirty sink, the bottom getting wet, as she combed through it.

"You walk around with Percocet in your purse?" I asked, furrowing my brow. I'd heard about the Oxycontin epidemic and wondered, for a nanosecond, if Lexie was using to take the edge off of motherhood.

"Yeah," Lexie responded, it was clearly no big deal to her. "Josh had foot surgery last month and he's got three left. I'm sure he won't miss one or two if we give them to Robert."

"Really? You keep old prescription meds in your purse?" I had never even thought of holding onto the leftovers of a prescription. The concept of carrying around anything stronger than a cough drop, Butt Paste or Neosporin was completely foreign to me.

"Oh please," she replied with a sigh. "Remember, I was a drug rep before I had kids, plus Josh is like a little bubble boy, you never know what he's going to need. I've got a mini Walgreens in here. Now I need you to bring me a camera. A decent one, like your thirty-five millimeter. I only have my phone camera and it sucks in the dark."

"What?" I asked, startled. "*Now?*" I strained to see the clock on the microwave. "Are you crazy, it's 1:45 a.m. What would I tell Mark? I'm in my p.j.'s for crying out loud." I looked down at the blue cotton jammies with electric guitars and trucks that I'd bought for the whole family last Christmas.

"So get changed. And don't even tell Mark, just leave him a note. You'll be back before he's awake anyway," Lexie urged.

I thought about this, wondered what he would say if he woke up and found my note, then wondered what if he *didn't* find my note and I got in a crash and didn't make it home before he left for work without realizing I was gone, thus leaving the boys alone in the house. Apparently the pause was just too much for Lexie to take. She started in on me again.

"Come on, you're the one who was inspiring us all to go out and 'do something big.' Remember? Right the wrongs? Sock it to the cheaters? This could be our first mission!" I could hear the excitement in Lexie's voice, just like mine had been that night, and it was somewhat contagious. But I was still apprehensive. This wasn't at all what I had had in mind.

"Yeah, I remember. But I certainly didn't mean go out and kidnap people. I was thinking more along the lines of setting up cameras to catch the vandals who spray paint the Strand or booby-trapping a bike or stroller so that tar and feathers pour out on the people stealing them, you know. Something do-able like that."

"Tar and feathers? Who are you, Wile E. Coyote? Well, you should have mentioned that when you were talking like Che Guevara. And this *is* doable and it's going to get done. Right here, right now. Let's go."

"If I recall, Che didn't kidnap anyone," I blurted out, not having the faintest idea of what the hell Che did except live in South America and wear a beret.

"Kelly! Stop being such a wuss and get over here!" I could picture her in the bar yelling into her phone. But I was so conflicted, I couldn't decide what to do. I hated disappointing Lexie, or anyone for that matter, but especially Lexie. She was one of these people that did not hide her disappointment well and would definitely hold a grudge. I'd seen her get mad at people before, and it was not pretty. There was nothing passive aggressive about her, unlike a lot of moms who would let problems just fester, she tended to say exactly how she felt and I did not want to be on the wrong side of her, especially now when I needed her. My silence must have made her think because she changed tactics, a true salesman. "Seriously, Kel, get over here, please? Just bring me the camera, we can decide later if we want to go through with the rest of the plan. But first we have to take the photos."

I looked at the clock again and did some quick math in my head. Could I make it to Culver City, deliver the camera and get back in time to get an hour or two of sleep before everyone woke up? The traffic on the 405 would at least be moving at this time of night. Did I have a tough day planned or could I skate by loaded up on extra caffeine? Lexie did have a point. I was the one who had stood on my soapbox and urged everyone to take action. And even though this wasn't *at all* the action I had in mind, it was action nevertheless, and if I wasn't willing to take some, how could I possibly expect others to? Plus, I rationalized, maybe blackmailing Robert would set him straight, and saving a marriage was making the world a better place in some small shape or form, right? Maybe we wouldn't even go though with the blackmail portion. For now, I just needed to bring my camera to Lexie, which seemed innocent enough. And as far as an initial mission goes, it probably wouldn't get any easier than a simple delivery.

"Okay, fine. But don't drug him, that's way creepy. Jesus, I can't believe you're talking me into this. If Mark finds out, he'll think I've gone loco."

"That's my girl," Lexie said. "Remember those unique abilities you were talking about that us moms have? The ability to lie through our teeth to better the world? Well, giddy up."

Twenty-five minutes later I parked my car around the block from the Sunshine Motel by the Howard Hughes Center just off the freeway as instructed. I crept to the parking lot of the motel, hunching down and staying out of the streetlights. The building itself was L-shaped and painted a bland yellow color, just your basic two-story motel with a parking lot in front of the rooms. I found Lexie easily. She was leaning up against her car, which was parked in the lot by the street, completely out in the open, checking her watch and looking up and down the street. I snuck closer and crouched between a car and a large oleander and began tossing pebbles to get her attention. It took a couple of tries, but she finally looked my way.

"Kelly?" Lexie said, squinting into the darkness. I hushed her and motioned for her to join me. She walked over and as soon as she was within reach, I popped up, grabbed her and pulled her down.

"Hey!"

"What are you doing out in the open, all exposed like this?" I whispered. "Someone could see you."

"Get off me," Lexie said in her normal, not-stealth-at-all voice as she caught herself from falling. "Jesus, you almost made me break a heel. What took you so long?"

"I had to leave Mark five different notes, in case I'm in a crash on the way home and get amnesia. Here," I whispered, handing her the camera, "I parked down the street and snuck in behind these bushes. I'm pretty sure no one saw me. Where's Lauren?"

"She's inside the room alrea..." She stopped herself short, and took a good, long hard look at me. "Holy shit," she said with a gigantic grin. She pulled me up to standing and held my arms out to the sides. "Just look at you!"

I had dressed for the occasion; head to toe in black, including Mark's black ski cap and my little black-knit ski gloves. On my face I had smeared a bit of black face paint, which I admit, might have been overkill, but for our first mission I wanted to go all out, be completely prepared and hidden.

"Are you planning on knocking off a few liquor stores on your way home?" she said, trying to contain her laughter.

"Sshhhh! Keep your voice down," I said, pulling her between the cars so we were hidden.

She continued to scan me until she got to my pants and then her eyes lit up like a Christmas tree. "Oh. My. God. Are those pants *leather?*"

I closed my eyes, thankful for the darkness and face paint that hid my hot red cheeks. "Yes," I said as defiantly as I could, opening my eyes and returning her gaze. "Yes they are, thank-you-very-much. So?"

"Well, Miss I-Don't-Snack-Between-Meals-And-I-Floss-Twice-A-Day, I just didn't think you had a wild bone in your body, that's all. You should wear those more often, they look great on you."

"I have had plenty of wild bones in my body, I'll have you know..."

"I'll bet you do, especially wearing those pants!" Lexie shrieked, smacking me on the butt and laughing out loud. "Every boner around is going to want to get in them."

"Knock it off, gross! That's not what I meant," I said, swiping Lex's hand away and blushing even harder. "What I meant was, I had a wild side, too. Maybe not *your* brand of wild, but I was young at one point. I did have my fair share of excitement. But let's face it, who wants to see a middle-aged mom carting her kids around Trader Joes in black leather pants?" I had bought the pants on a whim over fifteen years ago when I had decided to turn over a new leaf and be more adventurous, style-wise. It didn't work. I had always felt out of place and had only worn them out twice. I was surprised—thrilled really—that they still fit. I enjoyed putting them on tonight for the mission, as if they had been waiting for me all these years to discover my true purpose. Instead of feeling like a poser, I felt like a renegade; focused, stealth and sleek.

"Kel," Lexie coaxed, "you seriously look hot in those. I'd lose the face paint and the goofy gloves, but with the right top, you'd be smoking in that outfit. I bet you'd have Mark's jaw dropping to the ground."

Lauren came casually out of the motel room and strolled over to us in the parking lot. "What are you doing out here?" Lexie asked anxiously. "Why aren't you inside with Robert, getting him drunk?"

"Calm down," Lauren said coolly, putting her hands up in the air. "Everything is under control." She looked over at me. "I didn't know you were friends with Catwoman." I rolled my eyes and looked the other way.

Lexie giggled then introduced us. "Oh yeah, I forgot you two have never officially met. Kelly, this is Lauren. Lauren, this is my friend, Kelly. She heard from the Fonz that there was a rumble here tonight, she's hoping to take down Pinky Tuscadero." She draped her arm around my shoulder and gave me a big smile.

We said our hellos as she brought us up to speed on Robert who had passed out on the bed while Lauren used the bathroom. "I guess he was drunker that we thought."

"Well, let's just hope he doesn't wake up in the middle of the photo shoot," Lexie said, starting for the room.

I grabbed her arm. "Wait Lex, are we sure we want to do this?"

"Absolutely," she said. I knew Lexie was one of the most stubborn people on the planet and that when her mind was made up, it was impossible to change. But I still wasn't quite sure about this. It wasn't helping Hermosa, and even though we hadn't drugged Robert and hadn't officially done anything wrong, it still felt slimy.

She looked at me and gave me a big sigh. "Listen, Kelly. I know this isn't what you had in mind during your big speech, but you also didn't see him totally working Lauren. He needs to be taught a lesson. He needs to know what he stands to lose. Some people just need a nice little reality check to appreciate what they have." I still wasn't convinced and the look on my face must have said so because she toned her rhetoric down.

"Come on. Just think of this as a training mission. Seriously, if we botch this one then how can we expect to be any good at anything else, and this one isn't even slightly dangerous. We'll just take the photos, see how they turn out, then I'll let you make the call on whether or not we use them, okay? But let's get this party going. My ankle biters will be up in a few hours."

Knowing she would leave the rest up to me helped me to relax and I followed the two of them into the room, looking around to make sure we weren't seen as we went in. Sure enough, when we got there Robert Williams lay on the bed, passed out cold on top of an ugly polyester bedspread. The last time I had seen him was at the New Year's Eve fireworks down at the beach pulling his girls in a wagon. Back then he was all smiles in his surfer hoodie and flip flops, looking a hell of a lot better than he did now with his cheeks all blotchy and his mouth half open with a puddle of drool collecting at the corner. He wore a blue button-down shirt with the sleeves rolled up and tan slacks, as though he had come straight from the office. One shoe was off, exposing a black sock with a big hole in it.

The room itself was three stars at best, like one of those convenience hotels you stay at because they are so close to the airport. There wasn't much in the room except the bed, a nightstand, and a dresser with a TV on it. The carpet was worn and the most recent guest had obviously been a smoker. I wrinkled my nose as I shut the door behind me and made sure the heavy, patterned drapes were completely shut before turning to Lexie who was conferring with Lauren over the various poses and levels of nudity required to get a few great shots as though she was directing a Vanity Fair photo shoot.

I looked sideways at Robert and, to my surprise, actually felt sorry for the guy. "Lex, maybe you misunderstood his intentions. He looks so inno—"

Robert snorted loudly and turned over and I couldn't help but shriek and duck behind the bed, my heart racing. Lexie, too, jumped out of her skin and made it to the bathroom in a second, pushing Lauren in with her. When Robert was settled and quiet again, we peeked out at each other from our hiding spots.

"That was close," I whispered, peering over the bedspread that gave me the creeps with its plastic feel and the probability that it hadn't been washed in this decade.

"Too close, let's get on with this," Lexie said.

I convinced Lexie that nudity wasn't necessary, that just being in this incriminating position would accomplish the same thing. So Lauren unbuttoned her blouse and draped herself all over Robert in different risqué poses and Lexie snapped away playfully telling Lauren to "Work it, own it. That's hot, baby. That's hot," as I watched from the sidelines.

Thirty minutes later we were back in our cars on our way home leaving Robert to snooze away. I argued with myself the whole way home and into the next couple of days. I made lists of all the pros and cons of the various scenarios that could happen, role-playing what I would do if I were Stacy and a friend like me discreetly, or anonymously, or even directly handed over photos of my husband having an (almost) affair.

In the end I decided two things: the first was that Lexie was way into this. She hadn't stopped talking about it since it happened, like it was her baby, her mission. It got her excited and at this point our cause needed some energy, some inertia, and I needed a comrade-in-arms to cattle prod our little team into action.

Lisa was on board, but super busy. Jackie wasn't aggressive enough and Ramona was just too old. Up until now Lexie had been going along with me and my quest to rid Hermosa of its seedy and dangerous side, but only half-assed. If blackmailing Robert was going get her head into the game, then I decided I would have to be all for it. The second was that cheaters, criminals, ruffians, thugs, you name it, the people destroying our beautiful town, did not play fair. They were menacing and intimidating and scary. They used illegal tactics and had no respect for the law nor for the people who lived within the law, which should have been obvious to me because they were *criminals*. But I decided that if we were going to beat them, we were going to have to bend a few rules, too, and I was going to have to be okay with that.

Eight

The stolen wallet incident hadn't deterred me from my daily routines. I still took the boys with me around town, only I'd upped my caffeine intake and was now on triple espresso alert. I figured the extra jolt would help me to not only keep an extra eye out but would help me to burn rubber—double-stroller style—should I need to quickly avoid a kidnapping, drive-by shooting or some other sketchy situation.

What I noticed in this heightened awareness was that Hermosa was looking downright shabby. At the beach alone there were at least half a dozen things that made the town look ghetto: the swings were either torn or completely broken and the paint was peeling; the lids on trashcans had been ripped off so the seagulls got to the trash, spreading it out across the sand in every direction; the bathrooms that were always dirty, always wet, never had any soap or toilet paper, now seemed just a magnet for derelicts to hang out and do drugs or teenagers to vandalize, and the wooden handrails on the pier were beyond disgusting. They were worn from the fishermen using them as cutting boards and caked with sedimentary layers of dried fish guts or were oozing with something fresher that inevitably Griffin would get his stubby little hands into and use as finger paints.

So I took it upon myself to clean up our town the only way I knew how, by mothering it. I began scolding the teenagers for leaving their trash on the beach. I preached hygiene to the nannies who sat idly by in the park, chit-chatting at the picnic table as they let the children pee and poop behind the bushes where kids regularly played hide-and-seek. I let my boys go to town with sidewalk chalk and washable paints on the graffiti that was always on the walls of the beach sidewalk (and not the cool, artistic kind of graffiti, either, unless you find a large, poorly drawn caricature of a penis spouting semen like a blow hole to be aesthetically pleasing) turning the giant penises into rocket ships and space monsters.

It was empowering, and addictive. I had long wanted to harass the little punks that just got up and left their fast food wrappers on the sand, but never wanted to do it in front of my boys for fear they might pick a fight, tell me off, or even worse, completely ignore me. However, I was now convinced that our town's appearance was related to the escalating crime and I was willing to do whatever I could to clean it up, even if that meant taking on some mouthy high schoolers.

"They didn't listen to me at first," I told the thirteen moms who'd shown up for our April MNO, "in fact, they turned their backs and flat out ignored me, even started walking away."

We were at The Cove, Manhattan Beach's newest hot spot that was oddly juxtaposed next to a strip mall Cost Plus World Market, but even so, the atmosphere was surprisingly cool. We sat outside cuddled in sweaters around a stone fire pit on deep cedar benches and Adirondack chairs with comfy cushions in various shades of blue, drinking frilly, sweet cocktails and noshing on small plates.

"But then I went ape-shit crazy, shaking their trash in their faces as they tried to detour around me. I screamed at them about taking care of their own neighborhoods and shamed them about littering and contributing to climate change. All but one of them went back, the girls first, of course, then the guys—all but one. I think they were a little bit scared of me, which was awesome."

I laughed recalling the mixture of disbelief, awe and terror on my boys' faces when I got done with the teenagers. Priceless. "The too cool to clean-up guy mumbled something at me so I let him have it and get this, other parents who were witnessing this from the Strand and the swings began yelling at him, too. If it ever happens again I'm going to take his picture and circulate it around so other people can keep an eye on him, let his parents know he's being a menace."

The whole experience had been empowering and I could tell by the attentive faces that it was resonating.

"Let's start an Operation Beautification committee," my friend, Jennifer, whom I'd met at Pee Wee Sports, suggested.

"And I can start a crowdfunding site so we can raise money to replace the swings and the trashcan lids the second they're damaged," said another friend, Erin, from Mommy and Me.

"I'll work on getting the handrails sanded and re-painted and maybe some real cutting boards installed," said my friend, Maggie, whose husband was in construction.

Everyone was excited and I knew they'd get involved. We'd post our progress and show off our momentum. We were going in the right direction with all this great grass roots energy but deep in the pit of my stomach I feared we'd never catch up. Sprucing up the town would maybe deter a vandal, but the real criminals wouldn't care.

Lisa arrived late, as usual, just as most of the other ladies were starting to leave. She said hello to everyone and settled in next to Lexie who made space for her. She looked tired from a long day and was still in her work heels, and I could see her shoulders visibly relax as she dropped her bag and sat.

"Here, try a sip of this. It's almost as yummy as our waiter," Lexie said, raising her eyebrows up and down while handing Lisa a pomegranate mojito. She took a sip of the tangy-minty combination and smiled her approval.

We chit-chatted under the stars for another thirty minutes until all the others had left, leaving just me, Ramona, Jackie, Lexie and Lisa with the fire pit to ourselves. I called us all closer.

"Huddle up, ladies," I said, physically moving their chairs to form a small circle. "Let's get down to business." I looked at Jackie with one eyebrow raised and said in a hushed voice, "Do you have the package?"

Jackie nodded and grabbed her personalized tote bag decorated with puffy paints and imprinted with a photo of Sierra smiling by a pool, and pulled out a very professional-looking black portfolio case. The word "CONFIDENTIAL" was painted across it. She handed it to me. I was expecting just some blown up photos and a small, ransom-style note tucked into an envelope—that's what I would have done—but this was Jackie and I should have known better. When I reached in and pulled out a full-fledged scrapbook, I was totally confused.

"You scrapped this?" I asked, in awe of both the high-quality work and the odd notion of a blackmail scrapbook. She smiled and nodded. The group gathered around and looked over my shoulder as I began flipping through the pages. Jackie had artfully designed the photos of Robert and Lauren in different layouts with different backgrounds and embellishments on each of the ten or so pages. The last page read, "You didn't cheat—this time—but these pictures tell another story. Are you sure you want to give up on your marriage and lose everything? Think about it."

"Oh God," Lisa said, almost losing her drink as she leaned forward to get a better look at the photos. "Is that Stacy's husband?"

Lexie nodded. "Lovely man, isn't he?"

"How did you get these?" Ramona asked.

Lexie explained the story all the way up to the point where I ran into Jackie the day after the photo shoot. Jackie wanted to be involved so we let her put together the blackmail packet, which we all agreed was amazing. I had to particularly compliment her on the impressive font, which looked very menacing.

"Thanks," Jackie smiled, blushing a little. "It's called *Smack*. I was going to use *Hollyweird*, but it was a little too girly and I didn't want to give anything about us away. Then I thought about *Howl*, or *Trick or Type*, but those seemed too Hallowe—"

"It's perfect," Lexie interrupted. "And far better than just cutting letters out of a magazine and gluing them on."

"Well, I thought about that, and chip board, too. Or I could have used my Cricut cutter or foam cut-outs or grommets and other embellishments. But once again, I thought that would have been giving away too many clues as to our identities."

"Right, good call. Grommets would have lead him right to your doorstep," Ramona said.

"This is really serious," Lisa said, taking the book from me and thoughtfully looking through it again. "Stacy would be devastated if she saw these. What are you going to do with it?"

"That's what we've got to decide tonight," I said. "I want us to decide as a group. One for all and all for one. Do we deliver these to Robert and hope that it scares him straight? Take them to Stacy? Maybe anonymously? Or do we burn them in this lovely fire pit right here, right now?" I held the scrapbook out over the flames; they seemed to jump higher as if to get a taste.

We discussed it all for only a few minutes before Lexie got impatient.

"Come on, let's take a vote and get this show on the road," she said.

"Fine," I said, feeling pressured. "If everyone is ready, we can just take a vote. Everyone in favor of delivering this lovely book to the big jerk, raise your hand." To my utter amazement, everyone raised their hands, even Lisa, whom I had assumed would take the high road or at least abstain for moral reasons.

"Yes," Lexie said, making a fist and flexing her bicep like a golfer who's just sunk a money putt.

I looked at Lisa, searching her face for some answers. "Wow, really?"

"What's the worst that can happen?" she shrugged. "He won't know it's us, and who knows, maybe it will knock some sense into him. But mostly I couldn't stand the thought of burning this gorgeous scrapbook." She looked at Jackie and winked.

"Alright then, it's settled," I said, feeling anything but. "Now, how do we get this to him without being caught or without anyone else seeing the photos by accident? We can't exactly mail them to his house or office."

We ordered another round of drinks and tossed out ideas, finally settling on a plan of action. It was decided that Lisa and Ramona would be the ones to deliver the packet so they were involved as well.

Jackie was to deliver information on Robert's schedule, since she was going to see Stacy at a My Gym class in a few days. We all agreed to meet at the swings by the pier the following Friday morning at ten o'clock for a debriefing. The package was to have been delivered by then.

"Ladies," I said seriously, looking each friend directly in the eye. "It goes without saying that this is a top secret mission. Not a single detail leaves this circle of trust." I indicated all of us with an emphatic hand gesture.

"Dude, you watch entirely too many spy shows," Lexie said, popping in a piece of gum and shaking her head.

"'Circle of trust' is a line from '*Meet the Fockers*', not a spy show," Jackie said to Lexie as Lex glared at her. "I'm just sayin'."

"It doesn't matter," I continued. "The point is—"

"Robert DeNiro's character was a spy in that movie," Lisa whispered across the circle. "CIA." She looked at me. "Sorry."

I took a breath and continued. "As I was saying, the point is that we will have completed a mission together."

"True, but so what?" Lexie asked, checking her phone for messages.

"So, not all friends complete missions with each other. They shop, they see movies, they go out to eat," I said.

Lexie gave me the raised eyebrow. "Aaannnddd?" she said, putting the phone back in her purse and gesturing with her hand for me to hurry up and get to the point.

"And that elevates our responsibility to each other." I looked around and whispered, "By keeping it secret, even from our husbands, it strengthens our bond to each other."

"Oh," Jackie squealed, "like a secret club! Or Vegas. What happens at MNO, stays at MNO." She smiled and I couldn't help but smile back, she was so cute and young and reminded me of what it felt like to still enjoy going to Vegas.

"Or like the mafia," Lisa interjected. "Having everyone's hands dirty creates the notion that we are all in this together."

"Exactly," I exclaimed louder than I intended, pointing at Lisa. I

91

looked around to make sure I didn't draw any attention then continued. "So I was thinking," I whispered, "maybe we should make up a secret handshake or code names for each other or something."

"We could pinkie promise?" Lexie mocked in a silly voice.

"I'm not cutting or spitting on my hand if that's what you have in mind," Ramona growled.

"A code name would be fun," Lisa said, ever the one to play along. "What about your slogan, Lexie?" Lisa asked. "It's 'Mom Power' or something like that, right?"

"Mama Power," Lexie corrected, nodding.

"Works for me," Ramona said.

"You okay with that, Lex?" I asked as Lexie smiled and shrugged. "Okay then, *Mama Power* it is." It was then that I felt it again. The same electric zing of hope and excitement I had felt the night after the school incident. The feeling that we could, against all better judgment and with the odds stacked against us, actually win this thing. I raised my glass and whispered a toast, "To Mama Power."

They raised their glasses to meet mine. "To Mama Power," they repeated as we smiled at the gesture that we all knew was silly and goofy. But at the same time, it was a serious reminder that we had more power than we knew, just like Lexie had said in her interview. And sometimes, for better or worse, if you repeat something enough times, you really do start to believe it.

Nine

The beach play date on Friday couldn't come fast enough for Lexie and me and I found myself actually feeling thankful that we caught Robert, if not for anything else but the fact that it got Lexie excited about doing these missions. Ever since that night at the motel it was almost all she could think about. By the time Friday finally rolled around, I had received at least ten speculative texts from her: *Do you think the package delivery worked? How did Robert react? Were Lisa and Ramona caught in the act? Would I like to go for a walk with her and nonchalantly walk by Robert and Stacy's house?*

We met at the swings as planned. I arrived early so I could run my munchkins around and tire them out so they'd sit still and have a snack during our meeting. After an hour of nonstop tag and tickle, I was thrilled to see Jackie show up with Sierra in her stroller while simultaneously spotting Lexie walking my way, holding a latte, looking gorgeous in her sunglasses and sundress.

I looked around and decided that this was the perfect place for a confidential meeting. The beach itself was practically empty and there were only a handful of walkers, joggers, and bikers and two lone surfers. I greeted the gals and we pushed the kids on the swings, all of us anxious for the others to arrive.

Finally, twenty minutes later, Ramona and Lisa sauntered up, each with a Starbucks in their hand, chatting and laughing like they had known each other their entire lives. They played coy as they joined our group, discussing the gorgeous weather and asking us if we'd seen the sale at the surf shop.

"Enough small talk, spill the beans. What happened with Robert?" Lexie demanded after taking as much as she could.

Ramona and Lisa shrugged and we all sat on the warm sand to hear the story.

"Well," Lisa began, "we knew that Robert was in town and that he left early for work. So Ramona here camped outside his house and followed him to work. Once she knew where he parked, she called me and I met her in the parking structure. Lucky for us, he works in Century City in a building with a pretty big parking structure." She looked at Ramona and nodded, "You tell the rest." Typical Lisa, always being inclusive.

"We changed into disguises—wigs and scarves—and while I stood by the elevators keeping a look out, Lisa put the envelope containing the scrapbook on Robert's windshield covered by a flyer for El Pollo Loco. Then we waited at the other side of the parking lot in Lisa's SUV."

"I worked on my laptop and Ramona watched through binoculars pretty much all day. I got a ton of stuff done since nobody was there to bother me. It was kind of nice."

"Who you calling 'nobody'?" Ramona said, her brow furrowed.

"You know what I mean. Nobody *annoying*, like my boss. I'll work with you any day."

"I'd definitely do that again," Ramona said. "I haven't been out of the house for six hours in a row in I don't know how long."

Lexie cleared her throat grunting, "Get back to the story."

"Oh, sorry. So Robert came out around 4pm, got to his car, saw the book, checked it out. He looked really confused at first, but that quickly turned to panic. He glanced around, threw the book in his car and sped off," Ramona said.

"And that was that. It was kinda fun," Lisa said with a shrug.

Ramona smiled. "Agreed. When he came out and found it, my heart was going a million miles a minute."

"Alrighty then," I said, feeling like we'd accomplished what we set out to. I nodded my head and looked at the others. "So what's next?"

Lisa looked at me hesitantly. "What do you mean, *next?*"

"You know exactly what I mean," I said, pointedly. "We've got work to do, bigger fish to fry, a community to save. So now let's do something that benefits the town. What's it going to be? Catch the A-holes that keep writing graffiti everywhere? Get that lingerie shop on PCH closed down, since we all know it isn't *just* a lingerie shop and it attracts all kinds of weirdos?"

"How about catching the losers that pitch beer cans through our basketball hoop at two a.m. on their way home from the bars?" suggested Jackie.

"You should just take that thing down," Lisa said, wrinkling up her face.

Jackie shrugged, then suggested, "Well then, what about taking down the oil company that's leaking tar all over the beach? I hate that."

"Yeah, I hate that, too. And I like that you're thinking big, but maybe we should tone it down a wee bit," Lexie said pinching her fingers together, "do something a little more manageable..."

"Something that wouldn't involve the EPA or a multinational mega-rich conglomerate who would sooner kill us than clean up their mess," I added.

"I'd like to catch the yahoos that let their dog poop on my sidewalk and then don't pick it up," Lisa said.

"That *is* annoying," Ramona agreed, winking at Jackie. "But is it really *illegal?*"

"I think you were on the right track with the graffiti suggestion," Lisa said, refocusing. "It should be something local..."

"And something meaningful..." I added.

"And manageable..." Lexie agreed.

"I got it," Ramona said in a voice more enthusiastic than we had ever heard. "My neighbor, Mrs. Hedges, she's eighty-five-years old. She keeps an extra refrigerator in her backyard on her patio. It's where she puts juice boxes and pop and extra stuff for when her grandkids come over. She also keeps cases of her son-in-law's beer in there and lately all the beer has been disappearing."

"Someone is stealing *beer* from *senior citizens*?" Jackie asked. "That's almost as bad as taking candy from a baby."

"Oh yeah, that project sounds manageable *and* fun," Lisa added.

"Then it's settled," Lexie said, picking herself up and dusting the sand off. "Mrs. Hedges is our next mission."

I smiled as I got up, looking at all my friends and realizing that I was no longer the one on the soapbox, that we were becoming a real unit. And while catching beer thieves wasn't exactly making leaps and bounds toward getting rid of the violent criminals, it was a step in the right direction. And if we could figure this one out, our little commando team would be ready for the big league.

We made plans to meet at Ramona's house at nine p.m. the following Thursday. To my delight Lexie volunteered to take the lead on planning, and Ramona would instruct Mrs. Hedges to stock her fridge that day. Then we started collecting toys, cleaning off sandy fingers and toes, loading stuff back into strollers and walking to our cars and houses.

"Quick question," Ramona asked before we all scattered. She had one hand on her hip and the other blocking the sun. "Do you all tell your husbands what you're doing?"

We looked at each other for a moment as we collectively mulled over the question, then Lexie's answered for us all with a firm, "Hell no."

Everyone nodded in agreement for their own various reasons. I figured that if I brought it up to Mark, especially after the school incident, it would only start a conversation about whose responsibility it was to catch beer thieves (the police) or meddle in someone's personal life (not mine). We all agreed it would be best if our husbands just thought we were meeting for something as generic and benign as a Mom's Night Out. Which is how, later, when we desperately needed them, not a single husband knew where we were or that we were in trouble.

Ten

Ramona's home sat at the top of the Hill section of town a mile or so from the beach. Hers was one of the oldest homes still standing and looked it. It was a white stucco Spanish Colonial two-story with the iconic red clay roof and shutters painted sea foam blue. It stood proudly in the middle of her lot—which had been rezoned over the years to now be three lots—while at the same time appearing lonely with so much yard and gigantic palms and eucalyptus trees surrounding it. Of course it paled in comparison to the other McMansions on the street, the ones that were more Mediterranean in style with smooth stucco in various earth tones, balconies that were more ornamental than functional, with barely a strip of grass left for a yard. But according to Jackie, Ramona didn't care. She loved her home. She and her late husband, Ben, had scraped together every last nickel in order to buy it back when it wasn't unusual to have goats roaming freely in their yard. I asked her once if she ever thought about selling, knowing every realtor and developer in the South Bay was salivating over its potential. She told me she got offers every day but that she would never, ever even consider it. This was her home.

I arrived at her house Thursday evening after getting the boys down and giving Mark a quick peck in passing as he came in the door from work. I carried the black duffle bag I'd stashed in my car earlier so Mark wouldn't ask questions and oddly enough, I was the last one to arrive, even though I was right on time. As I came up the stairs I took in Ramona's amazing 360 degree views of the mighty Pacific to the west, the expansive lights of L.A to the north, the black silhouette of the San Gabriels in the distance to the east, and the Palos Verdes Peninsula to the south. The view included my best friends slumped on Ramona's comfy old sofa, their feet up on her coffee table, margaritas in hand. They all looked as though they had been there for hours and were settling in for the night. I instantly began to worry.

"Is this a perfect night for a mission or what?" I asked, my tone a tad too enthusiastic, dropping my duffel on the well-worn hardwood flooring and gladly accepting the margarita Ramona handed me. Her house was sparsely decorated, only a few knick-knacks here and there, some small photos hung in tiny frames, much different from my walls that were crammed with oversized canvas pictures of my boys. "It's so dark out there with the new moon, and not a single star in the sky," I said sitting on the edge of the sofa arm.

"This is L.A.," Lisa said, "there's never a star in the sky."

"Well, it seems darker out there than usual to me," I practically sing-songed. "Or maybe I'm just never outside at night any more. Or maybe I'm just excited for this mission, aren't you? It's all I've been thinking about for a week." I eyeballed them, and when no one would make eye contact, I knew I would have to cattle-prod. "So what are we all doing sitting here like bumps on a pickle? Let's get this stakeout show on the road. Come on." I took a big gulp of my marg and exaggerated the act of standing up.

Lexie groaned and looked at the others. "I told you she wouldn't cave." She focused her gaze on me. "What are the chances you'll sit down, put your feet up like the rest of us, and postpone this stealth party 'til we have more energy?"

I let out a sigh that came out sounding more like that guttural, phlegm-coughing sound old men make. "Zero. The chances are exactly zero. Those beer thieves are not going to catch themselves. Now what's the plan, Stan? I'd like to get home by midnight so I can get five hours of sleep."

Lexie had volunteered to lead this mission and knew I would hold it over her head for the rest of her life if she pooped out. I met and held her exasperated gaze until she blew the hair out of her eyes, took one last sip and forced herself to stand. "Okay, okay, let's go." Lisa and Jackie did as they were told, albeit slowly like a bunch of grannies while Ramona, a legitimate granny, stood ready at her back door. I was about to make a crack about it when I realized we weren't properly outfitted.

"Wait a second," I said, pulling my duffle bag over. "You guys can't go out like that." I began pulling things out and handing them around. "Here, put these on. You're going to need them."

I pulled out enough stuff—sweatshirts, T-shirts, wind pants, sweatpants, hats, scarves and gloves—for everyone to dress themselves head to toe in black. I saw Lisa and Jackie exchange a look but before anyone could revolt, Lexie nudged them. "Just humor her," she said. "It's easier than arguing." She rolled her eyes and pulled on one of Mark's sweatshirts I'd turned inside out to hide the silkscreen.

"You'll all thank me when you're out there and know that nobody can see you. Now here, hold still."

"Oh, you've got to be kidding," Lisa said, shaking her head slightly as I rubbed black Halloween make-up under her eyes and on her cheeks, then followed up with one big black dot on her nose like a dog.

I smiled, satisfied. "Camouflage."

Jackie began to laugh until I came after her as well. When we were all ready, Lexie instructed us to turn our cell phones to vibrate and follow her.

We proceeded single-file out Ramona's side door, looking more like a bunch of frumpy cat burglars than the sleek, stealth, ninja stakeout team I had imagined and I made a note to self: next time bring yoga pants instead of sweats. We followed Lexie through Ramona's backyard and out her gate, ducking down and moving quickly into her neighbor's yard and the dark quiet of the neighborhood. The cool air along with the movement seemed to pep everyone up and when Lexie stopped and pantomimed in the dark in exaggerated motions that she would be the look out and give the signal when it was okay to move, we all paid attention. Slowly, we crept through the back yards of eleven houses while holding onto a hand or piece of clothing from the person in front so we would stay together. Then, one by one we sprinted across the last street following Lexie as she ducked behind some bushes and stopped at the top part of Mrs. Hedges' backyard.

Once together, we huddled up. The refrigerator in question was on the back patio, positioned against the wall of the house and next to the sliding glass door. Lexie whispered instructions as to where we were to position ourselves so we had the large appliance surrounded. "Ramona and Jackie, you stay behind the bushes."

"Oh no, not the bushes again," Ramona mumbled.

"Lisa and Kelly, hide yourself somewhere close to the refrigerator."

"Got it," Lisa said.

"I'll take the front yard," she said, and started toward her location. I pulled her back.

"Then what?" I whispered.

"What do you mean, 'then what?'" Lexie whispered back.

"I mean *then what?* How long do we wait? What do we do if we see someone? What if we don't? Does Mrs. Hedges even know we're here? What if she comes out with a shotgun or calls the cops? *What's the plan?*"

Lexie looked a little taken off guard. She was excellent at thinking on her feet, but thinking things through and doing detailed planning would have taken some time. "Well..." she said slowly.

I raised my eyebrows. "Oh I see," I said in an exaggerated tone. "So we wait about five minutes and then the thief will magically appear on cue and we'll all surround him and tell him how terrible it is to steal from people, right? I think I saw that on an episode of *Clifford* this morning. What if there are several thieves? What if they are big dudes with guns? What if we wait for hours and end up falling asleep and get eaten by possums?"

"Okay, listen everybody," Lisa said, giving me a nudge that meant shut up. "Here's what we're going to do. We'll wait for an hour, max.

If someone shows, we do surveillance only. Get as much information about the suspects as possible—license plates and detailed physical descriptions. We'll then feed the info to the realtor, er, I mean police," she said, eyeing me, "and let them do their jobs. No need to take things into our own hands and get killed over a little beer."

"I sure hope Mr. Hedges doesn't own a shotgun," I noted. "We're like sitting ducks out here."

"How could anyone see us, we all blend into the night," Lex said, waving her hands five inches from my face.

"Okay," Jackie said shivering. "I hope they come soon, it's freezing out here. I can't believe I gave up sitting on my warm sofa and watching *Dancing with the Stars* to hang out in an azalea all night."

Lisa ushered us all off to our assigned locations where we commenced "Mission Espionage." At about ten o'clock, after forty-five minutes of nothing, I was cold, bored and tired of my legs having pins and needles from being jammed uncomfortably beneath me. I figured if I was ready to throw in the towel, the others must have been ready thirty minutes ago. I began to whip out my phone to text a suggestion that we call it a night when I heard a car pull up and park down the street followed by Lexie's impression of a pigeon, "Coo coo! Coo coo!" her signal that someone was coming. I froze in my position, waiting and watching as my pulse picked up.

A young man wearing jeans, a white long-sleeved T-shirt and a baseball cap fitted tightly over his head silently opened the gate and slipped into the backyard. He was tall and thin and had arms that seemed overly long, like an orangutan's. He kept his head low, barely moving it as he looked right and left and stayed near the house and away from the windows. He moved casually and silently in his classic black and white checkerboard slip-on Vans, which I noticed from my vantage point under the patio table.

When he reached the fridge and pulled it open, the light for a brief second shone on his face and I could see that he was young, no older than eighteen. At this point he was close enough for me to jump out and grab. I thought about it for a second, imagining myself wrapping my arms around both his legs and taking him down like I had at the school. But then there was a sudden movement in the bushes on the hillside followed by a very audible grunt. He froze and scanned the yard, then in one seamless movement grabbed two cases of beer, shut the refrigerator with one of them and bolted out the side gate.

As soon as he was gone, Lisa and I slunk out from our hiding spots and looked at each other wide eyed, then motioned toward the hillside. "Ramona? Jackie?" I whispered to the yard. Lisa and I quickly made our way up into the bushes where we found Jackie pulling Ramona up and brushing dirt and leaves off her.

"Oh jeez," Lisa muttered, as we both rushed to help, "what happened?"

"Nothing, nothing. Just old age and bad circulation," Ramona said, embarrassed. Apparently she had been sitting in the same Indian-style position for most of the last half hour and when she saw the kid come into the yard she tried to rise up on her knees to get a little better view but lost her balance because a good chunk of her lower extremities were asleep. We checked her over as she waved us off, insisting she was fine. By then Lexie had joined us from the front yard.

"What happened?" she asked, panting.

"Possum attack," Jackie said, keeping a straight face. "But Ramona killed the little sucker with her bare hands."

Lex ignored her and got right down to business. "So? D'ja see him? Who got a good look?"

Both Lisa and I proceeded to describe him for Lexie, right down to the tattoo of a mermaid on his forearm.

"Good job," Lexie complimented. "I saw him from a distance, but it was too dark for me to get a description."

"What about the car? Did you see anything out front?" I asked.

"I totally got it. I got the license plate," Lexie said, smiling, with a little clap. "It was so much fun, too. When the guy went into the backyard, I snuck down to the car and got the number. There was only one guy in the car, the driver. It was an older silver BMW with a bent back bumper. I texted the plate number to myself so I wouldn't forget."

"I think I know this car," said Ramona. "Did it have any bumper stickers?"

"Yeah, several. One 'AVP,' one 'HHS' and one that said, 'The Weather is Here, I Wish You Were Beautiful'."

"The HHS is for Hermosa High School," said Lisa. Her oldest daughter, Scarlet, was going to be entering high school in the fall and had put HHS stickers on her notebooks. She'd tried to put one on her mother's car but Lisa had refused, not wanting to admit to herself that she was old enough to have a child in high school.

"Yep," agreed Ramona. "And I'm pretty sure whoever owns the car lives on Jasmine Street. I walk by there all the time with Smedley. I've noticed this car because the person who drives it parks facing the wrong way."

"Well, you'll definitely be able to spot it now," Lexie said with a giggle. "I slapped about ten of my 'Mama Power' stickers on it."

"You didn't," Jackie gasped, putting her hand to her mouth.

"I did," Lexie said, smiling and nodding to the group. "So, before they notice and yank 'em off, do you think you can walk by tomorrow and see if it's the same car?" Lexie asked Ramona.

"No problemo," Ramona said.

"I can ask Scarlet if she knows who the kid with the mermaid tattoo is. She and her friends are completely boy crazy. They know every details about virtually every guy within a twenty-mile radius."

"Excellent," I said. "Once we know who he is, we can either narc him out to his parents or the cops. Or cajole him into confessing and teach him a lesson, which might be more fun," I added, nodding.

Before the others had a chance to ask me what I had in mind, Mrs. Hedges' automatic sprinklers came on, drenching us. We screamed and ran, in practically every direction, bumping into each other, finally finding our way out of the yard and back to Ramona's house, laughing the entire way.

Eleven

There is not a park in Hermosa that the boys and I had not visited at least 100 times. When you have little kids and virtually no yard, going to the park is simply what you do. Lucky for us, we had a handful of really good ones within stroller distance and we rotated between them, including the one we were at now, Fort-Lots-O-Fun, one of my favorites. It literally looked like an old western fort with a giant, 15-foot high gate and fencing made from tall, barky posts placed side by side like giant pencils, the tops sharpened to keep out the bad guys. Towering eucalyptus and pine trees shaded the play structure, which included a pretend jail we took turns breaking out of and a mercantile where we bought pretend sarsaparilla and rattlesnake jerky. The best part? From atop the slide you could see the ocean shimmering in the distance.

I had very quickly taken in that view before ducking my head and bracing myself against the walls of the covered slide in order to hide from Casey and Griffin who were counting to twenty down below. I whipped out my phone, knowing I had a minute or two before they found me, to glance at any important texts when I saw Lexie's response to the MNO eVite I had sent out before the boys and I left home.

"Camping?! Are you crazy?" she wrote and I had to smile a big toothy grin. We'd talked briefly about camping before, Lexie and me. I grew up doing it and was excited for when my boys would be old enough to enjoy it—they were almost there—and thought it would be fun to go with another family, Lexie's family to be precise, of which neither she, nor Josh, were campers. But I was sure they'd like it. Sitting around a campfire in a beautiful forest, drinking good wine, telling stories, making s'mores for the kids as they caught bugs and got filthy and wore headlights on night walks and saw more stars than they ever could have imagined.

But the camping I had invited everyone to for our next MNO was nothing of the sort. "This isn't *real* camping," I said when I called her back later as Griffin napped and Casey played with his wooden trains. "My invite said if you *like* camping, you'll love this."

"I hate camping."

"How would you know? You've never even been."

"I know myself really well."

"I think you'd like it. Besides, this is just the best part of camping, the bonfire! And it's on the beach. There's no tent to set up, no bugs to spray, and I'll do all the hard work. Easy breezy."

"We'll see. But don't expect a big turnout, we've got the Gucci Gals, remember?"

I remembered. The Gucci Gals is what we call the moms who were always, *always* dressed nicely. Many of them actually carried Gucci diaper bags. They never had their hair in a ponytail, they wore full make-up consistently and their children rarely wore anything less than Hannah Anderson or Juicy Couture. They were not likely campers.

Which was exactly why I chose Dockweiler Beach for this next MNO. It was twenty minutes north of Hermosa and the only beach in L.A. County that allowed bonfires. This was not going to be one of our swanky, hip, tinsel-town outings. There was the dirt, sand and smoke factor, plus Dockweiler was known to be a little sketchy. The rumor was that gang members hung out there, which I had a hard time believing, but that was the reputation.

This venue choice, I figured, would weed out the moms who wouldn't get down and dirty, which was what I wanted because lately I had been making a point of reading the police blotter and it was not pretty. Just this past week the pizza place on Bayview Drive had been robbed at gunpoint, a gang-related knife fight took place outside one of the bars on the promenade, and a waitress disappeared on her way home from her shift. The crimes were happening more often and becoming more and more violent. Our crew needed to kick our efforts up a notch or ten and *now* and I wasn't sure the five of us were going to be enough. I was starting to scout for a B-Team, ergo the Dockweiler venue. Plus, I figured this would test how well our core unit responded to unknown stresses in the field.

All week I had been taking detours on the way to and from Casey's school and Griffin's classes to check behind Ralph's, Von's and Trader Joe's to stock up on wooden palates. My Highlander was now packed to the ceiling with them, plus I had lighter fluid and matches, camping chairs, blankets, a boom box with fresh batteries, stuff to make s'mores and of course, several bottles of wine. I was so excited.

I pictured us all under the night sky as the waves crashed less than 100 feet away. We'd be curled up in sweatshirts, our tan legs tucked inside to beat the chill. We'd be listening to the Beach Boys and Jan and Dean, telling stories and laughing, chilling old-school California style. We'd feel the fresh, cool, salty air on our faces, the warmth of the fire on our legs and the cool of the sand on our buried toes. It was a little kumbaya and hokey, but I could think of nothing else that would make us feel so free and alive and remind us of what we were fighting for. There had to be a few more adventurous moms amongst us who would want a little of that.

I arrived at the parking lot early to set up. The weather on this Friday evening, late in May, could not have been better. I kicked off my flip-flops once I hit the edge of the pavement and my feet sank into the soft sand, still warm from the day's sun. I chose the third pit north of the parking lot so we'd have some privacy then texted the location to everyone, tossed my phone in the car and began unloading.

Within twenty minutes I had everything set up. I turned on Jan and Dean's Greatest Hits, lit the fire and plunked down in my chair facing the parking lot with ten minutes to spare before May's MNO officially began.

Nearly two hours later, I was still alone and in my chair next to the fire, still waiting for all the moms and feeling dejected and disconcerted. I had forced myself half an hour earlier to stop looking up, looking desperately at every car that entered the parking lot, every person who passed by, hoping for a face I'd recognize. I just sat there, numb, poking the fire with my s'mores stick, searching the flames for answers to how I could fight this fight alone.

"Kelly?" I heard someone say from far off, as if in a dream. And then again, closer this time, "Kelly?" and then someone else whispered, "Is she okay?"

I blinked hard and tore my eyes from the flames. When I looked up I saw Lexie, Lisa, Jackie and Ramona standing just on the other side of the fire pit, each with their own look of concern. Lisa immediately came and sat next to me in the sand. "Are you alright? We've been yelling for you from the parking lot. Didn't you hear us?
"

"Where is everyone?" Jackie asked, scanning the beach as she kicked off her flip-flops and dropped her tote bag.

I looked at Lisa despondently. "Nobody," I mumbled, gesturing wildly with my s'more stick to the whole beach. "Nobody came."

"Is she drunk?" I heard Jackie whisper.

"Maybe on *sugar*," Lexie responded, picking up the graham cracker box that was stuffed with Hershey's wrappers and a sticky marshmallow bag that was by my feet. She glared at me and demanded, "How many s'mores have you had?"

"I dunno," I mumbled, trying to swallow the one still in my mouth. "Maybe fifteen?"

"Give me that," she said, grabbing my s'more stick. "What are you, four?"

"I got depressed," I said meekly. "Really, really depressed. And a little bored. I mean, what the hell?" I said, motioning to the empty chairs, my voice rising. "Where is everybody? Where were you guys?"

"We called about a million times," Lexie said. "Why didn't you answer your phone?"

"It's in the car," I admitted. "I didn't want to have any valuables with me out here at the pit. And then, when it started getting dark and late, I was sure someone would come and I didn't want to lose our spot or have my stuff stolen just to go get my phone."

"I'm so sorry, this is all my fault," Lisa said. "Jackson cut himself really badly just before it was time to leave and I had to bandage him up and calm him down. Pete might have taken him to the hospital for stitches."

"It's my fault, too," Jackie said. "Brian just got home when it was time for me to leave and the transition for Sierra was not such a smooth one."

"Don't look at me," Ramona said flatly, hugging an old Mexican blanket to her chest. "I was ready at five." She had on a grape colored oversized fleece, an orange corduroy skirt, white tube socks and Birkenstocks.

Lisa placed a blanket over my legs and they all settled in, setting their chairs, blankets and other necessities around the fire.

"Here," Ramona said, handing me a plastic cup of red wine. "This will make you feel better."

"Go easy on that. I don't want you barfing s'mores on us," Lexie said.

Lisa narrowed her eyes at Lexie then turned to me. "Here, try this," she said, taking the aluminum foil off a casserole pan she'd brought and spooning a steamy heap of what was probably her amazing baked ziti into a Solo cup and handed it to me. "You're going to need some protein."

"I can't believe nobody showed," Jackie said, still scanning the beach. "I mean, yeah, it's a little work to get everything together and down here, but it's totally worth it. Look at it, this is awesome," she said, gesturing to the fire, the sky, the ocean.

She was right. The beach was completely dark except for the fire pits that dotted it like exotic tiki torches every twenty-five yards. The sky, too, was pitch black making the sound of the crashing waves even more dramatic. The lights of the houses and towns lit up the twenty-something miles of coastline from Malibu to Palos Verdes, forming what's known as the "Queen's Necklace." There were even a few noticeable stars in the sky. The breeze had become damp and the air smelled of campfire and salt.

"You should have seen the sunset," I said, sipping my wine and slipping back into my beach chair, my eyes drawn vacantly to the fire. "Now that was awesome. But," I sighed, "nobody showed." I was not trying to make them feel bad by any means. But I was worried.

"We showed," Lexie said, abruptly standing and putting another pallet on the fire, sparks shooting out from all sides. She dusted her hands and sat back down. "Just not exactly on time."

I shook my head from side to side and said meekly, "I'm not sure the five of us will be enough. I have to tell you, I was hoping to recruit some other moms, back-ups or a JV-squad or something, to help with our various missions because, if any of you read the police blotter this past week, the criminals appear to be waging a war. And winning.

"That's not exactly a scientific gauge of how we're doing," Lisa said. "We should call the police and see if the hotline is helping and what kind of activity we're seeing on Facebook and Twitter. I agree that we need to step it up, but let's see where we really need to focus our efforts. Let's get some metrics going so we can see where the problems are concentrated, what types of activities are the most prevalent, and what time of day these events are taking place."

"I can do it," Jackie chimed in. "I love graphs and charts." I looked at her and could tell right off that she would take color-coding and pie charts to a whole new level. "We could present it to the whole group at the next big MNO."

"Ya know, forget those other moms, those weak, wimpy little wusses," Lexie said, stoking the fire with my s'mores stick.

"Lexie," Lisa said in her scolding tone.

"What? Kelly's right. I read the police blotter, too, this week and we have a serious problem. If the others can't hack a fucking *bonfire*, then they aren't up to snuff. My neighbor's house was broken into yesterday in broad daylight *while she was home*. This situation is getting out of control."

"You're kidding," Jackie gasped. "What happened?"

"She was upstairs in her kitchen and thought she heard something. When she went downstairs, she saw someone in her bathroom rifling through her medicine cabinet. She screamed and the dude ran out. These people are brazen and we need to focus on sending a message that criminals aren't welcome in our town. That if the police aren't around to get them, the people will."

"Well, we can't just kick the others to the curb," Lisa said between bites of ziti. "We need their eyes, their ears, their iPhones. They need to feel included so they continue to stay alert and call in reports. That's actually a really good story. We should put it on the Facebook page to get everyone on guard."

For the better part of the next hour we discussed strategies for getting the others involved. We were coming up with some good ideas, all of which would be pretty easy to implement. But while we were brainstorming ways to keep trouble in our town at bay, trouble came to us.

Three young men appeared out of the dark right behind me. They were young, early twenties, looked strong and mildly intoxicated. If the others felt like I did, they were scared out of their pants.

In tight jeans, T-shirts, jackets and gym shoes they looked like they spent a good deal of their day at the gym. Flirty and smirking mischievous little smiles they crashed our bonfire without a hint of reservation planting themselves on the sand between me and Lisa and on either side of Jackie, whose eyes went wide.

"What do we have going on here, ladies?" the one next to me asked. He had blonde, disheveled hair, a ridiculously small goatee and the cocky overconfidence that comes with youth.

"Looks like we're having ourselves a little beach party," another said from across the fire. He had brown skin and dark hair that was shaved so close I could see his skull.

"Can we help you?" Ramona asked calmly, not seeming to be nervous or scared at all.

"No, we're cool," the third one said, ignoring her and eyeing Lexie. This one was brunette with short hair, a Dodgers baseball cap on backwards, and a glint in his eyes like a cat who'd just found himself a mouse. "We just thought we'd hang with you guys and chill for a while. How about sharing a little of your libations?"

"Uh, sorry guys, this is a closed party," Lisa stated, her eyes wide, darting back and forth between the men.

"We just thought you could use some male company," Cap Guy said, scooting closer to Jackie who shifted away from him ever so slyly. He smiled at her lasciviously and slurred, "There definitely seems to be a lack of men in this circle."

"On purpose," Lexie said in the stern yet softly consolatory tone I'd heard her use a million times with her children, although this time I'm sure she was biting her tongue so she didn't add 'asshole.' "We are all happily married with children and are not in any need of additional company. Why don't you all have a brownie and go and find some kids your own age to hang with." Bravely she stood and offered the box of what I assumed were her gourmet cabernet brownies to our unwelcome visitors, holding them so high they had to stand to take one.

I slowly and quietly sifted through the sand with my fingers for the nine-iron I'd buried under my chair as I watched them glance at each other. It looked to me as though they were trying to gauge what their next move should be, communicating with their eyes to see how far their pals were willing to go, weighing their options.

They seemed relatively harmless, just a bunch of drunk punk 20-year-olds, but what did I know? They could easily be the dreaded gang bangers who plagued Dockweiler, terrorizing people and giving it such a bad reputation. I realized with a sinking feeling that, again, I was so very naïve when it came to criminals and potentially hazardous situations.

"This is a tough crowd," Blondie said getting to his feet slowly, carefully trying to keep his balance. He was definitely drunk.

"Tough and gorgeous," Cap Man said. He gave Jackie the once over then locked eyes with Lexie as he stood. "I like that. Maybe we'll just take the whole box." He rested both hands on the opposite side of the container from Lexie and pulled ever so slightly.

Tension poured out of me like water draining from a pool. All we had to do was give them the entire box of brownies, fine by me, and they would leave. Hell, I was willing to throw in all our wine and s'mores, too, if they would just go away, now and nicely.

Relieved, I looked to Lexie, expecting her to feel the same. Instead I saw her jaw clench, her expression still rigid. She got the same look when one of her kids was disobedient too many times and for too long and had pushed her beyond her last nerve.

"I think one each is enough," she said, staring back at him, her crystal blue eyes flashing in a way that was both captivating and intimidating, like she was either going to seduce him or turn him to stone. And she held on tightly.

I felt as though the wind was knocked out of me and I heard Jackie let out a quiet gasp. Lexie was infamous for her bravado; it had gotten her in over her head on more than one occasion. There was that incident at the day spa and the time she'd goosed Goofy at Disneyland. She'd paid for both transgressions.

And here she was now, standing up to three guys who could easily pound us all into the sand. I watched her, hoping she had some insight from her "ghetto intuition" as she like to call it, to know that these guys were harmless. Because we'd just had an out and she blew it. At the very least, I thought, if we died tonight I knew that I was no longer solely responsible.

My eyes were locked on Cap Man. He was eyeing Lexie intently, willing himself to sober up. Everything was silent and still, all of us waiting for him to make his next move. And then I heard something that was just barely audible from somewhere by Ramona, a click that sounded mechanical. He heard it, too, I saw him flinch ever so slightly, a moment of recognition. "Fine, fine," Tiny Goatee said, reaching around his buddy to grab a brownie. "Thanks." He placed on hand on the other guy's shoulder signaling it was time to leave. "Come on dudes, let's go. These MILFs don't want to play."

Cap Man took another look at Lexie then dropped his gaze to the brownies, reached in and grabbed one and shoved the whole thing in his mouth. He gave her a cocky grin, turned and shot Ramona a quick glance before strutting off with the others.

We watched them go and when we were convinced they were gone, I broke down. "Oh my God, you guys, I am so sorry." My face flushed hot as tears quickly came to my eyes and I wiped them away with one sleeve, my other hand was still locked on the golf club. "Those guys could have been gang bangers! I could have just inadvertently killed us all. I could never forgive myself if something happened to any of you."

Lexie sat down, still holding her Tupperware, and patted my knee. "Those weren't gang bangers, honey," she said, trying to calm me down through my sobs.

"How do you know?" Jackie asked, her eyes still wide.

Lexie scoffed and shook her head. "They were just punk kids. I grew up with guys just like that. They're just out for some fun, and fun for them is intimidating people."

Lexie was tough, I had to give her that. She grew up in a not-so-great part of the Inland Empire. She would occasionally tell me tales of her childhood, how her mom was an alcoholic, her dad long gone. How she would come home from school to find her mom and the boyfriend du jour passed out in various places in the apartment. She wasn't at all embarrassed about her roots, rather she wore it as a badge of honor, a reminder, I think, to many in the South Bay who came from money that she had put herself through school, had been successful in her career, had done it all on her own.

"But how did you know?" Lisa asked, a look of intense interest on her face.

"Well," Lexie said, "they didn't have any tattoos, for one. They weren't wearing colors, two. And the blonde guy's hair was too long." She shrugged. "Plus, they just didn't seem the type. Gang bangers just aren't that relaxed. These guys seemed more like drunk surfers to me."

"They still could have been dangerous," I said, wiping my nose on my sleeve. "They could have been muggers, or rapists or something. And I got us all into this mess."

"Kelly," Lisa said, "look at me. We aren't lemmings. We are all grown women who made the decision to be here because we wanted to be. We've all heard the rumors about Dockweiler. We all know the risks. We would never agree to a MNO in, say, Compton. If something were to happen it would not be your fault, got it? We're in this together." She looked at me intently and added, "And not just this bonfire, either. I'm talking about everything. Okay?"

Her words hit home and as I looked from face to nodding face, I realized they were all just as committed to my cause to clean up our town as I was. I smiled, relieved, and said okay. I let out a little laugh as I pulled out my golf club. "I don't know how much damage I could have done with this, but I would have gone Tasmanian Devil to protect you all."

To my surprise, Lisa opened her clutched fist showing us all a canister of pepper spray she'd brought. "Me, too."

"Me, too," Jackie smiled, showing us the grip she had on my weapon of choice, a bottle of red wine.

"Me, too," Lexie said, pulling the box of brownies away from her hand, revealing that she had a wine opener with the knife part out hidden up her sleeve.

"Me, too," Ramona said, and I noticed that she had her entire arm tucked into her tote bag, as though she were rooting for something in the bottom. It hit me then as I watched her that the mechanical clicking noise I had heard, the one that made the man take pause, had come from somewhere very near, if not inside, her bag. She slowly pulled her hand out and then, with a gleam in her eye and a very subtle smile, she opened it to reveal nothing but made her hand flat and cried out, "Hiyah!" then sliced both hands very fast and very enthusiastically through the air.

"My hands are registered as lethal weapons," she deadpanned. "I could have taken those guys out with one swift chop!" She continued slicing up more air trying to keep a straight face and contain her laughter, but was doing a horrible job of it.

We laughed uncontrollably for a solid five minutes, Ramona continuing to entertain us until she finally collapsed into her chair and caught her breath.

"Now," she suggested, "why don't we all taste what's in that box that's worth risking our lives for."

"Forget the brownies," Lexie said, standing up and tossing the box on her seat. "Let's do what we came here to do. C'mon, the ocean is calling!" And with that she began stripping off her clothes.

I watched, my mouth agape, completely speechless, until Ramona snapped me out of my trance, shocking me by yelling, "You don't have to tell me twice." By the time I looked over at her, she was already up and flinging her tube socks over the back of her chair. I looked at Lisa and Jackie who looked as stupefied as I felt. Poor Lisa, frankly looked more terrified than she did when the men had sauntered in.

"Wait," I stammered, "this is crazy, it's cold, it's dark—"

"It's like *Mom's Gone Wild!*" Jackie chirped, joining in and jumping out of her seat.

"No way, no way, no way," I could hear Lisa mumbling as I watched everyone disrobe.

"Lexie, let's talk about this—" I began.

"Come on!" she yelled over her shoulder, already jogging toward the water. She spun around, arms wide open. "There's no one to see you so what do you have to lose? Quit thinking and start stripping!"

I glanced over at Lisa who looked like a deer in headlights. "Come on you two," Ramona said, taking off her shirt revealing her apparent dislike of bras. "Kelly, you wanted bold action? Well, this is bold and action. Pretend you're that Jason Bourne guy you're always yammering about. Lisa, at least and put your toes in, it will work miracles for your stress level. Now mom-up, both of you." She ran for the water with purpose, like she was going to swim to Catalina.

"What is this, hazing?" Lisa cried after her, her voice going up in pitch. "I will not bow to peer pressure!"

Jackie shrugged and smiled as she started for the water. "Whatever it is, I love it. I can't wait to tell Brian," she yelled over her shoulder. "You guys are crazier than his single buddies!"

I looked at Lisa, whose expression had now turned from scared to miffed. "Just up to my ankles and that's it," she growled at me

115

through clenched teeth as she rose from her chair. I knew her problem was her body image, which wasn't nearly as bad as she thought. Mine, however, was a fear of sharks and freezing cold water, both of which were made worse at night when you couldn't see or warm up. But Ramona was right, I needed to mom-up and this was exactly the type of drill that would train us for whatever may lie ahead.

And so I began to strip down. By the time Lisa and I reached the water, my teeth were already chattering. I took one step into the frigid water and shrieked. I heard Lexie shouting to me over the roar of crashing waves and saw Jackie duck dive under one. I looked over at Lisa and to my surprise, she had a huge grin on her face as she waded out knee-deep, then stopped, closed her eyes and lifted her head and arms to the sky. I took a deep breath, looked up at the moon, and decided right then and there that I wanted to be the kind of person who would jump at the chance to skinny dip in the dark— the kind of person who wouldn't hesitate at the edge of the water.

Then I ran. Into the surf, jumping over the waves, screaming and hooting. When it got deep enough, I held my breath and duck dived below the water, giving my system a shock that took my breath away but enlivened every cell in my body. I swam out to find the others and we body surfed, or tried to, until we could no longer feel our hands or feet. I realized as we dragged ourselves back to the fire, picking Lisa up in the smaller waves, that we wouldn't be needing that B-Team after all.

Twelve

Lisa wasted no time discovering the beer thieves were seniors at Hermosa High. Her daughter, Scarlet, knew all about them. Their names were Gage Brewster and Will Portman, the big men on campus. Both had full-ride volleyball scholarships for the following year to USC. People were saying they were Olympic material.

Now that we knew this, we had some leverage.

Our plan was two-pronged. The first goal was to make Will and Gage apologize and make amends to the Hedges' satisfaction; the second was to teach them a lesson, embarrass them a little so they'd learn a little humility or at the least some manners, especially since kids were looking up to them.

It was a week after the bonfire when we put our plan into gear, starting with me spying on the one with the car, Will, early one morning. The night before Ramona had put an envelope on his windshield containing a letter that demanded he apologize to the Hedges. My job was to make sure he got it. And so with my boys strapped in their boosters in the backseat eating bagels and watching Clifford, I surveyed his car through binoculars from a block away, snickering to myself at how invisible I was.

Will came out of his house looking every bit the young, virile athlete. He was tall and thin yet muscular, and wore jeans and a blue T-shirt with Wayfarer-style sunglasses hanging off the neck of his shirt. He practically bounced down the steps of his house, his thick hair bouncing with him. He didn't carry a single thing: no books, no backpack, not even a pencil that I could see. I only caught a quick glimpse as he grabbed the envelope off his windshield, tossed it in the passenger seat without so much as a curious glance and took off but it was enough to for me to get a picture of his life and how, with only thirteen days left before a killer summer was at hand, he must be feeling like he had the world by the tail.

I texted this info to the group and Lexie, who was stationed in the parking lot outside the high school, texted us all when she saw him arrive. Our inside team, Ramona, Jackie and Sierra in her stroller, were already roaming the halls, pretending to be looking for someone, and they saw both boys go to class. They then had someone deliver a similar envelope to Gage during first period. Both envelopes contained a cheesy letter that said, "We witnessed you stealing beer from 814 Gladiola Street. Underage drinking is illegal. Stealing is illegal. Apologize now, face your victims, make amends to their satisfaction and we won't contact the police. Ignore this message at your own peril. WE ARE WATCHING YOU." Jackie and I had written the message over the weekend and had to keep each other from falling over we were laughing so hard trying to find words that would resonate with teenagers.

The boys, of course, had understood our message. They met each other at their locker, which was now covered with "Mama Power" stickers, after first period and proceeded to freak out. Jackie had put her new high-tech, super-sensitive, NASA-developed baby monitor above their locker in order to hear every word of their conversation as she and Ramona watched the two meatheads from the end of the hall.

"Whoever is fucking with us, is dead meat," Will said, punching his locker.

"I will kill them with my bare hands," Gage replied. "Nobody messes with us. This had better not be on Punk'd." He shouted this last bit to the hall as people walked by staring, keeping their distance.

So even though the plan went smoothly and they didn't see us, it didn't exactly work, either. They were nowhere near coming forward and apologizing, which, I think, we all kind of expected and why now, three days later, we were meeting at the beach to enact Phase II.

Near the foot of the pier is a bronze statue of a surfer catching a wave, melded together with a volleyball player spiking a ball and a swimmer looking under his arm to take a breath. It was an expensive sculpture donated to the city by some wealthy local couple when the pier was remodeled ten years ago and was meant to add elegance and sophistication, but kids and seagulls were constantly climbing on it, making it more of a hangout for families than the intended work of art. We decided to meet there because it was right next to the volleyball courts and we could bring all of our kids and have a big picnic, making us more inconspicuous.

We did our homework and found out that Gage and Will worked out at these courts every day after school. For two hours their coach drilled them, made them run sprints to and from the water and worked on their techniques. Afterwards, the fun began. Their friends would join to watch them take on whoever dared to challenge them, usually college guys or just some locals who thought they might be good enough to take them down. But at six-foot-six and six-foot-eight, Will and Gage made a pretty gruesome team, it was easy to see why they were being called Olympic material. Except they didn't act like Olympians, they acted like jackasses.

They enjoyed humiliating and taunting their opponents. They strutted and posed, flexing their muscles. They cat called girls strolling by on the Strand, sometimes even holding up signs that ranked the girls numerically. Ramona, asked around and found they had straw-wrapper fights and loosened the lids to all the parmesan dispensers in the pizza place; they complained about their food at Java Hut in order to get it for free; they demanded samples of all the ice cream flavors and then didn't buy a scoop at Lambert's. Will and Gage were the kings of the sandcastle and they were oblivious to anything else, especially, we hoped, a bunch of middle-aged moms.

"Let's get down to business," I said, slyly breaking out a bottle of Sauvignon Blanc and pouring it into plastic cups. Our kids were all playing nicely, we had to make the most of our window. "First off, kudos on all the surveillance texts and the seamless delivery of Phase I. Communication is key to any successful mission. And I, for one, would have loved to see the faces on those two clowns when they opened their letters. Brilliant idea, Ramona, having them delivered at school, where their friends would see them." We raised our glasses to toast our successful first step.

"Looks like Tweedle-dee and Tweedle-dum are here," Ramona said, motioning with her head to the court where Will and Gage were just starting to play. "So I'm a go for Phase II."

She had volunteered because she felt she would be the least suspicious. Without wasting another second, she stood and quickly threw a loose-fitting purple dress over the orange one she was wearing and took her purple hat and shoved it in her bag. Then she wrapped her head in a lime green scarf, said "Back in a flash," and headed off towards the juice bar closest to the pier.

We watched her go and then directed our attention to the kids and Will and Gage. "They're gonna love seeing the bumper of their car," Lexie said with a smile.

"You didn't. Not again," Jackie said.

"Oh yeah, I did." Lexie said with a grin.

"I wish we could put some on *their* bumper," Lisa said, nodding toward the young guys that were standing thirty feet from us. She was referring to the drug dealers that were almost a permanent fixture of the pier. They generally appeared in pairs and hung out toward the side, where they could make a clean escape up the Strand if need be, but still have easy accesses to the crowds. I'd never seen them alone and sometimes, mostly weekends, as many as four would show up. It was rare to see the pier without them, the same way it was rare not to see a homeless man or two along with all their stuff under the pier.

Today, because it was Friday I suppose, there were three. They were all clean cut, mid-twenties young men. They dressed in the surf T-shirts and wore cargo or board shorts, sometimes jeans. They never looked ratty or dirty, one would simply think they were a group of friends hanging out at the pier, taking in the scene, occasionally going for a skateboard ride—except they were there each day, every day, sometimes as early as ten in the morning if it were a weekend.

On weekdays they started around eleven when the restaurant workers began appearing for their lunch shifts, always with a purposeful expression on their faces, like the salespeople at the mall who try too hard to make earnest eye contact then offer a free sample of something in order to lure you into their store. Everyone knew who and what they were, and they had a diverse clientele: the homeless, the beach bums, the twenty-something waiters and retail workers, the thirty and forty-something business people. They were always pleasant, offering a polite "hello" to me and the other mothers, sometimes commenting on how cute our babies were. It was offensive and awkward since I felt obliged to smile and say hello back instead of sneering and telling them to fuck off, which I really wanted to do.

"I hate those guys," Lexie said with a sneer. "You know one of them offered Cash a joint a last summer? Said he could have it as a free sample. He's *eight*, for Christ's sake!"

"Seriously?" Lisa asked, looking over at them. "What did you do?"

"I took the joint back over to him, crumpled it in his face and told him to shove it up his ass and that if he ever so much as looked at my kid again, I'd blow his fucking head off. That's what," said Lexie.

"Atta girl," I smiled, again both awed by and proud of Lexie's boldness. "What did Josh say?"

"Ooooooohhhh, he was pissed. I calmed him down so he didn't drive down here and try to punch their lights out," she said, dropping her voice and leaning in towards us, "because let's face it, those brawny dudes would smash Josh like a grape." She sat back up. "I haven't been that fucking blow-my-lid mad since I can't remember. They are so slick and slimy. Why the hell don't they get arrested and put away? I saw them lead a pack of high school girls under the pier last week. It makes my blood boil."

"I've heard the cops just can't catch them in the act. They're too understaffed to really address the problem and like you said, these guys are slick," said Lisa. "It's not even like they try and hide it anymore. That one meth-addict, the one who sleeps under the library bushes whose face is practically burnt off? He follows them around like a mouse looking for crumbs."

We sipped our wine for another minute and helped ourselves to snacks, watching the kids play and laugh while taking in the whole beach scene. The older ones took their boogie boards and headed down to the waves and as we were watching them go, Ramona came back, a little out of breath wearing her other outfit and plunked down on the sand, a big smile on her face.

"The eagle has landed," she said.

We all got into position to watch the show and within three minutes a Jamba Juice worker, decked out in his apron and visor, arrived at the volleyball courts with two jumbo smoothies and called out for Will and Gage. They boys looked at each other bewildered and dashed for the man. To their surprise he handed them both extra large smoothies, which they took with huge smiles, toasting each other. They then raised their cups to whoever was around watching them, their little token of appreciation to the secret admirer who had sent the drinks to them *this* time, then proceeded to strut around as if they'd been given the keys to a new car. When their show was over, they began to strut back to their court but the juice man called them back and handed them a manila envelope. Together they tore it open with their straws in their mouths, still sucking. They ripped the top open and pulled out another anonymous note printed on the same white card stock glued onto black posterboard and decorated with calligraphy, just like before. Jackie murmured to us what the card said while we watched from behind sunglasses as the boys read their copy:

You still haven't apologized.
We have your fingerprints.
We have a photo of you stealing.
We are watching you now and always.
Don't be stupid, you could lose everything.
And don't blame the juice man, he knows nothing.

We all giggled. Another cheesy, semi-mysterious letter with the last line thrown in to both amuse us and protect the juice man. The two beer thieves sobered up quickly after that, looking around to see who might be watching them. They were trying to size up everyone on the beach and pier, but it was Friday afternoon and there were just too many people around. Instead, they took their rage out on their volleyballs, kicking them across the sand and tossing their juice cups, which they finished first, down on the sand as well. They sat there for a while broken off from their entourage, whom they had verbally berated, and we could tell they were trying to figure out what to do.

These two had never felt like caged animals before, I was sure, but suddenly they were realizing how real our threat could be, how they could truly lose everything. But apologize? I watched their body language and it didn't look like it was in the cards, like apologizing was beneath them. They looked as though they'd rather pound every person they knew than do that. We watched with glee as the wind was taken out of Will and Gage's sails.

"This is better than Tivo," I said, munching on a tortilla chip, watching from the corner of my eye. They got up, dusted themselves off and started to play again. This time, however, most of their shots went straight into the net.

"I'm glad we added the bit about the juice guy. These guys are stupid enough to think he's the one messing with them," Lexie said. I shook my head as the boys fumed around the court, glad we had a Plan C.

"You guys don't think they'll figure out it's us, do you?" asked Jackie, a little worried, rubbing Sierra's back while she sat in her adorable onesie on the warm sand chewing a plastic shovel.

"No way," said Lisa. "They're morons, I mean look at them." They had started up a new game and Will was picking a fight with a college-aged kid who had spiked him in the face. The older guy was just as tall, but had a lot more meat on his body. Gage was trying to pull Will away, but he continued his trash talk. It looked like a scene out of Jerry Springer. "And they aren't sorry, either."

"Looks like Plan C is a go. I've got their coach's address, Lex and Lisa, you'll send me the photos you took? Jackie, you up for writing another anonymous letter?"

"You bet. But since we're going to continue to do this sort of thing, do you think we should get some professional training of some sort? Something that would make us feel a little more prepared?" Jackie asked.

"Agreed and I'm already on it," I said, recalling my revelations on the drive home from the bonfire. "I was going to run this by you guys anyway. Casey's martial arts instructor said he'd be happy to start a self-defense class for moms, so I thought I'd invite the whole MNO crowd. Plus, I was thinking I could set up a secret agent style boot camp in my house."

Lexie smirked as if to say, "I got this," then sat up on her knees, dusting chip crumps off her shorts. "Ladies," she took a breath, "you're totally selling yourselves short. Just by being a mom you are trained better than half the secret agents out there."

"Excuse me?" Lisa asked, pulling her glasses to the tip of her nose to look over them, "what, pray tell, are you talking about?"

"I'm serious," Lexie replied, sitting up straighter. "Who is naturally better prepared to handle disasters on a regular basis than a mom?" We looked at her in silence. She let out a deep breath and rolled her eyes, got to her feet and stood looking down at us like a teacher, her lesson about to begin.

"Kelly, when Griffin dashed away from you into the Target parking lot the other day, who did ten yards in under a second to catch him and still saved her cart from crashing into a car?"

I looked at her apprehensively, remembering how I had told her that story and how freaked out I had been when Griff had ripped his little hand out of mine and dashed away. "Me?" I uttered.

"That's right," Lexie said, pointing at me. She then turned to Lisa. "Lisa, when Jade started crying the other day in your playroom and Jackson said he didn't know what happened to her, who saw that he had smacked her upside the head with a light saber in the reflection of the television?"

"Oh, I did," Lisa recalled. "He did not get away with that one."

"Yes," Lexie said, stabbing the air in Lisa's direction with her finger before turning to Jackie. "Jackie, the other week at Kelly's when that glass got knocked off the counter and almost broke right beside Sierra, whose freshly-honed cat-like reflexes snatched it out of the air Matrix style?"

Jackie looked bewildered, but answered dutifully, her face bunched up in a question. "Uh, my freshly-honed cat-like reflexes?"

"Exactly!" Lexie said, clapping her hands together enthusiastically, she was getting revved up. She turned to Ramona. "Ramona, who sacrificed herself by miraculously catching the surfboard that fell off the wall in my garage and almost took out half my kids?"

"I wouldn't exactly say I caught it," Ramona said under her breath. "It kind of just landed on me and fell the other way."

"That's right! You did!" Lexie shouted, looking to us all as if she was trying to prove some long-debated conundrum and that last piece was all the confirmation she needed. "Who picked a child-proof lock in under two minutes to get out of her own kids' bedroom when she accidentally locked herself in?"

"That would be you," I said with a grin, adding, "but not the first time. That time you were stuck in the room for an hour with two sobbing kids and a two-year-old roaming the rest of the house unsupervised."

"And the second time," Lisa pointed out, "you had your phone so you called a neighbor to get you out."

"But the *third* time it was me, thankyouverymuch, who picked the lock with a safety pin in about ninety seconds flat," Lexie said, "and I bet I could do it now in under twenty, on all of your bathroom locks." She began to pace like a commander in front of her soldiers.

Her swagger was not only amusing, it was contagious. I caught Lisa's eye and we smiled, shook our heads, and smiled wider when we looked back at Lexie. "Who had to jump four feet from her deck onto the nearest palm tree and then shimmy down it because her toddler locked her out on the deck while she was grilling dinner and her husband was asleep upstairs and couldn't hear her screaming?"

"Me!" I replied, my hand reflexively jumping into the air. "That rash took a month to heal." I remembered how scared I had been, jumping from my patio to the tree, and how pissed I was that Mark couldn't hear me yelling for help as he snoozed away. Casey had been past hysterical when he locked me out. He was almost two and so flustered when he couldn't undo the lock as I tried to explain it to him through the sliding glass door. He was crying and screaming and I couldn't understand how Mark could sleep through that racket. My desire to comfort him was what drove me to jump, it was borderline primal.

"Who drove herself to the hospital—normally a twenty minute drive—in just under ten during peak traffic *while* in labor?" Lexie asked the group.

"I did!" Lisa said, beaming. "Made it with a half hour to spare."

"I have one," I said, sitting up on my knees. "Who stopped an older sibling from slamming the car door—not accidentally, may I add—on her little brother's hand by diving into the crack, thus breaking everything in her purse and skinning up her knees?"

"Me," Lexie said proudly, cocking her head and raising her glass in the air.

"Oh, here's one," Jackie said, putting down her chip and brushing the salt and crumbs off her fingers. "Who hotwired and borrowed," she made finger quotes in the air, "her neighbor's car so she could pick up friends and see *Elvis*?"

Everyone's head whipped toward Ramona and we gasped. Lexie's eyes brightened as she took a few steps toward Ramona, offering her hand for a high five as she said, "Oh no you didn't!"

Ramona sat there, unfazed, a look of indignation on her face and pressed her hand into Lexie's. "Oh yes, I did. I wasn't going to miss *the* event of the summer. And my parents wouldn't lend me their car. They even locked it up in the garage."

Lexie smiled her award-winning smile as if Ramona's comment had just driven home her point and I made a mental note that a good playdate activity would be for Ramona to teach us all the mechanics of hotwiring. Lexie stopped and faced us, hands on hips. "Ladies, who can sneak around the entire house without making a peep?"

"We can," we all said in unison.

"Who can successfully hide Christmas presents from little people who spend hours each day looking for them?"

"We can," we repeated, a little louder this time.

She opened her arms wide and shouted her next question to the sky. "Who can push a double stroller filled with at least two kids, sand toys, towels, water, snacks, boogie boards and who knows what else down to the beach, across the sand, play for hours, then lug it all back up insanely steep hills stopping for groceries while balancing a latte?"

"We can!" we shouted back.

I had to give it to her, she was so charismatic. I could imagine her on horseback, her face painted half blue and half white, declaring that "they may take our lives, but they will never take our freedom," her speech was that good. I actually believed we could do this; we could take on criminals with half a chance at winning. And it felt good. It felt big and empowering. I slyly glanced at the others, to see if they were drinking the Kool-Aid as much as I was.

Jackie's eyes were wide open and she was nodding at Lexie, her fist was ready to punch the air with the next, "We can!" Lisa was listening intently, a small smile on her face that either meant she was in, or just amused at Lexie's hubris. Ramona was definitely listening, but I couldn't see her expression due to her giant cosmonaut-style sunglasses. She was hard to read anyway, all stoic and deadpan.

Lexie then looked at us all pointedly. "Damn straight we can. And that's because we're moms. We're a breed apart. I'm done being bashful about it. We can do twenty things at once and still not lose our cool. We can survive on three hours of sleep and still focus on honors homework. We can perform all our duties with sore nipples, sore backs and sore feet. There isn't a boot camp in this world we wouldn't ace because," she picked up her plastic cup and brought it into the center of the group waiting for everyone else to follow suit, "moms rock!"

"Moms rock!" We chorused and clicked cups, reveling in the knowledge that we did, indeed, belong to a very special, elite group.

Lexie's pep talk seemed to elevate us all, giving us a much needed confidence boost. I, for one, felt inspired and more powerful than I had since the initial revelation I had months ago that my friends and I should be the ones to take on the bad guys. With Lexie's little you-are-more-powerful-than-you-know seed planted squarely in my head, it was like having my very own version of Obi Wan Kenobi cheering me on and whispering "Use the force, Kelly." And her speech couldn't have come at a more perfect time. It felt like we were getting ready for something. Like we had messed around with Will and Gage and Robert enough and it was time to take on something bigger, something eviler, something more significant. It was as though, had our lives been a movie, this would be the montage sequence with inspirational background music and us getting ready for the big fight, like in Rocky when he's jumping rope, punching the bag, then finally running up the steps and jumping for victory, ready to take on Apollo. We were there, we were running up the steps.

What I didn't know, what no one could have predicted, was that Lexie's message had struck a chord in one of us and inspired her to an unimaginable level. And instead of including us, she went rogue. We wouldn't find out until the end of the summer just what she'd been up to.

Thirteen

July brought the gloriously sunny days that Hermosa Beach was known for. People flocked to the iconic beaches made famous the world over by *Baywatch* and the *Beverly Hills 90210*. Concerts on the pier drew crowds of families on Sunday evenings, while the outdoor patio seating and warmer nights made the bars swell and spill over onto the promenade just about every night of the week. The larger crowds, it appeared, gave better cover for the criminal set and in the past there had always been a spike in crime over the summer months.

But not this summer. At least not so far. Lisa had enthusiastically delivered this tidbit to me over the phone with all the supporting facts and metrics and I had screamed so loudly that it actually drew Mark away from his office to check on me.

"We're making progress," I screamed, throwing my fist in the air in triumph. He nodded and smiled and went right back in while I listened to Lisa. "Chief Daniels says that our constant canvasing and reporting of incidents has made a real impact. It has enabled his force to be more effective and efficient."

She had plenty of stats to back up her statement. Burglaries were down. Petty theft was down. Violent crime was down. Everything except drug-related crimes. We, of course, gave the information to Jackie who was able to transform the metrics into an eye-catching work of art chart that we texted to all the moms and posted on our

Facebook page.

There was other good news, too. Ramona had been on a walk on the 4th of July and returned home to call us all with an urgent report. She had witnessed Will and Gage painting the outside of the Hedges' house so she talked to Mrs. Hedges and it seemed the boys would be missing out on the best beach day of the year, the one where extra police had to be brought in because the atmosphere was comparable to Mardi Gras, where girls paraded around in American flag string bikinis, where beach volleyball took center stage and they surely would have been treated as kings—all in order to keep their scholarships.

Mrs. Hedges had told Ramona the boys had arrived a few days prior with their coach and knocked on her door. The coach told her they were at her disposal as long as she needed them until school started, and if they gave her any lip, to call him directly and he would happily remove them from his team. It seemed he had received an anonymous envelope with a certain amount of incriminating evidence, a photo and the promise of the testimony from several sworn eyewitnesses that the boys were thieves and underage drinkers and would be turned into the police unless they made amends. The coach wouldn't tolerate any trouble-makers on his team.

So things were actually moving. We were doing it, making a difference. We were making progress on other fronts as well, including our self-defense training, which we took to calling "Fight Club." We didn't care that the name wasn't super original. I think we were all surprised by how little we knew about keeping ourselves safe, and even more surprised by how incredibly awesome it felt to kick stuff.

At this point, I was basically eating, drinking, breathing the role of the commando. My boys were used to me being a high-octane mom, but now they got one with stealth mode, which they loved, and I had to admit I felt like I was born for this sort of thing. We practiced spying on Mark using mirrored glasses and toy periscopes. We disguised ourselves with various hair and make-up outfits I had from past Halloweens and tried to fool our neighbors. During playdates we ran an obstacle course around the outside of our house, timing the participants and throwing water balloons like grenades off the porch (only if it was a mom).

We set up a "laser beam" hallway with bright red yarn crisscrossing the hall that the kids were pros at crawling through and shimmying underneath on their tummies. Us moms, however, needed lots more practice and no one could do it without getting the giggles. Lisa got so caught up in it she tripped and pulled the whole thing down, much to Casey's dismay.

On the playground, my boys and I were the stars with our games of cops and robbers. Casey even commented presciently one day after the three of us had successfully completed a mission against the rest of the kids that "the team you're on really makes all the difference." I gave him a wink and a fist bump, thinking *out of the mouths of babes*, as I simultaneously took stock of the blood, snot, and tears on my T-shirt, feeling grateful there were no other bodily fluids on me and wondering what brand of laundry detergent Jason Bourne used.

So we were on our way, and it wasn't just me being all gung-ho about everything. The others were getting into the game, too, "drinking Kelly's Kool-Aid," as Ramona put it. Lexie practically pounced on anyone she caught littering and Jackie had gone Facebook cray-cray, posting all the arrests that were results of a mom tip. Even Lisa got involved, begging me to let her plan this month's MNO and promising it would have something to do with *the cause*. I was happy to oblige and now that it was the night of our July MNO, I couldn't wait to see what we were doing because all she would divulge was that we needed to "dress comfortably."

Lexie, too, seemed excited when I went to pick her up. I didn't even have a chance to put the car in park when she darted out and hopped in.

"That was fast," I said, looking her over to make sure we were dressed similarly (we were, but somehow she still looked more stylish).

"I'm not letting the door hit me in the ass on my night of

freedom. Let's go before my little nibblers realize Daddy's watching them."

I programmed the address Lisa gave us into my car and headed north on the 405. As usual, it was backed up so we got off and I had Lexie direct me through side streets. Once we got past the airport we began cruising down streets with dead grass and chain-linked fences and houses and stores with bars on their windows. We were no more than ten miles from Hermosa, yet we were in a completely different type of L.A.

"This is the last time we let Lisa plan MNO," Lexie said, looking around locking her door.

We pulled into a strip mall next to a store with a giant doughnut on the roof. One of the shops had a few bullet holes in the window, others had their windows boarded up.

"This is the place," I said, cutting the engine and looking around. "Think my car is safe here?"

"Fuck the car, I'm more worried about us," replied Lexie. "Maybe we should we bail and get margaritas instead?" She looked at me with both eyebrows raised and a big smile, like a dog begging for a bone.

I smirked and gave her a half smile. "On the other hand, maybe it's one of those uber-exclusive, smoking hot clubs where celebs hang out because it is discreet and dumpy."

"Unlikely," she replied, looking around suspiciously.

Lisa's car was in the parking lot, along with at least a dozen others that didn't all look like total beaters. There was a Tesla, a Range Rover and several BMWs, which I pointed out to Lexie. "Drug money," she replied in a high-pitched sing-song voice. The address Lisa had given was above a dirty white door under a sign that said "LAGC." It was a one-story building made of white painted cinder-blocks. "What do you think that stands for?" I asked.

She looked and turned up the corner of her lip. "Losers Admiring Gum Calligraphy? Lackadaisical Aardvarks Gluing Cornucopias?"

I raised an eyebrow and turned to the door, slowly easing it open and we both slipped in. The brightly lit room was large with a high ceiling. It was a store, but unlike any store I'd ever been in. Most of the room was open, except for a few round clothing racks and some folding chairs set up in rows, like you'd see at the DMV. A long counter, the front covered in plywood, the top plexiglass, ran the entire length of the side of the room. Behind the counter on the wall were rows and rows of guns. Hundreds of them in all shapes and sizes, lined up like little soldiers.

We spotted Lisa, Ramona, and Jackie in the back of the room. They were perched on the edge of a worn lime-green couch that looked as though it had been picked up off the side of the highway. Jackie saw us, smiled and waved us over. We hastily made our way over the poured concrete floor to join them, taking in the place that reeked of stale cigarettes and sweat as we moved.

The man working behind the counter was big and burly with a crew cut, goatee and black T-shirt; he definitely looked the part of "gun shop clerk." He was helping a couple of guys in their early twenties and I watched them hesitantly while I walked by as they inspected each gun the man handed them, pretending to aim them, feeling the weight in their hands, checking to see where the bullets went.

The round hangers displayed all kinds of merchandise—T-shirts, bullet-proof vests, other stuff I had no clue what it was used for— and then the bathrooms, which were plastered with posters of women in swimsuits wearing combat boots posing in sexy positions with large guns wrapped around their necks. I felt my mouth reflexively frown and I instantly felt dirty. I fought the urge to flee.

We joined the others at the couch and Lexie eyed the loveseat with a big brown stain then pulled up a folding chair, dusting it off before sitting on the very edge. "Are you out of your mind?" she said to Lisa under her breath. "What is this place?"

"Welcome to the Los Angeles Gun Club, gals," she said, a satisfied grin on her face.

I snapped my fingers. "Rats. So no aardvarks or cornucopias?"

"Are you kidding me?" Lexie whined, looking around. "A shooting gallery? *That's* what we're doing for MNO?"

"Uh huh," replied Lisa smugly. I think she liked seeing Lexie out of her element.

Lexie crossed her arms and looked around in disgust. "Oh come on," Lisa said. "Think of it as an education, and not just that you're missing out on an opportunity to have drinks on Robertson." She nodded towards a guy who came out through a heavy steel door on the opposite side of the room. He was wearing cut-off jeans shorts, work boots, a white T-shirt and was carrying a sawed-off shotgun. "See? Bet you didn't know your average construction worker has an affinity for…hunting."

"I am now officially scared to live in L.A.," said Jackie.

"Are you sure we're in L.A.?" I mumbled. "Feels more like Texas."

"If this were Texas, you'd have brought your kids," Ramona remarked.

"You don't have to be scared, just more aware. Hermosa is a little bubble, but that doesn't mean you can just relax and not worry about who is around you, *as you know*. You'll thank me for peeling the wool off your eyes," Lisa responded.

Lisa explained that as part of our training, she thought we should know about guns and what they are capable of. We had all seen them fired a million times in movies and shows, but what were they like in real life? She figured we should all at least try shooting one, if not for any other reason than to truly be able to respect the power the gun-wielder possesses. She therefore called Rachel, who said she would be honored to teach us all whatever she could. "And, here she is," Lisa said, nodding her chin toward the front of the store.

Rachel came through the door like a little beam of light. Her petite size still surprised me, so did the way people in the store reacted to her. She saw Lisa and waved, then proceeded to greet the man behind the counter with a big smile and a friendly hug. Everyone she saw smiled back at her and said hello. Her mere presence kicked the drab place up at least five notches. She finally made it to us and greeted us all enthusiastically. "So, are you ready to shoot?"

She suggested we get registered with Zeke, the burly clerk. She took us over to the counter and introduced us all. Then, after filling out some forms and being issued our official shooting gallery cards, headsets and safety glasses, we followed Rachel through the stainless steel door into another world.

Suddenly the ceiling was lower and the entire space much darker. The walls were painted gray which gave the whole place a claustrophobic feeling of dread. The room was set up just like all the shooting galleries I had seen on TV with little rows separated by concrete pillars and bulletproof glass. Each row had a target that hung from a clip attached to a wire that could be brought closer or pushed farther away by a switch on the wall. All types of people were shooting: a couple that appeared to be on a date, an old lady with her grandson, several young men in groups as well as individually. There were benches by the wall behind the shooting stalls and that's where we plunked ourselves down to take in the action.

Rachel let us watch for a while, then gathered us around her as she pulled out a small, red and yellow "Hello Kitty" backpack from her leather Chanel tote. I felt like I was in an adult-version of show and tell as she unzipped the backpack and pulled out a small package swaddled in a light blue cloth. She unwrapped the cloth and held up her gun.

"Now this is my piece," she said, turning it around in the air for us all to see. "It's a standard, FBI-issued 35 millimeter hand revolver. It works like this," she pulled out and unzipped a navy blue terrycloth makeup bag with a picture of a cuddly panda on the side. Inside were loose bullets and we watched as she loaded a magazine and snapped it into the gun. I glanced at the others, glad to see they were as stupefied, bewildered and worried as me at how the gun fit together. She explained what all the various parts were as she loaded and unloaded it several times, slowly at first so we could see, and then faster. I asked her to do it with her eyes shut. Rachael happily obliged, loading it in seconds flat.

She then demonstrated how to hold it firmly in one hand while resting it in the palm of the other, extending both arms toward the target. She showed us how to aim by looking down the nose of the gun and lining up the notch on the end between the two points on the head. The target was a silhouette of a person cut off at the waist. "When you're shooting, aim for the biggest part of the body—the chest. Once you get the hang of it, we'll try for the head to test our accuracy."

We followed her to one of the bays, and watched as she slowly pulled the trigger back and fired. The explosion was tremendous even with the ear protection and we all jumped and flinched. The gun gave quite a kick, which Rachel seemed to absorb with her whole body. And there was a tiny bit of smoke. We looked at the silhouette that hung fifty feet away, a hole now smack dab in the center of the target's head. She pushed the button on the wall and moved the target back another twenty feet and shot again. Bullseye. She moved it again to eighty, then again another twenty feet. Two more perfect shots. Finally the target was as far back as it could go. Rachel got into her stance, extended her hands straight forward and pulled the trigger three quick times in a row, emptying the rest of her ammunition dead center into the head of the target, demonstrating perfect technique and composure.

She pulled the switch on the remote and held her target up with its head blown apart. "Viola!" she said smiling benignly, as though she had just demonstrated how to use a Cuisinart. Our jaws all dropped. "Believe me, it's much easier when the target stays still."

Then it was our turn. Ramona was a good shot and at least hit some part of the target practically every time. Jackie was virtually thrown to the floor by the kick and was visibly shaken by the ordeal. Lexie was quite a good shot up close, but when the target was moved back beyond sixty feet, her nearsightedness kicked in and she couldn't hit it to save her life. Lisa was a bad shot at first, but true to her nature she tried again and again until she got it down and by the end of the lesson, was able to hit the target in the chest at one hundred feet.

When it was my turn, I walked up trying to channel my inner Bourne even though inside I felt shaky. I glanced tentatively at the granny in the stall to the left of us and then stepped across a taped line into our booth. I was surprised by the weight of the gun, surprised by the whole ordeal to be honest, but the weight was what really stunned me. I had been expecting for some reason something much lighter and less sturdy, probably because of how they are always flung around and handled so easily on TV. But this thing was solid. Solid and metallic and mechanical, which I guess makes sense because it is a machine; a machine made for projecting small metal objects at a speed greater than 1,700 miles per hour.

Rachel positioned the gun in my hand, showed me again what all the various parts were, helped me get into my stance while keeping one hand on the gun, and backed away. She was so calm, collected and friendly, we could have just as easily been working on our golf swing. I took aim, tried to steady my hand as best as I could, closed one eye and fired. The kick almost knocked me off my feet and I stumbled backwards. Rachel was quick to steady me, one hand on my back and one on my hand that held the gun, giving me words of encouragement. I got set up and tried again, this time ready for the force. I fired, absorbing the shock into my shoulders the way I'd watched Rachel, and clipped the side of the target. "Now you're getting it!" Rachel said with an encouraging smile.

I tried several more times and did a little better. Then I tried pretending I was back at the school and I was a cop who had just crept up on the men who were stealing the computers. But try as I might, I could not get into character. This wasn't fun. I couldn't make it into a game anymore.

We shot for about an hour until everyone had had enough. When we came back through the heavy steel door, we were totally exhausted and felt as though we'd run a marathon. We washed our hands thoroughly—as instructed by Rachel—to get all the residual lead off, a precaution against birth defects that was even posted on a sign in the ladies room. Jackie looked like she was going to take an entire shower in the sink. Then we meandered out and crashed back onto the stained couch, too spent to worry much about the strange clientele or catching hepatitis.

"I had no idea that was going to take so much out of me," Lisa said, slouching. Rachel explained that it's a high-stress environment and shooting requires many muscles, especially ones that you don't use often, to be flexed at the same time. "Plus, you're concentrating, which can be taxing," she added.

"That explains why Josh needs a nap after he finishes the Sudoku puzzle every Saturday morning," Lexie said.

"Do you guys realize I could have just gone crazy and killed you all in there?" I asked, still awed at the sheer power contained in something the size of a paperback novel. "I mean everything could have changed in less than one second." I shook my head because I could not quite wrap my brain around the power contained in that little piece of metal. "Your husbands, widowed. Your kids, motherless. And they sell these like candy. Sure, there are some background checks in some places. But gun shows? Walk in, lay down some cash, walk out with as many guns you can hold. No questions asked."

"Well thanks for not taking us out, Kel, we appreciate it," Lexie smirked.

"Shooting galleries are actually pretty safe places," Rachel explained. "You've got a better chance of getting shot at a DMV, post office or high school than at a shooting gallery. Statistically speaking."

"I feel so much better," Lisa muttered.

That night, I lay wide awake snuggled next to Mark, my family safely tucked into our secure little home. I'd never had the slightest interest in guns before, but now I could not get the thought of that little weapon out of my head, it was like a magnet, pulling and repelling, depending on its orientation. It was so powerful, so accessible, and so easy to pull the trigger. I couldn't imagine being in a situation where one simple squeeze of my finger could take away a life—or save one—depending on the circumstances. In all this pondering I never considered that just such a scenario could be in my future.

Fourteen

Summer came to a close with a few new developments. The first involved the money the mayor embezzled. The police concluded their investigation and it appeared we would not be getting any of that money back. The City Council therefore, decided the only fair thing to do was to give their overall budget a haircut so we not only wouldn't get any more police, but now we also needed to make up funding for our schools as well. Lovely.

The second was a bit more positive. One of our "Eyes on the Streets" moms had actually witnessed someone stealing her stroller. Instead of freaking out, she texted our group and because there were now so many of us on patrol, we were able to track the thief all over town until the cops could apprehend her. When they did, they found an apartment full of stolen bikes and strollers. It was satisfying to know we had nabbed her, but even more so to know the system was in place to catch others, and it was working.

The final event of the summer took place at the beach and involved Lexie, Jackie and Ramona. It happened the first week that school was back in session and it took until now, almost three weeks later, for Lisa and I to be clued in because that's how crazy everyone's schedules were. But finally, we were all at Ramona's for an MNO she insisted on hosting. We were waiting on Lexie of course, but trying to convince Jackie to start the story without her since we knew Ramona wouldn't blab.

"Come on," I said over my shoulder, "spill the beans already. You know Lexie wouldn't wait for you." I was standing at Ramona's picture window looking out at her panoramic view of Hermosa that extended for miles beyond the city limits in every direction. The lights of Malibu and Palos Verdes were beginning to twinkle on and the homes on the undulating hills of the South Bay looked charming and peaceful. It was so clear I could see one of the Channel Islands 60 miles off the coast. It looked like a container ship.

I turned and walked back to the couch where she and Lisa sat and plunked myself down next to her. "Spill."

"Oh, alright. But it's your fault if she's mad," Jackie said.

"I relish the moments Lexie's mad," Lisa said, nudging Jackie's knee with her socked foot. "Now spill."

"Okay, fine," she said, taking a deep breath. "So a couple weeks ago Jennifer Garner appeared in *In Style* looking gorgeous in a pair of Lexie's "Mama Power" yoga pants and sales went through the roof. Lexie couldn't keep up so Ramona and I were over at her house helping fulfill orders. Sierra needed to go down for her nap so we decided to walk to the promenade for a coffee so she could sleep in her stroller. It was gorgeous out, sunny, hardly any people around. But as we got to closer to the pier, Lexie recognized the guy standing by the statue as the dealer who'd offered Cash that joint. Naturally she got all huffy and was about to go shout something at him, like that would do any good, but Ramona here stopped her."

"That girl could stand a little restraint in her life once in a while," Ramona said, standing behind the couch munching hors d'oeuvres and listening to the conversation.

"What did the guy look like?" Lisa said.

"He was sorta cute, actually. Young, muscular, tan, shorts and a t-shirt. He's just standing there like he's waiting for someone, with one foot propped on the bottom rail of the pier, sunglasses on, smiling at everyone," Jackie said.

"Your basic asswipe," Ramona added, looking out at the ocean. I couldn't help but chuckle.

"So Ramona here," Jackie continued, "puts her hand on my stroller and keeps us moving because apparently I was slowing down to look at him and she didn't want to draw any attention to us. We park ourselves outside of Peet's on a bench and Lex and I run in for cappuccinos. When we come out, he's still there chatting up this young couple. We're about one hundred feet away from him but he barely notices us, probably because the of stroller. Moms, I guess, aren't his biggest customers."

"More likely because of me," Ramona said.

"What does that mean?" I asked.

"The Promenade is for the young. There are kids whipping by on bikes and skateboards, shoppers. Everyone's beautiful and checking each other out. Us old folks are non-existent."

"That's not—" Lisa started.

"I'm not complaining," Ramona continued. "It is what it is. There are too many interesting things to look at than those of us who are nearly dead. I'm okay with it, I like being invisible."

Jackie glared at Ramona and rolled her eyes. "So we sit down and watch the dude for a while and he's amazing, total salesman. He's flashing his beautiful smile and then before we know it, they're following him down the stairs below the pier like little ducklings. They all come back up a few minutes later, the couple takes off and the guy starts looking for his next sale. Bam! Drug deal done right in front of us."

"It was preposterous," Ramona said, shaking her head.

"And Lexie's about to go and punch the guy in the face, just for fun. But Ramona gets this idea to use my monitor to listen in. So before Lexie and I know it, she's grabbed the monitor and disappeared. So now I'm worried and trying to call her back without waking Sierra…"

"Worried is an understatement. Wigging out is more like it," Lexie said, breezing into the room. "Sorry I'm late," she said, tossing her jacket and bag on the ground and landing in a big chair with a big breath. Ramona handed her one of the sidecars she had premade and Lexie accepted graciously. "Please continue," she said, looking at us over the rim as she took a sip and exhaled, giving Ramona a thumbs up.

Jackie continued. "Okay, yes, so I'm wigging out a little because Ramona sometimes thinks she's Evil Knievel—"

"And I tell her there's no use worrying about Ramona, for Christ's sake, she can take care of herself," Lexie said.

"Thank you," Ramona said with a little nod.

"The one to worry about is Kelly here...thinks she's Jason Bourne,"

"Hey, I do not," I said, kicking her.

"Whatever," Lexie continued, shooing her hand at me. "So I distract Jackie by getting her thinking that Ramona would look cool in an Evil Knievel pantsuit with stripes and stars and shit, and we start betting about whether or not she has one." Lexie looked to Ramona with her eyebrows raised.

Ramona looked back at her. "What? Oh, yes, I have a pantsuit, of course I do," she said, "but it doesn't have stars and stripes if that's what you're asking. It's just basic black. With fringe. Very comfortable, I might add."

"Yes," Lexie said, making a fist in the air and grinning at Jackie. "I knew it."

"Anyway," Jackie continued, "now the guy has found this kid that doesn't look older than fifteen and he's working him. They're about to go below the pier and Lexie and I are terrified that Ramona is still down there. Lexie actually starts jogging towards the guy, but suddenly Ramona's behind me and calls her back and we listen to the whole drug deal on the monitor." Jackie was getting all wound up and was now sitting on her knees on the sofa. "And get this. He offered the kid samples, like it was Costco! What's next, a rewards card?" Her eyes were about to pop out of her head.

"I wish I'd been there," Lisa said. "I would have liked to have seen that kid, see how old he was."

"He looked like he was still in high school," Ramona said, passing over a tray of cheese and crackers. "And the dealer offered him all sorts of things, like it was a drug buffet."

"Right there, under the pier, right beside the lifeguard's main station. That's incredible," I said, imagining my boys at that age, feeling a little sick to my stomach.

We sat there in silence for a moment.

"Well," Lexie said, getting up and walking to her bag, "this won't solve the problem, but it will take your mind off it for a while." She pulled a magazine out and tossed it on the coffee table. "Check it out."

Jackie grabbed the magazine and began leafing through it. "What are we supposed to be looking at? Celebrities buying toilet paper? I'm so pathetically out of touch with pop culture that I have no idea who any of these people are."

"You can't be out of touch yet," I said, "you're barely into your thirties."

"Oh, you'll know who this is," Lexie said, kneeling down and spinning the magazine toward her. She found the page and turned it back towards us. It featured a close-up shot of Angelina Jolie in a brown, ribbed tank top carting one of her kids through a parking lot. "Viola," Lexie said with a satisfied smile. We all bent over the magazine to get a closer look.

"Angelina?" I gasped.

"Yep," Lexie said with a huge satisfied grin and an exaggerated nod. "And, if you look closer, you'll see she's wearing a Mama Power tattoo on her arm and a Mama Power tank." The tattoo was on Angelina's tanned, toned bicep and made her look particularly fit and strong. The tank top fit snuggly, showing off her perfect figure and flawless skin. The design, a mosaic of jewels sewn subtlety to create the initials "M.P." for "Mama Power," was striking.

"Look, her kid has a tattoo, too," Lisa said, pointing to the back of the hand of the child Angelina was carrying. "Man, if anyone needs Mama Power it's her. I can't imagine trying to protect my kids from all those crazies out there who want a piece of that family."

We began to gossip about which star would be best to invite to a playdate, but Ramona decided we'd had enough chit chat and it was time to get down to business. From behind the kitchen island that was filled with the type of food served at the last party Ramona had hosted decades ago—bacon wrapped around cocktail franks, saltines topped with fake cheese spread, a JELLO mold that contained canned fruit cocktail and was topped with what must have been Cool-Whip, plus an assortment of pickles—she brought out a laundry basket overflowing with papers, books and equipment and walked it over to the coffee table and plopped it down right on top of the magazine.

"Sorry, didn't mean to smash Angie Lee," she muttered.

We all shut up and looked curiously at the stuff as Ramona started taking it out, piece by piece, spreading it around to us. "I wanted to host MNO this month to show you this stuff," she said. "It's a project I've been working on most of the summer, ever since we delivered juice to Tweedle-dee and Tweedle-dum. And, I think it may actually help us solve the problem. Go ahead, take a look."

We began to pull out library books, notebooks, gadgets and glossy eight-by-ten black and white photographs of people, all of them men, down by the beach. It was amazing, there was so much information and stuff, *spy stuff*. I was used to seeing this sort of gadgetry, I had it all over my house, except I had the cheap, plastic version and this was the real McCoy.

"I believe it's time to get to work on kicking these drug dealers out of our town for good. I invited you all over for this month's MNO to officially make that our next mission and I've been doing a little research to get us going," Ramona said as she stood over us, fingering a brochure on some type of handgun.

She told us how she had been spending all her free time staking out the drug dealers at the pier and collecting data on them and their customers. She had notebooks filled with times, dates, characteristics of the various drug dealers, descriptions of events, descriptions of customers, typical patterns they all used as well as everyone's body language. There were photographs of all the dealers and many of the customers she had seen, the kind of photos taken with a telegraphic zoom lens you might see on a television show. There were tons and tons of library books. Books on espionage, gadgets, cyber spying, intelligence gathering and weaponry. There were print outs on how to tail a car discreetly, how to hide a bug, and how to disguise yourself a million ways. Pamphlets were everywhere. One for the shooting range we had been to with Rachel, one for night-vision goggles, one for a high-powered listening device and a few others for stun guns and pepper sprays.

Ramona took out the last gadget, something that looked like a Swiss Army knife on steroids, and set the laundry basket on the floor so we all had a clear and complete look at her "project." I let my eyes wander all over it. It was hard to believe that a little old lady had gathered all this stuff as her hobby. Sitting here, seeing it all, made my heart race with the thought, the tiny quiver of a thought, that we could do something to curb the stranglehold the dealers seemed to have on the town. I found myself momentarily speechless and from the looks of the others, they were stunned as well. When my voice returned I gasped, "This. Is. Awesome."

"Seriously," Jackie said. "Wow." She blinked as though the sun was in her eyes and she repeated the word several more times.

"Been doing a little light reading lately, then, have we?" Lexie said, sitting down and picking up a pamphlet on Tasers.

"So you've been doing surveillance down at the beach all summer?" Lisa asked.

"Yep," Ramona replied, pulling up a chair and sliding her wrinkly fingers along various books and printouts.

"From where?" Lisa said, glancing up at her over a close-up black and white photograph of one of the dealers, her brow furrowed, her interview instincts kicking in.

"All the different restaurants, mostly. Coastal Café worked especially well because it's close and crowded," Ramona answered nonchalantly, like she had been doing stakeouts her entire life.

"And you took these pictures?" Lisa asked, holding up one of the many eight by tens on the table. It was a black and white photo profile of a man in his 30's. He was wearing sunglasses and was close enough to see that he had stubble on his chin.

Ramona nodded. "Bought a new camera, took a class at the community college on how to work it with the zoom lens, learned to upload files and get them printed at Target."

"What are these names at the bottom?" Lexie asked, looking at a shot of another dealer with the name "Snake Eyes" written on the bottom in thick Sharpee.

"Oh, those are just names I made up for all the dealers so I could keep them straight in my own head. There are a lot of them."

Lexie sifted through the photos, calling out the names. "Snake Eyes. Cheesy Mustache. Shadow. Shades. Num Nuts. Scar. They're like the loser Seven Dwarfs."

"Here's your guy," Ramona said, leafing through them and handing her the photo of the man they'd listened in on, the one who'd offered Lexi's grade-school son a joint.

"Stubble," Lexie said, looking at the photo. She looked back up at Ramona. "Can I rename him Asswipe?"

Ramona chuckled. "Be my guest, honey. If the shoe fits."

"How long, each time I mean, would you watch them?" Lisa asked.

"Oh," Ramona said, looking to the ceiling as she sat on the arm of the couch. "I'd say I stayed about forty-five minutes to an hour at one restaurant, then I'd change clothes and hair and add some sunglasses and cross the promenade to go after another one for a bit."

"And they didn't ever notice you?" Lisa asked, her eyes wide, her head cocked to one side.

Ramona tensed. "Only once." She leafed through the photos. "This one." She held up a photo of one of the meaner looking dealers.

"Scar?" Jackie asked. "A guy named *Scar* noticed you?"

"I don't know if his actual name is Scar. He just has a lot of acne scars, so I named him that. And yes."

She told us how one evening in late July she waited until the dealers left the pier and followed them up the promenade until they went separate directions. She had to pick one, so she followed the one that was heading in the same direction as her car but she lost track of him after he rounded the corner. She kept walking, though, looking for him and two blocks up he was suddenly there, behind her this time, following *her*. She increased her pace and could tell he was now stalking her.

She circled back to the promenade, walking as fast as she could without breaking into a run, her heart beating wildly as she wound her way through people and racks of clothes on the sidewalk, finally ducking into a boutique clothing store. Hiding behind a cardboard display, she could see the man had been stopped by two lost tourists and when he went to resume his hunt, he had lost track of her. She was so scared she stayed in the dressing room under some clothes until closing then drove around for thirty minutes until going home to make sure she wasn't being followed.

"I have never been so glad to see Smedley in my entire life," she admitted. "After that I was much more careful. I did a lot of surveillance from my car, or I'd try and time it so I was in a shop when they quit and walked by. These men, they're creatures of habit, which is why I wanted you all here tonight."

She set her drink down and walked down the hall returning a second later with a new laptop computer. She held is up and smiled proudly, "Who says you can't teach an old dog new tricks? You gals have inspired me to get out there and do something important with the rest of my life. This here has been a good start," she said, nodding at the computer.

Ramona proudly told us how she had been taking classes to become computer literate and had been able to get on email and even hook up a webcam so she could start to see and communicate with her children and grandchildren. "It's a step in the right direction," she said, with a small nod. "But, that's a conversation for another night. Tonight," she continued, "the thing I wanted to show you is this." She pulled up a webpage showing a map with a beeping dot on it. We all looked at it for a second and then realized it was a close-up map of downtown Hermosa Beach.

"What's the beeping dot?" Lisa asked.

"That dot," Ramona said, tapping on the screen, "is actually a GPS tracker I bought that is stuck to the inside bumper of the vehicle owned by one of those drug dealers. Tonight, I thought you might like to join me in watching where they go after they leave the pier."

"No way," I gasped. We all moved in for a closer look.

"How on earth did you manage that?" Lisa asked, always the one to keep her cool.

A huge grin broke across Ramona's face. "It took some time, but I was finally able to follow them to their car, see what they drive, where they park. Like I said, these men are creatures of habit. They always park right next to the liquor store on Monterey Avenue. After that it was easy. I'd park myself in front the surf shop a little before 3:30 in the afternoon when they generally show up, or be in my car half a block back around 11:30 at night when they left. On a weekday that is, they leave later on the weekends. Getting the tracker there was trickier. I was going to borrow that play from Kelly and use some duct tape and a phone, but then I ran across this GPS tracker that has a heavy duty magnetic case. This internet thing is amazing." She shook her head and made a little "um um" sound.

I watched the dot in silent amazement as it blinked, representing so many of the things that were wrong with where we lived and society in general. Blink, blink, blink. I stared at it and felt a twinge of nausea. The dot reminded me of a heartbeat, only the heartbeat of a non-feeling, multi-headed beast.

I snapped out of my trance when Lexie called me to look at pamphlet for night vision goggles, wondering if they were like X-ray glasses and would allow the wearer to see through clothes.

"Because that would be pretty cool," she stated. "We could take them to the beach and look at the lifeguards."

"I don't think they work that way, Lex," I replied. "And don't you think you'd look a little devious staring at a lifeguard with those strapped on your head?"

She shrugged and put a bacon-wrapped cocktail weenie in her mouth. We spent the next hour pouring over Ramona's research, asking her questions, trying to take it all in, brainstorming plans for ridding our town of the dealers.

Then Jackie screamed.

"It's moving", she said, pointing to the computer screen. "The dot. It's moving!"

We all gave a jump and turned toward the screen. Sure enough, the dot was slowly making its way up Pier Avenue to the Pacific Coast Highway. We gathered together to watch as it went.

"Let's see," Ramona said, watching the screen like a child watching the NORAD satellite feed of Santa going all over the world, "tonight is Thursday so it will either be Slick or Num Nuts driving."

"Damn, Ramona," Lisa said, "you really know these guys."

"Know them and despise them," she replied without taking her eyes from the screen. "I've watched them sell to the waiters and waitresses at all those bars down there. I've seen them try to chat up impressionable groups of young girls, getting all flirty with them. And they act like they own the place, their bravado just bugs me. I will be glad to be rid of them."

The dot turned right on PCH and headed south.

We pulled our chairs around and settled in with our drinks and munchies, watching the screen as though we were at a slumber party glued to a movie. It continued to make its way down PCH as we discussed its location like TV announcers.

"...they're by Trader Joe's now."

"...'bout to hit the library. They now have story time in Spanish on Fridays."

"...they're by the park where Stosh broke his arm."

We watched intently as the dot cruised through Redondo Beach then turned off PCH and started to wind its way up into Palos Verdes. I inched forward on my chair. I was dying to know where they were going.

"You guys think they live up in PV?" Lexie asked, looking closer. "They wouldn't sell here *and* live here would they? I bet they're just cutting through to get to Orange County. You know, all those *Real Housewives* need their fix."

"If they were going to O.C.," I said, "they'd have taken the 405 to the 5." Lexie began to argue with me when Lisa hushed us both.

"Look," Lisa said, pointing to the screen, "they just passed the golf course. The homes there *start* at three million."

Ramona zoomed in so we could see the names of the streets that the dot was moving along. It turned left on Poinsettia, then right onto Eucalyptus, then wound its way on one of the roads that hugged the coastline, Via Del Mar. It then turned on Mira Monte Drive, a road that switched back and forth so much it started to make me car sick just watching it. Finally, it came to a stop.

"That's quite the neighborhood," Lisa remarked. "One of Josh's friends lives up there. We are talking people who have some serious cash."

"Doesn't Oprah live up there?" Jackie asked.

"No, she's in Santa Barbara. I heard Stevie Nicks had a house up there at one point, though. I think I read that she sold it."

"Do you think they're doing a house call?" Jackie asked.

Lisa shook her head and looked seriously at Ramona and the others. "I don't know. I think people who are loaded and buy drugs send someone out to get them rather than invite the dealers back to their house. What do you think Ramona?"

"I think I better find out," she said with a dead seriousness in her voice. We watched the dot for a while longer to make sure it stayed put. Ramona zoomed in to get a better idea of where exactly it stopped as the rest of us began brainstorming the different reasons the dealers could have for going there. The drinks had taken effect and we laughed as we tossed out ideas including getting a flat tire, visiting Num Nut's rich grandparents before moving on, as well as dropping off their leftover product and profits at the drug lord's multi-million dollar estate, and everything in between.

"Come look at this," Ramona said to the group. We gathered around her to see a photo from Google Earth of the house, or more accurately, very posh Mediterranean-style villa, that was located where the dot was blinking. "I'm about 95% positive this is the one. But I can tootle on by tomorrow and take a quick looksie, see what I can find out."

"Man," I said in awe, "technology is crazy. I used to be up on this stuff."

"It's hard to stay current when you're busy wiping bottoms and singing 'Slippery Fish,'" Jackie smirked. "So what's next?" she asked, turning to Ramona and warming her hands on a cup of Bailey's and coffee that Ramona had produced earlier.

"Yeah," I said, looking up eagerly from the computer. "What's the plan and how can we help?"

We had tossed out the idea of one of us going under cover to buy from them, even ran the idea by Officer Hogan, but he had told us they had once set up a similar sting operation. They'd nab one dealer, but the next day another would replace him. They tried it for a week but they just kept coming back and the police didn't have the manpower to continue.

"Couldn't we just picket them? Like we did when that porn shop tried to open?" Jackie asked. "I bet we could get enough moms and dads to be down there every night for a month with signs that said something like 'No Drugs in Hermosa'."

"They'd just move to a different location," Ramona said.

"So? At least they'd be out of Hermosa," Jackie said.

"They'd be back. Location's too good. Easy money," Ramona replied.

"Alright then, how's this?" Lexie said, sitting forward. "We'll wait until Ramona figures out how they get their shipments in, then we'll plant one of those GPS things on the boat or plane or however they transport in the drugs. We'll charter a boat or plane to follow them, have Ramona learn some bomb making skills, sneak in to the factory in the dead of night and blow the drug-making factory to smithereens. We'll be home in time to make pancakes."

"I detect a hint of sarcasm," Jackie said.

Lexie sat back, rolling her eyes. "Sorry, but you guys are dreaming. There is no way we are ever going to get rid of these guys. It's hopeless, like getting mildew out of your towels. Once it's there, it's always there."

"Ew, I hate that," Jackie said.

"Me, too," I said. "I throw those towels away."

"What ever happened to 'Mama Power'?" Lisa asked looking at

Lexie with a raised eyebrow and a wry grin, looking ever so much like the mascot of Lexie's company. "I thought that could fix anything."

"It can," Lexie said, "but it can't work miracles. The thing has to be fixable. How do you stop a monster that grows another head every time you chop it off? I'm thinking we should go after something easier, like tracking the morons that tag the Strand with spray paint for our next mission."

"Don't worry, we'll get them," I said. "They're on my list."

"I agree that the dealers are going to be tough," Lisa said. "But not impossible. We just need to be patient and creative."

"I hate being patient," I said, crossing my arms.

"I love being creative!" Jackie said.

We left it at that, all of us trying our best to figure out a plan. It was daunting, though, and oddly enough, I felt myself siding with Lexie, thinking it was an impossible situation. It was like David and Goliath, only where David is a fumbling, bumbling amateur and Goliath is a huge, strong, ruthless well-oiled machine.

I went home, kissed my precious boys who were tucked snuggly into their beds goodnight. I checked in with Mark, made a cup of tea and went to the computer. I Googled "drug dealer movies," hoping for some sort of clue, some "banana in the tailpipe" trick like Eddie Murphy's character used in *Beverly Hills Cop* that would help us topple the bad guys. But I didn't find it. Not in one movie.

But what I did find was a theme. Over and over again the fumbling, bumbling idiot who got in over his head was pretty much shot, tortured, thrown off a bridge, or stabbed to death. Whatever the case, it was never pretty. *Savages, American Gangster, Scarface, Blow, True Romance,* in all of these movies the good guys never got out unscathed. It seemed, as I made a little grid on a scrap piece of paper tracking the characters, their strengths, weaknesses and outcomes, as if movies really paralleled real life and this little exercise would predict our future, that the ones who were the most unhinged, the most unafraid, were the ones to prevail.

I closed my eyes and let my head rest in my palms, the smell of Tension Tamer not doing a single damn thing to tame my tension.

We were doomed. We were the Judge Reinhold character without Eddie Murphy's street-smart Axel Foley to keep us out of trouble. I saw the picture of the man Lexie nicknamed "Asswipe" in my head. His dead eyes, his charming grin. Unlike him and the rest of his crew, we *were* afraid and we *weren't* unhinged. We were just the opposite. Rule followers, law abiders.

I shut my computer off and trudged up the stairs, my legs feeling like they weighed a hundred pounds each. I popped two Advil for my head, which was beginning to pound, and began reconsidering the idea to picket the pier. It would take constant, consistent long-term effort and the men would probably figure out a new place to sell, Manhattan or Redondo if they weren't there already. We would be patching a hole in a dyke that was forever springing a leak, and we only had so many fingers.

I had no way of knowing, of course, that I wasn't the only one googling things. As I dozed off, ready to opt for the less risky alternative, Ramona, I'd later learn, was still at her computer. Looking up bomb making techniques.

Fifteen

In other parts of the country October brings crisp, frosty mornings, the breaking out of winter caps and mittens, and the annual pilgrimage to the local pumpkin patch where acres of orange spheres could be hand plucked off the vine. Not in L.A. The surfers and hipsters wear winter caps only because it's stylish. Our pumpkin patches are made by transforming a vacant parking lot with hay bales, adding a petting zoo, bounce house and randomly placing pumpkins around. And instead of adding layers, we shed them because our warmest weather comes in October, which always takes me by surprise.

I was thinking of this as the boys and I got out our Halloween decorations and I found their old costumes. Thick, bushy, fuzzy animals seemed adorable when I bought them online, like Casey's lion costume when he was two, then his skunk costume and Griffy's bunny costume the next year, because I still hadn't learned. All worn for less than five minutes before the kids started to boil and wail in the 90 degree heat. Luckily we had spare pillowcases that were easy to make into toddler-sized togas.

Decorating the house with small children is only made to look fun in parenting magazines. In reality, it is an exercise in restraint, and I was trying to practice just that, as I attempted to get both boys to produce decent black handprints that we would eventually turn into keepsake spiders and bats, if only they would stop putting their hands all over everything else. I was about at my limit after the paint had been spilled twice, when I got the call from Jackie.

"Can you meet at the beach in thirty minutes?" she asked.

"Definitely," I said, relishing the idea of getting out of decorating hell. "What's up?"

"Ramona's found something."

I did not have to be told twice. Ever since her MNO and the production of vast quantities of her research, I had hardly thought about anything else.

I quickly put together some snacks and other necessities, loaded the kids in the double-wide and strolled to the beach, pretending to run the stroller into obstacles, turning at the last second as the boys giggled and cheered.

I found my crew in our normal spot by the swings and dragged the stroller backwards over the sand. Jackie was freaking and trying to pry something out of Sierra's mouth, and Sierra was wailing desperately.

"What is this?" Jackie said, looking closer at the item she dislodged. "Oh, gross!" She held out the object for us to see. "It's someone's acrylic fingernail! Yuck! Sierra, honey, no! We don't eat things we find in the sand!" She held a bottle of water to her daughter's mouth, unsuccessfully, as Sierra fought and screamed. Jackie finally set her down, letting her get back to the sand. "Only my child would find a friggin' fingernail on this huge slab of beach and then put it in her mouth. Disgusting!"

"It could be worse," Lexie said as Ramona and I nodded.

"Not to say that's not gross," I added, hoping to make her feel better by legitimizing her feelings.

"Oh yeah?" Jackie said, defiantly. "Well, guess where I found her this morning? In the toilet! Actually standing in the bowl, just splashing around in her p.j.'s. Happy as a lark. The toilet!"

"Oh, that's nothing," Lexie said to Jackie's obvious surprise. "There's only three of you, how dirty could your toilet be?" Jackie made a face.

"When my kids were little," Ramona said, "everyone smoked. I can remember taking the kids to visit my parents, who were both big smokers. The babies were still little but Ridge was about two. Every chance he got he was either putting cigarette butts in his mouth or licking the ash trays clean."

"Nasty," I said, as Jackie grimaced.

"I used to take Cash grocery shopping before those smart little cart liners were invented and they put wipes out. I'd look down and he'd be gnawing the cart handle. All I could think of was that some man had probably just gone to the bathroom, masturbated, not washed his hands, then handled that very cart my precious baby was now licking."

"Only you would think that," Ramona said.

"True, but I never thought my child would be popping fresh goat poop into his mouth as if they were M&M's like Finn did when he was eighteen months at the Adventure City petty zoo."

"Nooooo!" Jackie said, her face was bunched up in a grimace. She looked like she might start to rock herself.

"Yes," Lexie said, as though she was proud of the fact.

"That is gross, indeed," I said, feeling suddenly competitive. "But this is worse."

"No, please," Jackie whined, "this is out of control, guys."

"Last summer we took the kids back to Missouri for a family reunion at the Lake of the Ozarks. We had just landed at the Detroit airport so I'm letting them run around, burn off a little energy while we wait for our bags. Griffin toddles up some stairs and I watch him start splashing in something then Casey is right next to him, splashing, too, before I can get there. I'm thinking it's a spilled Coke or water or something, no big deal. I walk over to them and—you won't believe this—it's puke! They are splashing in a humongous puddle of someone's puke!"

Even Lexie groaned at that one. "You had me at 'Detroit Airport.'"

"Vomit has got to be one of the worse offenders," Ramona said. "I could spend days telling you vomit stories about my three."

"But you won't, right?" Jackie said sternly.

"Well, this is my best—or worst—however you want to look at

it," Ramona continued. "We were also at the airport about to get on a flight, an overnight one to Paris. Ben wanted to expose the kids to different cultures early, get them to broaden their horizons so they wouldn't just be little beach bums. So the twins—Jasmine and Cooper—were six, Ridge was eight. Just before we get on board Jasmine projectile vomits all over herself and me. I'm telling you we were drenched in the stuff. We have to spend all night and most of the next day looking and smelling like throw-up. I'm surprised we didn't cause a chain reaction on the plane."

"Okay, so I've got another one—" I started.

"No!" Jackie said, "No more, please!"

"Oh, come on," I said, "this is like the Final Four of gross toddler behavior. It will make you feel much better about Sierra's fingernail."

Jackie stared and turned up her lip.

"Like I said, Griff has texture issues. Luckily, he's beginning to grow out of it. He used to love rubber, especially when he was teething and the plumbing in our house is terrible so we have always just left the plunger next to the toilet."

"No," Jackie interrupted, holding up her hand, "please don't." She puffed her cheeks out.

"Yes," I said, smiling and nodding. "One morning I'm getting dressed and I walk into the bathroom to find him gnawing away on the rubber end of the plunger." Everyone groaned. "Yeah, I about died."

"Speaking of rubber," Lexie said, barely allowing time for the groans to die down, "Lisa's youngest, Jackson, found a used condom under the lifeguard shack when he was two. Lisa said she saw him stretching and biting on something by the time she got to him he had the whole thing in his mouth and was chewing on it like gum. She said when she saw what it was, she almost fainted."

"I would have died," Jackie said. "Right there, I would have been begging for death, rather than have to deal with that. You guys *have* to stop. Now."

We stopped, but not until we made Ramona judge who won the final bracket. "Both are close," Ramona said, contemplatively. "But they just splashed in the vomit, right? They didn't try to, say, lap it up?" I winced just thinking about it, remembering its smell and texture. "That one's out then. I'd have to say condom, animal poo, plunger, then vomit, in that order," she pronounced like a judge on reality TV.

"Lisa wins! She'll be so proud. Maybe winning Most Disgusting Child will cheer her up," Lexie said with a shrug and I couldn't tell if she were joking or not.

Lisa's mom had recently been diagnosed with ALS and was now living with her. It had not been easy but we all had been helping, especially Ramona who had been spending all her extra time at Lisa's house to take care of the younger kids while Lisa tended to her mom.

"So Ramona," I said, turning my attention to her. "What's going on?"

Lexie and Jackie nodded, echoing my curiosity. We settled ourselves, leaning in closer to hear over the waves while keeping an eye on the kids. And she told us not only what she'd found out, but also about something she had found, something she thought could help us, something she had forgotten she even had.

It started yesterday morning, Ramona began, when it was still very early. Smedley was yipping and jumping around, anxious for his walk so she was hurrying to put on clothes—bobby socks, running shoes, baseball cap and a Mexican poncho over her cotton nightgown, the one Ben had bought her when they were in Ensenada. She caught a glance at herself in the mirror and thought it was official, she looked homeless.

Not caring, she walked down the hall for the leash when she noticed the computer was still on and the tracking page was still up. She wondered why it hadn't hibernated so she checked it, expecting to see the dot at the same location as before, but was surprised to find it at King's Harbor in Redondo Beach.

"Well, what have we here?" she asked the computer as Smedley barked from the top of the stairs. Ramona was familiar with King's, it had been her and Ben's home away from home. It was where they moored their boat, which they had taken out practically every chance they could when he was still alive. She hadn't given a single thought to the place or the boat in the eight long, grief-stricken years since his death, but now, with the dot blinking in the place she held so close to her heart, the memories came flooding back.

Her mind wandered to their boat and she wondered if it was still there, still floating or half submerged. She and Ben had had such wonderful times on that boat. They would invite friends out and sail up north or out toward the islands, Ben always in his silly fishing hat, regaling their friends with his outlandish stories, the ones that made her laugh so hard she had to cross her legs so she wouldn't pee. She was much lighter then. They'd bring down the sails, crack open a bottle of wine and a bag of pretzels, then fish or play cards or just enjoy the beauty as curious dolphins and seals circled.

She had been paying the rent on their slip every month and knew most of the harbor folks, at least she did back then. Ramona figured if something was wrong with her boat, one of them at least would have sent her a letter. She snapped out of her thoughts and looked back at the screen, watching the dot blink as she tried not to think about how much she still missed the life she had with Ben. She refocused her mind and narrowed her eyes, squinting at the computer as she wondered aloud, "What are you guys doing there? Preparing for a nice cruise to Catalina? Maybe a fishing trip?"

She sat down at the computer, much to Smedley's dismay. He whimpered, did a little dance and barked. "Okay, okay, boy. Just give me a second." Ramona zoomed in on the dot to get a better look at its exact location but the map was ambiguous and just showed the general area. She scoffed and closed the browser, then sat staring at the empty screen, deciding what to do. Her initial thought was to shrug it off and take Smedley for his walk. But that was the old Ramona, the one who had sat in her house alone for the past eight years.

She looked over at Smedley who sat waiting, wagging his tail. "Well, what do you think, Smeds? Want to go for a ride? Smedley gave her an energetic bark and pawed the air, unaware of what he was agreeing to. "You sure?" Smedley barked again. "Alright. Let's hurry then before those dopes disappear." She got up quickly and took Smedley to the backyard to do his business, then they were in the car and heading down the hill.

Moments later, she and Smedley passed under the archway that read "King's Harbor" in pink neon with a picture of a giant fisherman catching a giant fish. She and Ben had always laughed at that sign since the biggest fish most people caught out of the harbor or the general area were no bigger than a popsicle. Smedley's memory, too, seemed stirred by the sign and he barked and wagged his tail. Ramona wondered if he could remember being on the boat; it felt like ages ago to her, it must feel like a lifetime to him.

They pulled into the parking lot which was only half full and immediately saw the black SUV parked in the middle, just as the computer had shown. Ramona parked discreetly a few rows back and attached Smedley's leash to his collar. She hadn't had time to think of a thorough plan for her early morning harbor espionage and was even a little surprised to find that the SUV was still here. Suddenly she felt naïve and self conscious. She was still wearing her nightgown-poncho outfit, for the first time in a long time, she actually cared what she looked like. What if she ran into one of Ben's old boating friends? She thought about calling it quits and putting the key back in the ignition and driving right back home, but then thought of the drug dealers and knew she had to at least attempt to see what they were up to.

She and Smedley got out of the car and headed for the water. It was a gigantic marina with hundreds of boats. There were five long, parallel main docks built on cement pilings that went straight out into the water. Each main dock had eight gated and floating branches-four on each side-accessible by a ramp; each could hold ten boats. Ramona used to love looking at all the rows of rows and boats, wondering where they had been and who they belonged to, the boating life could be so romantic. Most of all, she loved the names of the boats, ones like *Red Racer, Kimberly, Titanic*. It was fun to imagine who named them and what sort of people they were.

She decided to work methodically, starting at the far left, Pier 1, then hit Pier 2, then head down to piers four and five and finally finish up in the middle at Pier 3 where she could check on the status of her own boat. The dock was still wet with morning dew. She tried to look nonchalant, like a person just out for a morning stroll with her dog. She kept her head looking forward only her eyes darting left and right from behind her big sunglasses, hoping to spot the dealers. Smedley, for his part, wasn't exactly helping her to be discreet. He was in his element, loving all the new but somewhat familiar sights, sounds and smells. He was dying to run and check everything out and Ramona had to keep pulling on his leash and calling him back.

She got to the end of the first row, pulled a u-turn and headed back to the main sidewalk, walking a little faster since Smedley was pulling her like a sled dog. She was starting to see a decent amount of activity around the harbor as people took their boats out for an early morning sail and the folks who lived here began to stir. Every new person startled her a little, but as soon as she could decipher they weren't the men she was looking for, she would relax a bit, nod a hello, and continue.

They were almost two-thirds up the second pier when Smedley heard something that piqued his interest. He jumped and ran, pulling the leash right out of Ramona's hand. She yelled for him as he skidded to a stop at the end of the pier, barking like a mad dog. *So much for our stealth stroll,* she thought, looking around quickly. She snapped at him, cupped her hands around her mouth, calling to him as loudly as she could without making too much noise. He continued to bark like crazy then took one look back at Ramona as if to say, "Sorry, but I can't help myself," and jumped the ten feet down into the water. She screamed and ran for the edge, looking over to find her pup playfully being teased by a family of sea lions. They barked at each other as Smedley tried ever so pitifully to catch them. She yelled at him from the edge, knowing the seals could eat him alive at any minute, a fact that Smedley seemed to have missed.

After a few minutes of Olympic-worthy dog paddling, poor Smeds was spent and turned to his master to save him. The water was ten feet below her, much too far for her to reach and pull him out. She ran to the nearest branch and found the gate unlocked. Running down the ramp she called to her pup, coaxing him around the boat that was moored where she stood. He struggled to get past the boat, using the very last of his manic yap-yap dog energy, the leash now heavy with water. Ramona was also struggling. She got down slowly on her knees, feeling the soreness of her aging body. There was nothing to hold on to in the middle of the dock and she couldn't reach the water from her knees so she got down flat on her stomach while holding onto a metal cleat. She reached down into the water and caught Smedley by his collar. It was too loose to pull him up by, so she tried to get her arm over his body and her hand under his armpits. She heaved him up, grunting and using every ounce of strength she had, his little legs kicking the air, trying to scamper further onto her hand. As she got to her knees, her other hand slipped off the wet piling and she fell, her free arm flailing, trying to grab at the rope that was attached to the boat, but it was no use, she was about to find out what fifty-nine-degree water felt like first thing in the morning. Shutting her eyes and taking a deep breath she tensed, but instead of icy cold, oily harbor water smacking against her body, she felt an arm around her waist, abruptly grabbing her inches from the water as if she weighed nothing.

"Gotcha!" came a man's voice, his grip wrapped around her body like a vice. She screamed out of surprise, letting go of poor Smedley who sailed back into the air, his little arms and legs frantically scurrying like a hamster in an exercise wheel, his body landing in the water with a plop. "Didn't think I'd be catchin' myself a grandma this morning," her rescuer quipped. As she turned to see who had saved her, she let out an uncontrollable gasp and put her hands to her mouth as she came face to face with the dealer she had nicknamed Shades. Her heart was pounding already from her close call but this was like being hit with a defibrillator. "Maybe we should take you on over to the office. I could get a prize for you, except you don't weigh nothing," he chuckled.

She wanted to chuckle back, to try to act normal, but she was so petrified, so full of adrenaline, that she stood paralyzed in front of this tall, muscular man, desperately trying to think of what to do and say.

He looked at her, sensing her shock. "You okay? I didn't hurt you, did I? You better not sue me, maybe I should have let you fall in and then fished you out, huh? Speaking of fishing, let's get your pooch." Ramona watched as he bent over and pulled Smedley out by the scruff of his neck. He handed him to her as though he were a dirty Kleenex. "Smedley, is it?" He bent down so he was almost eye to eye with Smeds cradled in Ramona's arms. "You're quite the fierce watch dog, ya know? Maybe you should be named Seal Bait instead of Smedley." He laughed at his own joke, rubbing his wet hands on his pants as the little dog shivered with cold in Ramona's arms.

"Tony! Let's go!" The voice was low and gruff and came from the main dock above. Ramona turned and saw Scar motioning for Shades to come. His eyes and words were directed at the man, but his gaze was on Ramona and he glared at her a little too long for her comfort. Ramona recognized him as the one who had chased after her that day at the pier. Her jaw dropped open just a little and she quickly looked down and nuzzled Smedley, wrapping him up in the bottom part of her poncho to keep him warm as he shivered. She held her breath, hoping he wouldn't recognize her.

"I'm comin', I'm comin'. Take care, lady. No more chasing seals for you," he said to Smedley, pointing his finger in Smedley's nose. Smedley let out a low, guttural growl and the man moved back a little, then growled right back. "Next time I'll leave you in there, see how you like that!" He picked up two big coolers, and left Ramona standing there like a statue. She was scared stiff, but knew she had to act.

"Er, wait," she called softly, hoping Scar wouldn't hear her. She took a few steps towards him. "I didn't catch your name, so, I can, uh, thank you. Properly." He stopped and turned sideways. His muscles bulged from the weight of the coolers. He had one large elaborate tattoo of a woman with long hair and a huge bosom on his right bicep.

"Name's Tony, and you're welcome," he said. She was surprised by his politeness.

"Is one of these your boats, Tony?" Ramona's voice trembled ever so slightly and she willed it to go away as her mind began to quickly thaw. Her next sentence came out more clearly. "I'd like to bake you cookies. To thank you for saving my pup. I could drop them off on your boat?"

Tony rested the coolers on one knee and seemed to contemplate the idea. "Grandma's homemade cookies, eh?" He looked up to find his colleague who by now Ramona guessed was at their SUV. He took a moment to respond, as though weighing his answer. "What the heck," he said with a shrug. "Sure, cookies would be great. We're the third from the end," he jutted his chin out toward the boats. "The *All Nighter*."

Ramona looked back toward the boats, branding the name on her brain. "Well thank you, Tony. You'll have cookies by tomorrow." She wanted to ask if their morning catch was in the cooler to see his reaction, but lost her nerve.

"No rush," he said, starting for the parking lot. "We're only here once a week or so. You can leave 'em at the office, I'll check there. I don't want a little old lady crawling on our boat, you'll probably fall in." He winked and quickly walked away, leaving Ramona dumbfounded.

She looked down at Smedley, who was completely wiped out from his escapade. "Who is he calling a little old lady?" she asked Smeds, giving him a little squeeze. "What a jerk. Although he did save your furry little butt." She crept up the ramp, peaking her head up to see if the SUV was gone. The coast was clear. She walked briskly down Pier Two and made a U-turn up Pier Three. The key on her ring still fit the gate's lock and she slowly padded down the ramp. She put one foot aboard the *D.B. Cooper* and stopped, taking in a deep breath and remembering how she and Ben had poured over names for their boat, finally settling on the epithet for the elusive bank robber because Ben had a thing for outlaws and D.B.'s story, he said, was both mesmerizing and madness, just like their life together. She boarded her boat and left Smedley shivering on a cushion while she went below, quickly returning with several towels that were musty, but dry. "You are just a treat this morning, Smeds," she said, rubbing his fur. "As if wet dog wasn't bad enough, we have to add mildew to the mix, huh?" Smedley sat calmly in her arms as she dried him, then she wrapped him up, put him in her lap, and sat back to take in her boat. It had weathered her absence surprisingly well. It needed a good cleaning, but to her amazement, nothing seemed broken or stolen. She even surprised herself by feeling a little twinge of interest in taking it out on the water rather than the deep-set sadness she was expecting.

"Well howdy stranger!" She looked up to see a kind, familiar face approaching. "I had just about given up ever seeing you again. How the heck are you?" It was Ben's old friend, Bill Fullerton. He was a handsome man, even now in his seventies. He wore a blue T-shirt with a white button down over it. His sleeves were rolled up to his forearms and his shirt was loosely tucked into his Levis. He had on flip flops and carried a newspaper in one hand and a tall paper cup of coffee with a bagel balanced on top in the other. Ramona remembered that he had retired from his position as a chemical engineer at one of the big aerospace companies a few years before Ben died and was doing handyman jobs to keep busy. Ramona had always loved the times she and Ben had spent with Bill and his wife, Sofia. They'd take the boats out or just sit around on them in the harbor drinking wine, playing cards, talking and eating all night. Bill and Ben seemed as though they could have been brothers. They had the same deep belly laugh, same mischievous streak, same thirst for adventure and the same generous heart.

Ramona's smile was automatic. "Well, hello yourself. Doing fine, thanks. I was wondering if I'd run into anyone I would recognize down here. It's been a while."

"A while?" Bill huffed warmly. "A month is a while. A season is a while. I don't think I've seen you in, what, seven, eight years?"

"Okay, okay," Ramona took the ribbing well.

"I was beginning to think I was going to have to send you a bill for maintaining this heap of yours, just to get you down here," he joked, gesturing to the boat. "I practically drowned several times trying to save it from sinking," he said winking at her. His smile was warm, genuine and contagious. Ramona found herself entranced.

She shot back a reply. "Well, if you'd learn to swim, you wouldn't have that problem, now would you? What kind of boat captain can't swim, for crying out loud?" They both laughed and she invited him aboard. Smedley jumped at him, trying both to give him a kiss and steal his bagel. He set down his coffee and paper out of Smedley's reach and gave Ramona a warm, strong hug.

They then sat down to catch up on each other's lives. Bill had been one of the pallbearers at Ben's funeral. Ramona, though, was unaware of Sofia's passing three years ago. As Bill told the story of how she had a massive stroke while she was alone at their home, Ramona could tell that the pain was still sharp. He probably felt even worse since he wasn't there to help, just as Ramona hadn't been there for Ben. It was added guilt and sadness that piled on top of grief like sedimentary rock. She apologized for not being there for him, for not knowing.

Before she knew it, it was three hours later. She felt as though she could have talked to Bill all day, he made her feel so light and young again, the way she had felt with Ben. But Smedley let her know that it was lunch time and he was ready to go. They walked up the floating dock to Pier Three together and said their good-byes, promising to get together next weekend to clean up her boat, maybe even take it out on the water to see if it still worked. He hugged her again, picking her up off her feet where she got a perfect view of the *All Nighter*. He put her down and turned to walk back toward his boat.

"Bill, wait," she said, grabbing on to his arm. He turned and she let go, a little embarrassed. For the past three hours she hadn't even thought about it, but suddenly she realized she still looked like a bag lady. She stood up straighter, trying to make the best of a bad situation, tucking a strand of hair under her hat. "Do you happen to know anything about that boat or the people who own it?" She pointed to the dock where she had almost gone for an accidental morning dip. "It's the third one from the end, the *All Nighter*?"

Bill didn't even need to look. He shook his head as though he knew them too well. "There's something fishy about that boat and the folks who own her, no pun intended. I can't put my finger on it, but I'd stay as far away from them as you can." He told her how a few years ago several young guys were "whacked out on something" and were attempting to dock their boat. They were so out of it, they crashed into Bill's boat as well as several others. When Bill and the staff from the harbor office confronted them and tried to help, they became belligerent. They yelled obscenities and one of them had taken out a gun. The harbor patrol had been called by this time but the men left before they arrived. "What's going on?" Bill asked her. "Why do you want to know about those guys?"

"Oh, no reason, really." She tried to sound detached and casual, but she got the feeling he wouldn't buy a nothing sort of answer, especially after seeing him raise one eyebrow at her. "Oh, okay," she continued, "but it's embarrassing."

"Go on," he said with a wink. "I like embarrassing."

She blushed a little and was thankful for the second time today to be covered by big sunglasses and a hat. "Smedley chased after a family of seals this morning and as I was attempting to fish him out, I almost went in myself. One of the men from that boat saved me just in time from falling in the water. I was going to make him cookies as a thank you." The thought of telling him the truth, that she'd been spying on them for months, that she'd been collecting evidence to use against them, and planned to take down their whole operation, made her chuckle.

"I wouldn't waste one chocolate chip on those bozos," he replied. "They've got another boat docked on Pier Four, the *Al Rescate*. They seem to be some sort of serious fishermen because I always see them bringing big coolers and tons of gear from the boats to their truck. But," he shook his head, "I don't buy it. I know fishermen, and those guys are not it." She nodded as though she was heeding his warning, remembering that he had always been a good judge of character.

"But hey, if you're going to the trouble to bake, my favorite is oatmeal raisin. I'll cut you a deal and take a batch as payment for several years' worth of boat maintenance."

He grinned at her and Ramona noticed for the first time that his eyes twinkled when he smiled, betraying his wrinkles and white hair and showing off the mischievous little boy that lurked within. "I'll see you next weekend." He turned and headed down the pier toward his boat, looking off at the horizon and the dazzling water.

Ramona watched him go for a moment then looked at the beautiful ocean herself. It would be a dazzling day out there. She looked at her boat and thought to herself, *we'll get you taken care of, don't worry.* Then she looked across the way to the *All Nighter. We'll get you taken care of, too.*

Sixteen

Ramona's story left us in awe and we sat on the beach until dinner time brainstorming about how the dealers were operating. This new clue had given us a new plan, one that wasn't as daunting as getting rid of the dealers, and some new found hope. We now just wanted to find out what their process was, where they got their product, where they deposited their money and the like. If we could document that stuff, we could turn it over to the police and let them take over. Ramona promised she would spend some time at the marina, working on her reconnaissance.

That was two weeks ago and now, on the afternoon of Halloween, we were looking forward to her update at Lexie's annual Halloween bash. The party didn't officially start until five, but here I was at three, loading the kids in the car as the sun beat down on us and the heat wave continued.

We drove toward the beach and luckily found a space near Lexie's house right away. I plugged the meter with quarters I kept in an empty Playdough container, then let the boys run wild down the walk-street. Putting on my sunglasses I took a deep, satisfied breath of sea air and smiled as I took in the ocean, glittering a little more than two hundred yards away. I loved this time of year. Loved that my kids would experience a safe, fun Halloween but not one of those sterile versions where you trick-or-treated at the mall.

Lexie lived in the most coveted—and therefore pricey—area of

Hermosa Beach. It was closest to the water and cars could only access the homes through alleys in the back, leaving the front of the of the homes facing one another over a 15-foot wide pedestrian "walk-street;" hence, the perfect place to trick-or-treat. The walk-streets went a few blocks east from the Strand and ran the length of both Hermosa and Manhattan Beach's coast. A teenager would need more than a pillowcase to handle all that real estate. We had been coming to Lexie's for trick-or-treating now since Casey was born and the popularity of the neighborhood for the Halloween ritual seemed to be growing exponentially. It got to the point where around eight o'clock, there were so many people out it was like leaving a stadium right after the final whistle. That part I didn't enjoy, but our group was always one of the first out as well as the first back so we could drink wine and enjoy the madness from the safety of Lexie's yard while the kids poked through their loot and worked the gate to give out candy.

I marveled at the transformation of her neighborhood. Practically every home was decked out with Halloween decorations that would make a Hollywood set designer envious. One was completely covered in thick webs with spiders the size of Mini Coopers scaling up the stucco; still another featured what looked to be a mad scientist's laboratory with potions of every color as well as jars of snakes, frogs and rats scattered over the lawn. Everywhere I looked I saw caldrons already steaming with dry ice, jack-o-lanterns cut in elaborate patterns and designs, and body parts littered on the patios.

The heat changed the tone of the festivities, but only a little bit. It was just hard to imagine being in a chilly Sleepy Hollow when the surf was up and it was eighty-five degrees, but I didn't mind as I flip-flopped my way to Lexie's yard and let myself in through the gate my munchkins had failed to close.

"Hello?" I called.

"In here," came Lexie's voice from the kitchen.

I followed the voice in, and saw that Griffin and Casey were already happily playing with Cash, Savannah and Finn in the living room.

"Thank God you're early," Lexie said, thrusting a whisk at me. "Here, whisk!"

I took the tool, but didn't move. Instead I stared at Lexie, who was wearing a Snow White outfit. "Holy fairytales," I said, my jaw dropping. "It's been a while, but I don't remember Snow White showing that much cleavage." I scanned the rest of the costume. It was skin tight, of course, looked striking on her, but was just plain wrong. "Or wearing fishnets for that matter."

Lexie slowed her frantic pre-party pace down long enough to smile, bat her falsies and strike a sexy pose. "Well," she said in a sweet voice mimicking the fabled princess. "That was old-school Snow White."

"So what are you? The Snow White who works the corner?" I scoffed.

"Ha, ha. Hardly. I'm *Party* Snow White," she winked and raised both eyebrows a few times.

"Oh my God," I gasped. "Seriously? As if making nurses and cowgirls sexy wasn't bad enough. Have you no respect for our beloved classical fairytale icons? What do your dwarfs think of 'Party Snow White'?"

"They're all sleeping it off back at their little cabin," she squinted her eyes and made a sultry look. "Let's just say I rocked their little worlds. I doubt they'll be back up any time soon. Those little guys had years of pent up sexual energy in their little bodies. Seven at a time, baby, a new personal record."

"Ewww!" I said, making a face and shaking my head. "I didn't mean the fictitious little men from the story! You shouldn't even tease about that. I meant *your* little dwarfs. Your children, sicko! What do they think of a Snow White who could be spinning on a pole? And," I grabbed Lexie's arm and pushed her cap sleeve up a little to reveal a temporary tattoo of barbed wire running around the circumference of her bicep. "What's this? You gave Snow White tats? Lexie!"

Lexie pushed her sleeves down to cover the tattoo, insisting that the kids loved her costume and that Josh *really* loved her costume.

Eyeing me she picked up both my arms and held them out to my sides.

"Now don't tell me." She looked me up and down, pursing her lips. "You're a middle-aged stay-at-home mom whose sex life is on the downward spiral. I really don't think anyone will guess that one." She dropped my hands and gave me a mischievous smile. Lexie had a thing about everyone—grownups included, make that grown-ups *especially*—dressing up for her party. It was mandatory.

"Ha ha," I said, dropping my stuff into the corner and making a b-line to the kitchen counter. "This middle-aged mom is able to transform into a kick-ass Princess Leia faster than you can charm a fury little woodland creature, so you better watch it or I'll have you booted right back to Tatooine."

Lexie made a face. "Tatooine?"

I feigned exasperation. "The planet that Luke grew up on? The one with the two suns? Get it? I have two sons. It's a natural fit."

Lexie rolled her eyes and began to busy herself about the kitchen again. "Whatever, Princess Better-Get-Laid-A. All I can say is you better be the Princess Leia in the bikini chained to Jabba or you've lost all respect from me."

"Really? The scantily clad chained princess is the one that gets your respect?"

"Well, she did strangle him with that chain."

"Good point."

As Lexie put the finishing touches on cleaning and decorating for the mad rush of overly excited children and their ready-to-drink parents, I jumped right in, mixing up cornbread, checking on the simmering chili, and mixing up a huge bowl full of salad. Soon the house was filled with kids, dads, moms, grandparents, babysitters and friends. Everyone was eating and drinking, talking and laughing. I had to laugh when I saw Ramona, who'd dressed as a 60's style Go-Go dancer, and had to look closer to even recognize Jackie who was a picture perfect Dorothy from the Wizard of Oz with Sierra dressed as an adorable Toto.

"Don't tell me," I said to Jackie. "You made your entire outfit."

Jackie shrugged. "It wasn't so hard." She pointed to her curly hair that had been shellacked into braids and sprayed to withstand a tornado. "Now, getting my hair to stay like this, that was difficult." Her shoes, which had been perfectly bedazzled with hundreds of red jewels, were certain to be the envy of every little girl at the party. She had made Sierra's costume as well, probably the only hand-made costume in the entire South Bay.

Lisa soon made her entrance as a pregnant nun. Her youngest, Jackson was a transformer. Jade was a princess and Stosh wore a simple "Scream" mask with black clothes. Lisa was sad but not surprised when Scarlet, her oldest, had said she wanted to opt out of the party for the first time ever, preferring to hang out with her friends.

Lexie was the first to greet her, giving her a hug and complimenting her on her outfit. "Oh my, Sister," Lexie smiled, patting her belly, "you've been bad. I love it!"

"Thank you, my dear," Lisa said in a quiet nurturing tone. She looked at Lexie's outfit. "I see you've had a Catholic upbringing yourself."

"Oh yeah. And check this out," Lexie pointed out that her outfit had Velcro on the seams and she pantomimed that she could easily rip it off, revealing black Madonna-style lingerie underneath.

"Well, at least someone will be having some tricks and treats tonight. Lord have mercy. Pete's return was delayed and he won't be back now until Tuesday. Amen!"

Lexie repeated her "Amen" and asked how Lisa's mom was doing. "She didn't want to come to the party?"

Lisa smiled at the thought and said her mother would have loved to have been part of the festivities, especially if she were able to enjoy them with her grandchildren. "She's too tired right now. She said she would be happier staying home and handing out candy." Tears welled in Lisa's eyes. "I'm sorry," she said to Lexie. "I have a hard time talking about this."

Lexie put her arm around her and gave her a squeeze. "It's going to be okay," Lexie said. "I've got a surprise later that will help take your mind off it."

By six o'clock the sun was starting to set and Lexie and Josh started rounding people up to head out for trick-or-treating. Push cars and wagons were filled with children while backpacks were filled with wine. Josh walked through the party with open wine bottles handling out tumblers and filling them up with "witch's brew" for the road. Everyone grabbed their cameras and moseyed toward the gate, spilling out on the walk street. The older kids ran ahead, criss-crossing to hit every house, waiting impatiently at the end of the block for the parents to catch up. The little ones toddled down the street, taking in all the excitement with wide eyes. They hesitantly took one piece of candy from a cauldron, sometimes only to place it back in the next one. The neighbors oohed and ahhed over all the costumes while simultaneously trying to scare the older children with spooky laughter and creepy decorations. Neighbors greeted neighbors, everyone marveling at the creativity, decorations and the spectacular night.

The streets began to fill up so we returned to Lexie's. The children immediately dumped out their candy, sorting, counting and eating their bounty. Mark had arrived and helped Josh wander the party again, refilling glasses while chatting about sports.

Lisa and I were sitting on the patio talking and watching the kids and the chaos when Lexie quickly appeared. "I need you two for a little project," she said with a wink. "I told my sitter to keep a lookout for your kids, Lisa. Kelly, get Mark to watch yours and meet me in the garage in two minutes."

Lisa looked at me and I shrugged. "She's got something up her sleeve."

"And a lot more in her bra," Lisa smirked.

I laughed and offered the pregnant nun a hand up. "We better hup to it, I don't want to see what 'Party Snow White' is like when she's upset."

When we arrived in the garage, Ramona, Jackie and Lexie were already there. "Okay, let's get started," Lexie said as if running a board meeting. She reached her hand into a big bag and before pulling anything out, she looked up at us with an expectant smile, "Are you guys ready to have some serious Halloween fun?"

We just stared at her, dumbfounded, as Lexie turned back and pulled out a rubber clown mask, the kind that goes all the way over your head, and handed it to me. "KISS dude," she pulled out another pull-over mask and handed it to Ramona. "Nixon," she pulled out a fleshy, rubbery mask of the disgraced president with hard plastic hair and handed it to Jackie. "Princess," she pulled out a bunch of blonde ringlets topped off with a tiara attached to more fleshy rubber and handed it to Lisa. "And good, old Jason," she said, holding up a hockey mask. She took a deep breath and let the bag drop to the ground, looking up as we continued to just stare at her. "Well don't just stand there," she scolded, "Put them on!"

"But," Jackie protested, "I'm Dorothy. This won't match the rest of my costume."

"Yeah," I agreed, "who ever heard of a Princess Leia with a clown head?"

Lexie rolled her eyes, placed hand on hip and slid the Jason mask over her head. The hockey mask completely blocked out her identity, including some stringy, fake hair that covered her perfectly shellacked Snow White hairdo.

"See?" her voice was a bit muffled by the mask. "The contrast looks a little creepy." Whisking off the mask she took a deep breath. "But that's not the point. Just trust me on this one. We're not going to a costume contest. Now put them on, please."

Ramona was the first to comply. She shrugged and threw it on, adjusting the eyeholes until they fit perfectly then she looked around. We all giggled at her. From the neck up she looked like a heavy metal hard rocker from KISS with mounds of black, stiff hair and a star painted over one eye. From the neck down she still looked very groovy.

The rest of us followed suit as Lexie barked at us. "Okay, okay," Lexie said excitedly. "Now listen up." She motioned us into a huddle. "I've been wanting to do this for over a year. Here's the plan."

Five minutes later, we were all on bikes cruising down Manhattan

Avenue toward the pier. Following Lexie's lead, we cut through the grassy park north of the upscale Beach Hotel, then pulled into the valet and asked to stash the bikes behind his counter for ten minutes. Lex grabbed her backpack from the basket of her bike, took a $20 from her bra and tipped the valet to watch the bikes and we scurried off toward the pier.

The promenade was packed with twenty and thirty-year olds, all reveling in the craziness of the night. We held hands, weaving in and out of the partiers like a giant snake. Twice I had to bat people away, telling them we weren't a conga line. We slowed our approach, stopping about fifty yards from the base of the pier, then all of us tried to fit behind a giant planter that held a huge bird of paradise and some jasmine. All five of our masked heads popped out from behind the foliage to try and get a better look.

"Okay," said Ramona, "there they are. It's..." she squinted through the mask, stretching and pressing it closer to her face so she could see better. "Scar and Cheesy Mustache."

"Quick question," Jackie whispered, "if we're wearing masks, why are we hiding behind a tree?"

"It's more fun this way, plus that's how they do it in Scooby Doo," replied Lisa, who seemed to be relishing the excitement. I imagined our adventure was a welcome reprieve from what her life had been over the past few weeks, taking care of her dying mother while her husband had been out of town on business.

"Are we sure we want to do this?" I asked, suddenly a little anxious at seeing their faces up close. These two weren't the smaller cute ones.

"Absolutely!" cried Ramona and Lexie simultaneously.

"I'm game," said Lisa.

"Me, too," said Jackie.

"Alrighty then, here ya go," Lexie said. She unzipped her backpack and handed the supplies to Jackie, Lisa and me. "As soon you're in position, give Ramona the signal. Everyone to this planter afterwards. If we get separated, meet at the bikes."

My heart was racing as Jackie, Lisa and I disappeared into the crowd of tipsy partiers, all dressed as their alter egos—anything with fishnets, stilettos and little else for the girls, and anything that took zero effort for the men. It was crazy crowded and we zig-zagged through until we were on the opposite side of the pier from Ramona and Lexie. Jackie waved a red scarf in the air. The signal for Lexie to go.

Lisa took watch as Jackie and I worked. From her vantage point, she could barely make Lexie out through all the people. We finished in a flash, and Lisa informed us Lexie was in place, chatting with the dealers, I'm sure being flirty and sassy. We began making our way toward them, walking carefully behind Lisa who was blocking, trying not to get bumped. My hands were shaking a little, and I told myself this was crazy, but with all our momentum, I didn't dare abort mission now.

We knew it wouldn't take long before one of the dealers tried to close the deal and get Lexie to go under the pier so we picked up the pace. Soon we were directly behind them and could hear Cheesy Mustache saying "We don't have any tricks, but we definitely got some treats."

"Oh yeah?" Lexie responded. "What kind of treats do you have?"

"All kinds of treats," replied Scar, his voice was gruff and I was close enough to see him eyeing Lexie's cleavage. "What are you looking for?"

"Oh, I don't know. Something to make the evening a little more...fun and interesting," she said, turning on the charm. She stepped away from them slowly, they followed, until she had them facing the water, their backs to the promenade. It was gross to hear her be so nice to the same people that offered her child a joint, one that could have been laced with something stronger.

The rest all happened in a blur. I could hear Cheesy Mustache saying, "Why don't you come with me and we can discuss it in private?" He motioned toward the stairs behind her. At the same time and I handed Lisa my handiwork while Jackie handed the one she was carrying to me.

"Okay," Lexie said, giving us the signal with her hand, a big thumb's up. I began counting down from five, and took in a slow, calming breath. "But I'm with a group tonight. Do you have enough with you for a crowd of say, twenty?"

The two dealers glanced at each other and laughed out loud. Scar turned back to Lexie and said with a sly, slightly sinister grin, "Don't worry, we got plenty."

Lexie's body tensed slightly. "Good," she said as calmly as she could muster, "because my friends and I plan on doing a lot of tricks tonight. Starting now."

Lexie nodded toward the crowd behind them and when they turned, we sprang. "Trick or treat, dickwad!" Lisa yelled, slapping a huge shaving cream pie upward and into Scar's face as fast and hard as she could. He yelled in shock and grabbed for his nose and I thought for a second she might have broken it. Cheesy Mustache turned just as quickly and got the same treatment from me.

"Smell my feet, jackass!" I called out as I thrust the pie in his face with all my might. He grabbed the pie pan that had stuck to his face and hurled it to the ground, frantically trying to wipe away the thick choking foam.

"Run!" Lexie screamed, grabbing us by the hand as the pie tins fell to the ground and the stunned men struggled with the messy, stingy goop. We dashed to the bikes when Lisa noticed we were missing Jackie.

"Where is she?" Lexie cried, looking around. We were nearing the planter where Ramona lurked when we looked back and spotted Jackie through a small opening in the crowd, still hunched by the men's skateboards.

"What is she doing?" Lexie yelled.

"I don't know," I screamed through my mask. I was sweating and it was wet inside the mask from my breathing, plus the smell of sweet plastic and my adrenaline mixed with the wine was beginning to make me feel nauseated. Before I could say anything, Lexie turned and ran back. We watched, petrified, as Jackie got up and began running toward us, trying to steer clear of the doubled over men still madly flinging shaving cream from their hair, eyes, noses and mouths as the crowd gawked at them. She began a full-out sprint but was too late, Scar had seen her running, had guessed she was part of the prank, and had let out a guttural growl as he reached his right hand and caught her by the back of her skirt. Jackie screamed and was jolted off her feet and onto her butt. He let go and went to grab her body when Lexie caught up and gave him a front kick to the face knocking him off balance.

Lexie picked up Jackie and the two of them raced to join the rest of us, already running toward the hotel. "Move it!" Lexie shouted as she and Jackie folded into our group and we dashed around and over to the bikes, all of us looking back over our shoulders every few seconds. We grabbed the bikes, hopped on and peddled out, through the adjacent park and up the alleyway as fast as we could without hitting anyone. Finally, with a stitch in my side, we pulled into her garage, one after the other, until at last Ramona came speeding around the corner, parking as Lexie hit the garage door button.

We flung off our masks, all of us out of breath and sweating, panting and quietly watching the door completely close, afraid that at the last moment Scar or Cheesy Mustache's hand might pop in, causing the automated door to open, leaving us cornered and defenseless. But it didn't. We let out a huge sigh of relief followed by screams of accomplishment. Our hair and makeup was a mess because of the masks, but we didn't care. We were all grinning from ear to ear, our ecstasy fueled by adrenaline. We hugged and laughed, high-fiving each other, making sure everyone was all right.

"Score another point for the moms!" I said, overflowing with enthusiasm. "Let's see, with the school incident, Robert, Gage and Will, the stroller thieves and now this, we're at Moms 5, Bad Guys 0!" I hadn't even thought of keeping score since the night of the school incident but after taking stock of all that we had accomplished in the past six months, we seemed to be on a roll. It even felt like we might be a tad bit untouchable.

And as we rejoined the party, all of us in a very celebratory mood, I kept thinking about how the bad guys really weren't so scary after all. Those men, those drug dealers, had always been such a huge, menacing, dreaded force to me. They'd seemed infallible, larger than life, above the law. Even in the middle of a sunny day, when Casey was a baby and I would push the stroller by on one of our walks and they'd say their polite "hello" in the most non-threatening kind of way, they still scared me. They were *drug dealers,* for crying out loud, and therefore dangerous. My imagination over the years had them kidnapping women, shooting them full of drugs to get them hooked, then cooking their babies up in a frying pan while they themselves were on some PCP-induced high.

But tonight the tiniest of chinks had been broken from this notion of mine. I realized that they were, after all, just men. And this recognition brought forth another: that they were fallible, they could make mistakes. Mistakes we could use to our advantage, if we were smart about it. I knew it was the smallest of a chance, a slight-chance-in-hell kind of chance, a winning-lottery-ticket kind of chance that we could take them down. But I believed in those chances. I was a lottery-ticket-buying kind of person.

And so even though our juvenile prank did nothing to make the town safer or to rid us of their presence, it was a baby step, and in retrospect, an important one. Because knowing that they were in fact human, and that they didn't pull guns and shoot us right there by the pier or turn into giant ravaging demons, somehow gave me an extra ounce of confidence. And sometimes an extra ounce is all you need to do something incredibly brave—or incredibly stupid.

Seventeen

I can't imagine the grief in losing someone you love with all your heart. Yes, I've lost people, all my grandparents, for example, and that was sad. But I was young and they weren't exactly an intricate part of my life, their absence did not leave a hole so large in my heart that I thought I might never recover like the death of Ramona's husband did to her.

But now, all these years later, things were changing. She was changing. She was spending large chunks of time at Lisa's to help out with the kids so Lisa could tend to her mom, and she still popped over to Jackie's to help out with Sierra every day as usual. And in addition to keeping up her pier surveillance, she was now spending loads of time at the marina working on her boat. Her demeanor was changing, too. She was now upbeat—still sarcastic, of course—but in a more upbeat way. Even her appearance was changing. Upon request, Jackie had taken her to the spa and shopping, and she was now sporting a spiffy new haircut complete with highlights and almost a complete new wardrobe from J. Jill. She even joked about getting Botox injections. I figured the changes were a natural progression of finally getting over her grief, of getting back into life but Jackie informed me she thought Ramona might have a new boyfriend. The name 'Bill' was mentioned a lot on their walks.

Ramona's new computer skills helped her reconnect with her kids. She was sending emails and Skyping regularly and had bought a ticket to visit all three of her children over the winter holidays, spending two weeks with each one which explained the rush of her latest appeal. She asked me again if she could host November's MNO to be held on her boat and she had two requests: 1) I was to invite as many moms as possible, the whole entire gang and even more if I knew them, she wanted "ladies spilling off the boat," and 2) she wanted it to be a spectacle, something that would draw attention to us and not just by body count. Naturally I complied, it sounded fun and different, and I thought she just wanted to show off her boat, maybe her new style.

So on a cloudless Tuesday evening smack dab in the middle of November, I picked Lisa and Lexie up and drove us down to the marina. We unloaded my car, chitchatting about our families, Lisa's mother's health and Thanksgiving plans, and began following Ramona's instructions that would lead us to her boat, all three of us pulling coolers filled with wine and food. Bill and Ramona had watched Sierra most of the day, and Brian had come home early so Jackie could do her thing, which was apparent the second we emerged from the parking lot.

All I could think of as we approached was that Disneyland must be a notch less magical now that Jackie no longer worked there because suddenly it didn't feel like we were just meeting friends for drinks, it felt like we were V.I.P.'s going to some incredible Hollywood gala.

It started with a make-shift archway decorated with hundreds of twinkling white lights that she had somehow erected at the entrance to Ramona's pier and as we walked through, a path lined with luminarias lit the way to a smaller pier with a gate that was open and decorated with even more lights. The luminarias lit the path to the boat, which looked like a Christmas tree. Strings of colored lights, the kinds with big round bulbs, ran the length of the mast and the sail lines. The railings running around the perimeter of the fifty-foot sailboat's deck had been wrapped diagonally in white lights. A machine was projecting beautiful blue stars that would grow and explode like fireworks onto the huge sails. Brightly colored throw pillows and colorful wraps were perfectly situated on the decks and benches, inviting people to sit down and snuggle up. Tea lights were on the deck, and larger floating candles, at least fifty of them, surrounded the boat, bobbing up and down in the water. It was an enchanting.

"Hey! You guys are here!" Jackie said from behind us.

She was walking up the pier with a tall, older man none of us recognized. We set down our things and began to heap the compliments on her.

"Thank you guys, oh and this is Bill," Jackie exclaimed, suddenly realizing we were all beginning to stare at the stranger. "He's Ramona's friend, and he's helped me a ton this afternoon."

"Nice to meet you," he said, getting our names straight with a firm handshake.

"He was just showing me his boat," Jackie explained.

"And I'll now be returning to it," he said with a wink and a smile. "You girls have a fun party and don't worry about taking anything down, I can do all that tomorrow. Tell Ramona I said goodnight."

"Will do. Thanks, Bill," Jackie said, turning to us with a huge isn't-he-great kind of smile mouthing "Ramona's new boyfriend!" to us just as Ramona emerged from the lower deck.

"What are you land-lovers doing?" she called to us, just as we had started to gossip about Bill. "Let's get this party started!" She opened the gate and we picked up our stuff and climbed onboard, the celebratory vibe palpable.

"Ramona, this boat is incredible," Lisa said.

"Thanks. She was Ben's baby. He was a born sailor." She took a quick step back outside the gate with her hands on her hips, admiring the decorations. She turned to Jackie, "You don't think you're going a little too crazy with the decorations, do you?"

"You mean I'm going overboard?" Jackie chuckled. Ramona rolled her eyes then came inside the gate, opened up a bench and took out a stack of lime green sunhats.

"I almost forgot," she said plopping one on Jackie's head. "I was hoping for purple, but they were out. I got one for everyone. What do you think?"

"Nice!" Jackie said. "If you'd have told me, I could have brought some material to tie around the brims." Ramona raised an eyebrow at her.

"Just for a little added color," Jackie said defensively.

"They're lime green, honey," Ramona replied. "They practically glow in the dark."

As we set up the food and drink Ramona put a hat on each of our heads and instructed us to pass them out as people arrived. Then she looked to me. "Did we get a good number of RSVP's?" There was an odd tone in her voice, which I chocked up to nerves. I was quick to allay her fears, telling her I thought we'd have a good turnout, somewhere in the neighborhood of fifteen moms, which seemed to make her happy because she uttered a quick, "Good," then went below.

Soon other guests arrived in ones and twos. Most had never been down to the marina before, even though they lived within a few miles, and they were shocked to see what a beautiful place it was. It was a perfect night to be on the water. The Santa Ana winds had just started picking up, which usually meant bad news for brush fires across L.A., but made for the perfectly rare, warm evening at the coast. As darkness fell, the moon rose and made the water ever more resplendent as it shimmered with both candle and moon light. The wine was flowing, the hors d'oeuvres devoured, the conversation lively and the hats were a hit.

We must have welcomed about twenty-five moms, which made the boat a little crowded. There were a few people down below in the cabin, but mostly people wanted to be outside so the deck space was full, even spilling out onto the floating pier. Jackie called Bill and he brought down some chairs and a table for us. Every now and again I looked for Ramona to see if she was having a good time, enjoying the MNO she had so adamantly wanted, but it was hard to tell. I made my way over to her to ask how she was doing. Before I could speak, she took my arm along with Lisa's and began guiding both of us off the boat, a fake smile plastered across her face as she murmured to her guests, "Just going for some ice, we'll be right back."

We made our way to the end of the pier, Lisa and I shooting each other questioning glances. Ramona stopped at the entrance to the next pier where, I noticed, the street light was out. We were completely concealed by darkness.

"Sorry about that," Ramona muttered, nodding toward the boat as though she had just stepped on our toes instead of hijacked us from the party she insisted we help her throw. "I figured you two'd be the best for this," she paused, trying to pluck the right word out, "situation."

"What situation?" Lisa asked, perplexed.

Then she told us her plan, and everything snapped into place: the party, the hats, the *scene*. Ramona hadn't wanted this to draw attention to herself. She'd wanted just the opposite. She had wanted a diversion. She didn't care two cents if people liked her boat or her new style. She wasn't hosting because she was over grieving and was ready to celebrate being alive and having good friends to share it with. Her plan, she told us, was to sneak aboard the *All Nighter*, with Lisa and me as lookouts in case the dealers happen to stop by. She knew from spying on them all week that they had loaded their boat with coolers. And she was dead set on finding out what those coolers contained.

"Have you lost your marbles?" I asked, gawking while she begin to strip down in front of us, wiggling out of her pants and pulling off her top to reveal an outfit that consisted of black leggings and a tight black turtleneck, both of which clung to her skinny little body and made her look downright delicate. She ignored our pleas to return to sanity, to do this some other way, as she held on to me to steady herself and pulled off her shoes. Handing me her clothes she put on a black knit beanie and held up her hand to shush us both.

"We don't have time to argue," she said in the my-word-is-final tone we both recognized from mothering. "Your job is to stay here and stop any dealers from coming down that way until you either see me come back or hear me give the signal. If, by chance, a dealer gets by you, which if we're lucky and I'm fast won't happen, then I want you to sing to warn me. Got it?"

Lisa sort of nodded, but I was confused. What was the signal she was going to give us? What were we supposed to sing? I was still trying to think of convincing arguments to talk her out of this stupidity when she turned and jogged down the pier, disappearing into the night.

"Wait, what?" I panicked and turned to Lisa who looked frightened as well but was doing a much better job of holding her anxiety at bay and herself together, something she did expertly. "What were we supposed to sing? What was the signal? Has she lost it? She's gonna get on their boat?"

"I don't know," Lisa replied quietly, turning her back on Ramona and looking the other way, already taking up her assigned duty. "We stand guard, don't let anyone through, sing if there is danger."

Damn, she was good. I knew Lisa had been in some sticky situations back when she was single and making documentaries in dangerous parts of the world and she just seemed to fall into this high-alert, triage, manage-what-you-can mode. I tried to follow her example.

"Okay. Okay. She'll be okay," I said out loud but mostly to myself. I took a deep breath and turned to stand shoulder to shoulder with Lisa, my eyes scanning the area. "Now, what do we sing?"

"She didn't say. I just hope she hurries and doesn't get caught 'cause I'm not much of a singer."

I nodded, taking in that piece of information. "And when she comes back? She'll either walk by us or give us some sort of signal?"

"That's what she said."

"What's that signal?"

Lisa just shrugged and shook her head and I noticed she checked her watch. I checked mine as well. It was just past ten. I glanced over at our party and noticed that it was, indeed, a spectacle, all those bright lights and green hats, the lively conversations, the occasional shrill of laughter. It would be nearing a peak right about now, I guessed. Most of the moms were usually home by eleven, except, of course, those of us who were friends with Lexie and were now programmed to stay out later. Ramona must have known that it was now or never. If she had waited any longer, the party would start to die down. If she went any earlier, we might not have had a critical mass yet. Watching the crowd I was frankly surprised the cops hadn't been called yet.

"So I guess we could pretend we're over here on a smoke break, huh?" I suggested.

"Yeah, good idea," Lisa responded. "Do you have any cigarettes?"

"Ew, yuck, no. You?"

"Uh, no. Never smoked in my life."

"So much for that idea. Is it me, or did she look like Mike Meyers when he plays a Sprocket?" I asked.

Lisa half-chuckled and replied, "I just hope she knows what she's doing. That boat could be booby trapped."

"Are you serious? Oh my God, I didn't even think of that." I turned to see if I could see her at all. "Why didn't you tell her that?" I swatted Lisa on the shoulder.

Lisa scowled. "This woman has been ten steps ahead of us for months. I would be shocked if she hadn't thought of that herself. Now," she put her hand on my shoulder and gently pushed me aside so she could continue to be on the lookout. I turned and joined her and we stood there, shoulder to shoulder, thinking up scenarios of things we would say to people, to the dealers, if they did indeed show, as our eyes darted around restlessly and Lisa checked her watch every thirty seconds.

"How long did she say she would be gone?" I asked after what felt like fifteen minutes but upon checking my own watch, turned out to be only six.

"She didn't," Lisa responded, her tone a little edgy. She then nudged me with panic in her eyes nodding toward the parking lot and a dark figure moving quickly toward the sidewalk, headed our way.

The shadowy person turned up our pier. We could tell he was a man as he got closer. He wore dark jeans and a tight long-sleeved T-shirt, and he was walking straight towards us, his face fixed on his phone as he walked. We fumbled for each other, pretending to have a conversation, but then thinking we should approach the man and in the confusion he quickly darted right past.

"Ah!" I cried. "Wait, sir!" I called after him, panicking, looking quickly at Lisa then trying to look casual and not drop the armful of Ramona's clothes. We decided that if anyone were to pass, we would act like we were out looking for someone to take a picture of our entire group back on the boat. The man continued on as if he hadn't heard me at all.

"Sir! Sir!" I called after him as we both scrambled quickly behind to catch up. He was fifteen strides ahead of us and heading Ramona's way, and fast.

"Hey!" Lisa finally shouted, running up to him and tapping him on the shoulder. The man stopped and turned, taking his earbuds out, the music blaring out.

"Yeah?" The streetlight caught his face and I recognized him from Ramona's files. He must have been in his early 20's, still baby-faced, an attempt at a beard on his chin.

"Oh, hi," Lisa replied shakily. "I'm wondering if you can help us out. We need someone to take a photo of our group over there." She pointed but he didn't even look.

"Sorry lady, I'm kind of in a hurry," he said, shaking his head. He started to turn and walk away but Lisa boldly stepped in front of him.

"Come on, she pleaded. It will only take a second. I'll make it worth your while, I promise." She raised her eyebrows and smiled gently.

He glanced over at our party and in that second, she hooked her elbow around his and began leading him back to Ramona's boat, launching into chat mode. "Seriously, this will only take a sec. Are you hungry? We've got some great appetizers. And maybe a beer? I can't tell you how much I appreciate this."

He glanced quickly at the parking lot, then to my astonishment, gave in to the idea muttering, "Okay, but let's make this quick." We walked back to the party together, Lisa and I practically running to keep up with him.

"Keep your eyes on the pier," I muttered to Lisa when we arrived, "and I'll organize this end." I saw Lisa nod slightly as she stood with a plastic smile on her face shoulder to shoulder with the man who I could now see, in the glow of a thousand twinkly lights, was built like a prize fighter, his tight T-shirt hugging his arms that looked as though they could crush rocks.

I yelled to the ladies something about this nice man agreeing to take our picture and got us all in position so we would fit in the shot, then squeezed myself in on the edge, trying hard not to look away from the other pier so long that I'd miss someone walking by. The man stood back, held Lisa's phone up and took the picture, then quickly gave it back without so much as a word. In that quick second, I was able to grab my camera from my bag and hand it to him, smiling. "Can you take another with mine, please?" I asked, giving him my best puppy dog eyes.

He sighed, but took it and complied as I beamed to the crowd, "This will make such an excellent scrapbook page!" He fumbled with my 35mm, but found the right button and took the picture. The second he was done, as I predicted, three other moms pulled their cameras and phones from their bags and pockets with lightning speed and the man found himself suddenly dripping with at least a dozen gadgets.

"Get him a beer!" someone shouted and a bottle of Sierra Nevada Christmas Ale was produced as if out of thin air and thrust at him, softening him a little as he glanced at his watch, then the parking lot, then with the slightest of smiles took a quick swig of the beer and began snapping away, not even waiting for us to smile. Five minutes and twenty pictures later, he was exasperated.

When he finished the last photo, he nodded quickly to Lisa who was thanking him profusely, picked up his beer bottle and was gone. Our group broke up and began to mingle again and Lisa and I found each other, hopping off the boat, watching from the smaller pier as he high-tailed it up through the gate and down Jackie's beautifully lit path.

I was about to ask Lisa what we should do when she grabbed my hand and cried, "Look!" She pointed across the water to the other pier and I saw him. Another darkly dressed figure, similar to the man we just encountered, walking briskly toward the boat. We watched him stop at the gate and figured he was working the lock, and I knew we had only moments before he would be there, on the *All Nighter*, where we could only guess Ramona was still snooping inside.

"We don't have time to get over there," Lisa said, keeping her eye on the man.

"What are you guys doing?" I heard Lexie say, feeling her next to me but hearing her as if she were far away, like in a dream.

"Quick, sing a song!" Lisa ordered, holding my shoulder and shaking it a little. "Uh......" I began, racking my brain for a song, any song, which shouldn't have been hard because I almost always had something jingly in my head but they were all songs from kids' shows, and it wouldn't have made sense to belt out Mickey Mouse's "Hot dog" song. The stress was making me draw a blank and I felt completely frozen.

"Now!" Lisa cried.

I looked to Lexie who stared back bewildered, her eyes wide with concern, as I realized I was starting to shake. The man was steps away from the boat by this time and I knew I had to give the signal so I quickly aimed my voice directly at the *All Nighter* and sang at the top of my lungs. *"Hey, once I was a funky singer! Playin' in a rock and roll band! I never had no problems, yeah..."*

My tempo was off, I was way too fast and I never actually could sing on key. I must have looked completely ridiculous because everyone at the party stopped their conversations and stared at me. But I continued, walking quickly through the crowd as I sang with all my might until I got to the part of Ramona's boat that was closest to the *All Nighter* and there I stepped up onto a bench so I was over the heads of almost everyone.

I tried to position my body sideways so I looked like I was really hamming it up for the party but mostly so my voice went over the water and alerted the crazy old trespasser. I forced a smile on my face and began to bounce a little so it looked like I was trying to groove and get the party started, instead of just looking like I was off my rocker drunk. I began to snap my fingers and sway my hips as well, and crooned the second verse. *"Burnin' down one night stands, and everything around me, yeah! Got to stop to feelin' so low, and I decided quickly, yes I did, to disco down and check out the show!"*

I could see the man reach the *All Nighter*, saw him hear my song, look up and take note of our party, stopping for one brief moment to watch the spectacle I was making of myself and I hoped to God that it had been enough to help Ramona get out of there if she hadn't already.

The others continued to watch me and I scanned the crowd, taking stock of how much damage I was doing to my reputation as a normal person, until I found Jackie looking at me with a confused expression but who, upon making eye contact, smiled sweetly, encouragingly. And then I felt Lexie. She had climbed up on the bench next to me and was using a beer bottle as a microphone. I looked over and saw her glance at me out of the corner of her eye, giving me her glorious smile, and together we belted out the chorus. *"Yeah, they was dancin' and singin' and movin' to the groovin', and just when it hit me somebody turned around and shouted—"* Jackie made her way to the bench and jumped up next to us just in time for the best part. *"Play that funky music white boy! Play that funky music right! Play that funky music white boy! Lay down the boogie and play that funky music till you die!"*

The whole boat exploded. Every mom joined in, grooving back and forth and up and down, bumping hips with each other and for a moment, remembering how it felt to be young and free, the way we were when that song was new. When we got to the chorus again, it was as though we were at a concert, right there with the band, Wild Cherry, front row and just off center stage. *"Play that funky music white boy! Play that funky music right! Play that funky music white boy! Lay down the boogie and play that funky music till you die!"* There was no background music, just our a cappella voices but even so, it felt like we could be heard for blocks in every direction. I doubt any of the moms on that boat had rocked out that hard in years.

As all the ladies were still in mid groove, I saw Lisa snag a bottle of wine from the cooler and sneak off the boat. I grabbed Lexie, whispered that she needed to keep it up, saw her nod her understanding. I jumped down and rushed off the boat and after Lisa. I caught up with her as she turned the corner to the other pier. She told me in quick, panicked sentences that she had seen the first man board the *All Nighter* seconds after I had started singing and that we had to make sure Ramona wasn't trapped.

Our speed walking stopped at the gate to their pier, which they had left propped open and we let ourselves in, slowing to a seemingly casual walk, scanning left and right and calling out under our breath for Ramona in case she was hiding somewhere on one of the other boats. As we got closer we saw the two men and could tell one of them was definitely the one who had been taking our picture. They were working in the cabin of the medium-sized Bayliner and it was clear they were in a hurry. The other man gave the camera man orders we couldn't hear. Then he began to take some brown boxes that were lying on the deck below.

Worried Ramona might still be aboard, possibly even hiding somewhere or worse, hog-tied, gagged and soon to be kidnapped by the men, Lisa and I approached them. The second man looked up at us. His face was pock-marked by acne scars and he wore what I could only assume was a permanent scowl. Lisa smiled at him and acted nonchalant and a little tipsy. I was impressed by her convincing improvisation and could tell she wanted to get as close as she could to the boat so she could take a good look inside.

"Hey there!" she practically sang, pretending to stumble a little as she walked closer. The man nodded in a no-nonsense, no-solicitors, don't-bother-me kind of way.

"I'm sorry to bug you, but I was looking for the man who helped me—" Before she could finish her sentence, the camera man came up from below. He looked shocked and little embarrassed to see two middle-aged women in a lime-green hats asking for him. The other man gave him a stern look, telling him with his eyes that he was to get rid of us, and now.

The camera man looked up at Lisa as she scanned the cabin behind him. "Yeah?"

She handed him the bottle of chardonnay she had taken from the ice chest and he took it with a surprised look. Then she gushed, thanking him profusely, going on about how people don't help each other anymore, how the kindness of strangers was underrated, if ever he needed someone to do him a favor, etc. She was slurring some of her words, trying to occupy as much of the man's time as possible in order to give Ramona a fighting chance to get out of there if she were able or to give us a sign that she was trapped. I watched the boat but listened more than looked, straining to hear a muffled yell or a whimper, anything from the inside of their boat that might sound like a cry for help but it was hard since the multitude of moms were now belting out Jackson 5's "ABC's" from across the water.

Abruptly, the boss cut the conversation off. He belted out an order and the camera man quickly set down the wine and obsequiously untied the boat and brought in the ropes. With that, the boss started the engine and without even so much as a glance at Lisa or me, backed the boat out as the camera man gave us a quick apologetic look before they disappeared into the darkness of the ocean.

We watched them for a minute or two until it felt safe then started to call out in desperate loud whispers that quickly turned into shouts. "Ramona? Ramona!"

We ran up and down this branch of the pier, looking on, in and around the boats as best we could. We scoured the area but after a few minutes of crazed searching, we ran back to the party to see if maybe, somehow, she had gotten past us and made it back to her boat on her own.

We walked quickly, continuing to shout Ramona's name as we went, our eyes scanning the area. As we rounded the corner, we could see all the moms spilling off the catamaran as two police officers watched. We looked at each other apprehensively as we neared the party, part of me was thinking, hoping, Ramona had called them to report on her findings, but those hopes were soon dashed.

"We were busted!" a gleeful mom called out as we neared the boat. "It was awesome!"

"Yeah! Great party! Tell Ramona thanks for us, I haven't been sent home by the cops in twenty years!" voiced another.

We saw Jackie and Lexie hugging guests and acting as hosts as everyone left. "Good evening, officer," Lisa said, playing up the role of good citizen. "What's going on?"

"We've had complaints of disturbing the peace, ma'am," the officer replied. "Party's over." His hands were on his hips where, we noted, he had quick access to his equipment. A necessity for the job, I supposed, but a bit overly dramatic considering the offenders were all compliant. His partner read the scene more accurately and stood there pretty relaxed, a slight grin on his face, a lime green hat on his head. As the middle-aged moms left, I couldn't help but ponder the irony of a bunch of ladies being busted for loud singing while drug dealers and possible kidnappers had just snuck out from beneath their noses.

"Is Ramona here?" Lisa asked Jackie and Lexie, looking anxious, if not terrified. They nodded their heads no, worry reflected in their eyes as the last of the revelers left the boat to go home and brag to their husbands about how their party was broken up by the cops. It would be the talk of the mom-circuit for days.

"That's what we'd like to know," the serious officer continued. "As the owner of this boat, we could issue her a ticket."

"Come on, Steve," the other officer said. "Let's go. Try to keep it down from now on ladies." He gave us a smile, which Lexie returned with a few bats of her eyelashes.

As soon as they were out of earshot Lisa demanded, "We've got to find Ramona. This is serious. Are you sure she didn't come back here?"

Both Lexie and Jackie looked at her like deer in headlights. By now Lisa and I were in full panic mode and began delegating search and rescue areas of the harbor for all of us to take.

"Maybe she's down at Bill's," Jackie said. "I'll go check."

"Maybe she has some flashlights in here," Lisa continued, rummaging around in all the nooks and crannies of the boat. "We've got to find her in the next five minutes or I'm calling the Coast Guard!"

"Don't call the Coast Guard, I'm right here," said a small voice out of nowhere. We all looked around but couldn't tell where it was coming from.

"Ramona?" Lisa gasped. "Is that you? Oh my God, Ramona! Where are you?" Lisa practically screamed, doing a 360, her eyes wild with panic.

"Look overboard, on the ladder. The backside of the boat. I think I'm going to need help getting up." We ran to the back of the boat and looked over. Down, next to the motor, the lower three-quarters of her body still submerged, we found her clinging to the ladder. We all cried out for her, she looked so tiny, so feeble, like a survivor of a tsunami clinging for life. Lexie and Lisa were there first and each took a side, hanging themselves halfway over the boat while Jackie and I held their legs as they pulled Ramona up. She was completely soaked with the exception of the very top of her head, which was still covered in her beanie. She was visibly shaking.

"Let's get you warmed up," Lisa said, issuing orders for Jackie and I to find towels and boil water while she and Lexie helped Ramona walk, dripping, to the galley downstairs where she collapsed onto one of the seats, dripping and shivering all over. We soon had her covered in towels, sipping hot tea, and soaking her feet in a bucket of warm water that moments before had held iced beer and wine. In no time we had her warmed up and looking like someone who was waiting for a spa treatment.

Once she was warm, it didn't take long for her to try to stop the fuss we were making as we each took a limb and tried to rub some circulation back into her. "Alright, you can stop now," she said to no avail as we kept on rubbing her until she threatened to kick us off her boat. "I'm okay, I'm okay. Seriously. Thank you."

We stopped doting and sat back on the cushions, relief washing over us like a warm shower. Jackie was the first to speak. "What the hell were you doing in the water like that?" she demanded.

Lisa followed up quickly, "Seriously, what happened? And what's with the singing?" I could still see the worry in Lisa's eyes and imagined that her heart, if it was anything like mine, was still beating somewhere near the rate of a hamster's.

"You gave those creeps a good bottle of wine, that's what," Ramona quipped, looking at her tea, then up at Lisa with a smile hiding on the corners of her mouth. Lisa shook her head and smiled faintly, and I could see her let out a big sigh, the tension in her shoulders visibly decreasing. She sat down next to Ramona and practically smothered her with her hug.

"I was so worried about you," Lisa cried, wiping a tear from her eye.

"I would have been up a creek without a paddle if I hadn't heard the signal," Ramona said. "Thanks for that. But next time, give me a little more than thirty seconds, okay. I'm old, remember? I don't move as quickly as I used to."

"Next time?" Lisa scoffed. "Ha!"

"Would someone like to inform the rest of us what is going on?" Lexie said.

Lisa filled them in on Ramona's plan to board the dealer's boat in order to gather as much information about them as possible. "So that's why you guys disappeared so suddenly," Lexie said.

Lisa shook her head. "The singing was Ramona's signal to get the hell out of there PDQ."

Lexie looked at Ramona and scooted a little closer. "That's pretty ballsy. But how'd you end up in the water?"

Ramona told us that the second she heard the signal, she came up from the dealer's galley to see the man at the bow of his boat. There was nowhere to go but overboard. She slipped into the water as quietly as possible, missing him by seconds, then swam across to her own boat and held on to the ladder until the coast was clear.

"It would have been a great escape except I was worried I would be seen because of all those ridiculous candles floating in the water," she scoffed.

"So," Lexie asked, her eyes wide, "what did you find?" We all looked at her, waiting, the only sound the quiet lapping of the water against the boat.

Ramona took a long sip of her tea, not making eye contact with any of us. It was as if she were having some internal debate, weighing the consequences of telling us, of getting us further involved. Then she looked up and said definitively, "I found money. Loads of it."

Eighteen

We all realized after Ramona's discovery that this was not a simple Mom and Pop shop. It was a much bigger operation, probably with multiple points of sale all over Los Angeles, all of it funneling back through our little slice of heaven. It felt like if we involved ourselves any further we would be entering a whole new level of danger, a level we weren't prepared for, a level that wouldn't be fun to even pretend we belonged in. We were all more than ready to hand the whole project off to the police and be done with it. Even Ramona wasn't resisting that idea, but before we could do it the holidays attacked.

Ramona left to visit her kids on the other side of the world and each of us went into our own little worlds. For me it was like being in the ocean, each new activity a wave that crashed and took me under until I kicked for the surface and could take a quick breath, only to be taken under again. There was the orchestrating and attending of school parties, neighborhood parties, and company parties. Halls had to be decked, cards sent, and cookies baked. Crafts were made, presents were bought and wrapped, some shipped while others were tucked secretly under the tree. Company came, dinners were cooked, movies were watched, and of course there were those elves. Those fucking elves.

This was the first year my boys seemed cognizant of the mystical powers the big man in the red suit held and I felt a joy I never had before to watch the awe that came over them whenever they saw

Santa, or his mischievous helpers. They were, it seemed, at their pinnacle of cuteness and I could not get enough of them. I took a gazillion photos, made tons of movies, bought a voice recorder and had the kids tell silly stories and sing songs into it. I jotted down everything we did each day as well as the adorable things they said while tucking love notes into their scrapbooks for them to find one day. I made every effort to capture this precious time, to preserve these memories and always, *always,* in the back of my mind, I was doing it so I could look back on this time when things were perfect. Because underlying it all was this fear that the whole thing, this life I had built and everyone in it that I loved, was going to be yanked out from under me. That something bad was going to happen to us. What if a car jumped the curb and hit us? What if a deranged ex-husband hunted down his ex-wife and kids at the playground and opened fire while we were there playing? And now, what if these drug dealers did something to hurt us? I knew I was being ridiculous and paranoid and I tried to push those thoughts out of my head, I really did, but they were always there, lingering, like my hangover on New Year's Day.

Mark said I was being irrational, that there were better things to worry about. That if I didn't knock it off, I was going to cause something to happen, like a self-fulfilled prophecy or a jinx, which I, in turn, said was irrational. Maybe these are the kinds of discussions married people have in January as they are taking stock of their lives and noting the passing of time. But while our household was busy imagining death and despair, it actually came to Lisa's. Twice in one month.

The first tragedy was a fifteen-year-old freshman at Hermosa High named Nicole McKenna. She was best friends with Scarlet, Lisa's oldest daughter, and Lisa had been the first, after Nicole's parents, to be alerted. Lisa was home alone, except for her ailing mother who was sleeping, when she got the call. Everyone was still on break from school and work and so Pete had taken their younger two to the La Brea Tar Pits. Both Scarlet and Stosh were out with friends. Lisa had to track down her daughter, tell her the news and take her to the police station to give her testimony as to what had happened, which, according to Lisa was in the Every Parent's Worst Nightmare category.

Nicole, it was patched together, had been at a party with Scarlet on New Year's Eve but had left with a boy she liked to attend another party in Santa Monica at his brother's apartment. The boy's brother convinced them to try Ecstasy, thinking it would the fun thing to do for the first time on New Year's Eve. Unbeknownst to anyone, it was laced with meth and she began to react immediately, passing out, vomiting. The brother kicked them out of the party; he'd wanted nothing to do with the scene and the frightened boy she'd come with took her to the pier. He left her hidden behind a restaurant while he ran to call for help, using a payphone so he couldn't be tracked, which is where she had a heart attack and died, alone, next to a trashcan.

It was an awful, horrifying story. Shock and grief spread through the high school and the entire South Bay, stabbing at everyone's hearts. Scarlet was beside herself. Lisa immediately got her into counseling but that was about the only place she would go, the rest of the time she spent in her room either sleeping or crying. It wasn't until the last week of January when Pete was able to coax her back to school, and at the end of that week, the last day of January, Lisa's mother died.

It didn't come as a big surprise, although she had been doing better over the holidays, so much so that Lisa had a glimmer of hope for a recovery. She was able to make it to the table for most meals with the family, even though she didn't always eat. She watched all the Christmas movies with Lisa's youngest two, Jackson and Jade, both of them cozied up by her side on the sofa. She learned to play video games with Stosh from his PlayStation and Wii. She helped Lisa stuff and address their Christmas cards, a task that was originally delegated to Scarlet but quickly abandoned by the first cell phone ring. Christmas morning Lisa had noticed her mom's eyes were bright and she looked happy and engaged as they sat on the sofa sipping mulled cider and nibbling coffee cake together. They watched the kids unwrap their gifts as her mother stroked the children's soft little heads when they brought their presents over to her, their faces beaming.

But almost immediately after Christmas she went downhill and Lisa's hopes were extinguished. I was on my way to pick up Casey from preschool when Pete called with the news that Lisa's mom had passed in her sleep. Lisa, he said, was busy taking care of details, but I imagined she was so heartbroken she couldn't tell me directly. Naturally we all rallied around her and her family, circling the wagons and showering her with love and whatever help we could offer: dinners, help with funeral plans, childcare and the general chaos that is life, especially in a house with four children. Ramona, I think, was over there morning to night every day for a month. She claimed to love it, though, because she was now missing her own grandchildren she had met for the first time over the holidays.

If anyone needed a vacation, it was Lisa. I couldn't provide that, but I could get her out with her friends for an evening. And miraculously we were all able to meet at Adventureland, our local playzone, on a Tuesday afternoon the first week of March to figure out our schedules.

I pulled into the parking lot and helped Griffin out of the car, holding onto both boys' hands like a vice so they didn't dart across the parking lot. They had played here a million times but somehow never seemed to tire of the climbing mazes, rope swings, slick slides, sport court and ball pit. I couldn't help but smile as I watched them sprint to the equipment shouting "Race ya!"

It took a minute while I scanned the place before I spotted my friends in the toddler room and I had to let out a laugh. Sierra was busy playing with toys by herself in the corner while Lexie, Lisa, Jackie and Ramona all sat criss-cross applesauce in the middle, chatting away. I stashed my shoes in a cubby and joined them, kissing and hugging my hellos and letting slip a comment about the well-supervised children.

"They all seem happy," Jackie said with a shrug, looking around the maze above her. "We were just saying that if we were allowed to have food and drinks in this place, it would be the hottest ticket in town."

"If I had a latte right now, I'd be in heaven," Lisa agreed. She looked tired and worn out.

"If I had a margarita right now, I'd be in heaven," Lexie added, giving me the perfect segue into the MNO conversation.

Over the roar of screaming and giggling children, we sat in the toddler area trying to figure out the where, what and when of our next MNO. It shouldn't have been so tricky, but we kept getting interrupted and had to referee a squabble or check on an injury, and just when we thought we had it, someone would need to be taken to the bathroom. Finally, there seemed to be a lull in neediness and we were able to have a bit of a conversation.

"How about a trip to the spa?" Lexie suggested, trying to sound innocent. "I haven't been in ages."

"Duh," I replied, "that's because you've been banned for life from the place. After what happened last time, I'm never going to the spa with you again."

"Agreed," Lisa said grimacing. "Not so relaxing."

Lexie huffed. "It's not like L.A. is a one-spa town. There's more than one."

"They've circulated your photo to all of them," Lisa said. "We got you out of your first mug shot once already, I'm not doing it again," Lisa quipped.

"Oh that wouldn't have been my first," Lexie stated nonchalantly as we all stared. "What?" she said, looking around. "It's a long story. Trespassing. Stolen samurai suit. Too much vodka. 'Nough said," and with that she waved off the rest of the inquiry.

"I have an idea," Ramona offered. She lowered her voice so we had to lean in just a little to hear her. "Do you guys think you're ready for a *real* stakeout?"

We all remained quiet, waiting to hear more except Jackie, who cackled, "Oooh wee! I just love a good steak out!" We all looked at her. "Sorry," she giggled. "That was a line from *Clifford* this morning. The dogs were detectives. That was my Cleo impression."

"I love that episode," I said, smiling. "We're huge Clifford aficionados."

Lisa looked at Ramona. "What, exactly, are you talking about, when you say *real stakeout*?"

Ramona smiled. "Well, unlike the spontaneous one we did back at the Hedges' house, where I fell into the bushes, I think we've all honed our skills a little over the last year and maybe we're ready for a real one. Like in cars. Watching a house. Gathering information, binoculars, cameras with big lenses and stuff. You know, like a real stakeout. How about it? It's different, possibly exciting, and here's the thing..."

She went on to explain that the drug dealers she'd been watching seemed to be gearing up for a big summer. That despite the slight increase in police activity since Nicole's death, the *All Nighter* and the *Al Rescate* down at the marina had tripled their comings and goings.

"Where do they go?" Lexie asked.

"I have no idea," Ramona answered. "But I'm working on it."

"They can't be selling that much product just on the pier," Lisa said.

"They aren't. They have a few other spots they like, I've tracked them." Ramona looked coyly at us all. "It would not surprise me at all if they were the ones to sell that boy the stuff that killed Nicole."

Of course all of us had thought of that, but nobody could prove it. But to hear it out loud from our up-close and personal expert was still a shock.

"I don't know," Jackie said, looking cautiously at Lisa. "Lisa's been through the ringer. Maybe we should do something not so crazy, like a chick flick or a mani-pedi? I think she needs to just chill."

"Please. Don't pass up a good stakeout on my account," Lisa said. "Especially one that might put those guys away. Besides, a little action might do me some good. A chick flick will probably just make me cry. And trust me, I'm tired of crying." She gave us a weak little smile. Jackie put her arm around her and gave her a squeeze.

"That's the spirit," Ramona stated. "Listen, I know it's not a chick-flick," she looked at Jackie, "or a kegger," she looked at Lexie, "or a top secret mission," she looked at me, "but if I can get a couple of photos of the leader of this crew, well, I think that would be enough to take to the police, then they could deal with these assholes."

"Let's try to keep the profanity down in the toddler pit," Lisa said under her breath.

"Oh yeah, sorry, I forgot," Ramona said covering her mouth and looking around to see if any of the little people by the Velcro wall had heard her. "Anyway, I just want to drive up to the house in the hills and watch for a little bit. Try to see what they are doing inside and get some photos. They keep talking about this meeting at the end of the month, someone important will be there."

We all shrugged and looked at each other. "I'm in as long as we do a kegger next time. With beer bongs," Lexie said flashing her smile.

"A stakeout it is," I said.

We marked out calendars for the Tuesday before Easter. Ramona smiled. "It's settled then. My house. Pre-stakeout drinks start at seven."

Nineteen

That Tuesday could not come fast enough for me. All week long in anticipation I had the boys practicing spying, taking cover, rolling to get to better coverage disguising ourselves. And now, on the night of the actual event I was so thrilled we were doing an honest to goodness stake out that I even put on my leather pants knowing full well that Lexie was going to make fun of me. It didn't matter. We were close to catching them, Ramona had said.

I had it in my head that this would be easy, a cake walk. We'd just roll up silently, drink a little wine and chat in the car while Ramona clicked away with her telephoto lens. We could then send the info on to the authorities—the DEA or the FBI, whatever—and get these guys out of our town, out of our community, out of our lives, for good.

I was ready. To be honest, I was really tired of being worried about it all, about them. Tired of being vigilant when we went to the beach. I wanted to get back to being worried about normal stuff, like being attacked by killer African bees or catching malaria. I was done with these idiots, these menaces to society. And I was willing to do my part to accomplish our task for what I hoped was our last mission. I had somehow distilled everything Ramona had said down to the fact that we only needed this one photo, and for that I was going to take my role seriously. Thus, when Mark whistled at me as I kissed the boys good night, I smiled smugly. No doubt he thought us gals were going dancing. I wasn't even out of the house yet and I'd already deceived the one person who was supposed to know me best. Heh, heh, heh.

On my way to Ramona's I played some spy tunes and got my game face on. I even had a retort planned for Lexie. But when I walked in and heard her call out, "Hey! Cat woman!" instead of teasing her right back my jaw dropped when I saw that she, too, was wearing black leather pants. And a matching halter. I had to drop my tough guy persona because I couldn't help but smile.

"Oh my God!" I said as she greeted me with a hug and I let out a laugh. "Did you buy those special for tonight?"

"Second hand store, baby," she replied. "I've been telling myself the previous owner was a Playboy Bunny."

"No fair," I scoffed, "you look like a model in yours."

"You *both* look like models," Lisa chimed in.

"We should get you a pair!" I exclaimed, my eyes lighting up. "How fun would that be?"

"They don't make leather pants for people my size," Lisa said passing around a tray of deviled eggs and adding before she could be interrupted, "If they do, they shouldn't. They belong exclusively on the thin, hip crowd, not the portly middle-aged crowd."

"You're not middle-aged *or* portly," Jackie said to Lisa. "You'd probably look better than you think, they can be very flattering." Lisa gave her a *you-gotta-be-kidding-me* look. "Okay, okay, so they aren't the best look for everyone, including myself. I'll stick with my yoga pants, thank you very much."

"We should get Ramona some. I'm sure they make them in purple. Or orange. Or neon-paisley-patchwork-plaid." Lexie said, her arm dangling over my shoulder. "Where is she anyway?"

"She called from the marina about an hour ago," Jackie said. "Said she was running late but she'd be here. Gave me instructions to get the food out and start the party without her. Here, try a crab cake. They're really good."

We settled into Ramona's living room, gabbing about life and what was going on with our kids and husbands, noshing on the 70's style appetizers that were surprisingly tasty while sipping rosé. I had almost forgotten we were supposed to be going on a mission when Ramona came home.

She soared into the room like a hawk, quiet and fast. I could smell the night air on her. Her hair looked a little disheveled and her face was pink, either from running up the stairs or from the chilly night air and together they made her look youthful, alive and a little edgy. She was clearly invigorated.

"We did it," she exclaimed as she joined us. "We caught them!"

"Caught who?" I asked?

"Who's 'we'?" Jackie wanted to know, her eyebrow raised.

"I meant I," she said guardedly to Jackie. "I caught them, *the dealers!*" then, turning to me, "I figured out part of their process, where they go in those boats."

"Where?" we all asked together as if on cue.

"You'll never guess," she said, shaking her head. "Catalina."

The room erupted into gasps and questions and she settled us down with her hands. "I'll tell you a little bit now but then we've got to hurry. I bugged the dock and they mentioned the name of the guy they're meeting with tonight, 'Alfonzo.' They said he was at the house waiting for them. I think it might be their boss so I want to make sure we get up there soon so listen."

She quickly told us how she'd been trying to track them each time they left the marina farther and farther out into the ocean, but couldn't follow them too closely or too far because she knew she'd be discovered. "But today I got lucky. That or they got sloppy."

Following a hunch, she had sailed to Catalina last night and had moored her boat at Avalon, the only town on the island. In the morning she proceeded to sail around Catalina, and she kept sailing. All day, doing loops around the island, keeping an eye out for the dealers while trying not to look suspicious.

"Wait," Lexie said. "You did this all by yourself?"

Ramona brushed Lexie's question off and continued with her story. Lexie listened but looked around at all of us and I noticed Jackie mouth the word "Bill" to her.

"It worked," Ramona continued. "I kept my distance but I knew it was them," she said, telling us how she watched them through her high-powered binoculars pull their boat up to a make-shift dock on the deserted back side of the island, then the captain let two men off who disappeared into the brush with several coolers. A few hours later the same boat picked them up and they returned to the Redondo marina.

"Did you see any smoke?" Lisa asked.

"No," Ramona answered, her eyes meeting Lisa's as though they shared a secret. "That would be too obvious. I bet they cook at night."

"You think they are actually cooking meth over there?" Jackie asked, almost under her breath.

"Possibly, whatever they're doing it's a brilliant location. That side of the island is completely uninhabited. The brush and trees are thick, the hillside's steep. There's no real place to dock a boat. DEA planes or boats can't see through the foliage. If they're cooking, the ocean breeze would carry the fumes away, but I don't know. They're obviously doing something, maybe just packaging the stuff they get from other places. I'd bet my life they've built some kind of bunker."

We all burst into various forms of congratulations, all of us marveling at her detective work, her tenacity. "It's not over yet," she said cautiously. "We still have work to do."

She immediately fell into the role of commander, addressing us as if we were her crack, top-secret commando squad whose mission was to stake out the home of the kingpin she had yet to identify. The excitement and anticipation in the room was palpable. In a drill-sergeant-like manner she explained our night's mission: to get photos of anyone, she repeated *anyone,* inside the house. This included housekeepers, girlfriends, children, and of course, the drug dealers. Plus, we were to gather the license plate numbers and the make or model of any car on the property. Ramona had analyzed the situation and somehow decided it would be best to take two cars—Lisa's and mine were chosen because they were both black—so we could get different viewpoints of the house. Lexie and Jackie were to ride with me while Ramona would ride with Lisa.

Ramona left for a moment then returned with a large black duffle bag of supplies. From the bag she handed a pair of binoculars to Jackie, who took them and immediately began to practice, looking more like a bird watcher than a spy. She handed both Lexie and Lisa a 35mm digital camera with a high-powered telephoto lens and explained that all they needed to do was point and shoot.

She then took out a map and laid it on the table. We huddled over a blown up version of Palos Verdes. It had the location of the house we would be staking out circled in red marker plus she had blown up a satellite view of the property courtesy of Google Earth. She showed me and Lisa exactly where to park and gave us tips on the best routes in and out of what would appear to be a well-cased neighborhood.

After fielding a few questions, Ramona cleared her throat and spoke. "I'm not much for sentiment, but I want you all to know how much this means to me. You could be out at the movies or sipping chocolate martinis or some other God-forsaken drink at some hip bar and instead you are spending your precious MNO time sitting in a boring car, and for that I thank you.

"I've spent more hours than I care to admit watching these assholes. I've got lots of intel on them, and I'm hopeful that tonight's mission will provide the last bit to put them away, especially in light of what happened to Nicole. The world will function better without them."

We nodded and hugged her, telling her there was no place we'd rather be, that we were in this together.

"Thank you, thank you. That's enough," she said, waving us off, embarrassed by her sentimental bravado. "Now get your gear. Let's go."

"Wait!" I cried, "I've got some gear, too!"

I dashed over to my bag while I heard Lexie utter, "Oh God, here we go again." I ignored her, rummaging through the diapers, wipes, crayons and plastic spoons and came up with Casey's plastic walkie-talkies. "Here," I said handing one to Ramona, "now we can keep in touch without phone records."

Lisa furrowed her brow. "What's wrong with phone records?"

209

I shrugged. "It's always the piece of evidence that's the cornerstone of the case."

"For the *bad* guys," Lexie injected.

"Details," I shrugged, smiling. "It's more fun this way. Besides, better safe than sorry."

"Take 'em," Ramona said. "Cell coverage is patchy up there."

We picked up our gear and headed out the door toward our cars. Lisa and Ramona were gone in a flash, something Ramona had recommended because she didn't want us all arriving at the same time. Meanwhile, Jackie slipped into the back seat of my black Highlander, sandwiching herself between Casey's and Griffin's car seats while Lexie took shotgun. I hopped into the driver's seat then, looking sly, turned to Jackie and Lexie with a grin. "Are you guys ready for this?"

They looked at each other with a weary expression, then back at me as I blasted the theme song from the Bourne Identity. "This will get us into the mood!" I called out, doing an "action-spy" dance in my seat. Jackie and Lexie covered their ears and exchanged glances. "Don't think I can't see you," I yelled. "I have eyes in the back of my head."

"And not much between your ears," Lexie yelled back.

"Somehow I don't feel very stealth," Jackie shouted over the music. I turned down the stereo.

"Just trying to psych us all up," I said. "Don't you feel better?"

"To sit in a car and stare out a window? Mission accomplished," Jackie affirmed.

"Come on, Nancy Drew, let's go before Ramona makes us do push-ups or run laps," Lexie motioned with her head. "I need you to make a stop first."

"A mystery stop," I said, narrowing my eyes as I turned on the car and rubbed my hands together. "Most excellent."

I put the car in gear and drove down the dark side streets of Ramona's neighborhood then turned south on PCH. We were about to turn up the hill to Palos Verdes when Lexie instructed me to keep going and to pull into the well-lit parking lot of Safeway.

"Hmmmm," I raised an eyebrow and cut the engine. "A seemingly normal grocery store. Could be a front for something more…dangerous."

"I'll just be a sec," Lexie gave a shake of her head, slid out of the seat and dashed inside. Ten minutes later Jackie and I were still waiting. We had listened to all the spy songs I had downloaded on my phone and Jackie had crimped, braided or BeDazzled everything that wasn't nailed down in my car. We were beginning to worry that Ramona really would make us do push-ups or jumping jacks as penance for being so late.

"What the heck could she be doing in there?" I asked, squinting and trying to see Lexie beyond the boxes that were stacked up against the front windows.

"I don't know," Jackie replied. She had unbuckled her seatbelt and was leaning forward between the front two seats. "Maybe Safeway sells night-vision goggles? Or pepper spray? Tasers?"

"Binoculars," I said, thrusting out my hand like a surgeon asking for a scalpel. Jackie sat back, rummaged through her bag and handed me the pair Ramona had given her. I put them to my eyes and began scanning the store. They were nice. I was used to the fake, plastic toy version but these were smooth, high powered, heavy and professional. "There she is. I see her."

"What's she doing?" Jackie asked, squinting through the windshield.

"She's in the checkout line…she's got her credit card out…she's flirting with the bagger guy…she's headed toward the door pushing her cart…she's got…she's got…"

"What?" Jackie asked eagerly scooting up closer. By now we had both convinced ourselves that there might seriously be a secret aisle of Safeway we'd never been down before that sold spy equipment. "What's in her cart?"

"It looks like…like…

"What?! Like what?"

"Cupcakes."

"Cupcakes?"

"And juice boxes."

"What?!"

"And a whole watermelon."

"What's she planning on doing, giving the dealers a snack?"

"I have no idea," I said still looking through the binoculars. "Maybe she's hoping to take them out slowly with tooth decay?"

"I see," Jackie said. "A surreptitious plaque attack. Very clever." She laughed maniacally, tossing her head back.

Her laugh was enough to break me out of the commando character I'd been adamantly playing since Ramona's house, and we both got the giggles. We were still at it when Lexie opened the door.

"What's so funny?" she asked, loading the groceries into the back of the car. She also had several packs of Goldfish and peanut butter crackers.

"We were just marveling at your sly plot to rid our fine town of drug dealers by giving them all a well-balanced snack," I said.

"And we see there are no toothbrushes in your provisions. We applaud your attempt to kill them off, one cavity at a time," Jackie added.

Lexie chuckled and rolled her eyes as she climbed back in and shut the door. "It just so happens that I'm snack mom tomorrow at Cash's school and we'll be celebrating his birthday. I'm totally out of food and it was either stay home and be Martha Stewart or go out with you guys."

"Martha is so totally overrated," I said, putting out my fist for both Lexie and Jackie to pound.

"Damn straight," Lexie said, tapping my fist with her own.

"Though some of her stuff is seriously cool," Jackie said, tapping both our fists.

"Let's rock," Lexie said, buckling her seatbelt.

We were soon racing up the steep, windy hillside that was dotted with multi-million dollar Mediterranean-style mansions on huge estates that boasted perfectly manicured and terraced landscapes. The road hugged the steep hill and in places came so close to the edge that you could see the rocks jutting out of the ocean hundreds of feet below. It was a stunningly beautiful evening with the moon casting a shimmering path across the Pacific. The winds were mild, making it warm enough to not even need a jacket—a rarity at the coast, even in summer—and I felt the satisfying sensation of loving where I lived, that it was where I belonged, and knowing it was worth fighting for.

We soon arrived in the drug dealers' neighborhood and, as instructed, I shut off my headlights as we drove the last few blocks. All the homes in this section of Palos Verdes were humongous and sat on lots that were three acres at bare minimum, a shocking amount of land compared to the houses that were built on 2500 square foot lots in some places close to downtown Hermosa and the beach.

Ten-thousand square feet was the average size of these houses. Ramona had called a real estate agent and posed as a potential client so she knew the stats. They included in-home theaters, wine cellars, spas, pools, outdoor kitchens, fire pits and incredible three-hundred and sixty degree views of the Pacific Ocean from Malibu down to the Orange County coast, Catalina, the lights of L.A. and the San Bernadino mountains to the east.

Many were protected by high-security fencing and tall hedges. They had vast lawns landscaped with indigenous bougainvillea, palms, citrus trees, rosemary, Birds of Paradise, and jasmine. Real estate moguls, foreign investors, sports stars, investment bankers and the occasional Hollywood celebrity occupied this serene hilltop paradise.

The particular house we were casing sat high above the road and shared the crest of the hill with only one other property to the east, giving the drug dealers perfect, unobstructed Pacific views. The house itself was a fairly new Mediterranean-style mansion. Ramona had looked it up online and found it had seven-bedrooms, fifteen-thousand square feet, an indoor and outdoor pool, multiple living areas, and a bowling alley. It was beautifully landscaped with citrus and palm trees close to the house, a patio large enough to land a helicopter, and fabulous fountains randomly situated all over the property. The entire perimeter was lined with ten-foot high wrought iron fencing.

"Wow," Jackie said as we pulled up and parked, as instructed, across the street from the property on the dirt shoulder of the road. "Business must be good."

Lexie shook her head in disgust. "Too fucking good. I hate these guys. Just looking at their house makes me want to puke on it and then blow it up."

"I wonder how many homes like this they have," I said in awe.

Jackie unbuckled her seatbelt and leaned forward between me and Lexie. "You think they have more than one?" she asked incredulously, peering at the mansion.

"Wouldn't surprise me," Lexie said. "Assholes."

"I bet they paid cash," I stated. "Unbelievable."

"Man," Jackie said, almost in a whisper, "this is not what I pictured at all. I kind of thought we were going to case out a small broken down house with laundry hanging outside and a chain-link fence, maybe some sad-looking broken toys on the lawn. Or at least some non-descript typical suburban house. Not the Taj Mahal."

"You're thinking of the crack houses where their customers live. Where the parents are so doped up the babies have to raise themselves," Lexie said, disgusted.

"I can handle the thought of grown-ups screwing up their own lives," I said, the rage in me beginning to boil. "But when they abandon or abuse their kids, it makes me crazy. And the dealers love that they've hooked customers. They give out free samples, for crying out lout. I swear I could kill them."

My last statement was just an expression, people use it off-handedly every day. I couldn't kill spiders, or the mouse that had moved into our garage. I trapped these things and released them down the street. But I had come to really, really hate these guys. They were doing nothing to make the world better. Just the opposite, actually. On purpose. For profit. It surprised me when I wondered—briefly and to myself—if I really could.

Twenty

It didn't take long for us to get bored. After texting Lisa that we were in position and watching the house for a good ten minutes without seeing a shadow stir, Lexie decided it was time to get the party started.

"Know what pairs well with a stake-out?" she said, busting out a bottle of cabernet from a new winemaker in Paso Robles she wanted us to try. "This cab. Now check out these skills every spy-slash-secret agent should possess."

In slow motion with the occasional "Ki-yah!" or similar sound effect, she whipped out a bottle opener, zipped off the wrapper, popped out the cork and poured three glasses without spilling a drop.

"Nice work, soldier," I said. I, too, was bored, but determined to take it seriously and stay in character.

"I had no idea I was so close to greatness," Jackie said.

"Oh, I have skills," Lexie said, looking at Jackie from the corner of her eyes.

We talked idly for a while until Lexi pulled a word game from her bag. Between that and the wine we got to laughing and wisecracking just like it was a normal MNO at someone's house instead of the confines of my car outside the headquarters of a serious drug dealer. They tried to get me to play, but I decided *someone* needed to watch the house, to take this thing seriously.

"Hey you guys, look here," Jackie said, after we'd been there for at least forty-five minutes. Lexie and I looked back to see Jackie with her camera out, pointing it at us. "Smile!"

Shocked, I looked over to see Lexie hold up her glass of wine as if toasting Jackie, looking every bit as though she could be in a magazine. I looked back at Jackie in horror as she clicked off a few photos. I made a grab for her camera. "What exactly do you think you're doing?"

"Well," Jackie said eagerly, "I'm going to scrapbook this stakeout." She sat back and fumbled around in her bag then brought out a *Keepsakes* magazine. She quickly turned to a page she had dog-eared and set it up on the center console to show us. "Look," she said, excitedly, tapping the page with her finger, "Ali Edwards did this fantastic layout that I can tweak just a little bit and make it perfect. I'll put the title right here in this fantastic camouflage chipboard I just found at Michaels. I was thinking 'Stakeout with My Sisters,' or something catchy like that. What do you think?" She looked up with a grin to find Lexie smiling, and me glaring at her.

"What do I think?" I snarled. "I think you need to put that stuff away!" I pushed the magazine back at her and surprised even myself with how harsh my tone was. "Especially the camera. Are you nuts?"

Jackie looked a little confused but insisted, "Oh, don't worry, I've got the camera on my night setting. The photos will turn out great, even in the dark. I'll email them to you. Here, I can show you now—." She began to switch the camera into 'view' mode so I could see but I stopped her.

"Put that down," I said, looking quickly at the house then back at her. "That's not what I'm worried about. Do you want them to see us? With your flash we might as well light up a neon sign that says 'STAKEOUT IN PROGRESS' or send them an email that we're out here. We're supposed to be stealth, remember? Not to mention, there's just something inherently wrong with scrapping a *stakeout*. It's like buying Twinkies at Whole Foods." I felt terrible the instant the words were out of my mouth but I couldn't help myself.

Lexie looked at me and then back at Jackie, who looked hurt and defeated. "Don't worry about sarge here," she said to Jackie, "she can

216

get a little swept up in the moment," and then under her breath, "hence the leather pants." She took a deep breath and then declared, "I say if we don't see any action in another ten minutes or so, we call Ramona and tell her we're taking this party to the overlook. You obviously need another drink," she said reaching for my cup and topping it off. She took a sip straight from the bottle, wiped her mouth with the back of her hand. She looked at me and grabbed for the binoculars I was holding. "Whole Foods *should* sell Twinkies. That damn place takes itself way too seriously." She raised her eyebrows at me then put the binoculars to her eyes and scanned the house, which had lights on, but still had shown no sign of life.

We sat quietly for several minutes, all three of us staring ahead at the house, sipping our wine. I felt terrible about scolding Jackie, and Lexie's reply made me think back to that MNO at my house when I cajoled everyone into taking our rare evenings together and making them into a bad guy patrol. The anniversary of that meeting was right around the corner. It had been almost a year and we felt like we had really accomplished quite a bit. Our latest metrics showed that petty crime was down in all categories. The Crime Blotter in the South Bay News hadn't reported a major incident, like an abduction or a shooting, in at least three months. But Lexie was right, the others had only agreed to my little project if our first priority was having fun together.

I took a sip and looked over my shoulder to Jackie and asked, "Did you say Ali Edwards did that layout?"

"Uh huh," Jackie replied.

"I just love her designs," I said looking over my shoulder apologetically.

"Me, too," Jackie said, breaking into a big grin. She got the magazine back out. "She's my absolute fave. Let me show you how cool it's going to look."

We huddled over the layout as Jackie began illustrating her vision for her perfect scrapbook page, complete with a jet-black background, camouflage chipboard and spy-style embellishments like a bomb, missile, cell phone and dark glasses. As we looked it over, me wishing desperately that Jackie was in charge of my kids' baby books, we heard a faint, scratchy but audible voice saying, *"Hello? Hello? Are you there?"*

I looked up from our huddle and kind of cocked my head to the side. "Shhh! You guys, do you hear something?" Lexie and Jackie froze and listened.

"Hello? Hello? We have a problem here guys!"

"What is that?" Jackie asked, head darting left to right.

We tried to pinpoint where the voice was coming from and then realized it was coming from the front of the car, somewhere down by Lexie's ankles.

"The walkie talkie!" I blurted out when Lexie lifted her purse off of the floor. "I forgot we had it."

"It's me, Lisa," came the response. "We have a serious problem."

Lexie snapped the gadget right out of my hands, smiled and pressed the button. "Uptown One this is Downtown Two," she said playfully, making her voice a little lower and adding a bit of a southern accent for some reason. "What's your ten-twenty, Mother Bird? This here's Rubber Duckie and we have a major convoy and we're now sittin' at LZ1. Ten-four roger that, come back."

"Enough already," I said laughing and grabbing it back.

"What? You're the only one who gets to use the walkie-talkie? Lame." She turned to Jackie in the backseat and said in a whisper she clearly wanted me to hear, "I bet I have better radio skills. Did you just hear me speak in code? We're less than one hundred yards from the drug dealers home and I totally just narced them out, but they would never even know it if the call was intercepted. Ha!" She looked at me mischievously. "Go on, Chief. Let's hear your radioese."

"No way," I spat back. "None of what you said even made sense. You can't just string together quotes from movies where people were using radios."

"Although the line from *Proof of Life* was a nice touch," Jackie interjected.

Lexie smiled graciously, "Thank you. Such a great movie."

"If I had been that woman and Russell Crowe's character came to help me, I'd have done him in a nanosecond, too," Jackie said. "No contest."

"Ladies, please," I interjected, "could we get back to the mission at hand? Our associates are in need of our assistance." I spoke loudly and clearly into the walkie-talkie for some reason, as if I was talking to someone who didn't understand English. "Uptown One, this is Downtown Two, what seems to be the problem?" I let go of the button and held the walkie-talkie up for everyone to hear.

Lexie was smug. "See? You're even copying my line."

Lisa came back over the gadget and with a panic-stricken edge to her voice. "Serious problem here guys. Ramona has just jumped out of the car. She said she was going in for a closer look."

We looked at each other, completely dumbfounded, then looked the hundred yards or so toward Lisa's car, trying to spot her.

"In? In *where*?" I replied, shock causing me to drop completely out of character.

"I'm not sure exactly, but for now she's headed into the yard." Lisa replied, "She drugged the guard dogs by dropping meat coated in crushed-up Ambien over the fence using a remote control helicopter. And I'm not kidding—I think she's lost it. I was right here as she did it. She told me to watch for her through the binoculars. Said that if anyone catches her, she'll fake Alzheimer's and that I should then go to the front door and say I was looking for my poor demented mother who often gets lost around here."

"What the fuck?!" Jackie was the first to say, echoing all our sentiments as she grabbed for the binoculars and moved up so she was now sitting on the front console between Lexie and me. "Did she just say Ramona *drugged* the guard dogs? With *Ambien*? She can't be serious. There's no way she's serious. This has got to be a joke."

"Lisa," I said hesitantly into the walkie talkie, "Could you please repeat that?"

"Guys?" Lisa's voice rang out over the walkie-talkie. "There's more. I just looked inside her duffle bag and it's not good."

We could hear her ruffling through the bag, calling out items as she went. "She's got shoelaces, extra binoculars, several hand guns, a small tape recorder, a black sweatshirt, some duct tape, a few spare pre-paid phones still in their boxes, a small Winnie the Pooh make-up bag filled with bullets, a Taser gun, pepper spray, and,…oh fuck."

My stomach jumped at this. Unlike Lexie and Jackie, Lisa almost never swore. I'd only heard her curse once, when we saw a dog get hit by a car. I knew her profanity was reserved for only the most drastic situations. I held my breath and we all froze, waiting for her to continue.

"You guys, she's got tear gas, some grenades and what looks like several homemade pipe bombs in here."

We all gasped. If I didn't know how serious a person Lisa was, especially in light of what she had recently dealt with, I would have thought she was pranking us.

Both the volume and pitch of my voice went up several notches. "Lisa, why didn't you go after her?"

"I couldn't," Lisa replied defensively, almost shouting. "I was shocked, and she took off like a friggin' rocket. For a little old woman, she's fast! 'Spritely' does not cover it. I couldn't exactly tackle her in the middle of the street."

"Holy shit," I said more to myself than anyone else, feeling nauseated as my stomach did a flip. I let the walkie-talkie fall out of my hand and into my lap, turned to Lexie and Jackie. They were both as shocked and scared as me. "What do we do?"

Lexie grabbed the walkie-talkie. "Lisa, this is Lexie. Do you know where she is now?"

"I lost track of her almost immediately," Lisa answered. "She's wearing a dark green jump suit, a black sunhat, black fuzzy slippers and a black Hello Kitty fanny pack. She just disappeared into the landscaping."

"Hello Kitty?" Lex and I both said in unison, looking at each other.

"What do you think she has in there?" Jackie asked, still scanning the fence line with the binoculars.

"I don't know, but I bet it's not friendship bracelets and hair bows," Lexie said.

"We need to call the cops," Jackie insisted, taking the binoculars down for a second to look at us. Lexie picked them up and began scanning the fence line.

"And tell them what?" Lexie asked. "That our geriatric friend has flown the coop? That she is now trespassing on drug-dealer territory? Oh, and that we have several pipe bombs in our possession?"

"Yes, whatever," Jackie replied, "I don't care. Anything to get her out of there. She can't be in her right mind."

"Calling the cops would totally wreck all of Ramona's hard work," I said, thinking Ramona wouldn't get the picture she needed and I wouldn't get to stop worrying. "The dealers would know she's on to them and they'd temporarily pull up operations. She'd be pissed and I, for one, do not want to face the wrath of Ramona," I said. Of course the smart move would be to call the cops, but we were so close. I wanted to salvage the mission, no matter what the cost.

"I'd rather face her wrath than attend her funeral," Jackie said. "I'm calling the police."

"Wait!" Lexie said. "I see her!"

"Where?" both Jackie and I inched closer to the windshield, squinting.

"She's on the other side of the fence. Near that big rock outcropping. How the hell did she get in there? Oh my God, it looks like she's putting leashes on the dogs. Shit, I didn't even see those dogs. And...and now she's attaching the leashes to the fence." I looked hard and could barely see a tiny, fragile silhouette scrunched next to the fence, her white face the only thing that didn't blend perfectly into the night.

"This. Is. Crazy," I said, almost in a whisper, shaking my head and wondering what Ramona was really up to. I looked over at Lexie and gave her a weak smile. "I'll go get her."

"What? Are you fucking out of your mind?" Lexie shouted. "We don't need *two* Rambos out there!"

"Someone needs to," I said resolutely, trying to sound more confident than I felt while convincing myself that it would be quick, that I could talk her out of whatever she was trying to do. "She's just at the fence line. I'll go talk some sense into her, and then I'll be right back. As long as no cars come by or no one new shows up, we should be fine. And if they do, we'll just use the Alzheimer's excuse. Besides," I said, giving Lexie a slight shrug and the edge of a smile, "I *am* dressed for the part."

Before she or Jackie could stop me, I slid out of the car and ran across the street, hunched down, the way I had been practicing with my boys for months. The traffic was nonexistent so I really didn't expect someone to see me, but you never knew, someone might have been out walking their dog or driving home from dinner and I just didn't want any added attention. I really didn't want Jackie or any of the others to call the cops, it would ruin all of Ramona's hard work and we were so close. I would have to get to her and talk some sense into her. As much as I wanted these guys caught, there had to be another way.

When I got to the fence line where Ramona had leashed up the dogs, she was gone. It was so very dark, there wasn't a single street light anywhere. The lights of L.A. sparkled below like a sea full of Tinker Bells, but up here it was pitch black. I frantically scanned the area, looking up the vast property toward the house. Then I spotted her, dashing up the hillside, hugging the hedges on what I assumed was the property line.

"Ramona!" I whisper-yelled, but it was no use, she was too far ahead to hear me. I would have needed a megaphone to get her attention. I trotted along the fence line, keeping my eye on her, calling again and again, my heart pounding. I had so much adrenaline pumping through my body I felt like I'd eaten a box of chocolates, washed it down with a pot of coffee with a Red Bull chaser. I'd nearly decided to go back to the car and get the consensus of what the other gals thought we should do. Then I found the gate.

It was hidden by some bougainvillea and Birds of Paradise and left slightly ajar, no doubt by our crazy friend, who figured she'd be coming back out this way. I looked at it and thought of the dealers, of how badly I wanted them gone. Then I thought of Ramona, who so clearly seemed to be in control. She had cased the dealers at the pier. She had tracked their boat to the marina, picked the lock, disarmed the alarm and found their money.

She had tracked them to this house and knew all about them, their operation, their boss, their property taxes for Christ's sake. All she needed, she said, was one little photo and she could turn over all her evidence to the police who could then bust them out of our town and our lives. She must have done her homework. She must know what she's doing. I pictured her sitting under a windowsill, hidden in her camouflaged outfit, clicking away with some sort of high-tech spy camera completely undetected by the men inside.

But then I thought of how she had fallen over in the bushes—*twice*. And I pictured her falling outside the windowsill, the men catching her, everything we'd all worked for crumbling to pieces. I thought of her age, and how people I knew who were younger were having hip and knee replacements. *Just one photo*, I whispered to myself knowing that if I didn't act immediately, I'd lose track of her inside the huge jungle of a yard. I looked back at my car where I knew Lexie and Jackie were watching me through the binoculars and raised a finger to let them know I'd be back in a minute. And honestly, at the time, I really did believe I'd be back in a minute or two. Five at the most. Then I slipped inside.

Twenty-One

My mind was all over the place as I sprinted for the edge of the property, trying to catch up with Ramona. What if the yard was booby-trapped? What if the gate had a silent alarm? What if the dogs woke up? What if it took Ramona longer than she thought to get the picture? Would she be willing to throw in the towel? What if she wasn't? Should I leave her? Could I tackle, hog tie and drag her back with me? What were the gals doing back in the car? Could they help?

The house was a football field's length up a fairly steep hill. At the top was the back patio and a pool, both lit by glaring security lights. I stopped quickly to shoot off a text to the gals in the car, then caught sight of Ramona fifty feet ahead of me scrunched below hedges and made a mad dash for her. Hoping to get her attention, I tried out some bird calls to no avail and when I was finally on her, I added peacock attack to my list of worries since they were known to roam wild on the hill, and I must have sounded like one in heat.

She jumped about ten feet when I grabbed her shoulder. She whisper-yelped, "Oh! Jesus Christ, Kelly!" and put her hand to her heart. "You practically gave me a heart attack! What are you doing?"

She looked mad, actually, not only shocked, but really angry like a totally different person, and I was a little taken aback. "You might need some help," I said defensively. My voice sounded small and childlike. "To get the photo?"

"Do you know how dangerous this is?" she hissed, her eyes stabbing at me in the dark. "Those men in there are not joking around. This is not one of your pretend missions."

"I know," I said, keeping my voice down, trying to sound like I knew what I was in for but not really understanding until right now, at this moment, when I saw the fear and anxiety in Ramona's face. My stomach lurched and I felt the cabernet churn as I realized that the calm, collected, totally-in-control Ramona I had so much faith in had been replaced by one that was out of her league, and knew it. I couldn't physically drag her down the hill, she would probably karate chop me. What was I supposed to do now? Run back to the car without her and let her fend for herself, especially after she had just openly admitted this was a dangerous situation? I told myself there was safety in numbers, that we just needed to hustle, that again, we had that illustrious element of surprise going for us. I knew it was naïve, but I honestly felt that even if we were caught, they wouldn't do anything to us except maybe call the police and report us for trespassing. I felt my body go rigid with anxiety but I kept my voice calm. "So let's do this thing and get out of here. Now."

Ramona gave me a hard look, as though weighing her options, and I guess decided I would be more of a help than a hindrance because she narrowed her eyes at me and began talking through barred teeth. "Fine. You're to follow me closely and do exactly as I say." I nodded.

"We go up to the house and find a window I can see in...*without getting caught*. I don't think the yard is armed and I took care of the dogs. We'll photograph whoever is inside, hopefully this guy they've been talking about. Then we get the hell out of here."

"Roger that," I said meekly. She glared, as if having second thoughts, but then turned and ran.

We made it up the edge of the yard to the side of the house. Now I was thankful for the pitch dark. I followed Ramona closely. We eased our way along the side and stopped at the first window. I was so hopeful—a window! It was like the pot of gold at the end of the rainbow.

I should have known it wasn't going to be that easy. Ramona had said we needed to find a window and we found one. I took her literally just like Casey does me when I tell him "just a second" and he counts to one and says, "There, that was a second." Wishful thinking had clouded my judgment.

Ramona proceeded to pull a little gadget that looked like a small bicycle pump from her fanny pack. "This is a night-vision periscope with a telephoto lens," she whispered and I watched her in awe as she extended it up to the window. I took the quickest second possible to wipe the sweat that was dripping down my forehead and rub it on my leather pants, not caring that I was probably ruining them. It didn't matter, they had served their purpose; I was throwing them away at the end of this night. I watched Ramona, my body tense with anxiety and anticipation, her one eye on the periscope as she turned it 180 degrees. We hunched under the window, shoulder to shoulder, silent and intense. That's when Lexie caught up to us.

"Are you two out of your fucking minds?" she hissed, making us both jump. She came crawling towards us along side the house panther-like on all fours, looking more like a stripper from a Motley Crue video than a spy in her tight black leather pants and halter that showcased her cleavage, despite the jean jacket layered on top.

"Lexie!" I whispered, my stressed face breaking into a smile. I couldn't help myself. Seeing her made me feel instant relief. Everything always worked better—spa dates excluded—when Lexie was around. She was bold and aggressive. She could make even the worst event or activity fun with one of her hilarious stories or her animated spirit. And she could talk herself out of almost any situation—especially one where men were involved.

"C'mon, let's get back to the car," Lexie ordered, grabbing my hand and giving me a tug. "This is crazy."

"We're at the window," I whispered, as if that was supposed to mean anything to her. "Ramona's got a night-vision-periscope with a telephoto lens!"

"We're at the window, Ramona's got a periscope," Lexie mocked in a sing-song voice, bouncing her head side to side. She glared at me, her voice returning to its edgy side of normal. "What are you, five? It's gonna be the window where you get shot to death. And I don't care if she has a super-secret-nuclear-blasting-invisibility-stun-gun.

This is dangerous, not to mention illegal and *not* what we all signed up for."

She looked directly at Ramona who was collapsing the periscope.

"And my guess is, that if you don't see anything in this window, you're going to want to try another one, and another one until you do find what you're looking for."

Ramona looked at Lexie with cold determination. "You two head back to the car now. I'll be fine. If I'm not back in twenty minutes, call the cops and come to the front door saying your elderly mother has escaped again and is wandering the neighborhood. That's why I wore these dorky slippers." She put her foot out, wiggling a huge black cat slipper with a nightcap on its head.

"Wow. You really thought of everything," Lexie said sarcastically. "Those will look great on your cold, dead feet. How are you going to explain away your little spy gadget here, or whatever else you may have in that fanny pack of yours?"

"I'm almost eighty-five-years-old. My days of explaining myself are long gone," she said matter-of-factly.

"Well you're jeopardizing Kelly's and my life now, too. Explain that one. So let's go, Ramona. Now…before you get us all killed."

I half expected Lexie to start counting to three and wondered for the briefest second who would win that standoff.

Lexie's words hit home and I could see Ramona weighing the risks versus the benefits. She looked at me and turned to Lex. "Take Kelly. I'll try one more window. The one around the corner has a light on. If no one's in there, I'll give up… I promise," she added softly.

I looked pleadingly at Lexie, who was completely put out. "It's just one more window, Lex," I whispered. "She may need some help. C'mon, what's five more minutes gonna do?"

Lexie glared at me and Ramona as if she could turn us to stone, but she conceded, probably figuring that arguing would take longer than five minutes anyway.

Staying close to the house, we followed single-file behind Ramona, all of us now adopting Lexie's panther-style crawl. We turned the corner and stepped in a muddy flower bed; no one complained as we moved on. Twenty feet further and we reached a window spilling light out onto the lawn. Ramona got out her gizmo. Lexie and I watched her slowly raise it and look into the room.

"See anything?" I whispered.

"Yeah, that's what we were wondering."

The words came from a deep voice just a few feet away. Another deep voice to the left asked, "Did you get a good enough look?"

I jumped and let out a tiny screech, spinning to face two large men looming above us out on the grass. One wore board shorts, a long-sleeved Hurley T-shirt and flip-flops, the other was in jeans, classic black and white Vans, a plaid shirt over his black tee.

"Because we'd be happy to show you the inside," the shorts man said, taking a step closer to us.

Fear and panic shot through me, like being struck by lightning from the inside. As I tried to breathe, Lexie got to her feet, dusted herself off, flipped her hair ever so slightly and smiled calmly at the men. "Oh, hi. We were just searching for our cat. We tried your bell, but no one came to the door so we let ourselves in your yard."

The men looked at her silently so she soldiered on. I stood and helped Ramona, who'd tossed the periscope under a geranium.

"It's our friend's cat, really. We're staying with them down the street, you see, and the cat got out. We thought we saw him dart up here so we were just looking for him, you know, before the coyotes get him. He's kind of gray, long-hair, so big," Lexie held her visibly shaking hands about a foot apart. "Have you seen him?" She cocked her head to the side a little, giving the men the same slight smile that had gotten her past bouncers at exclusive Hollywood clubs and out of innumerable speeding tickets.

They glanced at each other quickly. Shorts Man grinned wryly "Perhaps he ran inside. Why don't we go look?" He took a step toward us, ushering us toward the patio.

Plaid Shirt joined him. "Yeah, I bet he's inside. Normally we'd say there's no way a cat would be in the yard because we have these two great big dogs, but somehow they seem to be taking a hard-core nap right now. Which is," he laughed a little, "really odd but also lucky for you, because they would have torn you to shreds." He gave us a plastic, menacing smile and motioned us to move with his friend.

Lexie stood her ground, which pleased me to no end. The thought of going into the house where there could be more of these guys scared me to death. I racked my brain for a plan and got nothing. I couldn't think. I couldn't move. My body felt like I'd been filled with cement. I wanted to run, to flee past the men somehow, maybe give them a round kick to the groin or a punch to one of those sensitive areas we'd learned about in Fight Club. But I was literally scared stiff.

"Hmmm," Lexie said as though taking their offer seriously and looked at her watch. "You know, it's getting late. We really should be getting back. Why don't I just give you my phone number and if you find him, you can call me," she said with a quick Pollyanna shrug. "Do you have a pen? It's 310-256-78—"

The men cut her off and moved in, stepping close enough that I could feel their body heat. "Let's go," Plaid Shirt said. His tone meant business. He pointed one beefy finger inches from Lexie's nose and pointed. "That way. Now."

"Okay, okay," Lexie said, as though she knew the jig was up. She stepped out of the flowerbed first and I grabbed Ramona's arm to help her, amazed that my body would move at all. It felt like a dream when Lexie begin to talk again, as though she was miles away, yet her voice was close and audible.

"Okay, okay, muscles," she began to joke light-heartedly. "You caught us. We're on your turf. This is all just a big, big mistake, though," she said, eyeing Ramona. "Now if this is the part of the game where you intimidate us and threaten us, could you get on with it out here, please? I've got a birthday party to throw tomorrow for a six-year-old as well as a boat load of errands and carpooling—"

She was cut off by Shorts Man, who was eyeing Ramona closely. "Hey! Doug!" he said, elbowing his friend, his eyes growing wider.

"What?" Doug answered, never taking his eyes off me or Lexie.

"Remember that day I told you I was down at the dock and I saved that mangy little dog who almost drowned?"

"Yeah?"

"And there was this hippie-looking little old grandma there? Who said she'd make me cookies?"

"Yeah?"

He walked closer to Ramona who recoiled ever so slightly although I could tell she was trying to stand her ground. He reached over with his brawny, tan arm and whipped Ramona's sun hat off. "Dude! *This* is the grandma! The one that was down at the boat!"

The sudden motion of snatching her hat stunned Ramona, her hair was disheveled and her face shocked, but only for a nanosecond before she found her composure. She stood there, expressionless and silent. Doug, eyed her. Then the corners of his mouth slowly began to rise.

"You know, Tony, I think I've seen her before as well." He began circling her as if stalking prey and to my horror, she began to wilt. Part of me expected her to become a badass ninja, kicking and punching the men before crashing their heads together and piling them in the flowerbed. Instead, she dropped her gaze, her back slowly bent and her head drooped. In an instant she looked old and frail, like she'd lost her a walker, a far cry from the woman who was biting my head off just moments ago.

"Where, man?" Tony asked.

Doug stopped directly in front of Ramona. He was a foot taller than she and he bent down so his face was inches from hers. His move was meant to intimidate and it seemed to be doing the trick.

"I've seen her at the pier. Several times, to be exact. She's the one that's been watching us. I almost caught her once, too," he said, standing up straight, "but somehow she slipped away."

Ramona had told us about hiding in the dressing room of that boutique. I couldn't help wishing he had caught her back then, in broad daylight, on a busy street full of people. Maybe that would have knocked some sense into her—into me—because here we were now, in the dark, on their property, at their disposal, with no one around to help.

We had followed Ramona's lead; put all our faith in her. I had been so blinded by hope and the potential victory of our mission and so caught up in our easy victories, I didn't think the dangers were real. I wondered if Ramona was thinking the same thing, feeling the same remorse. I watched her standing feebly under the men's gaze; she looked as small as a child.

And then she collapsed.

"Ramona!" I cried, jumping to catch her as her limp body crumpled at my feet. Lexie shrieked and dashed to her side, grabbing her head before she hit the ground. We called to her frantically, Lexie and I, tapping her gently on the face, trying to wake her up. Doug and Tony simply stood and watched. We laid her out on the grass, propping her head on my lap as Lexie checked for a pulse and held her ear to Ramona's mouth to see if she was breathing.

"We've got to call an ambulance," I cried, pulling out my phone.

Doug swiped the cell phone from my grip and looked sternly at his friend. "We've got to check with Mike. Bring her inside."

The order startled and frightened me, rendering me momentarily speechless, but it had the opposite effect on Lexie. She jumped to her feet and began to spit her protest at him, crying that we needed an ambulance *now*, that our friend could be dying or having a stroke or a heart attack, that she was 79-years-old and that he better "fucking give the phone back, *now*."

Doug ignored her and repeated his order. "Bring her inside."

The burly dealer bent down and scooped Ramona up as though she weighed nothing, and started toward the house leaving us in the yard. Doug looked at Lexie and issued another order. "Your phone, too. Hand it over."

Lexie promptly told him to go fuck himself and even tried to grab my phone back. He deflected her, grabbing her wrist with one hand and twisting it behind her back. She shrieked with pain. He frisked her with his free hand and came up with her phone. He let her go, giving her a little push in the back and said calmly, "Inside," pointing with the phone to the house. "Let's go."

A slew of insults poured out of Lexie, but she stopped immediately with a gasp when he lifted his shirt to expose the fact that he had a handgun tucked neatly into his pants. "Now," he repeated, his voice almost tender, "Let's *go*."

I felt like the wind had been knocked out of me. Guns had been scary before, just at the shooting range. But here, in the real world, where if they were fired it would not be at paper targets, they were positively terrifying.

Lexie and I exchanged horrified looks. We were trapped and knew it. I thought briefly about running, and knowing Lexie, figured she was thinking that too. I knew if I made the first move, to punch him or trip him, she would follow suit. We could then dash down the hill and into the night, out the gate and to the cars where we could drive away. From there we could call the cops and circle back to get Ramona. That was, if we weren't shot in the back as we fled, our deaths being justified since we were trespassing. Out of the corner of my eye I saw Lexie start to reach for me, I looked at her and could see her mouth the word "run" but she was a second too late. She screamed as she felt the cold, hard metal of Doug's handgun on her back. He pushed her forward with it and into me.

"I said move it, princess. You deaf or something?"

There was nothing tender in that voice now, our chance to flee was gone. I glanced at Lexie and knew her heart was racing as fast as mine. We fell in line, trying to catch up to Tony as he carried Ramona across the patio and into the house.

We stepped through a sliding glass door and into a beautiful room with a pool table and arcade games lining every wall. I stopped and looked back at Doug, "Uh, shoes?" I said, not wanting to track in mud but waved me on with a flick of his chin and the barrel of his gun. We caught up to Tony and followed him up some stairs into a large open entryway. The front door appeared to have come from some medieval fortress and an enormous wrought iron lantern hung from the ceiling two stories above. I winced at the extensive security gadgets as we climbed a rounded staircase to the largest, most beautiful great room I've ever seen.

One side was a perfectly laid out kitchen gleaming with stainless steel, hammered copper and an island bigger than my entire kitchen.

The other side was partitioned by a giant leather sofa and chairs grouped around two enormous flat-screen TV's mounted each side of a rugged stone fireplace. Directly in the middle was a massive wooden table that could easily seat fifteen. The vaulted ceiling rose twenty feet up and the west wall was floor to ceiling glass; the view, under other circumstances, would be spectacular.

By the time we entered the great room, Lexie and I were on Tony's heels, trying to reach Ramona. Two men were staring at a laptop screen on the kitchen island, and when we entered they looked up in surprise. One of them, a fifty-ish man nicely dressed in a cheesy Hawaiian, shirt remained seated at the island while the other man, dressed in jeans and a blue fleece pull-over got up and came towards us. He was tan with sandy hair, probably in his late 30's and looked like your run of the mill Hermosa Beach resident.

Tony laid Ramona down on the sofa and Lexie and I rushed to her, checking her pulse, feeling her cheeks, trying to get her to regain consciousness.

The man in the fleece looked at Doug and nodded toward Ramona and us. "What's going on?" he asked in a calm but stern tone.

"Don't worry, boss," Tony said with a twisted smile, "we didn't shoot the grandma." He looked at me and Lexie adding, "Yet."

"What happened?" the guy in the fleece asked Doug, ignoring Tony's comment.

Doug recited the event of our capture like a soldier to his commander. He and Tony had been playing pool when they saw the dogs take off. They finished the game but when the dogs didn't return, they went looking for them and found them passed out and tethered to the fence by the rock garden. They came back to the house, armed themselves and began inspecting the grounds.

"That's when we found Charlie's Angels over here," Doug said, nodding at us. "They were trying to get a good look inside the house. They said they're friends of the neighbors," he brought the tone of his voice down a notch and stepped closer to the man, his eyes on us, "but I've seen the old lady before, Mike. She's been watching us *really closely* at the beach and Tony says he saw her down at the marina."

"I saved her wimpy little dog from being eaten by a pack of seals one morning just beside the boat when we were unloading," Tony said proudly. "She practically fainted when I handed her mangy dog back." Tony laughed.

Mike nodded slightly, taking in the information. He studied Lexie and me. "How about these two? Have you seen them before?" Both Doug and Tony shook their heads.

We let them talk as we worked on Ramona. She had a pulse, a surprisingly strong one at that, and was breathing. We hoped she'd just fainted but didn't want to rule out a stroke or something more serious.

The men fell silent and I looked up to see them watching us. Lexie took a quick breath, looked at me as if to wish her luck, then approached the man in the fleece.

"Please, sir—Mike, is it? We need an ambulance. This man here has taken away both our phones, but you seem reasonable. I don't know what is wrong with our friend," she motioned back to the couch, "but she's really old and may have had a heart attack or a stroke or something from all the excitement. She needs to get to the hospital."

"Yes," he said, eyeing Ramona and myself first, then Lexie. "She looks like she does. I don't think I caught your name?"

"Oh," she said, a little surprised at his manners as he put out his hand for her to shake, "it's Lexie."

"Nice to meet you, Lexie," he said, shaking her hand. "And, if you don't mind, what exactly are you, your colleague, and your *old* friend doing on my property?"

He didn't seem mad, exactly. Just suspicious. I tried to put myself in his place, wondering how an average person would react to people he found trespassing on his property, drugging his pets, and spying on them. I'd be suspicious, too. I held my breath keeping hold of Ramona's hand and hoping Lex could work her magic. If anyone could pull this off, it was her and to my surprise, she decided to come clean. Sort of.

"Like I said, our friend is old," Lexie said, trying to be sincere. "She's got the beginnings of dementia. She is convinced for some reason that you guys have stolen some of her prized collection of antique dolls, which we know is absurd. She went off on a rage this evening and wouldn't calm down so we drove her here to get a look at your house, to prove that someone who lived in such a fine house would not need to steal anything. We just meant to show her the house from the road, but before we knew it, she was feeding your dogs her meds and running up the hill to check you out."

There were a million holes in Lexie's tale, but she told it with so much conviction that it was plausible. "I know we're trespassing and I'm so sorry. I promise it will never happen again. We can see you're in the middle of something," she continued, "so if you'll just give us our phones and call off your trigger-happy men here, we'll call an ambulance and be out of your hair. We can even wait in the driveway if you want."

Mike studied her and I couldn't gauge his expression. He was eerily calm, a blank slate. I imagined his cold, stoic gaze was a result of his profession and I tried to push away the horrendous things I'd read people like him did to people like us. I didn't want to seem too scared or tip my hand in any way to the fact that we did, indeed, know what he did for a living. I wanted to keep things as light as possible, maybe just seem confused as to why they would overreact the way they had with us, forcing us inside with guns when we were simply chasing our crazy friend onto their property and spying in their window. But my stomach was in knots and I was clenching my teeth in order to prevent them from chattering.

"So," Mike said lightly, even politely, nodding toward Ramona, "your friend here needs our help."

I saw Lexie breathe a tiny sigh of relief, as she looked over to Ramona and me and then back to Mike. "Yes, but we really don't want to take up any more of your time. We're so sorry to have had to trespass, but we had to stop her. We'll be fine. We can let ourselves out and call 911 from there."

Mike looked at Doug. "Do you have these ladies' phones?"

Doug produced the phones and handed them over, as if he knew better than to argue or explain. Mike looked at them for a moment, tapping the screens as Lexie stood by drumming her fingers on her pants which I knew was to keep herself from reaching up and snatching her phone because she never let *anyone* toy with her like this. Mike glanced over the phone to Lexie.

"You have a new text message waiting for you," he said with a hint of amusement, raising an eyebrow. "It's from someone named Jackie Hayden. She says, 'What's taking so long? I'm calling the cops if you're not back in ten minutes!'" He looked at Lexie and raised both his eyebrows, waiting for a response.

Lexie stared back matter-of-factly. She was not going to be shaken by his little game, instead she played along. "We thought about calling the cops when she dashed through your gate. Some people shoot intruders on sight and we weren't even sure we'd be able to find her in this huge backyard of yours."

"Hmmm," he nodded. I couldn't tell if he was buying her story or not. "Doug," he commanded, "take Joe and go find this Jackie Hayden and whomever else she may be with. See if her story corroborates the one we just heard. If it doesn't, bring her in."

Oh shit, I thought to myself. *Not Jackie, too.* We need her out there. I prayed she had called the police, or her husband, someone who could come to our rescue.

"And what about calling an ambulance?" Lexie continued, an edge creeping up in her voice. "You know if she's had a stroke, she needs to get some help now. Every second counts."

Mike turned to face her. "You're right, maybe she should have thought about that before she drugged my dogs. Don't worry, we'll get to the bottom of this quickly. I'm sure whoever else is outside waiting for you will help put this one to rest. Or maybe there's more information in here," he said, holding up her phone.

"Let's see." He began scrolling through Lexie's texts, reading them aloud as Tony sniggered. "Here's one from Josh-slash-Honey. It's from yesterday. It says, 'Have dinner meeting, be home late.'" He looked at Lexie.

"So, you have a husband, or maybe a boyfriend. That's good information." He looked back at the phone. "The next one is from someone named Cash. He says 'Riding to Max's house, K?'"

He glanced again at Lexie and gently put the phone down on a table, out of her reach. "That's important, too. Now I know you have a child who probably isn't old enough to drive and has to ride his bike to his friend's house. These are very important messages from people I imagine are very important to you."

I could see Lexie's face get red, knew her blood was boiling. Mine was boiling for her, but I felt more sickened that this slime ball was saying the names of the most intimate people in her life out loud. I remembered how I felt at the school, how vulnerable losing my phone made me feel. How I knew that this man could easily look through both our texts and photos, easily figure out who our family members were, and just as easily, our addresses. I didn't have time to dwell on the fact because he turned his attention to me.

"And you," he said, walking over to the couch and holding out his hand as though we were at a cocktail party. "What is your name?"

"Kelly," I said quietly, shaking his hand.

"Kelly. Nice to meet you. Do you get equally important messages? Let's find out."

He didn't waste any time letting me know, as he had Lexie, that he held power over me. His technique was good. If we turned out not to be a threat to him, he could say it was all a joke, a misunderstanding, no harm no foul. But if we were a threat, he had zeroed in precisely and immediately on what was closest to our hearts. Talk about an element of surprise.

With a slight smile as though he was enjoying this, he picked up my phone and tapped on the screen, nodding and saying, "Oh," and "I see," and "Hmmm." He was putting on a show that was quite entertaining for the man with the laptop. I felt paralyzed and sick all at the same time.

I wanted to grab my phone and stomp on it, throw it through the window, anything to destroy the information on it. It was horrifying to realize I had dragged my family into this game that I had played so willingly—playfully even—and so irresponsibly. I was sickened by my actions and would have, right then, done anything to take them back. I had wanted so badly to protect my family and the people of Hermosa, but I'd done the exact opposite. I'd endangered the ones I loved the most.

"Oh, here's a good one," Mike said. "It's from yesterday. You wrote, 'Taking kids to soccer, then going to club for swimming. Want to meet there for dinner?' And someone named Mark wrote back, 'Sure, can be there by 6.'" Mike looked at me, smiling sincerely.

"That sounds nice. I'm sure Mark and your kids are awfully nice, too. Oh, and look, we have photos!" He tapped my phone a few more times and opened up the gallery loaded with pictures of my boys, my husband, my life. He scrolled through them uttering phony compliments. "Ah!" and "Cute!" and "Oh, this must be the St. Patrick's Day parade." Every so often he turned the phone to Lexie, including her in the show. She stood still as a statue.

I stared at him, zoning out as my mind went to the worst case scenario, the one where Mike sent his men for my boys and husband, kidnapped them at gunpoint in their sleep, then brought them back here where they would be tortured in front of me. I could hear Casey's and Griffin's cries of pain and horror, see their little faces as they screamed for me, see the hatred and blame in Mark's glare for bringing all this on our family when he had told me to leave it all alone, to let the police do their job. The mere thought of all this was more than I could bear and I shook myself back to the present, blinking to clear my blurry vision, sending streams of tears down my cheeks.

"Are you okay?" Mike was holding my phone up to me. "You really should take a look at these photos. The one of Griffin…is it?…in the bath is particularly adorable." My stomach wretched when I heard him call my baby by name. I knew I had to do something, that there must be some way out of this, some perfect play. I knew at least one of them was armed, and I had no plan for that.

I thought of Mark trying to raise Griffin and Casey by himself: shopping at the store, learning where the pots and pans were located, cooking something other than spaghetti, trying to keep up with laundry, cleaning, shopping, and two busy schedules let alone his own work. I wondered briefly if Mark had life insurance on me. He probably did, he was always one to dot his i's and cross his t's. He probably even had an accidental death clause and would be able to quit his job and be a stay-at-home dad. But would he want to? He could barely manage to take the boys to Starbucks and back for a pack of Madelines without being exhausted.

I thought of all I would miss: birthday parties, kindergarten, grade school pageants, the boys learning to read and write, soccer games, beach days, vacations, first crushes, the awkward years of middle school, learning to drive, prom, investigating colleges, my boys slowly turning into handsome, independent men.

I couldn't stand the thought of missing it all, not even one second of it. I should be home with them now, as in *right now*. I should be lying down with them in their beds, snuggled up tight. I hated myself for getting us into this position. This terrible, stupid, awful position that everywhere I looked resulted in us dying.

There had to be another option. We just had to find it. We did not have to sink to their level, to resort to violence. They were just bullies and I made up my mind that they could be reasoned with. A bunch of moms were not a real threat to their operation. They just needed to be convinced of this and they would let us alone and go about their business. I didn't even care if they sold drugs anymore; I just wanted to be home with my kids and husband.

"Sir?" I said, summoning all my courage. He looked at me as if this might be amusing, and nodded. I made eye contact as I began to speak, noticing that he had dark-chocolate eyes and a five o-clock shadow.

"Sir, I know your men here could have shot us on sight for trespassing, and I totally understand why you'd be pissed for having someone spy on you, I'd be upset as well. But let me explain."

I motioned to Lexie and Ramona. "We're just housewives who get together every month or so for some fun and laughs and excitement. We all have kids, *very, very young children*, who depend on us completely." I paused, hoping that if he had even a shred of decency, my statement might make some minute impact.

His expression didn't change, he continued to listen with a focus so intense I had to look away. "I can see that you're in the middle of something and we are so sorry for interrupting. Our friend over there has dementia, she gets confused easily and well, we just try and accommodate her as best we can on our nights out together. She's old, she doesn't get out much, her husband died years ago and she has no family to take care of her.

"During the week she has a day nurse, but once a month we all try to get her and ourselves out to have a little fun. We're all stay-at-home moms just looking for a little escape every so often." I couldn't tell if this was having any affect on Mike but Dorie's line from *Finding Nemo* popped into my head, *"just keep swimming, just keep swimming"* and suddenly I couldn't stop talking.

"You should have seen what we did last month for our MNO, that's an abbreviation for Mom's Night Out, it's what we call it when we get together, catchy, huh? Anyway, Ramona thinks her neighbors let their dogs go to the bathroom on her lawn and she can't stand that, so we totally TP'ed them. There was toilet paper everywhere! I think we used—what would you say, Lexie?—maybe thirty rolls? The place was covered!"

I glanced at Lexie with a grin and she returned a half-assed smile and questioning look. I plowed ahead anyway, gaily embroidering this tale as if Mike were my best friend. At this point I couldn't stop the nervous chatter even if I wanted to.

"By the time we were done, not only was the house covered in TP, but we also filled the lawn with pink flamingos, yard signs, flags, even a garden gnome picnic! There was toilet paper in their hubcaps, in their mailbox and in their garden hose. You should have seen it. And the month before that? You're not going to believe this, ha ha, we hopped the fence and went skinny dipping in the Hermosa Beach Country Club's pool! Well, I guess we didn't really 'hop' the fence, since a few of us are members and have keys, but you should have seen the security guard when he found ten naked middle-aged ladies swimming in his pool at midnight. He was so embarrassed, he didn't know what to do!"

I guffawed at Mike encouragingly. I just wanted to show him that we acted like a bunch of jackasses every month so why shouldn't we have wound up in his yard tonight. Certainly not because we suspected him of being a high-volume drug dealer and were trying to gather enough intel to put him and his colleagues in prison forever.

Mike watched me intently then glanced over to the man at the kitchen island. I saw them exchange looks, then the man in the kitchen returned to his laptop and drink and Mike stopped pacing and leaned back against the dining room table, folding his arms across his chest, eyes on me.

"So," he said, raising one eyebrow at both Lexie and me. "Once a month you get out and purposely act like teenagers again?"

Tony, who had taken a seat at the dining table in the middle of the room, chimed in, nodding his head. "My wife should do that. Maybe it would help her to not be such a bitch during that time of the month." He laughed at his own joke, looking at both Mike and the man in the kitchen to laugh with him to no avail. I felt horribly sorry for his wife.

Mike cracked a smile, the first of the night. It appeared he was starting to thaw. "My girlfriend goes shopping with her friends and out to lunch a lot. Those girls are always bitching that their husbands are gone all the time. They could use a little stupid fun, lighten up. They take themselves way too seriously."

I began to feel a little bolder, almost as though I had established a friendship with him. I thought if I showed empathy for his girlfriend, maybe he'd warm up to me. After all, friends don't shoot friends in the face, right?

"Maybe she needs friends that are a little more adventurous?" I coaxed. "I swear, I am happy as a lark just to do the housewife thing after a fun night out with my girlfriends, it fills me right up."

"Perhaps," Mike said, smiling and chuckling, "although I'm not quite sure she's the type to go *TPing*. Can you do that in four-inch heels?"

241

"Of course!" I laughed at his joke a little too hard and caught Lexie closing her eyes in embarrassment. "You just can't run from the cops very well if you're caught." I winked at him—inside joke. We're friends here, right? "Does she live here? We'll take her out on our next MNO. Seriously!"

"We'll see," Mike said, "she's not a mom, she may not get it." He glanced over at Ramona, who was still passed out on the sofa, a little drool starting to form at the corner of her mouth. "Your friend, do you think she still needs an ambulance?"

My heart jumped at the thought of getting the hell out of this house and getting Ramona to a hospital. "Absolutely." Lexie jumped in. "She's got a weak pulse, but if she just fainted, I think she'd have come to by now. There's something more serious going on with her."

Mike took out our phones and began playing with them as though trying to figure out whose was whose. We both stood there, trying to appear patient. I felt antsier than a five-year-old at the gates of Disneyland.

Mike figured out the phones and was handing them back when Doug walked in. A shocked Lisa and a bewildered Jackie marched behind him. A short, fat man we hadn't seen before brought up the rear, sweating. Mike glanced at Jackie and Lisa and then at Doug, whose expression made him hold back, leaving both my and Lexie's hands hanging in the air.

"Is there a problem?" Mike asked Doug.

"Yep," Doug said, giving Lex and me a distrustful glance while lifting Ramona's black duffle bag onto the dining room table.

Twenty-Two

Jackie and Lisa practically ran to huddle beside us at the foot of the couch. Jackie was visibly shaking and Lisa was trying to gauge the situation by reading our expressions. Then Jackie saw Ramona, let out a little scream and ran to her. Lexie followed.

"What happened?" Lisa whispered, looking from Ramona to the men.

"We don't know," I whispered back. "She just collapsed outside. They forced us in here at gunpoint." Lisa raised an eyebrow but the rest of her face remained calm.

"We found these two," Doug motioned to Lisa and Jackie with his chin, "sitting in a car down by the road. The little one," he pointed to Jackie, "is Jackie Hayden." He handed Jackie's phone over to Mike, who had joined him at the table. "The other one says she doesn't have a phone, says she left it on the charger at her house." Mike eyed Lisa and she stared back blankly.

Doug continued while I noticed Mike glance back tentatively at the man sitting at the kitchen island. He was no longer absorbed in his computer; we had his full attention now.

"We found the two of them going through this duffle bag," Doug motioned to the short guy to dump the entire contents out on the dining room table. Stuff came tumbling out with a loud crash, spilling across the table, some of it rolling off onto the floor. Mike looked suspiciously at the contents as Doug began to rifle through it. "Remote controls, bullets, cell phones, gas masks, tear gas, smoke bombs, rubber gloves, goggles, cereal bars, toy helicopters, carabiners, Krazy Glue." He grimaced at Mike.

"There's a pipe bomb in here and what looks like a remedial timer. It's like a MacGyver starter kit." The air caught in my throat as I looked disbelievingly at my friends. I suddenly felt sick as Mike picked up a notebook, the one covered with the Dora the Explorer stickers, and walked toward the windows leafing through it.

Meanwhile, the man from the kitchen had gotten up and joined Doug at the table. He silently looked over the contents as though they were for sale at a swap meet, picking up each item, checking it over, then setting it back down only to pick another one up. "It's like a small arsenal," I heard Doug say as the man acknowledged him by barely flickering his eyes.

"Mike," I pleaded to his back, speaking up to the shock of everyone, my eyes looking wild. "This stuff is not ours. I don't know how it all got in there, got in the car, but it's not ours."

Then I remembered Ramona and didn't want to throw her under the bus, but I had to come up with some plausible explanation.

"Ramona's husband was in the military," I lied. "He must have had all this stuff lying around! Maybe she was going to take it to the police to have them dispose of it, or to a museum or something? I don't know. Like we said, she's kind of out of it these days."

Mike had finished leafing through Ramona's notebook and was back at the table, leafing through a scrapbook Jackie had made with the headshots of all the dealers. He continued to flip pages, walking away from the table again, his expression now changed, hardened, his jaw set, his shoulders tense, and his eyes were now narrowly focused, on me. It was like a switch in his personality had been thrown.

"I mean, seriously, look at us. Do any of us look like we even know what that stuff is? It's absurd!" My voice was high with panic and there was no way I could control it. "I mean, I've heard of tear gas, but I wouldn't recognize it if it hit me in the head. And Ramona? Just look at her! She can't even remember her name most days. Do we look like a threat to you guys?"

"Enough!" Mike walked straight up to me and slapped me across the face, hard. It took my breath away and I heard my friends yelp as my face turned red and the tears began to roll. When I looked back he had his finger in my face, and was spitting his words at me, his face inches from mine. "I have heard enough out...of...you."

"I imagine you have rules in your family. I consider my operation like a close-knit family and we have two rules." He held up two fingers close to my face. "Always tell the truth and do what you're told the first time. It's simple and it works. I don't give second chances to people who break the rules," he hissed. "And you, you and your friends, are clearly lying."

Lexie stepped forward this time. "Seriously sir, we're telling the truth. We had no idea what was in that bag. Ramona simply said she wanted to come up here and spy on your house, see if you had her stolen belongings. That's why we are dressed like this, just to spy, nothing more." She raised her hands to show that she had nothing to hide and the rest of us followed suit. "We are who we say we are. You've seen the pictures on our phones. We've all got little children who need us. Check the car. I've got cupcakes for my son's birthday party out there—"

"And watermelon," Jackie added eagerly.

"And watermelon," Lexie concurred, smiling thanks at Jackie for the support. "You guys can have it all. Please. And I'm sure I can speak for the group when I say how terribly sorry we are and that none of us will ever bother you or your men again. Just please, we need to get Ramona to a hospital and the rest of us need to get home to our families."

Hearing Lexie say she was sorry made me think how sorry I was. I was sorry for following Ramona through the gate. I was sorry for wearing these stupid pants as if this was a game. I was sorry for not just sticking to what I knew, mothering the town, picking up the trash and fixing the swings, organizing fundraisers to pay for a police force instead of trying to be the commander of my own S.W.A.T. team. I was sorry for thinking that we, totally untrained, out-of-our-league, inexperienced moms could take on these monsters and actually win.

He snorted. "You *housewives* have no idea who you are dealing with." He stood in the middle of the room holding Ramona's notebook in the air as he turned around and spoke to his team. "This notebook details where we park, what we drive, how many operators we have, what we sell, where we sell it, where we buy gas, what we like to snack on, what we look like, where we live, how we get the product in and the money out. And it even mentions our outpost on Catalina. There are photos, close up photos, of the entire team selling product," he looked at Doug and Tony, "including you two. Our entire Hermosa Beach operation is detailed."

He slammed the notebook down on the table and turned to us. "Now whether it is *your* notebook or the old lady's is immaterial. It exists and it puts our operation at risk."

He looked directly at Lexie. "And if you think cupcakes and watermelon will fix *that*, then you really are stupid." He turned to Doug and Tony, who were now as serious as soldiers, and issued an order, "Tie them up." Then he walked to the kitchen island where the other man had returned and handed him the notebook. The other man began to leaf through it as Mike picked up the decanter and refilled both their glasses.

As Tony and Doug moved in, Lisa picked up where I left off. "Sir, please, we promise we won't bother you again *or* let our friend here bother you. You've got all her stuff, I think we should just call it even and go our separate ways. I understand you're upset, but tying us up, holding us hostage, is only going to make matters worse. And," she added with sideways glance at us, "I'm pretty sure I can speak for everyone here that we are all terrified of you. We will live in fear of you for the rest of our lives."

The other man snorted and smirked as Doug grabbed Lisa. She shrieked as he roughly pulled her arms together behind her back and zip-tied them pushing her to sit on the dining room bench. Mike wandered back to us, now with a drink in hand. He had the odd juxtaposition of being relaxed and menacing at the same time.

"Who says I'm going to hold you hostage?" he grinned at Lisa, his face inches from hers.

Tony now grabbed Jackie, practically carrying her over to the bench while, to my amazement, Lisa kept her cool. "Please," she pleaded, "we have families, small children. Our husbands will look for us, they'll get the whole South Bay involved, the police, the FBI, they will never stop. You think *we're* a pain in the ass, you could let us go now and this whole ordeal will be over. You'll never be bothered again. Otherwise, you'll have investigators and police here over and over and over again. I promise they won't rest until they find us."

"It's a little late for that," he said, striding to the island and coming back holding up the Dora notebook so close to Lisa's face she flinched. "And I promise you," he grinned again, like a psychopath, "they won't find you. Ever. You see," he stood in the center of us all, an edge to his voice as though he was really enjoying this, "there's a kelp forest a few miles past Catalina. Beautiful diving. All kinds of fish. It's also a breeding ground for great whites. We'll toss you overboard tonight, giving you a little cut to attract them so it's quicker. Then you'll either drown, since it's really hard to tread water with your hands zip-tied, then be eaten. Or the sharks will feast while your heads are still above water. Either way, we've never had a body turn up, right men?" he looked to his team for confirmation, every head nodded grimly. "And think of it this way, you're helping out a family—those mama and baby sharks get hungry."

"You'll never get away with this," Lisa whispered, choking back her tears.

Mike smiled the most menacing, cold smile I'd ever seen, his green eyes flaring. "Sweetheart, you have no idea what I get away with. Without any evidence, like a corpse, or witnesses, I can't be prosecuted. And I can foresee a big gas leak and a fire at your friend's house." Then he took his threats one step further. "And you've all mentioned several times now that you have children and care desperately about them. I'll make you a deal. If you go quietly, I'll leave them alone. If, however, I hear from my team that you gave them any problems, well, kids go missing every day."

The smile was gone. I could see in his flat, lifeless, demented eyes that he meant to carry out his threat and panic washed through me like ice water. My stomach lurched at his words and I choked back vomit. We were trapped, and they knew it.

Lexie began cussing them with every dirty word I'd ever heard plus a few in Spanish. Jackie broke down in sobs. This was surreal; I felt dizzy. Dread filled the room and the air got thick. I vaguely registered the satisfaction on Mike's face. He was pleased to see he'd terrorized us completely.

"Good."

He nodded to his men to get on with it. I thought about Griffin and Casey growing up and all that I'd miss. They were so young, they probably wouldn't even remember me. And Mark. I expect he'll remarry. He'll grieve first, of course, but be angry at the same time. Next time, I imagine, he'd pick someone more sensible. Less fun, no doubt, but someone who clearly wouldn't get herself into situations like these.

Mike turned and walked back to the kitchen with a little bounce in his step. He raised his hands, shrugging at the other man as if to say, "What are you going to do?"

At the same Lisa got up to follow him, probably to continue to reason with him and something about that dual action—his heartless audacity and her unwavering tenacity—snapped me out of my trance and hit me in the face with the realization that giving up would mean simultaneously giving in to the person who was destroying everything I loved while giving up on the women who had come so far with me.

I took another glance around the room, channeling my inner Jason Bourne. There were five of them, at least one was armed. There were five of us, one was unconscious. Not the best odds. The thing we did have going for us, once again, was the element of surprise. I had pretty much lost all faith in this element, but nothing was impossible, I reasoned. What we needed, was to get that gun.

Doug and Tony began to make their way over to me and Lexie. Jackie was still sitting on the bench a little to my left, sobbing, and Joe, the fat one, was on the bench on the opposite side just watching. I had Lexie shouting obscenities on my right and Lisa, Mike and the other man twenty feet away on the opposite side of the kitchen island. I took a deep, shaky breath. If I was going to make a move, and I knew I had to, it would have to be now. Time to go loud.

"No! Please!" I said to Doug, as I put up both hands up to hide my face as though I was cowering from him, a move our tae kwon do instructor had taught us last summer. Lexie was in between swear words and I caught her attention when I barked, "Lex, go loud!"

What happened next happened so fast, there was no time to think. Doug reached for my hand, which drew his face in closer, and I struck, hitting him as hard as I could with an upward palm strike to the nose, knocking him backwards. He reached for his bloodied face with both hands, leaving his crotch exposed. I kicked it hard, crying out, "Kiyah!" and watched him buckle over. Quickly I got in position for a round kick and was blindsided by a punch from Tony that knocked me off my feet.

Lexie took advantage of his distraction to slam her boot into his knee, then kicked him as hard as she could in the groin and slammed her elbow into his face. I shook off the punch and scanned for the gun, which Doug was clumsily taking out of his waistband. I ran and kicked it out of his hands and it went flying under the table. I went after it but he pushed me and my momentum carried me head first into the table leg. I felt a stabbing pain as I collapsed on my knees and grabbed my head, feeling the trickle of blood on my fingers, the thought of hungry sharks flashing.

Meanwhile, Tony had buckled as Lexie's kick took out his knee but had recovered and grabbed her leg, pulling her feet out from under her. She was in the middle of rolling away and getting up when Lisa screamed, "Lexie, gun!" I turned just in time to see Tony lift himself up onto one knee, pull a handgun from the back of his pants and point it at Lexie.

A loud report split the air and I saw Tony shiver slightly. I thought it was from the kick of his gun and my stomach dropped. I knew I had to get Doug's but I couldn't tear my eyes from Lexie. Her eyes were wide as she lay on the floor on her back, half propped on her elbows, staring at her assassin. But then he dropped his gun to his side and, as if in slow motion, he crumbled.

Everyone jumped to their feet, a look of utter shock on their faces. Doug froze for a second, then began inching his way toward Tony and his gun, looking around frantically as he tried to figure out where the shot came from. Another shot shattered the air and he too, spun backwards, banging his head hard on the floor as he landed.

Mike turned and ran for the back of the island when a familiar voice, high in pitch but strong and unwavering, called out from behind the couch. "Freeze!"

Mike stopped, carefully turning to meet the source of the voice. Slowly, from behind a handgun that had been wedged between the couch cushions, Ramona rose to her feet. Gone was the old, drooling invalid we had been so concerned about. In her place was a strong, commanding woman expertly grasping a handgun, her arms extended toward Mike, a fanny pack secured around her waist. At the sight of her we all gasped.

"Ramona!" Jackie shrieked. Shock and relief resonated in her voice and though my entire body.

"Kelly," she commanded, not taking her eyes off the three uninjured men, "get those two guns from Doug and Tony. Lexie, in my fanny pack is a pocket knife. Get it and cut Jackie and Lisa free."

"Grandma?" Mike said incredulously. "We forgot to frisk *the grandma*? Oh, this is incredible! Shot up by a bunch of feather-weight moms!" He laughed bitterly and glanced around, taking stock of his resources. His two top dogs were on the floor less than ten feet away from him, both of them now in a pool of blood. Fat Joe was ten feet away, on the other side of the table from us, his eyes wide, his arms frozen up in the air. The man in the kitchen had slipped off his barstool and stood crouched and scared—clearly out of his element—behind the island.

"So, Ramona is it?" Mike began. "You're the one who has been stalking us? Writing down our every move in your cute little notebooks? Drugging my dogs?" he gestured widely with his arms, his mouth smiling, his eyes like daggers. "You're the one with the dementia?"

"I told you to freeze!" she shouted, her aim steady on his chest.

"You and your team of scumbags can go straight to hell. I could say more but you're not worth my breath."

Lexie ran to Ramona, got the knife and began cutting Jackie free. Tony's gun had landed close to his body so it was easy for me to grab, but Doug's had slid way under the dining room table. I got down on all fours to retrieve it, which is when a small movement from the entrance of the room caught my eye. I looked up to see in the reflection of the chandelier another man creeping into the room, a handgun extended toward Ramona.

"Look out!" I yelled, at the same time I heard Lisa scream, "Get down!" She ran and jumped, her arms still zip-tied behind her, to shield Ramona.

The man was quicker. He open fire as he rushed into the room, one shot per second, all directed at Ramona. Everyone screamed. I could barely see from under the table, but knew I had to help. I took Tony's gun and loosely aimed, hoping I'd hit the shooter and not the table legs. I squeezed the trigger and dropped him with three horrifying shots.

Through the chaos, I could just make out Lexie calling me hysterically. I scrambled to get out from under the table when Fat Joe toppled the bench and pushed it—hard—smashing it into my face just above my punched out eye. Pain shot through me and I saw stars, but this was no time to give up. I pressed a bicep to my eye, clearing my vision enough to see him running for the staircase. I grabbed Doug's gun and aimed low, hitting him once in the leg and once in the butt and he fell hard against the marble floor.

Adrenaline filled my body, leaving me somewhere between feeling paralyzed and on fire. I made it out from under the table to find Lexie holding on to Mike's leg as he tried to kick her off. She was literally biting him through his pants as he yelled to the man in the kitchen about a gun in a drawer. Jackie was bent over Lisa and Ramona, both of whom were on the ground in front of the couch.

"Freeze!" I screamed, running to Mike as fast as I could. He continued to struggle until he felt the barrel of the gun in his back. "Now!"

Slowly he complied, turning to face me with disgust. I backed away a few feet, out of his strike distance. "You! Out from behind the island," I commanded. The shocked man gave up on his hunt and put his hands in the air, awkwardly clipping the island with his hip as he walked around it, stopping next to Mike.

Lexie got up with fury in her eyes and spat on Mike. "Go fuck yourself." Then she joined me. I handed her one of the guns, my hands shaking wildly, relieved not to be the only armed mom in the room. My eyes and my gun were glued to Mike and the other guy despite the blood dripping from the gash above my one unswollen eye.

"You got them?" I asked Lex.

"Oh, I got them alright." Staring at Mike she added, "I dare you to try anything, asswipe."

I ran to the guy I'd shot and took his gun and frisked Fat Joe as well, then ran back Lexie's side.

"Jackie! What's the situation?" I called over my shoulder, not willing to take my eyes off the men even for a glance.

"They've both been shot!" Jackie screamed.

"How bad is it?" Lexie called.

"I can't tell," she cried. "Lisa looks bad, Ramona seems okay."

"I'm alright," Ramona called out, "just give me a second." I wondered fleetingly how that could be possible, the man had shot what seemed like half a dozen bullets at her. I didn't have time to think about it because Lexie and I had to quickly come up with a plan. We got our phones and dialed 911 then made Mike and the other man lie on the floor in front of the island on their stomachs. Working quickly, we used their zip ties to tie their hands behind their backs and their feet to their hands—hog-tied seemed fitting.

"I'm good here," I told Lexie and she raced to help Jackie. I checked Tony and Doug for hidden weapons and pulses, finding neither.

I felt safe enough to look up long enough to see Jackie help Ramona take off her jacket. She was struggling to breathe and was cradling her arm. Lexie had Lisa on the sofa cradling her to her chest.

"How are we looking?" Keeping my gun pointed on the men as I inched toward my friends.

"We're holding on, aren't we Lisa sweetheart?" Lexie cooed in the motherly tone she used to console her children when they were hurt, though this time there was a hint of panic. She brushed the hair from Lisa's face with one hand while keeping the other pressed to Lisa's chest. Blood had soaked Lisa's shirt where Lexie's hand was and I could see it coming through her fingers.

Lisa nodded ever so slightly concentrating on her breathing, her mouth forming an "o" as her eyes closed. She was sheet-white, I could see sweat beading on her forehead. "You're going to be just fine, honey. I've got you, okay? Just keep breathing," Lexie coaxed.

"You hold on, Lisa," I said, running to get dishtowels from the kitchen to help stop the bleeding. "Just think about those beautiful children of yours, okay? Think about Scarlet and Stosh and Jackson and Jade." I put the dishtowel under Lexie's hand and shared a worried glance with her. "I'm calling Pete now and will have him meet you at the hospital. Try to focus on all the hugs you're going to get and how much those munchkins of yours need you. You stay with us now, okay?"

She barely nodded as tears streaked down her face. She seemed to sink deeper into Lexie and the thought that she could die shot a bolt of fear and adrenaline through me.

"We've got to get her out of here. I'm scared to death someone else is going to come through that door with a machine gun."

"I think she's going into shock!" Lexie shouted.

"Jackie," Ramona ordered weakly, "there's a blanket on the chair, grab it and cover Lisa."

Jackie did as she was told and I looked to Ramona and saw to my complete and utter astonishment, that she was wearing a Kevlar vest. She had been shot, multiple times, but the vest had stopped the bullets except for one that had hit her in the left arm, which was bleeding badly. I went to help her with one of the dishtowels as Jackie returned with an expensive, cashmere blanket. I hoped to see Lisa open her eyes as Jackie laid it over her, whispering, "There ya go, sweetie. Just hold on. Help will be here soon." She didn't stir. She was unconscious.

Ramona turned her gaze from Lisa to me, her expression hardening. "We haven't got a lot of time. The field teams may beat the ambulance here, they're due back any minute." She looked at her watch and stood with a grimace. Not missing a beat she picked up her gun and a dishtowel, and held them both against her bloody bicep as she walked over to our prisoners, indicating I should follow.

"You better hope the ambulance beats my team here. Because if it doesn't, you are fucking dead, grandma," Mike spat.

She ignored him and focused on the other man. "Who are you?" she demanded.

"Nobody, I'm nobody," he said, looking pissed but frightened. "I just run the books."

"So you know how the operation works?" she interrogated. "How they launder the money? Where they buy, or make, their products?" He swallowed hard and nodded.

"You have no idea who you're fucking with," Mike hissed.

"Neither do you," Ramona glared, now focusing her attention on him. "You have no idea who *we* are or what *we're* capable of. Let me tell you something, you little prick, you don't ever fuck with moms. Grandmas either, for that matter," she said, almost as an afterthought.

"You, Michael Nelson, are going to prison. I have enough on you for the drug dealing alone, to put you away for decades. Plus, how many people did you brag about feeding to the sharks? I think we can safely add murder to your list of charges not to mention kidnapping." Her confidence against this monster of a man was insane, I had no idea who this woman was anymore. This situation, this conversation where she was acting like Walter White, was blowing me away.

Mike laughed. "My lawyers will shred any evidence you have to pieces. And when I'm free, I'll find you and you'll wish you never messed with me."

His words cut through me. It was unimaginable to think that we could possibly survive this night only to worry about our safety and the well-being of our families for the rest of our lives while this monster went free. But Ramona kept her cool. She raised her gun and held it directly to his head and said, "Maybe I should kill you now, then?" He grimaced and stared at her, not even a hint of fear in his eyes. I shot a terrified look at Ramona. Shooting the other three men had been self-defense, I could reason, but this? This would be an execution. Was she completely out of her mind?

"Listen," Jackie said to everyone, breaking the tension. "I hear sirens!" They were still a ways away, but they were coming— finally!—and for a very short-lived moment I felt a tiny bit of relief. But then, as if it hadn't already, all hell broke loose.

"I can't feel her pulse!" It was Jackie again. She had Lisa's wrist in her hand and had been rubbing her legs. She looked up at us all with a look of unsurpassed terror that we all felt.

But a second later it was doubled when Lexie asked, "Did you guys feel that?" We all looked at each other like gazelles that had just caught the scent of a lion. "That's got to be the garage door," she said, panicking and looking around.

Ramona hobbled to the window and peered out from behind the drapes. "Shit," she yelled. "The teams are back."

"How many?" I asked, moving to Lisa to try to feel a pulse, hoping Jackie was wrong.

From behind the curtain Ramona cried out, "Three trucks pulling in now. They beat the cops and the gate's closed. They work in teams of two, so there'll be six men." Oddly enough, I wasn't even worried about the possibility of a shoot out. I felt fairly confident that, with my vantage point and accumulated guns, I could hold them off until the cops and ambulance arrived. But we didn't have time for any of that. We needed the paramedics to get to Lisa *now*.

Mike snorted and laughed. "I hope you're ready for the fight of your life. My guys are trained. What training have you completed? Potty training? Sleep training? You are sitting ducks."

Something snapped in Ramona and she walked over to where he sat. Then, gripping the gun with the hand that was covered in blood from her wound, she pointed it right at his head. "We're at least trained to be decent human beings, something you apparently are not."

"Ramona, no!" The thought of a point blank execution was too much and I cringed, but instead of pulling the trigger, she smacked him on the head with it, which set him off on a rash of obscenities. Without skipping a beat, she pulled out a small pack of diaper wipes and held several over his mouth and nose. He struggled for a second, then passed out. "Chloroform diaper wipes," she said shooting me a quick glance while moving to the accountant to knock him out as well, "who knew."

Lexie and I exchanged a WTF glance, but there was no time for contemplation about how we'd put that notion in her head because I was instructed to flip Mike over as she produced a small roll of duct. I was to place it over the mouth of the accountant first, then over Mike's. I did as I was told. Being the duct tape queen I was I finished with the accountant quickly and turned to Mike just in time to see Ramona withdraw a syringe from his mouth and tuck it in her fanny pack. I looked at her bewildered, but she turned away from me and issued an order, "Come on, gals, we've got to hurry."

Business must have been good that night from the sound the field teams made as they walked into the house, ready to drink a few beers and relax. They came in as a pack, walking up the staircase from the garage, laughing and joking. As they neared the top step, they were suddenly silent and we could hear weapons being drawn and just beyond that, the sirens, closer.

"Mike? Enrique?" we heard one of the men yell. Seconds later, we saw them, black silhouettes against the red and blue police flashers that were now coming up the driveway—they'd finally made it through the security gate—as the men slowly inched into the quiet great room.

They moved in together as a group, taking it all in. The room looked like a war zone. Bloodied bodies lay strewn across the hardwood floor. The first man was crumpled next to the door way with Fat Joe next to him, gagged, zip-tied, chloroformed and facing away from them; Tony and Doug were slumped in the middle of the room. Mike and the other man were lying on the floor passed out and duct taped, face up but still hog tied and dislocated-looking, near the kitchen island. Lisa and Lexie lay slumped up against the couch. Jackie sat on one of the barstools while I was on the dining room table, both of us with our hands tied behind our backs and our mouths gagged, mine with duct tape and hers with a dishtowel stuffed in it as we tried to look like scared, caged animals. As soon as we saw them we pleaded with our eyes and called to them as best we could through the duct tape.

"Jesus," one of them uttered as they slowly crept into the room.

"What the fuck happened?" I heard another say.

One of them reached out a large arm to me, painfully ripping the duct tape off my mouth. "Thank God!" I yelled, looking as delirious as I could, which wasn't hard since I was covered in blood from my gash and my eye was barely open. "Help!"

"Who are you?" one of them demanded. "Who did this?"

"Drop your weapons or you're next," Ramona commanded from behind a sturdy accent chair that was opposite the living area. "Now!" The men spun in the direction of the voice, aiming their guns at the chair. From my vantage point I could just barely make out Ramona's head and torso. This time she looked small, pale and extremely frail. Her injury seemed to be taking its toll, the dishtowel tied around her left arm was now soaked with blood, but she still held her handgun firm and pointed it directly at them.

"Please, please, please!" I cried, my code to let the others know I could see three guns. "She's crazy!" The men stood there, frozen, contemplating their move.

"Crazy like a fox," came Lexie's voice from the opposite side of the room, "and she said drop your weapons." They turned to see Lex, now alive and well, still holding Lisa with one arm, while the other pointed Tony's handgun at them.

"And she said *now.*" The voice was Jackie's. She had spit out the dishtowel and from behind her back where her hands were supposedly tied she pulled the other gun, the one we had found in the kitchen. Her arms were extended, her form perfect and the men now had guns pointed at them from three different directions. It was my turn.

I pulled Doug's gun from behind my back and calmly ordered, "Now means right now! On the floor!" Being the closest one to them with nothing to hide behind was terrifying, but I made myself stay calm. I moved cautiously around them, so they were completely surrounded and I'd have the wall of the staircase to hide behind. As I moved I told them the cops were here, that they couldn't win. "You have until the count of three," I commanded, "to put your weapons down. If you don't, we will shoot. You got that, ladies? Stay low and aim high if these jerks don't give up." I saw Jackie from the corner of my eye get behind the kitchen island like a sniper and close one eye. I did the same.

The room was now lit up with red and blue lights from what I could only hope was multiple cop cars and ambulances that must have finally busted through the gate. The sirens were still blaring and it was hard to concentrate. I could hear people banging at the front door, the cavalry had arrived, our rescue was in progress. We weren't going to be fed to the sharks. Maybe it was because of this, or because Lisa couldn't wait another second for help, or because I hated these men for what they so callously did for a living, or because I didn't want to chance them to really know our faces and be able to track us down later that I was ready to pull the trigger. Or maybe it was because I was willing to do anything to remain in control of the room and not risk another friend being shot.

"One!" I shouted, holding the solid, heavy gun in my hand, feeling its metallic, cold, density—its power—knowing what damage it could do. I readied myself to pull the trigger as the men stood there, paralyzed with indecision. It crossed my mind that one of them could be an undercover cop, but I immediately put the thought out of my head telling myself that only happens in movies. My swollen eye was actually helping my aim and I was surprised at how remarkably steady my hand was.

"Two!" I shouted, counting faster than I ever did with my boys, part of me wanting to give the dealers a fair amount of time to give up, the other part wanting to just get it over with. I started to shout out, "Three!" but someone louder than me came out of nowhere and commanded, "Freeze! F.B.I.! Nobody move!"

Suddenly shots were fired from all over the place. It was crazy, and loud and horrible. Two of the men fell back, clearly hit, but the others remained standing. One of them turned, his gun pointed, at what I couldn't tell. But I knew he was about to shoot so I pulled my trigger, three times, catching him at least once in the shoulder, making him fall back, his gun flying out of his hand.

Instantly, someone heavy as hell was on top of me, kicking the gun out of my hand, pulling my arms roughly behind my back and into another God damn zip tie. "F.B.I. Stay down!" the person commanded. I looked up to see the room taken over by officers wearing bullet-proof vests. Leading them all was Rachel.

"Rachel!" I screamed. "Get Lisa! She's shot! She needs an ambulance! Get Lisa! Get Lisa!" I screamed the same thing to the officer on top of me and then I watched from my place on the floor as the insane chaos of the night slowly came under control. Guns were collected. Pulses were felt. Lisa was loaded onto a gurney with Lexie still holding on to her, refusing to let go, yelling at me to join them at the hospital. Jackie and Ramona were taken in a second ambulance.

It was decided by Rachel that I would stay, at least for a while. I was finally picked up, my zip-tie cut, a blanket draped around me, a paramedic checked me out and left me sitting on the dining room bench with an ice pack for my eye. I scanned the scene. The floor was covered with blood and bodies. Police were everywhere. Photographs were being taken. The officers whispered amongst themselves, shaking their heads at the carnage, eyeing the stuff from Ramona's bag that was on the table, sneaking glances at me, a mixture of curiosity and surprise.

In the end, all the dealers lived except the one I shot at the doorway, Tony, and Doug. The others were taken to the hospital then, I presumed, jail.

Rachel came and took me to sit on the sofa where Ramona had

first pretended to faint, but not before I snatched her notebook from the island, clutching it to my chest. As a paramedic took care of me, I told her the whole harrowing story of our Mom's Night Out, from when Ramona first suggested it in the toddler pit at Adventureland up to when the FBI jumped on me. Then I personally put Ramona's blood-splattered Dora the Explorer notebook with all the information on the dealers in her hands. I wanted more than anything to get out of there, to be at the hospital with Lisa and the others, but I did not want any of those creeps to go free for lack of evidence.

"You're lucky to be alive," Rachel said, flipping through the book, "and that Lisa had the foresight to text me you guys were in trouble."

I took a breath. "When? She told the dealers her phone was at home."

"She's a smart cookie. She must have texted then ditched it. We'll go down the hill and look for it." She gave me a gratuitous half-smile that seemed to say, "I told you not to mess with fire." She looked far less glamorous than I had ever seen her. She was still cute, even in her vest and steel-toed boots, but suddenly her life, her job, no longer seemed exotic and exciting. There was nothing glamorous about what she did.

She got up to talk to a colleague, leaving me there to contemplate the room. I stared at the scene, shivering, but not from the cold. It was nearly three in the morning and I was exhausted. The torture, the guilt, the worry—my own injuries—were beginning to take their toll. I thought back to the moment when I saw the Penguins of Madagascar in my tub. For a few brief minutes tonight we had been that underdog, surprise attack, crack commando team. We had kicked ass and succeeded in taking down the bad guys. We had become everything I had dreamed, all the way down to the chloroform diaper wipes, and yet it hadn't been fun, we hadn't been laughing. And it had come at a price I had never, ever, imagined.

Twenty-Three

An hour later an officer dropped me off at the hospital and I didn't even let him come to a complete stop before I was out the door. On the way over I'd been able to have a quick conversation with a dazed and sleepy Mark, explaining as much as I could without losing it completely. Now I was focused on finding Lisa as I navigated the maze-like corridors with shitty directional signage, people shooting me incredulous looks everywhere I went.

Finally I found Lexie, Jackie and Pete in a waiting room on the second floor. When I saw my friends sitting there with Pete, all of them on the edge of an old, stiff, vinyl loveseat, sipping coffee out of Styrofoam cups, I couldn't help but let out a little scream and rush for them. Lexie and Jackie looked up and ran for me. We grabbed and held on to each other, all of us sobbing. I was now shaking again and Lexie hushed me and rubbed my back whispering, "It's okay, it's okay. We made it out of there. We're all safe".

"Lisa," I said, my voice cracking, my eyes anxious.

"She's in surgery," Lexie said, wiping her tears with the cuffs of her jean jacket still covered in Lisa's blood. "Her surgeon is one of my neighbors. She'll be okay, he's the best in California."

I took in her answer, seeing the gravity of it in both my friend's eyes, then in Pete's as he sat alone on the edge of the couch, looking at the ground, nervously bouncing one foot. "Pete," I ran and gave him a hug. "How long has she been in surgery?" I somehow managed to ask.

261

"About an hour," Pete answered, rubbing his tired eyes. "They send nurses out to give us updates. It's going to be at least another hour. All we can do is wait."

"She's a fighter," Lexie said, all of us nodding. "Did you see how she didn't stop fighting those guys? They say the bullet just grazed her heart."

"Her heart?" I cried, louder than I meant to, covering my mouth with my hands. Terror ran through me as I stood up to huddle with my friends and Jackie explained that the bullet had gone into Lisa's chest and had grazed her upper left ventricle. The hole itself was tiny and fairly easy to repair, they weren't worried about that. The problem was that she had lost a lot of blood. Her blood pressure had been practically non-existent when they brought her in and they were estimating that she had a class four hemorrhage. Stopping the bleeding, repairing the hole and getting more blood in her was their highest priority right now. I took a deep breath biting down on my lower lip as I took in the news.

"Oh my God, you guys," I whispered, feeling nauseous. "I am so sorry." My voice caught as I covered my face with my hands and sobbed, too horrified and embarrassed to look the friends I had endangered in the eye, totally aware that we could have been on our way to literally becoming shark food right now. "I can't believe how stupid I was, believing that we just needed to look inside one window. I never should have chased Ramona through that gate. If anything would have happened to you guys, to any of us..."

My voice trailed off as Lexie grabbed me and hugged me tightly and Jackie wrapped her arms around us both. "Lisa is going to be fine, okay?" Lex whispered. "You have to keep thinking that. And don't even think of blaming yourself for one minute, okay? You got that guy coming in the door, he could have shot us all. Lisa fucking jumped in front of a bullet to save Ramona. You guys are both heroes." She let go of me and made me look her in the eye. "By the way," Lexie scoffed, "there's no way Ramona would have listened to you, even if you tried to talk her out of her whacked-out madness. She was on a mission tonight and was hell-bent on completing it no matter who got in her way."

"I should have stopped her," I sniffed. "I should have caught up to her and then dragged her back to the car kicking and screaming."

"Are you kidding me?" Lexie asked. "Nothing, and I mean nothing, was going to stand in her way tonight. Did you see the arsenal she had? She probably would've tazed you, or chloroformed you, or injected you with some horse tranquilizer she had in her little fanny pack."

The tranquilizer comment jogged my memory. "I think she had a tranquilizer, or something." I told them about how I saw her syringe something into Mike's mouth.

Jackie freaked. "Jesus, who is she? This is surreal! I feel like she should pull off her face and underneath will be Tom Cruise as Ethan Hunt. She was wearing a bullet-proof vest for Christ's sake. And she had a pipe bomb in her bag. Who does that?"

"Don't get me wrong, I'm proud of her for taking those evil bastards out, but I'm pissed as hell that she almost got us all killed in the process," Lexie said.

"Where is she anyway?" I asked.

"Still down in the ER," Jackie answered. "I was just there. They patched up her shot arm with sixteen stitches and gave her some antibiotics and pain medication. She's got a few cracked ribs, too, from the bullets hitting the vest. Want to go see her?"

I nodded and looked to see if Lexie wanted to join as well. "You guys go, I'll stay with Pete," Lex said. "I don't know if I'll ever even be able to talk to her again."

When we got to the ER, Jackie waved at the security guard who smiled at her and grimaced at me and my swollen face, but then buzzed us both in. Jackie led me back through a maze of equipment, supplies, nurse's stations and chairs until we got to Ramona's room. The door was closed so we knocked softly and entered on tip toe, not wanting to wake her if she was asleep.

"Ramona?" Jackie whispered, slowly peeking behind the curtain that was drawn around her bed. "Ramona?" The room was brightly lit and I was suddenly aware of just how tired I was. I looked at my watch as Jackie gently pulled back the curtain, five a.m. The night was over. A new day was beginning. Under all normal circumstances Griffin would be coming into Mark's and my room right now to snuggle in with us for another hour or so until his brother woke up and the hustle and bustle of our day began.

"She's not here," Jackie said, a look of confusion crossing her face.

"Maybe they took her for more tests?" I shrugged.

We went to find the nurse in charge. "The old woman with the gunshot wound to the arm?" the nurse qualified. "She's still waiting for a room."

"But she's not in her room," Jackie said.

The nurse barely looked up. "Maybe she went to the bathroom. It's down that way."

We hurried off to look but she wasn't there. We checked her room one more time, just in case. No Ramona. We figured maybe she went to find Lisa. We stopped and asked the guard if he'd seen her but he said no, and that patients weren't allowed to walk around on their own. We thanked him, but by now we knew better. If Ramona wanted to get up to see Lisa, she would find a way.

We double-timed it back to the waiting area where we found Lexie and Pete standing, looking toward the operating rooms.

"She's out," Lexie called to us from down the hall, holding out her hand for us to grab. "They're taking her to her room now."

"How is she?" I asked.

"She's stable," Lexie said, with a weak smile. "She lost a lot of blood but they patched up the hole and everything seems to be working just fine."

I nodded and gripped her hand tighter. It wasn't exactly the good news I was hoping for. Somehow I was thinking maybe we'd get a miracle and they'd tell us she was fine, awake, cognizant, and that we could take her home tomorrow. But considering what the news could have been, I was ever so thankful.

They wheeled her out on a gurney and stopped briefly to let us say hello. We resisted the urge to rush to her, letting Pete greet her first.

Gently, he picked up her hand and held it to his cheek, whispering "Hey honey."

"She's still under the anesthetic," the nurse said. Pete nodded, keeping her hand glued to his cheek. He gazed at his wife who looked still and pale and broken with all the tubes coming out of her. Tears streamed out of his eyes as he squeezed her hand tighter and his words caught in his throat as he told her the things she needed to know, hoping she could somehow hear him. "You're going to be just fine, sweetheart. You need to stay here for a few days, then we'll get you home. The kids will be here later. They need you. *I* need you. We all need you to be well, okay? We love you so much."

The three of us got to say a quick hello and Pete placed Lisa's hand at her side then took hold of the bed to help wheel it to the ICU. He looked back at us as an afterthought and said to call him later for an update.

Lexie hooked her arms around Jackie's and mine as we watched Lisa roll down the hall, her husband at her side. We had all been longing to be with our kids, our husbands, but seeing Pete with Lisa made me ache for mine. I no longer just *wanted* to see them, to hold them. I *needed* to. I needed them like I needed food, water, air.

And then Mark was there, walking down the hallway, looking desperate and disheveled and determined. "Mark!" I called out, not wanting to waste a fraction of a second before I could be in his arms. He flew towards me, relief softening his wild look, but only for a moment until he saw my face. He stopped short in front of me, as though he was scared to touch me, to hurt me, but I grabbed him and held on as tightly as I could, the feeling of his arms enveloping me finally making me feel truly safe.

"Are you okay? What the hell happened? Is everyone okay?" he said frantically.

I let go and let him look at me. I was crying again. Having him there, retelling the horror of our night, explaining about Lisa, having to look him in the eye and knowing he'd told me to stay out of it made me feel so awfully ashamed. And his lecture, right there in the hallway, didn't help.

"Are you fucking out of your mind?" he practically yelled, abruptly taking his arms off me. "Do you have a death wish?"

"No," I mumbled, feeling very small, knowing I had this coming. Lexie tried to interrupt and explain it was all Ramona's idea but he quickly told her to butt out.

"Do you want the boys to grow up without a mom?"

"No," I replied, now quietly sobbing.

"What the hell were you thinking? That these guys would just what, roll over and let you guys take them to jail? Okay, ya got me," he mocked, throwing his hands up in a fake surrender.

"No."

"Then what? What is it that's so alluring? Is it fun to race around without anyone knowing where you guys are while you get involved in shit that is so far out of your league that you even can't comprehend how far out it is?"

"No, it wasn't fun, it was horrible," I said, meekly.

"Gee, ya think? What if Lisa dies in there?" he said, gesturing to the ICU. "What if that was you? How could you be so reckless with your life? With hers? With ours? All of you," he said, looking at Lexie and Jackie, too. He returned his focus to me and whispered. "I am so pissed at you right now. I don't even know what to say. How could you be so fucking careless?"

Everything he said was true. I had been so focused on getting rid of the criminal element in Hermosa, I had forgotten what truly needed to be protected. I had been lucky to come out alive and if anyone knew it, Mark did. In his line of work he saw truly awful things and I, all of us, could have been one of those truly awful things. A thing you never recover from.

"We're done. We're all done. This time for real. I promise."

Brian and Josh came bursting down the hall, both of them with the same desperate look that Mark had been wearing. Then there was the look of relief, then the news of what had happened at the house and to Lisa, then the reading of the riot act. As Lexie and Jackie were being chewed out, Mark grabbed me and pulled me into him, saying so only I could hear, "Jesus Christ, Kel, what would we do without you?" He pulled away enough to look at me but not enough to let me go. Anger and fear were in his eyes, but so were tears. "Enough, okay? This isn't funny. This is serious stuff."

Mark wanted to have my eye checked but I insisted I was okay, that the paramedics had looked me over, that I would get to a proper eye doctor later. We decided to check the E.R. for Ramona again one last time on our way out but she was nowhere to be found. We texted and called, as well as texted Bill, and Jackie said she'd follow up in a few hours. Then we headed for the parking lot where the street lights were starting to click off, the darkness of the night giving way to early morning, the songbirds wide awake in the bushes. We hugged our goodbyes and said we'd check in with each other in a few hours to discuss the logistics of the next few days, especially how we would split up taking care of Lisa's kids and her house.

Mark interrogated me the entire drive home, asking questions about every detail, glaring at me every so often. He also held my hand with a grip that said he was not letting go.

We walked into the house and while he handled the neighbor he had woken up to watch the boys, I let myself take it all in: the smell of last night's pizza still lingered; Candyland lay spread out all over the kitchen table; our camping tent was constructed in the living room; six freshly finger-painted pictures were clipped to a string that hung across our breakfast nook.

Then he was back, the neighbor gone with a concerned wave. "You guys were busy last night," I smiled, taking in the mess, trying to get Mark to say something, anything, to show his icy demeanor might soon thaw. He just nodded and raised both eyebrows mumbling, "We weren't the only ones."

He took my hand and lead me towards Casey's room saying, "Come on, let's get you to bed." I followed easily, my body on autopilot.

The darkness of his room, the little boy smell, the toys arranged so I could guess the scenario he had been playing, was like heaven. "I'll go get Griffy," Mark whispered as I nodded, unable to tear my eyes from my first born. I crept over books and toys and quietly let myself under his sheets until I was curled up against his sweet warm body. In the span of twelve hours since I had seen him last, he had grown a fraction older, bigger. I marveled at how long his body was becoming, how his sweet baby fat was disappearing from his cheeks, how he was growing into his ears. I kissed his head, smelling his hair, taking in the scent of his skin. Then Mark was there with Griffy, breaking two cardinal rules we had set by first getting Grif out of bed when he was still sleeping and then by letting him sleep with me.

I smiled at Mark who, this time, gave me a faint smile back, placing Griffin in his footy pajamas under the sheets next to me. I watched in awe as my baby opened his eyes, looked at me and said, "Hi Mama," then stuck his left thumb in his mouth and went back to sleep. I snuggled him closer, feeling the softness of his warm body on one side of me while Casey's foot searched for me under the covers, then hearing both of them take in deep, relaxing, dreamy breaths. And then I felt it, like I always did when we were snuggled in together. A magical chemical reaction, a rush of contentment. I couldn't imagine how any drug in the world could make someone feel any better than I did now.

Twenty-Four

Two unexpected things happened the next day. The first was Jackie found Ramona—finally—after an extensive search that took her from Ramona's house to the hospital to Ramona's boat, all documented via group texts we began receiving around noon. "*House search: No Ramona; Hospital: No Ramona; Ramona's boat: No Ramona.*" Finally around two we got the text, "*Ramona found! Bill says he found her sleeping on his deck. He brought her inside, has been asleep ever since. Says she checked herself out of hospital because didn't want any unnecessary tests. His story seems fishy & he's acting odd.*"

I chocked the "odd" comment up to thinking Bill was probably surprised and shocked by the whole incident. At least we found her so that was one less person I needed to worry about because the other thing that happened was that Lisa did not wake up. The doctors said to give her time, it was not that unusual, but I had knots in my stomach all day. Not that I had much time to think about it between taking a shift to watch her kids, watching my own kids, and being questioned by the police and the FBI. Pete started his own group text to let us know how she was doing.

Apparently she had become a bit of a minor celebrity in the ICU. The staff was used to seeing police officers walking the halls, but it was rare to see the FBI and DEA lingering. The gossip of who she was and how she was injured spread like wild fire and Pete told us he heard an orderly refer to her once as part of the "Momfia." Most of the hospital staff had walked the Strand at some point, and knew of the drug dealers who claimed the pier as their territory. They therefore took to making some exceptions to the ICU rules for us all, extending visiting hours and allowing extra visitors.

Which was nice, because the next day she did wake up and after a week, they said she was strong enough to go home. We celebrated by having our first and declared last MNO at the hospital the night before she was discharged.

It was a festive evening and we were all beyond thrilled to be together. There was lots of laughter, some joking around and of course, plenty of tears. The nurses kept coming in and telling us to keep the noise level down, lecturing us that there were other patients we needed to be considerate of, that just because the doctors had cleared Lisa to go home didn't mean she could party like a rock star.

Lisa was now off all her I.V.'s, her color was back and her eyes were bright. "You look *fantastic*," I said, sitting on her bed and squeezing her hand.

"Thanks," she smiled. "I lost about ten pounds, although I think most of it was blood. I call it the 'Get Shot Be Comatose Weight Loss Plan.'"

"Then you deserve one of these," Lexie said, opening a box of beautiful cupcakes. "Try this one, it's lavender-casis. It will blow your mind."

Lisa smiled. "Ramona brought these in yesterday. They're awesome. From Becker's, right?"

Lexie scowled. She still had not forgiven Ramona. "You sure the icing wasn't laced with arsenic? Or the cake bugged with a microchip?"

We were all able to at least smile a little at her joke. Now that Lisa was out of danger and we'd all had healthy doses of our families and knew everyone was safe, we were, at least on the outside, beginning to be able to relax a little about our terrorizing ordeal.

Jackie looked at Lisa tentatively, trying to gauge Lisa's take on Ramona. "Has Ramona been by a lot?" she asked trying to be nonchalant. "How's she looking?"

Ramona had apparently been by practically every night, sneaking in after visiting hours were over while Pete was still at home getting the kids settled in for the night.

While they talked, Lisa had noticed something different about Ramona. She thought that maybe it was just that she was embarrassed by the danger she put everyone in, and apologizing didn't come naturally to her. But for someone who was trying desperately to make amends, she was a little guarded. And, while she was very, very sincere about how sorry she was and kept repeating how much Lisa's friendship and the friendship of all the others meant to her, Lisa said she'd done enough interviews over the years to know when someone was hiding something, and Ramona was definitely hiding something.

Lisa looked at Jackie. "You haven't seen her? Her arm is still in a sling and she's not using it, but she's still full of her usual vim and vigor. She amazes me, she's got more energy than both of my teenagers. You're not going for walks anymore?"

Jackie shrugged and nodded. "I can't tell what's up with her. She's not returning my calls. She's definitely hiding something, though."

"Like an Uzi?" Lexie suggested. "Or a samurai sword? Can't you just see all eighty-five pounds of her brandishing a fucking samurai sword?" Lexie laughed heartily at her own joke.

"Wearing her big purple hat, too," I added.

Jackie laughed a little at the thought, picking a few sprinkles off her cupcake as she listened but quickly returned to her point. "Seriously guys, I'm worried. She's acting odd, I just can't put my finger on what it is."

"Yeah," Lexie said, pulling out a bottle of Dom Perignon from her duffle bag. "Well I wouldn't put my finger on anything remotely related to Ramona. It will probably explode." With that she popped open the champagne and pulled out some plastic flutes. "Celebratory champagne!" She handed the champagne to me and Jackie pulled out a bottle of sparkling apple cider and filled a glass for Lisa. Lisa raised her eyebrow at Lex and waved off the cider, pointing instead to the champagne.

"Please. I survived torture and a close-range bullet shot through my heart by evil, deranged drug dealers. I think I can toast with the real stuff."

"Here, here," Lexie said. She put the cider down and handed Lisa over her champagne. "Nice to see you're feeling like your old self."

"It's nice to be feeling like my old self," she replied then raised her glass and looked around the room at her friends. "To friendship. May it always win out in the end."

"To friendship," we all repeated, tapping our glasses together and looking at each other through misty eyes.

As if on cue, there was a small knock at the door. Ramona stuck her head in. "Excuse me," she said, trying to keep the atmosphere light as though she feared her mere presence would crush the mood. "Is this a hospital or a bar?"

"Ramona!" The champagne helped us to open our arms and invite her in, hugging her as tightly as we dared, trying to be careful of her bruised ribs and injured arm. She returned our embraces, then moved to Lisa for the same.

"I know you're still upset," she said, turning to Lexie, "so I won't even try to hug you." Her eyes were kind and filled with the hope that Lexie would forgive her, if not now, someday. Even with her injuries and bandages, I was surprised to see that she looked better than I'd ever seen her before. Her hair had been cut, colored and styled, and she wore cute, stylish jeans and a light, summery shirt over a tank top. Long gone were her heavy, formless hippie clothes, big hats and messy, long hair. It was as if a new Ramona had emerged from a cocoon.

"I'm not here to crash the party," she said, waving off a drink and our insistences to stay, our questions about not returning calls. "I just have something quick to say and then I'll be on my way." She then went out into the hall and came back in carrying a paper sack from Trader Joes in her good hand.

"Don't worry, Lexie," Ramona said as she came back in, "it isn't a bomb." Lexie smirked and I could tell her cold demeanor toward Ramona was cracking. Deep down I knew she really loved Ramona.

How could she not? They were cut from the same cloth—two outspoken, take no bull-shit, what-you-see-is-what-you-get kind of people—and I knew she planned to be as bold in her old age as Ramona was now.

"They're too heavy for paper sacks," Ramona continued, "you need at least a canvas tote for those. But I did bring a guest."

From out in the hall Rachel glided in looking every bit like a Bond girl. Her smooth, shiny hair was parted on the side and she wore a jeweled barrette to keep it out of her face. Her flawless skin glowed and her light make-up highlighted her perfect bone structure. She was the poster child for L.A. fashion in a cute, filmy top with a tight camisole underneath, form-fitting, low-rise jeans and Gucci heels. She slung what I was sure was the latest Prada hobo bag over her shoulder.

There were more squeals of joy and another round of heart-felt greetings and hugs as Rachel made the rounds. She quickly accepted a glass of champagne, declined a cupcake, and took a seat in a chair by the window. Ramona, watching with a smile on her face, took center stage. When everyone quieted down and she had our attention, she told us that she asked Rachel here to explain, in confidence, who the men in the PV house really were. But first, she had something she wanted to say.

"My actions were inexcusable, and I fear, unforgivable," she said taking a deep breath. "I've been able to tell Lisa this individually but the rest of you are hard to pin down and I'm running out of time so I came here with you all as a group to tell you collectively how very, very sorry I am. I really can't say it enough, but please know that I mean it from the depths of my soul. I endangered your precious lives, I could have left your children motherless, your husbands windowed, and that's something that I will have to live with the rest of my life." She stopped and took a breath, eyes lowered, shaking her head. When she looked up she was collected and wiped her cheek. "I needed to look you all in the eye one last time before I go, to let you know how much you all mean to me."

We all looked at each other quizzically, trying to see if anyone knew what she was talking about. She and Bill were leaving tomorrow, she said. They were taking his boat down through the Panama canal, then island hopping in the Caribbean before flying to Jakarta to spend time with her children and grandkids. "It's a dream I've had forever and Ben and I never got to do it before he passed. Bill is a widower and never had children. He loves to travel and is dying to play the role of surrogate Grandpa so it turns out, we make a pretty good team." She then thanked us for being so kind to her, for being such good friends, for including her in our little group and treating her like an equal. "If Jackie hadn't come along, befriending this crotchety old lady, bringing me with my heels dug in to your parties, my only kick in life would still be watching Smedley poop on Mr. O'Hanlin's lawn," she said laughing.

She dug into her bag and pulled out her antique martini glasses and shaker. "For you, Lexie. These have been through many, many good times. You are the life of the party and I admire your spunk. I hope you can continue to make merry with them." Lexie, taken aback at being given a gift she knew was dear to Ramona blushed and thanked her, not knowing what else to say.

Next she pulled out a small velour pouch. "Kelly, these are genuine pirate pieces of eight from the wreck site of the San Martin, which was due to sail for Spain in 1618. I found them scuba diving off the coast of Florida. They've been certified and you can read all about them in this little document. With your imagination and energy, I hope you and your boys will have many pirate adventures with them." Ramona handed the coins to me and I felt my chest tighten. I whispered "Thank you, we'll treasure these," and had so much more to say but when I looked at her, she had already turned to Lisa.

"Lisa," Ramona said, smiling at her. "You bring so much heart into this world, through your work, through your love for your children. But, take it from an experienced control freak, looking back I wish I would have let go a little more often and enjoyed the ride. To help you do so, I am giving you the keys to my boat." Lisa looked at her in disbelief and shook her head no.

"I'm not going to take your boat," Lisa laughed. "That's way too much."

But, Ramona insisted. She walked over to her and put the keys in her hand, holding them there while she spoke, looking intently into her eyes. "You have no idea how good sailing is for your soul. You and Pete attack projects like lions on wildebeests so I know you'll learn to sail in no time. Or, you guys can just take a bottle of wine down and have dinner alone on it. Boats can be incredibly romantic. Or you could take the entire family out and go to the Channel Islands. Adventure awaits!"

Lisa still protested. "No, really, I can't. It's your boat, it's too much."

"Well then, think of it this way," Ramona said, "it's just going to be sitting there gathering dust and Bill won't be there to keep it floating. You're in charge for the entire crew here, you can all use it." She added that she had arranged a maintenance crew to take care of it, so it would be ready at any time. Then she handed a sheet of paper with names and phone numbers to Lisa, telling her that these were some of Bill's boat friends and that any one of them would be happy to take she and Pete out and show them the ropes. "Plus," she added, winking and nodding her head to the others, "it's got a bit of a reputation as being a hot party spot for moms."

Lisa smiled and thanked her, relenting. "Okay, but I'll just be taking care of it until you return. Which is going to be when, by the way?"

Ramona turned back to her bag, "I'll get to that in a minute." She pulled another set of keys from her bag and turned to Jackie and took a big breath. "Jackie," she said with a smile. "I love you like a daughter. Your friendship has meant the world to me. You and that darling little girl of yours are more precious to me than you will ever know." Jackie smiled back at her and wiped away a few tears. "I want you to have these," she put her house keys into Jackie's hands. "The moments when Sierra came to visit and play at my house were the highlight of my life since Ben passed. I would feel so honored if she would continue to play at 'Wamona's playhouse.'" Ramona spoke of how she'd had some contractors over and that she was pretty sure Sierra and her mommy would be happy with the changes.

Jackie smiled through her tears and hugged Ramona, thanking her. "But you'll still live there when you get back right?" she asked.

Ramona took a deep breath and rubbed her sore arm. "Well, that's the thing," she said, looking at the floor so as to not hold Jackie's gaze. "I don't think we're coming back."

"What?" Jackie said, shocked and puzzled. "What do you mean, you *live* here." We all, even Lexie, echoed similar sentiments. Shivers began to go up and down my spine as I realized this wasn't just a see-ya-later kind of party crash, it was Ramona's way of saying farewell.

Ramona, who hated to be fretted over, basked a little in the fuss then tried to quiet everyone down. "Thank you," she said blushing, "knowing you would still want me around means more to me than you can imagine. But," she said, "the truth is, I'm dying to get back to my grandkids. I might not have been the best parent, I was impatient and couldn't wait for them to grow up, frankly. But it's not too late for me to enjoy my grandkids and I really want to be there for them, to watch them grow up, to know them and let them know me. Maybe I'll even get to know their mommies and daddies a little better, too. And, now," she took a big breath and look at us all, letting her eyes rest on Lisa, "that those dealers are gone and Lisa is healthy, it's time. Time for me to go." She half smiled at Jackie and picked up her hand to hold it.

"How can you do that?" Jackie stammered. "Just get up and go and never look back? You go from being this super-grandma-best-friend to bad-ass-psycho-ninja-drug-hunter to disappearing off the face of the earth just like that?" Jackie snapped her fingers. "Who does that?"

Ramona smiled weakly. "At my age, you start thinking that you better do what you need to do, because you might run out of time. And, after the other night, the danger that I put you all in? Well, it would be hard to live here and have to look you in the eye knowing how badly I betrayed your trust. I would feel ashamed every day."

"But we forgive you!" Jackie practically cried. "All of us. Even

Lexie." Jackie shot Lexie a look that said she had better forgive Ramona or else. "We want you to stay. We need you." We all nodded but I think we knew it was futile. We had learned that once her mind was made up, there was no changing it.

"I can't tell you how much that means to me," Ramona said, taking a deep breath. "I will miss you and your little ones so very, very much."

"Hey," Lexie said, suddenly standing up. "I've got an idea! Isn't next summer your 80th birthday?"

"Yes," Ramona replied. "Thank you for reminding me."

"Ladies," Lexie said, getting up off her chair, "I've been meaning to talk to you guys about taking long weekends, just us girls, to have a little fun. This is the perfect way to kick them off!" She raised her glass and looked excitedly around the room at her friends. "I propose that next summer we start our annual girlfriend getaways. The first one will be to find our globe-trotting friend here—where ever she may be—and help her celebrate her birthday!"

Lexie looked at us all as the thought of a few days of rest and relaxation, shopping and girl talk, sleeping late and drinking wine, possibly in a foreign country, sank in.

"I'm in," Lisa said almost immediately. She held up her glass.

"Count me in, too," I said, holding my glass toward Lexie's. I looked at Ramona and pointed. "But no guns! No stakeouts!"

"Okay, okay," Ramona conceded, holding her hands up. "No guns."

"That includes all rifles, automatic and semi-automatic weapons," I clarified.

"Got it," Ramona said with a wink.

"Or grenades," Lisa scolded, her eyebrow raised in mock reproach.

"Okay, no grenades," Ramona said in a fake whine, rolling her eyes like a teenager.

"Or anthrax," Lexie said, happy to jump into the game. "No airborne poisons or contaminants of any sort!"

"But the non-airborne kind are okay?" Ramona joked.

"No!" Lisa, Lexie and I all said in unison.

"Come on, Jackie, what do you say?" Lexie probed, sitting down next to her and nudging her with an elbow.

Jackie swallowed hard and looked at Ramona with big, sad eyes. Ramona returned the gaze as if to say that everything would be alright. Begrudgingly Jackie wiped her eyes, picked up her champagne and looked up at us all. "Fine. But you have to promise to Skype. And like a normal person, not hanging by a wire and talking on your shoe phone. I don't want to have to worry about you."

There was cheering and clinking of plastic cups. I heard Rachel utter, "I don't think anyone has to worry about her," under her breath. Then we hugged Ramona and wished her luck on her adventures. She smiled and took it all in, promising to keep in touch and to send all our kids postcards. She stopped at the doorway and turned to us one last time, holding up her good hand. Then she turned back and was gone. The room was silent.

"I think this is a great time for my spiel," Rachel said, getting up. In her hand she held a plain manila envelope. "So, I'm guessing it's pretty fair to say—now that your ring leader is leaving the country— you all will not be taking the law into your own hands again?" We all looked at her like kindergarteners being chastised by the principal. No one spoke, we all just shook our heads. "Good answer. Now, this will all come out in the trial, but Ramona thought you might like to be 'in the know' regarding the men whose bodies we identified and the others we arrested."

We all sat up straighter, shooting each other curious looks. "I thought so," Rachel said. She went on to inform us that the leader of the group was a man named Mike Nelson. He was a local dealer, selling all over L.A. with his headquarters here in the South Bay. He'd been building his business for about ten years and had 25 people working for him.

"He died yesterday, autopsy results show botulism, we're not sure how he was infected. Anyone?" She looked at us and my stomach jumped as I thought about the syringe. She made eye contact with me and said quickly, "I thought not. We're concluding he ate something that was bad." She continued saying Mike had four "lieutenants," Doug and Tony being two of them. The other was the man who had shot Lisa and Ramona and whom I had, in turn, shot and killed. All the other men at the house that night were lower on the totem pole, worker bees if you will, plus Alfonzo, the accountant, who was fully cooperating with the investigation.

The DEA had been able to locate their spot on Catalina and were investigating whether they cooked meth there. The last lieutenant was on the run, but Rachel was sure they'd be able to track him down and didn't think he would pose any threat to us. All of the men, she assured us, would be going away for a long time.

When she finished, we were all speechless. "Ramona thought you might be impressed, we at the FBI certainly are. How a little old lady and her crew of *chardonnay moms*," Rachel rolled her eyes as she spoke, "were able to single-handedly take out an organization like Mike's, one that Alfonzo tells us was in the process of beginning to work with one of the Mexican cartels…" she shook her head in disbelief. "Well, we're all just a little mystified by it. Ramona's notes, reports and testimony should help seal the prosecution's case."

"And speaking of Ramona, she wanted me to read this and pass these out to you after she left." We watched quietly, sipping our champagne, as Rachel opened the paper and began to read:

Dear Friends,

I was horribly wrong to endanger your lives. Your friendship has meant the world to me, has brought me back to life, and for that I can't thank you enough. I wanted to quickly explain that I had no intention of ever firing my weapon. I have never harmed a soul in my life, I even buy the humane type of flea repellant for Smedley! I don't even like to fish when we're out on the boat because of the harm it does to the little guys. But the way I see it, those men are better off dead than alive. I can't explain it, but I did go a little "bat-shit," as Lexie likes to say, when Mike threatened to kill us all and then go back for your children. People like that just shouldn't be on this earth in my humble opinion. Enough said.

Now, Rachel is going to give you all an envelope. Inside you'll find I've opened a 529 plan for each of your kids with some starter money to get things going. Don't argue and don't try to give it back. Your kids and you deserve it for what I put you through. Encourage them, as you already do, to make the world a better place for everyone. Take good care of yourselves. I love you all and miss you already.

    Your friend,

    Ramona

Rachel took the little envelopes and handed them out to each of us. We all received one envelope for each of our children with the name of the child written on it, except Jackie, who received one for Sierra and one with a question mark on it. We held them until they were all passed out and then looked at each other. "Should we open them?" I asked.

"I don't see why not," Lexie responded. We all shrugged and opened the envelopes, finding a certificate stating that a 529 plan worth $100,000 had been opened for each of our children.

"You've got to be kidding me," Lisa gasped. "She's giving me $400,000? Plus her boat?"

"I've got three certificates for $100,000," Lexie stated in awe, "one for each kid."

"Is she insane?" Jackie asked the group, looking a little panicked. "I mean, she's giving away everything. Her boat, her house, her money. Is she dying? Does she have cancer? Do you think she's just going off to die by herself because she doesn't want to burden us?"

"Don't worry," Rachel said calmly, "she's got more. *Lots* more actually."

Rachel then explained how the dealers would load their boats, the ones near Ramona's, with money, then they would take it back to Catalina where he owned a souvenir store that would launder it. The night of our ordeal, the accountant claimed that both boats were filled with over one million each, but by the time the investigators went down to check out their story, the money was gone. They figured one of Mike's dealers who didn't get arrested or killed that night probably knew about the loading practices and stole it. But, when Ramona came to Rachel with the envelopes a few days ago, it set off a red flag.

Immediately Rachel had her team look into Ramona's finances. "Turns out she owns five properties in Hermosa, including the house where she currently resides, plus a few other investment properties she and her late husband bought decades ago. We think she's worth about five million, give or take. I doubt she knows she's worth that much, just from the way she lives. But you never know, I wouldn't put much past her." Rachel explained that she and her team thought Ramona had been planning this whole thing, the drug dealer raid, the 529 plans, everything, for at least six months now. She had opened the plans back in March, taking the money directly from a property she sold at the beginning of February.

"So," Jackie asked, staring straight at Rachel with a skeptical look, "you guys think Ramona came back from being with her kids over the holidays, realized that's where she truly wants to be, sold a house to take care of us and began putting together the final pieces of her plan to rid the beach of the drug dealers so she could get back to her grandkids?"

Rachel chuckled a little, "As far-fetched as it sounds, yes, that's what we think. It's pretty easy to connect the dots. We just wish we knew where the drug money went." She looked questioningly at all of us. We all looked at each other and at Rachel shaking our heads. Rachel smirked. "Yeah, I didn't think so. You guys would have told me right off the bat."

We continued chatting about the case for a while longer, how they were investigating all the supposed "death by sharks" near Catalina, how they were working to seize the rest of Mike's assets, then Rachel got a call and had to go, leaving us to ponder her fresh information.

Twenty-Five

Two months later, I stood in my kitchen with Jackie and Lisa sitting across the island watching me make cheese raviolis from scratch for the evening's MNO. Tonight it was just the four of us—Lisa, Jackie, Lexie and me—since I hadn't had the energy to get the entire crew together yet. And we were staying in instead of going out. The plan was to have a good meal, a couple of great bottles of wine and binge watch *Downton Abbey.*

"You know you can buy hundreds of those at Costco for like ten bucks, right?" Jackie asked, nodding to my raviolis.

I smiled with a slight shrug. "Yeah, I know," I said, taking a ball of dough and rolling it out thinly. "But making these is good for me," I said with a shrug, "or so my therapist says."

"Why's that?" Lisa asked, popping an olive in her mouth.

"It's a process you can't rush. I'm working on not being so..." I took a moment to choose my words accurately, "seemingly over-caffeinated."

"Ah." She didn't argue.

"So, how's Ramona's house?" I asked, looking at Jackie. "What's that all about?"

She almost choked on her wine. "Amazing! Did I not tell you? She had had it totally pimped it out for Sierra, everything is toddler-sized and pink. There's a little kitchen, a little library, a little game room, and a room filled with dolls and a doll house. "It's like her own personal children's museum. She could spend hours there, which is

282

nice because she made me an Artist's Studio in the room next door."

"Nice! And the boat, Lisa? Have you used it yet?" I asked.

"This weekend, baby," Lisa replied with a smile and a faint blush. "Pete and I are going to take a picnic down around sunset, just the two of us." She said she still felt weird about using it, but we were all trying to get her over it. Since being discharged from the hospital, Lisa had quit her job and she and Pete were even thinking of taking the kids abroad for a year, homeschooling and making a documentary about the experience. It seemed we were all working on getting some sanity and little balance back in our lives.

"Good for you," Jackie said. She started to say something else but Lexie flew through the door like a hurricane.

"You guys are going to crap when you see this," she said, tossing her purse, shades and keys on my couch while hopping around and trying to take off her boots.

"You can take the girl out of the trailer park," Jackie mumbled.

Lexie padded on over in her socks and dropped the day's South Bay News on the island in front of us stating, "Seriously, you are not going to fucking believe this!" As soon as the words were out she quickly cupped her hand over mouth and looked around.

"It's okay," I said with a nod, "they're out back with the sitter."

"Oh shit, thank God," she said, totally relieved. She was desperately trying to get back in the habit of not swearing, at least not around children. It clearly wasn't going so well. "So look!" she said, thumping the paper, "hot off the presses!"

Lisa turned the paper to face her and began to read the top headline out loud as Lexie happily accepted a glass of wine. "Hermosa Beach Receives Multi-million Dollar Anonymous Donation," Lisa began reading. She looked up, one eyebrow cocked, then got back to reading. "Hermosa Beach officials have announced that the City Council received an anonymous donation of almost two million dollars on Monday. The city treasurer first noticed the wire and thought it was a mistake but upon further investigation, it was found that the donation was made to the city with the stipulation that it be split equally amongst the City Council, the Police Department and the School Board. Little is known about the anonymous donor except that the wire originated in the Cayman Islands. Council Members will be having a special session to discuss the donation in the upcoming week."

Lisa put the paper down and looked up at us all. "This is incredible."

I could hardly talk I was so shocked, the thought that we could get more full-time officers and add new computers at the schools flashed through my head.

"That's just unreal," Jackie stated. "And the donor is anonymous? Who does that?"

"Maybe it was Mayor Arvid," I suggested, my voice returning. "Maybe he's trying to redeem himself and can't seem to find the nerve to do it in person?"

"He didn't steal that much," Lisa replied, adding, "and he's not exactly the type to return the money he embezzled with a boatload of interest."

Lexie stared at us, awestruck. "C'mon, you guys don't know? Think about it."

"What? You know?" I asked, my eyes going wide. "How do you know?"

"Oh, I know," she said. "You know, too."

"How should I know," I scoffed. "I don't know anyone with that kind of money."

"Ramona," Lisa said, almost in a whisper, looking to Lexie to see if she was thinking the same thing.

"No way," Jackie and I said together, Jackie adding that Ramona's fortune was tied up in real estate and anyway she was saving it for her grandchildren and children, to make up for lost time.

"Yes way," Lexie said slyly, "and I didn't say it was *her* money, just that she was the one to make the donation."

As I was thinking and watching Lexie I could hear Jackie saying, "So whose money would she give? Bill's? His boat was nice, like super nice-nice as a matter of fact. I bet he's loaded but I doubt she would talk him into giving Hermosa a cool two mil." And then it came to me and I looked over at Lexie.

"You aren't thinking?" I asked, the words coming out slowly.

Lexie raised both eyebrows and smiled a conspiring smile. "I am thinking."

"But how," I gasped and Lexie shrugged as if to say, *Stranger things have happened.*

I stopped work on the raviolis and put my hands on my hips, my eyes locked on Lexie. "She wouldn't have! She couldn't. It's not possible," I blubbered. I was so astonished by the thoughts I was putting together in my head that I could barely get out a complete sentence.

Lisa jumped into the conversation, grinning broadly she held the paper in one hand and flicked it with the other. "She absolutely would! It's about the same amount, and it's from a bank in the Caymans."

"O! M! G!" I exclaimed, slapping the granite countertop as I said each letter, causing a puff of flour to rise up into the air. "You're right! She would! She friggin' would!"

By this point Jackie had figured it out as well, but was not about to buy into our theory. She sat back and crossed her arms and simply said, "No."

"No what?" Lexie said, always up for a confrontation.

"I know what you guys are thinking and you're wrong. There is no way Ramona stole Mike's money from the boats and donated it. It's physically impossible."

"You do remember who we're talking about here," Lisa chided. "I wouldn't use the word 'impossible' anywhere near her."

"And look," I said, holding up the paper. "It's more or less the same amount Rachel said the boats were carrying!"

"But how would she get it?" Jackie asked, shaking her head. "That money was sealed up on those boats and agents were all over them first thing in the morning."

"And Ramona checked herself out of the hospital almost as soon as she was checked in and disappeared," Lisa said convincingly. "You yourself said she looked exhausted the next day."

"When you found her. At the marina. *Where the boats with the money were,*" Lexie added, grinning.

"We all looked exhausted," Jackie argued.

"And look, the money came from the Caymans—" Lisa began.

"And Ramona and Bill are in Panama and were staying there a week. I just spoke with them three days ago."

"And Ramona would never lie, right? Oh no, not our sweet, little Ramona," Lexie said.

"Quick geography lesson," Lisa said pulling out her iPhone and bringing up her map application. "Once you get through the Panama canal, what's due north of you?"

"Jamaica," Jackie said, being stubborn.

"And just to left of that?" Lisa said, cocking her head. "The Cayman Islands. Both the Caymans and Panama are huge banking hubs because of their security laws. They shield and protect their customers like crazy. She could have deposited the money in Panama and zipped it to the Caymans. Or she and Bill could be in the Cayman Islands by now. It wouldn't take that long to get there, especially not on his boat. Who knows?"

"I don't know," Jackie said, looking hesitant. "Sounds a little far-fetched to me. I can't see her risking it. Dealers are pretty vengeful when you steal their money, you know."

"They aren't vengeful when they're dead. She probably figured the town would be better off with the money than having it sit in some evidence room," Lexie said. "And there wasn't time for any of the other guys that weren't working that night to have found out what happened then to rob their own boats."

"She is such a badass," I added, "don't forget she was a Merchant Marine."

"I think she wanted some good stuff to come from that money," Lisa reasoned, sitting back. "It wouldn't surprise me if that was part of the plan all along."

"I don't know," Jackie said, shaking her head. "It still sounds pretty crazy."

"About as crazy as a gang of moms with a senior citizen for a ring leader taking down a major drug dealer?" Lexie asked. "I'm telling you," she said matter-of-factly tapping the paper with her finger. "That's got Ramona's fingerprints all over it."

"I admit it's all weird," Jackie said, shrugging, trying not to tear up. "Maybe we could call her? Tell her we figured it out. Persuade her to confess."

"Ha! That woman is a vault. She's taking that secret to the grave," Lexie said.

Jackie shrugged. "Do you guys think Bill knew?"

"Fuck yeah," Lexie said, without a moment's hesitation, wrinkling her forehead and digging into my appetizer tray. "He's totally in on it. Could have even been his idea."

Lisa nodded, swirling her cabernet on the countertop. "Ramona's good, but she'd have a tough time doing all that by herself. She was bruised, had cracked ribs and a fresh gunshot wound, remember? All that money had to be heavy."

I shook my head a little. "I can just see them, down at the dock, scurrying about in the dark—"

"Wait a minute!" Jackie suddenly cried, throwing up her hands like she was trying to stop traffic. "You guys! We can totally find out what happened that night."

"How?" Lisa asked.

"Think about it. What's attached to her mast?"

"I don't know, a sail?" Lexie pondered.

"Oh my God, did she never tell you guys this?" She looked astonished and we, in turn, looked dumbfounded. "A nanny cam! She installed a nanny cam that's hidden inside a bear on her mast!"

"What?" Lisa was the first to ask, sitting up. "When?"

"Yes! She saw mine, thought it was a cool idea and got one. It's been up since, I don't know, Valentine's Day. I think Bill helped her install it. I guess with Nicole and your mom and everything going on, I forgot to tell you."

"Are you guys thinking what I'm thinking?" Lexie asked.

"This party's moving to the marina!" I cried. "Sorry gals, rain check on the raviolis." Organized chaos broke out in a mad scramble to gather up everything and clean up the kitchen. They knew my kitchen as well as I did and in no time everything was packed up and ready.

We piled into Jackie's SUV, all of us texting our husbands to let them know where we'd be, a new habit we'd all adopted. Ten minutes later we were in the marina parking lot, then practically running down the dock like a pack of wild first graders to the boat.

"Here we are!" Lisa said, jingling the key when we got to Ramona's gate. She unlocked it and we walked in, marveling at the stuffed koala bear that looked adorable hugging the mast about ten feet off the deck. We tossed our stuff aside and quickly settled in.

"You know how to work this thing?" Lexie asked Jackie.

"I'm on it," she replied, as I pulled out the wine and poured four small glasses. Lexie and Lisa busied themselves with setting up some appetizers.

"Bingo!" Jackie announced. "We are in business, people." We positioned ourselves in front of the TV with our wine and a plate of cheese and crackers.

"This is so exciting!" Lisa exclaimed, but her excitement was quickly diminished when all we could see was a dark, grainy silhouette of the marina, dark masses barely bobbing. "Are you sure this it?"

"Hang on, we have to find the right date. The taping mechanism records only the day, not the time," Jackie answered. She pointed the remote at the TV and we saw a time-lapse of several days and nights go by. "Here, this should be it, the night of the 'incident'. Look carefully for any action and remember, she's stealth."

"We remember," Lexie muttered.

We all moved a little closer to the screen as Jackie pressed fast-forward on the remote. The screen was so dark that I really couldn't see any difference between the two speeds, but I squinted and tried to focus. After ten minutes Lisa jumped and pointed, almost knocking over Lexie's wine. "Wait! There! I saw something."

Jackie stopped the recording and hit rewind for a few seconds, then hit play. Lisa got inches from the screen and pointed with her finger. "It's right...there!" She pointed to a small image in the bottom corner. "It moves!" Jackie hit play again and we watched, all of us except Jackie squinting to see.

She was right. There was a shadow, just barely visible, but clearly moving. It was a black silhouette of a person, and it moved onto the boat, disappeared, then was visible again. I was amazed I could even see it, it blended in so well.

"See?" Lisa said. "It's carrying something."

"It's a cooler," Lexie said. "Look, you can tell because the top is white." She was right. The person and cooler base were so camouflaged they almost completely blended into the night but the lid was white and visible and you could see the body carrying it better when you knew what it was.

We watched the shadow as it moved to the front of the boat, and brought the cooler to where another shadow was waiting. Then it returned to the boat and did the same thing over again.

"That one is doing something," I said, pointing to the shadow that wasn't on the boat. We watched it intently, trying to figure out what the shadowy figure could be doing.

"It's unloading the money!" Jackie cried. "Look! It's taking stuff from the cooler and putting it in something else. Then the other one brings the empty cooler back to the boat after dropping off a full one. It's got to be the money." We watched this for a good ten minutes until the figures were finished and they left.

Jackie sat down, disappointed. "Well that sucked."

"What? Why?" Lexie asked, astonished.

"That could have been anyone," she scoffed, crossing her arms. "We still don't know for sure if it's Ramona."

"Let's watch it one more time," Lisa suggested. "Maybe we'll see something we missed."

"Bill would have to be the one carrying the coolers up," I stated. "Even with Ramona's super-human ninja capabilities, she couldn't have done that with a fresh gunshot wound and cracked ribs."

Jackie rewound the tape and we all took our spots right in front of the screen. By the third time through my eyes were beginning to sting and I was starting to get a headache, but that's when I spotted something just at the very edge of the screen.

"Wait, what's that there?" I asked, pointing to a small, barely visible whitish shape near the foot of the figure unloading the money. "I can't tell, maybe it's just a plastic bag that blew onto the dock or something, it's only there for a second or two."

"It's got more shape than a bag, though," Jackie said, tilting her head sideways as she rewound and hit play again.

"And," Lexie said frantically, a huge smile stretching across her face, "it's scratching its ear with its hind leg!"

"Smedley!" We all shouted together, jumping up, hugging each other and giving high-fives.

"I knew it, I knew it!" Lexie said, pointing to the screen as we all looked incredulously at each other.

Lisa shook her head in disbelief. "Our Ramona, robbing and ravaging the drug dealers to benefit the citizens of Hermosa. A modern day Robin Hood."

Elated, we moved to the back of the boat and into the open air, taking our drinks with us so we could watch the wispy Southern California clouds turn from orange to purple to hot pink. Zipping up our sweatshirts and sweaters, we sat on the cushions and I threw a quilt I'd brought of Casey's that had astronauts, spacemen and grape juice stains on it over our legs to keep us warm as the cool, salty air began to permeate the evening.

I sat there, laughing and chatting on the back of that boat with these friends that I loved like sisters, and I felt something I hadn't in a long, long time: peace. Sure I'd experienced moments of relaxation over the past few years, but nothing like the deep-down-in-my-soul, everything-is-going-to-be-okay kind of peace that I felt right then. Peace that comes with believing that I could handle any situation that may come my way, and if, by some crazy chance life decided it was going to throw me a curve ball, I'd have this group of awesome people who would be by my side in a second.

It may sound like an exaggeration or overly dramatic, but I really hadn't felt that kind of solace since I'd become a parent, it was like the second I got pregnant my anxiety meter went up about 200 percent. I had attacked everything parent-related the only way I knew how: with a vengeance.

I'd done the same with the town that I loved dearly. I took fixing it to the extreme, deploying an army of citizens to keep an eye out while ridding the streets of all evil-doers. The latter of which ultimately climaxed in my friends and I being tortured, shot and, almost literally, fed to the sharks. And did my work accomplish anything? Absolutely. Was I proud of the ass-kicking we gave those dealers? You bet. Was it worth the risk and the price we almost paid? Well, I'll be thinking that one over for a long, long time.

What I had learned, though, was this: inevitably there will be crime in our lovely city; it is better to teach my children how to be safe than to try to protect and shelter them from everything dangerous in life; as my husband says, "Good enough sometimes really is good enough."

We had all stopped talking now as we directed our attention to the sun just before it dipped behind the ocean. I believe it is an unwritten law that when you are lucky enough to see the sun setting on the ocean, you stop everything from when the first sizzle hits the water until the last of the sphere flashes green and is gone, and you pay homage to the greatness of life. I guess I felt so at peace with the world and myself at this moment, that I had unknowingly begun to hum.

From the corner of my eye I could see Lexie staring at me, one eyebrow cocked. She listened for a minute before asking, "Is that the theme song to the *Greatest American Hero*?"

I listened to myself for a moment, my humming on auto-pilot. "I think so," I replied with a big smile.

"Better than *Play that Funky Music White Boy*,'" Jackie smirked.

"Probably," I laughed. "But it seems appropriate right now. You know those moments when you feel so small in the grand scheme of things and yet so alive, like this is my time to live and be on this planet and make the most of it all and I'm so grateful that I've got this incredible family and you guys as my brilliant best friends…"

I looked to Lisa, Jackie and Lexie, who nodded in agreement. "And I know you guys think about that night all the time and so do I. I don't know if I'll ever make sense of it, if we were right to kill those men, if they had it coming to them or did they leave families behind? Was the greater good done for society, will their customers just go and find other dealers…"

I'm sure everyone on the boat had pondered those questions and more hundreds of times and we'd all continue to contemplate them over the course of our lives. "But the one thing I am 100% sure of, though, is this." I looked earnestly into the eyes of Jackie, then Lisa, then finally resting on Lexie. "If I ever get in a sticky situation again, like where murderous, ruthless, torturous drug dealers are about to kill me, I'll know the best thing to do is to offer them cupcakes!"

I burst into a smile, joined instantly by both Jackie and Lisa. Lexie stayed serious, taking a sip of her wine as she looked off at the horizon and declared, "They were stupid not to take them." She looked back to us. "Seriously, I had one the next day, they were good, very good." She nodded matter-of-factly, swallowing a grin.

Jackie put her wine down and tucked her cold hands into her armpits. "Can't you just see Jason Bourne offering those other assassins a cupcake? Especially that Russian dude from the second movie?"

We all giggled. By the end of the evening, my stomach felt as though I'd had a personal trainer shredding my abs. Lisa then looked at her watch and announced it was time to get going. Dutifully we cleaned up, gathered our stuff and walked to the top of the gate.

"Oh," I said, as we stood there waiting for Lisa to lock it. "I forgot, I was going to show you guys something." From the inside of my bag, I took out a small, eight by eleven sized piece of poster board.

"Are you guys ready for this?" I asked, smiling.

"I was born ready," Lexie declared.

"I'm never really ready, but hit me anyway," Lisa said.

I flipped the card over to reveal some words I had written with a Sharpee a few days back that read, "Vote Kelly Birkby for City

Council." All three of them screamed and jumped up and down and hugged me, and then all four of us were screaming and jumping up and down in a big huddle.

"Of course with all that money to spend, every yahoo in town is going to want to be on the Council," I said as Jackie took the card from me to inspect it further.

"We'll totally help you out," Lisa pledged. "I'm unemployed now, I've got some time."

"And you're a super star, remember?" Lexie said as I gave her a look. We had not published any information about how we were involved with the drug dealer ordeal in order to protect ourselves and our families, per Rachel's recommendation, so I hesitated at her words. "From the school incident, silly. Not the other thing," she said, giving my shoulders a squeeze.

"And you have a network of helpers all over town. I'm sure everyone you know will help plant yard signs. Here," Jackie said, handing me back my sign that was now embellished with calligraphy and glitter and multi-colored paint. It was a veritable work of art.

"How do you do that?" I asked. She just shrugged.

"So baby steps, huh?" Lisa asked, nudging me with her shoulder as we grabbed our stuff and headed for the parking lot.

"Yeah, baby steps," I said with a nod.

Acknowledgements

I had the idea for this book about a decade ago. Through two moves, the building of a house, a major life catastrophe and, of course, life with little people, it has taken a constant backseat to other priorities (all moms will understand this) but the story has stuck with me. Along the way I have been encouraged by some amazing people to keep going and to them I am overwhelmingly grateful.

To John Shea, first and foremost, for making the dream of being a writer come true, thank you. From the first read when you told me, "You sure know how to beat a dead horse," to the umpteenth read when you declared it "good to go," you are never one to mince words, your sense of humor is whip smart, and your unwavering support is always surprising. I am so grateful that you are my person.

To my ridiculously sweet boys, Tyler and Tristan, you are the reason I am a hot mess of a worrier! Without you I never would have known the bursting-at-the-seams love and joy that I do when I look at you as well as the crazy desire to protect you like a mama bear. You guys are my world, thank you for being the wonderful little people you are.

There have several amazing people who have been willing to share their talents with me including the incredible Lynn Hightower, the most amazing writing instructor ever at UCLA's Writing Program. Thank you for your encouragement, your super sharp feedback and your willingness to give of your time.

To Rebecca Forster, the most serendipitous person I've met through this process, thank you for your wisdom, experience, and positive energy. You have been nothing short of inspirational. This book would have taken an extra decade if you hadn't shown me the way and shared your team of experts with me.

To the most magical editor and wizard behind the curtain there ever was, Jenny Jenson. If Hogwarts had a writing department, Jenny would be headmaster. Thank you, Jenny, for understanding my story and my characters, for being fun to work with and giving me notes that had me in stitches. I have learned more about writing from you than I have in years of writing classes.

Thanks also goes out to Hadleigh O. Charles for her incredible cover art and to Stef McDaid for his formatting and marketing expertise.

All the incredible moms I have encountered over the years deserve so much praise. From my first Mommy and Me group in Manhattan Beach to my current Cornerstone friends and everyone in between, you moms inspire me with your astounding parenting skills, relentless energy and fabulous humor. Parenting would have been one lonely ride and I can't imagine doing it without all of you. Moms rock!!!

Finally, to my own mom, Sher Printz, for being such a kind, supportive, generous soul. You are adorable and you've taught me so much about being a good person, taking the high road and appreciating the little things in life. I love you so, so much!

About the Author

Lara Shea is a surfing, gardening, beach/book/movie-loving mother of two boys and one miniature golden doodle. She has a B.A. in biochemistry and a M.A. in journalism from the University of Colorado. Seemingly powered by solar, she lives in Palos Verdes, CA with her husband and kids. Mom's Night Out is her first novel.

Lara on social media:

Lara-Shea.com

instagram.com/thelarashea

facebook.com/lara.shea.9

Twitter: @LaraShea1

Made in the USA
San Bernardino, CA
06 January 2019